THE MAGE HEIR

The Life Siphon, Book Two

Kathryn Sommerlot

A NineStar Press Publication

Published by NineStar Press
P.O. Box 91792,
Albuquerque, New Mexico, 87199 USA.
www.ninestarpress.com

The Mage Heir

Edited by Elizabetta McKat

Printed in the USA
First Edition
October, 2019

Print ISBN: 978-1-951057-62-6

Also available in eBook, ISBN: 978-1-951057-61-9

Warning: This book contains sexually explicit content, which may only be suitable for mature readers, and xenophobic, homophobic, and ableist language.

Exiled from Chayd and pursued by Runon, Tatsu's life twists into something unrecognizable when he escapes with Yudai into the mountains. Despite the growing danger trailing them, the biggest threat lies within Yudai and his voracious magic, a force spiraling outside his control. Their only hope is to head into Joesar in search of a way to contain the magic.

But Joesar's desert holds perils of its own, and the only answers Tatsu and Yudai find lead them farther into storms. Friend and foe blur until impossible to tell apart, and all the while, the unchecked siphon devours any energy it can find. If Yudai can't fix what the Runonian mages broke, the siphon could swallow the world, and Tatsu will watch the horror unfold.

No matter how tightly Tatsu's heart is tied to Yudai's, and after everything they have sacrificed for freedom, the past might catch up with them, murky and muddled, betrayal lying in Tatsu's traitorous bloodline.

To Rob and Caroline—
The cheerleaders who keep me writing

Prologue

TATSU WOKE WITH such a start he couldn't breathe.

Heart hammering, he spun up and onto one knee, grabbing his bow and notching the arrow before his thoughts had completely righted. He waited for one breath, and then another, poised and ready to release the arrow into the shadows of the trees. Everything around them loomed threatening, and the pulsing dread shouldn't have been a surprise—they were fugitives, after all.

His throat closed, pulsing along with his heartbeat. When nothing jumped out from the darkness, at least the idea of the soft sounds belonging to one of the queen's guards faded. No one had come to drag them both to the prison cells in Aughwor.

"Alesh?" Tatsu said, voice low, and was met with only silence. The low murmuring wasn't Alesh and Ral either, and knowing they'd stayed in Dradela eased Tatsu's mind a bit, though his stomach clenched at the thought of the queen guessing their involvement in Yudai's escape.

With their camp set up in a small clearing, the mountains stood half a day's walk away, close enough to feel the threat from both Chayd *and* Runon still breathing down their necks. If the queen hadn't sent guards after them, then Runon certainly had. The last thing Tatsu wanted was to underestimate Nota—no, *his mother*, no matter how difficult placing the designation on her was.

Underestimating mages had landed them into the whole mess in the first place.

Whatever stirred within the brush faded away—a small rodent foraging across the forest floor, perhaps—and Tatsu dropped his arms back to his sides. He focused on returning his heartbeat to normal rhythms.

He was jumping at shadows, and at such a rate, he'd exhaust himself long before they could hide themselves in the mountain peaks. Willing his body to relax, he settled onto his sleeping roll as the branches overhead waved gently in the night breeze. There was nothing strange about the trees, but Tatsu kept imagining he could hear them sing.

After traveling through so much of the drained land and its twisted aftermath, nature didn't hold the same comfort it used to.

From his vantage point beneath the tree cover, the moon remained obscured behind branches brimming thick with leaves, but Tatsu guessed half the night had passed, giving them three or four hours before the sun rose. Yudai, sleeping several paces away near the fire pit, was curled into a tight ball on his leather bedroll. Occasionally, he would murmur and turn over, but none of the sounds seemed to be enough to wake him. Small favors, if nothing else.

Tatsu closed his eyes, but unbidden, his mind pulled up a scene he'd spent weeks trying to bury: Zakio's body crumpled in the crimson-stained snow. He pressed the heels of his palms against his eyes hard enough to leave red spots dancing in his vision after he pulled both hands away, but the image persisted even as he resumed staring out at the trees. When he let his head fall against the trunk of the nearest tree, his hair caught in the rough bark.

At some point, he managed to nod off, still in his uncomfortable sprawl against one of the wider trees, and by the time he woke again, the sky had begun to streak with color. Leaning forward, he winced at the pain the movement elicited in his stiff neck. He was preoccupied enough with the tightness to only vaguely notice Yudai stirring across the fire, but the anguished yell a second later startled any residual sleepiness out of him. A split second of spinning showed they were still alone in the clearing.

The relief, if one could call it that, flashed in an achingly short moment.

Yudai sat up with both hands raised in the air, head jerking from side to side. Around him, stretched out like a too-bold shadow, his own sleeping outline had burned brown into the withered grass. The drained blades bent and curled over on themselves, even the ones that weren't crushed beneath Yudai's weight. In only a single night, life had been bled dry by Yudai's wild, uncontrollable magic.

Yudai glowered up at him, eyes glinting with vulnerability.

"No," he said, and that single word reverberated through Tatsu's limbs until he feared he could no longer stand. His chest heaved, a pang of copper blood on the back of his tongue.

The life siphon had endured.

Chapter One

FROM HIS VANTAGE point atop an outcropping of stone on the east side of the mountain, Tatsu stared toward the darkening horizon. The withered trees of the siphon's original devastation stood out blearily against the living landscape, and all sat shrouded in early shadow as ribbons of brilliant red streaked overhead. Twisted toward the ground, the old trees remained far enough away that they didn't pose a threat. Still, Tatsu stayed for a few minutes, enjoying the last bits of warmth on his skin from the setting sun as he gazed over the brown swath of long-drained land. With the season gradually cooling into autumn, they wouldn't be able to stay in the higher altitudes. Already, the sun's descent summoned a fierce chill that whipped against his cheeks, and the thought of remaining in the peaks, with relatively few provisions, didn't help the tightness in his gut.

As the sun dipped low behind the dark shapes of the mountain range, painting most of the visual in gray and black, Tatsu sighed and made his way back down the rocky slope. The path, long abandoned and overgrown with weeds, snaked through the higher cliffs and coniferous trees, high enough on an old trade route that Tatsu didn't see any movement in the trees below. While escape had been the goal, the lull gnawed at Tatsu's subconscious. If anyone *had* followed them, he'd seen no signs of it.

Hunting sorely lacked in the clusters of dark-needled trees. The abandoned paths only went so far, and after a while, they'd have to start looping over their own footsteps, which would impact any potential food supply.

As Tatsu wound his way along the path toward the small cavern they'd set up in, no noises, animal or otherwise, disturbed the peace. The mountain insects had already migrated down the slopes, and the birds and rodents would soon follow.

Yudai was sitting near the fire when Tatsu entered the cave.

"Anything?" Yudai asked. He didn't seem relieved when Tatsu shook his head. The white-drained ends of his hair hung ragged in front of his eyes, but the roots were growing in their natural black, and the transition between the colors formed a dark halo around the crown of his head.

"We have at most a few weeks of summer left," Tatsu said, taking a seat across the fire. He leaned forward to twirl the hare roasting over the flames, split by a makeshift spit. "Anyone on our trail will probably give up once the cold front comes down."

"And we'll freeze if we try to stay here," Yudai replied.

Tatsu kept his eyes steadfastly glued to the fire when he answered, "You're not wrong."

"You've been worrying about it for a week. I can see it on your face every time you return from hunting."

When Tatsu didn't answer, Yudai shifted on the ground, stretching out his legs and wiggling his toes near the warmth. "How long were you going to stew over this on your own?"

"That's not what I was doing," Tatsu said, but the argument was weak.

"Well, you certainly weren't being truthful."

"What have I been lying about?'"

"We can't stay here much longer, and a lie by omission is still a lie," Yudai said, sounding a bit put out. "We have to find somewhere else to go."

Tatsu peered across the fire at Yudai, who raised both eyebrows and said nothing. As the silence grew too imposing, Tatsu sighed.

"I've been going over our options," he said, taking his time with the words. "I just can't come up with an end point. We can't go to Runon—"

"No, we can't." Yudai's eyes flashed silver and angry.

"—and we can't return to Chayd," Tatsu finished. "The queen's response at this point will be much worse than simply using you for revenge."

"I'd rather die," Yudai said, low and more of a growl. His gaze dropped to his fingers splayed wide in his lap, curling and uncurling in tandem. "I'd rather die than be used as a slave again."

After another tense moment, Tatsu said, "I know. I won't take you back there; you know that. Right?"

Yudai raised his head, teeth chewing on his lower lip. "Where will we go?"

"Far. Rad-em, maybe, or Joesar. Or we'll take a ship across the Oldal Sea to Dusset and hope luck is on our side."

"Wonderful," Yudai said with a mirthless laugh. "That's worked out well so far. And what are we going to do when I start draining the world around me while we sleep every night? You know it's getting worse."

"I don't have an answer for you."

Yudai laughed again. "We're leaving a bright trail for anyone hoping to catch us, without any plan where to disappear to, crushed under the hourglass hanging over our heads."

"Are you yelling at me or the world?"

"Myself," was Yudai's frustrated response before he pressed his hands against his face and stilled, lost in his own thoughts.

The hare was beginning to char on the bottom, so Tatsu spun the spit and sat again. Even while staring at the sizzling meat, his appetite had started to fade away. Apprehension returned, throbbing in time with his heartbeat.

"They must have done something to you in Dradela," Tatsu said quietly as the cavern closed in around them, threatening in its inactivity. "There's a reason the drain started up again. It can't be a coincidence the change came only after the queen tried to use your magic for herself."

"Knowing that doesn't get us any closer to shutting it off."

Tatsu couldn't come up with anything to say in response, at least not anything inspiring. Instead, he crossed his arms over his knees and tried to push the thoughts from his mind.

"You think this is a result of being a prisoner in Chayd?" Yudai asked.

"It makes sense, but I doubt you were in any state to remember what the Chaydese mages gave you."

Yudai's mouth formed a hard line when he shook his head. "There was only a vague awareness of people around me and nothing else. It's not very helpful."

"Then we're stumbling in the dark," Tatsu said and sighed. After a few seconds of observing Yudai, dejectedly hunched over on himself, he added, "I wish I could find you something else to wear. The brown is insulting."

"Is it?" Yudai appeared genuinely surprised. "I had no idea."

"That's the color the lowest citizens wear. For royalty, it's...something akin to a slap in the face, I suppose."

Yudai seemed to consider the information. "It doesn't bother me. Brown isn't an insult in Runon."

"When we found you, you were wearing white."

"Nota has a twisted sense of humor," Yudai agreed. "In Runon, white is the color of funerals."

"Fitting." A tightness banded Tatsu's chest. Across the fire, Yudai pushed up to his feet, his face still lined with bitterness there didn't appear to be a remedy for.

"Less talk of dying," he demanded, "and cut up that hare. I'm *starving*."

THEY MOVED ON the next day, and the path they walked sloped farther upward through short, jagged switchbacks, though the route wove them around several large rocks and sheer drop-offs Tatsu stayed clear of. Frequent rests, required for the demanding climb, hampered their progress. Even though they didn't have a destination or an arrival time, the creeping pace made Tatsu's skin crawl. The uncomfortable buzzing under his skin had increased following their discussion, and more than ever, their only hope for survival depended on getting off the peaks before the siphon devoured everything. The looming limit on their time crept closer, and so, too, did Tatsu's apprehension.

When they were unable to find a cavern to set up camp in, they had no choice but to rough it in a small clearing between the trees. Tatsu didn't mind sleeping beneath the leaves, but Yudai's agitation seemed to grow as the sky darkened. He paced back and forth between two ancient tree trunks with his hands clasped behind his back, over and over, until the stars came out to twinkle above their heads.

"You're going to have to sleep eventually," Tatsu pointed out, voice mild, as the moon reached its zenith. His statement earned him a growl in reply. "Please sit down."

"This clearing will be dead by morning," Yudai snapped. When he turned to retrace his steps again, his fingers clenched together in fists so tight his knuckles blanched.

"You can't do anything about it, so there's no point in blaming yourself. It's probably making the whole thing worse."

The glare Yudai threw him was dubious at best, but evidently, the possibility was difficult to ignore. Yudai eventually settled himself between two patches of yellow-green weeds, and he ran his finger over his lip a few times before his eyes flickered up toward Tatsu. "Distract me."

"You could ask nicely."

One corner of Yudai's mouth quirked upward. "I could."

"Did you know my mother had other children?"

Yudai blinked and sat straighter, face slackening.

"Good distraction," he said, and from his tone, he was just as surprised by the question as Tatsu himself was. "I was actually wondering when you'd ask about that."

"Did you?" Tatsu's lungs swelled too big for his chest, pressing against his ribs in a mad attempt to break free. Part of him wanted to take the whole thing back, to inhale the words and swallow them down his throat—but the other part of him was so desperate for the answer that even the anticipation of an emotional gutting couldn't keep the words from breaking free.

"No," Yudai said. There was nothing on his face that betrayed any other truth. "Not until you showed up in the castle that day. But it makes sense."

"Why?"

Yudai's head fell to one side a little, and the white ends of his hair brushed against the curve of his cheekbone. "There was a mage in Runon, when I was young, who served as my mentor. He wasn't particularly gifted or strong, but he was a sensible man, and my father respected him. He never tried to hide his distrust of Nota. He told me she'd spent years trying to convince my father that marrying her and producing magical heirs was the best thing he could do for his kingdom."

Tatsu shook his head. "I don't understand what this has to do with me."

"Don't you?" Yudai sounded surprised again. "If she'd had a child that possessed no magical abilities, it would severely discredit her bid to be at my father's side. There would be no guarantee their offspring would share the gift. Her only hope was to hide the evidence of such a child to save her own chances at becoming queen."

Though expected, the hurt blossoming through his body shocked him with its strength. Shame rippled all the way down his arms, weakening his muscles until his fingers trembled against his thighs.

"It didn't work anyway," Tatsu said, so quietly he thought perhaps Yudai missed it.

But Yudai's face was open with sympathy. "No, it didn't. My father married an advisor's daughter. And every chance Nota thought she still might have had was destroyed when I was born."

"The most powerful mage Runon had ever seen." Tatsu tried to smile. He couldn't quite manage it.

He expected a smirk in return, but instead, Yudai's expression wrinkled further. "That's what they said anyway."

As Tatsu tried to pull himself out of his own thoughts, Yudai put a hand on his shoulder. "Don't do this to yourself."

"I'm just—I'm trying to understand," Tatsu said. "Understand my father, I mean. The Queen of Chayd knew about me and my heritage, but I don't know how."

"Your father probably went to the crown for protection. He was Chaydese, so the kingdom would've been compelled to help him. Without magic, you really weren't much of a threat to them."

Then Yudai chuckled, and his fingers tightened around Tatsu's shoulders. "Until you *were* a threat to them, and in a way no ruler ever could've predicted."

Not for the first time, the full weight of his transgressions hit him, but it seemed to knock more of the wind from his lungs than it usually did. Tatsu struggled to find his breath and right himself in the forest that had suddenly flipped upside down, leaving him with nothing to hold on to.

"*Phehon,*" he said as he squeezed his eyes shut.

"What's that?"

"The Chaydese word for treason. I'm a traitor to the crown now." He ran a hand through his hair as laughter bubbled up in his chest. "A traitor, most likely bastard-born, abandoned by my mother and fearfully isolated by my father, exploited by the queen I then betrayed to save the life of a man I hardly know."

"Prince," Yudai corrected. "A *prince* you hardly know."

"Oh, of course, that makes it all better."

"I feel as if you sometimes forget that fact."

Tatsu snorted and pressed his fingers against his temples. "I sincerely doubt you'd ever allow *anyone* to forget that."

He did feel slightly better, though, and the tension in his chest eased somewhat. He leaned back against one of the trees wrapped with sweet-smelling vines. Staring up at the stars twinkling between the leaves, the rock in his stomach didn't sit quite so heavily. Each moment he was still breathing and still free, the guilt faded away into a low hum in his veins.

"Well," Yudai said. "It could be worse."

"That's true. Tomorrow morning, we could wake up to find you've drained this whole mountainside."

Yudai narrowed his eyes.

"That's not funny," he said, but the lifting of his lips gave him away.

"Go to sleep, Your Highness."

Yudai grumbled for quite some time while getting himself comfortable amidst the grass, and Tatsu stared up at the moon, wondering if somewhere, somehow, his mother was doing the exact same thing.

HE WOKE TO a strange silence, the suspicious absence of humming insects and singing birds a warning. Senses on alert, Tatsu pushed himself up to take stock of their surroundings, but it took a second for his eyes to adjust.

No birds twittered in the leaves above them. Over the closest ridge leading down the mountainside, however, a few jays sang out in the middle of their morning serenades. The hush seemed to be limited to their immediate area, and when he looked left over the remnants of the fire pit embers, Tatsu saw why.

The outline of Yudai's sleeping form had burned into the ground, resulting in an expansive human shadow filled with withered grass blades.

As Tatsu struggled to form words with his too dry tongue, Yudai stirred awake and sat up with bits of the decayed turf clinging to his hair. He glanced to either side, and while his expression didn't change as he absorbed the morning reality, his shoulders stiffened. When his gaze met Tatsu's, his eyes gleamed.

"You said that when you found me in the castle, I was surrounded by black-market toxins."

"That's what Alesh said, yes," Tatsu agreed.

"And we need to decide on a destination before the oncoming season change decides for us."

Tatsu nodded, unable to follow.

Yudai bent over and ripped up a handful of the dead grass, apparently unafraid of the lingering effects the siphon always seemed to leave behind. Clumps of dirt and scraggly roots crumpled out from between his fingers to settle back onto the black-streaked ground.

"Then we go to get answers about what those poisons really did to me," Yudai said, full of finality, with all the weight of a man expecting to get his way. "We're going to Joesar."

Chapter Two

GETTING ACROSS THE mountains to the border of Joesar proved no easy task. It took several days to backtrack away from Chayd's territory, and Tatsu spent an entire afternoon traveling up to the high cliffsides he'd seen from the trade route they'd been following. He returned that night with two plump pheasants and a jack hare in its light brown summer coat.

He set about readying the animals, defeathering and skinning before carefully trimming off all the fat he could find with his knife. Yudai hovered nearby, somehow enraptured by the process.

"You can use this for soup," Tatsu said as he handed over the strips of fat and ignored the disgusted look on Yudai's face. "The fat will cause the meat to spoil faster, and we'll need this to last."

"You're assuming there won't be much hunting when we get to Joesar."

Tatsu leaned into his work, slicing against the grain with precise, deliberate care. "Joesar is mostly desert, and we'll be forced to travel at night, but the lack of food isn't even the worst of our problems."

"We'll die of thirst, then." Yudai sounded cross, but he dumped the fat strips into the cast iron cooking pot Tatsu usually kept strapped to the bottom of his pack and swirled them around with the wooden ladle.

"We don't know where we're going. I've never even seen a complete map of Joesar. Our best bet to finding information about the poisons is to head to the capital, but I don't have the slightest clue which direction it's in."

"Moswar."

Tatsu frowned, looking up from the growing pile of thin slices. "Is that a direction?"

"The capital of Joesar is Moswar," Yudai said. "I've never been, but I had to learn about the surrounding kingdoms during my lessons. My father had closed Runon's borders before I was born, though, so I never met any representatives in court."

"So you know the direction we should go?"

Yudai's face flushed a little. "Northwest. That's all I can tell you, and I wish it could be more. If I was ever taught anything else about Joesar's cities, it's gone now."

It wasn't much to go on, but Tatsu tried to school his features into something he hoped would pass as optimistic. "Well, it's better than nothing. At least we have a vague plan."

From the expression Yudai shot him, Tatsu hadn't fooled him at all. He continued to stir the fat bits in the stew as Tatsu finished cutting up the strips of meat to dry and keep as jerky.

"I would have known more about these lands," Yudai commented quietly, after Tatsu was done. "I would have been well-versed in the regions around my kingdom and their cities. I would have been taught more of their policies and customs as I grew into my time to rule."

"I know."

Yudai's eyes locked on the pot of boiling soup, and Tatsu wondered if he was seeing something Tatsu couldn't. "I can't stop thinking about it now, the life I should've had."

Then he laughed, the sound sardonic. He wiped a bit at his eyes with the back of his hand without bothering to disguise the action as anything else. His eyes, already a reflective sheen, sparkled like water droplets on fine silver jewelry.

"This is stupid, isn't it?" he said. "To feel this way now?"

"No. When we first got you out, the only goal was survival. There was no room for anything else. It's after survival is guaranteed that everything else catches up with you. You're grieving."

Yudai barked out a laugh. "That's a useful emotion."

"But necessary," Tatsu said, and Yudai's next look was long and shrewd.

Neither of them spoke for a spell. Yudai didn't turn away during the silence, but Tatsu did, folding under the weight of the knowing gaze.

"What about you?" Yudai's voice cut sharp.

"I don't know what you mean," Tatsu said to the slices of meat, but the dismissal sounded forced even to his own ears.

"Survival is guaranteed now, right? Mostly, anyway. So, what are *you* grieving?"

Everything was the honest answer, but Tatsu couldn't bear to let such truth fall from his tongue. His stomach pulled his heart low already—remnants on his tongue tasted bitter and ashy, coating the flesh all the way down his throat. With every breath, he mourned the loss and then felt silly for doing so in the same instant. The truth of it was that he grieved absolutely everything, even things he'd never really known, and he couldn't separate the strands from the mess where they'd tangled up.

"The image of my father," he finally settled on. "I thought I knew who he was, but I was wrong. And now it feels like I've watched him die all over again."

Yudai didn't offer any compassion in response. Instead, he said, "I know what you mean. Everything is different now."

"I wish I could say that it gets better..."

Yudai cut him off with another harsh laugh. "Of course it doesn't get better. You just have to deal with it. You learn to harden yourself against everything else."

Staring down at his hands, Tatsu wasn't quite sure that was the right answer, but he kept it to himself. He already felt exposed enough; Yudai's eyes seemed like they could pierce through his defenses at the best of times. Sitting by the crackling fire with the probing conversation strung between them, all of his shields had fallen away, melted to nothing in the dancing light.

When Tatsu raised his head again, Yudai was still staring at him, his expression seeking.

"Well, this has been a very uplifting conversation," Yudai said.

Tatsu laughed, surprised at how genuine the action was. "I'll try and tailor the rest of our interactions to bolster your spirits, then."

"Don't," Yudai said with force. "Don't you dare."

He looked uncomfortable when Tatsu raised both eyebrows across the flames at him. "You're the only one who treats me like a normal person. It's just...been a long time since anyone talked to me like an equal. Like I was something other than the prince or a magical prodigy."

"And?"

"It's *nice*." Yudai huffed, rolling his eyes. "Obviously."

The tension in the air returned, heavier than before. Yudai had curled in around himself, looping his arms over his knees as if he could disappear into nothing more than a ball of skin and bones. Afraid he would shatter the easy chemistry of their travels, Tatsu let the subject drop.

"That soup should be almost done," he pointed out. "Skim the foam off the top and divvy the soup up—we'll need all the energy we can get once we hit the edge of the desert."

WITHIN THREE DAYS, an expanse of rolling sand dunes appeared over the cliffsides. They were an hour or two from the desert, and already the air had changed into something drier and sharper. The old trade road they'd been walking didn't veer off into Joesar, so they cut their own path through the wild overgrowth clinging to the side of the last mountain like barnacles on the underbelly of a ship. Pulling away from the desert, the rocks butting up to the edge of the fading hills had been rubbed smooth from years of harsh, stinging winds.

As they grew nearer to the dunes, Tatsu's confidence wavered. He could get them northwest using the stars and the sun's arc, but all they had was a vague heading. They didn't know how long of a journey across the dunes it would be or what they'd encounter along the way. In a new, foreign land, few things threatened more than going in blind.

Tatsu thought about bringing up his worries to Yudai, but they'd woken up that morning to find the dead zone had expanded farther than it usually did. The increase could mean only one thing: the siphon was growing in power.

Yudai hadn't said anything about it, other than a few too-casual jokes, but his face was pinched at the sides. As he walked, his steps grew more careful and his fingers more controlled, as if he were afraid to touch anything for fear of the siphon bursting free.

Tatsu took the lead through the thick clusters of coniferous trees until, abruptly, the trees stopped, and before them lay a pebble-strewn, uneven cliff shifting down. Bits of the sand crept nearer and nearer to the grass, which thinned out until it was nothing more than tufts of prickly blades. Free from the mountains, the stretch of blue sky seemed never-ending without any clouds, and such clear skies would work against them.

Tatsu stopped before they reached the border so they could seek shelter beneath the last bits of the tree canopy.

"Now we wait?" Yudai asked.

"Now we wait for nightfall."

They settled in for the last hours of daylight, and Yudai's eyes fluttered closed almost immediately. Tatsu, however, couldn't get his heart to stop hammering, so he took the chance to commit what he could of the desert to memory. Knowing it wouldn't aid them much, for there was little beyond the dunes stretching out in front of them, he focused on the dips and waves in the dunes. The sand wove up and down in gentle hills, and past that, nothing emerged as a tool they could use in navigation. No mountains or trees dotted the horizon, only the vast nothingness of the rolling Joesarian desert. Even guessing the time needed to cross the expanse was impossible.

To their right, the Turend mountain range continued north to where it eventually met up with the Great Mountains of Runon. To their left, the peaks would slowly meet up with the Oldal Sea and the kingdom of Rad-em.

In front of them, the desert sands stretched on and on, tinged orange beneath the setting sun.

Tatsu waited until dusk to wake Yudai. He tried to look busy as Yudai stood and brushed bits of dirt off his pants, frowning down at the small ring of decayed undergrowth.

"At least you won't be able to drain much in the desert," Tatsu said.

"Small favors," Yudai agreed but didn't seem cheered by the prospect.

As the sun dipped below the undulating horizon, they set off into the sands. The air sizzled for only a half hour or so before it rapidly dropped the lingering heat. It settled around Tatsu's shoulders like a cold cloak, but the cold was no worse than it had been along the mountain paths. The dunes beneath them were harder to deal with—the granules shifted under their boots, too dry to stick together as they sank into them. Each step was a heaving lift to forcibly remove their feet from the sand, and overhead, the moon rose as a perfect half-circle, unobscured by clouds.

The desert remained quiet, save for the breeze rustling the sand in swirling arcs across the hills. Every once in a while, they came across a part of the dunes where the land flattened and grew rockier, strewn with fist-sized stones battered and weathered from the elements. These patches were far easier to walk across, but what energy he saved during those short bursts, Tatsu redirected to intensify his own focus. While traversing through the flatter areas, he caught glimpses of the zigzag paths left behind by desert sidewinders. They likely hid in the shadows of small rocks during the relentless sunny days and did their hunting at night; he hoped their party created too big a target to entice the snakes, because he didn't know how large they could grow out in the sands.

He stopped them every few hours or so for water. Even at night, the desert's dry heat made it easy to fall prey to dehydration, and Tatsu was acutely aware of their limited supply. He rationed it as best he could and pushed their pace as much as possible without exhausting them both.

Yudai didn't seem impressed with the endless dunes.

"What's the point to having this much sand?" he grumbled, grunting as he lifted his leg high to step over and across a shifting ridge. "You can't grow anything, and nothing shows up naturally."

"There has to be something, or else no humans would've settled here."

"I don't think there *are* any humans here," Yudai pointed out. "We haven't seen anything but sand for hours. It's a barren wasteland."

"That's not true," Tatsu told him as they paused for just enough water to wet their tongues. "There were several reedy plants at the last stop that likely grow fruit near the midpoint of summer, and I saw at least one lizard near the rocks large enough for a meal if cooked right. Besides, didn't you see the desert hawk that's been circling us on and off all day?"

Yudai stared at him incredulously for a long beat before his face contorted in disbelief. "A few plants, a lizard, and a hawk? You're arguing an ecosystem with *that*?"

Tatsu shrugged. "I'm only saying there's likely more here than we realize, or else no one would ever have journeyed through the sand."

Yudai sputtered out something incoherent, and Tatsu caught snippets of words like "disturbed" and "reaching" before they started out again. At least Yudai's grumbling provided decent background noise as Tatsu worked out their plan. The sun would rise soon. Already, the sky behind them had started to streak with pink light, and against it, the last bits of the Turend Mountains peeked out over the sloping hills. The desert would be nearly impassable at the height of the day, and they needed to find somewhere to sleep. Unfortunately, since they'd started out, Tatsu hadn't seen any rock formations large enough to provide shade, and they had only an hour or two left.

Dawn proved even hotter than he'd initially anticipated. Before the sun had been fully roused from its slumber behind the horizon, the air began to swelter and haze. They stripped off their outer layers and wrapped them around their heads to shield their faces, but it didn't seem to do enough to stave off the worst of the sun's relentless rays. The rolling sand beneath their boots only served to reflect the heat back up at them, catching them in an inescapable pocket of broiling oxygen, until the sweat ran down Tatsu's face in such large rivulets that swiping his tongue over his lips rewarded him with bursts of salt.

"We have to stop," Yudai moaned, wiping his hands under the white-black strands of hair and coming away with damp fingers. "We can't keep up like this."

"Ten more minutes," Tatsu said. "To the bottom of this ridge so we can set up the tent parallel to the wind."

Once there, it took several tries to secure his leather skin to the ground without trees to tie the edges around.

He used his pack for one side, to pick it up off the sands, and the other he secured with their cooking pot and a bit of the kindling he carried. Only a small crack existed between the leather and the ground, but the space was enough to catch the wind and allow it to flow through. The sand beneath the tent burned too hot to lie on directly, so Tatsu spread out the sleeping roll, and they both collapsed onto it. He stripped down as much as he dared, in case they needed to get up and move quickly, but it wasn't nearly enough. Staring up at the underside of the leather, sweat continued to bead and roll across his forehead, likening him to a hare roasting inside cast iron.

"I can't sleep," Yudai said, groaning. "It's so hot."

"We need the rest," Tatsu said, though he wasn't able to relax any better. Outside, the sun beat down on the sand, the heat rising up and wavering across the horizon when he squinted out at it from their boiling respite in the shade.

At some point, he did manage to drift off, only to wake in fairly regular intervals at the moments his body started to overheat. Evening finally arrived with bursts of color across the still cloudless sky, but his temples throbbed with the limited amount of sleep he'd gotten. His limbs hung heavy and foreign, as though filled with the same sand they were moving across.

He sat up and began pulling his layers back on. To his left, Yudai did the same, moving sluggishly. The heat weighed heavy on their shoulders, slowing all of their actions.

"I'm exhausted," Yudai admitted.

"Me too," Tatsu said and sighed. "We'll see how far we can get tonight."

Lack of energy slowed their pace considerably. Tatsu couldn't tell exactly when his boots began to feel heavier, but the drag increased throughout the night as they traveled by the stars. He kept them moving northwest as best he could, charting from the constellations he'd known since childhood. A snake slithered across the granules, and a large arachnid clung to the side of several small rocks, but the desert's muted night hours held little else. Above them, another desert hawk made lazy circles in the sky, punctuated by a few screeching calls. Around the middle of the night, when the air reached its coldest point and they shivered against the chill, the clouds rolled in, and their route disappeared. They had to double back a few times after that to wait for a glimpse of the navigational stars between the clouds.

By the third day, Tatsu's whole body might as well have been oozing across the dunes behind them. His legs ached from the extra exertion needed to move across the sand; his cheeks and lips were cracked, chapped from the wind and heat. Their water stores dwindled to half, and he'd seen nowhere to refill.

As dawn crept nearer, the wind picked up around them. What had been a calm roll of blue moon-tinged sand only an hour before, now came alive in a swirling mass of air. It reminded Tatsu of Yudai's magic in their escape from Dradela, accompanied by all the grains of sand the wind could pick up. They both removed their outermost tunics and tied them around their faces to shield their noses and mouths, but the intensity of the storm increased with each minute ticking by.

"There," Tatsu yelled over the roar of the wind. A small stretch of rock slightly taller than them sat in front of them—an incredible stroke of luck. "We can find shelter from the wind!"

Making it to the rocks proved difficult, but they managed just as the sandstorm seemed to reach its peak. Tatsu had only meant they could use them to crouch down behind the stone and let the land take the brunt of the storm; he certainly hadn't expected to find a small cavern carved into the rocks, low and black in shadows. Visibility dropped to almost nothing as he fell against the side of the stones. He could have wept in relief as they both stumbled inside, sand raining from their clothes and hair.

Outside, the howl of the storm battered against their rocky shelter, and when Tatsu pressed his fingertips to his cheekbones, pain blossomed along the rubbed-raw skin. He didn't know how long sandstorms in the desert lasted. Summers in Chayd would sometimes bring dust storms in from the coast, and the whitewashed buildings in Dradela would later be covered in a fine layer of dirt, but he'd never seen anything so devastating before. The wind echoed in his ears, low and steady, accompanied by erratic clicks.

"*Gods*," Yudai huffed from behind him.

"We'll stay here until the storm passes," Tatsu said.

He shrugged off his pack, and it hit the ground with a strange sort of crunch. The lingering sting of the sand had so rattled him that it took a moment for the sound to register. Far too slowly, his eyes adjusted to the darkness. Yudai's fingers wrapped around his elbow in a grip tight enough to summon pinpricks of pain.

"Tatsu. Do you hear that noise?"

He had to be talking about the clicking—the odd sound hadn't gone away, even when the reverberations of the wind dissipated. Tatsu couldn't see the rear of the cave without light, and everything outside had been engulfed by wind and rage. He froze in response, muscles clenching. The two of them stood motionless until Tatsu gradually made out the dips and swells of the rocky interior around them.

To his left, the wall was moving.

"Yudai," Tatsu whispered and couldn't have gotten anything louder past his lips if he'd tried. "Go. Run."

"What are you talking about?" Yudai hissed. "The storm is that way!"

"We have to get out of here." Tatsu took a single step backward until he realized he'd left his pack on the floor where it'd fallen. His eyes stayed glued to the movement on the wall he'd initially identified as jagged rocks—it was instead hundreds of scurrying, clicking exoskeletons, walking over and under and between one another in a revolting mass of legs and mandibles.

They'd walked straight into a scorpion nest.

"Tatsu?" came the shaky question from over his shoulder. Tatsu reached for his bag, thinking only about their water supply kept within the leather, their only source of survival in the desert. Instead of his strap, his hand closed around a wriggling insect. A second later, pain flashed through his palm, and then another pang stung his hand near his wrist. He yelped and yanked the bag toward his chest, bringing several of the creatures with it. Another prick of pain along his knuckles, and he stumbled, finally dislodging the rest that had crawled onto his pack.

"Run," he gasped, pulling his throbbing hand toward his chest as he slung his bag over his shoulder. "Yudai, run!"

There was nowhere to go but into the sandstorm. Tatsu pulled his tunic closer to his mouth, throwing his other arm up to shield his eyes from the worst of the wind.

With Yudai barely visible in front of him, he ran into the mass of whirling sand until the only thing visible was the screaming tan of the storm: no rocks, no sky, no horizon, only the wind shrieking around their ears and the sand biting at their cheeks.

Tatsu tried to push his tunic closer to his mouth when sand leaked in through the side and caught between his lips, but his arm, aching and stinging all the way up to his shoulder—had it always been hurting so far up?—didn't obey his commands. It fell to his side as he stumbled, and the sand around him went black at the edges.

"Yudai," he tried to say and wasn't sure that he had. The wind whipped at his clothes, but the world tilted to the side as everything started to topple over on itself, taking his body with it. He was only vaguely aware he had fallen because it seemed as if he floated instead, up into the storm threatening to steal them both away.

Yudai screamed his name, but anything after got lost in the haze, billowing down to envelop him. The last thing he remembered seeing on the wind and sand was a hawk, that blasted desert hawk again, cutting through the worst of the clouds, and he wondered if the bird would finally find itself a warm meal out of their remains.

Chapter Three

HE HAD NO concept of how long he'd been out. When he finally came to in a burst of awareness both jarring and excruciating, the only sensations registering were darkness and the cool water pressed against his forehead. It took several moments for him to muddle his way through the fog enough so he could crack his eyes open, only to immediately pinch them closed when the piercing light assaulted his vision. His head swam and his stomach roiled, but his throat closed, too dry to force the discomfort down.

After pushing through his nausea, Tatsu tried again. The second time, he managed to keep his eyes open long enough to take stock of his surroundings: tan leather stretched over his head, several clay bowls next to his reclining form, and a rack of large, smooth antlers holding a few wicked-looking blades. None of it rang familiar; bile burned up through his throat and into his mouth.

The flash of movement to his side escalated his pounding heartbeat until a hand came down gently on his right arm.

"*Loanai*," a woman said in a tongue he didn't recognize and then added in Common, "Do not worry. I will bring you water."

Tatsu's throat was too sore to respond. A splash of cold hit his lips, and he opened his mouth to greedily gulp it down, but the flow of drink ended before he was fully quenched.

"More," he rasped.

"Not now," the woman said. "Your body is too sick. If you can keep it down, I will give you more as the sun sets."

Tatsu had to close his eyes again. Even the sunlight filtering through the thin patches of the leather tent stung like fingernails against his eyes. He swallowed several times, body still alight with pinpricks of pain, and tried to shift his position.

"Where?"

"In the Cabaj dominion of the desert," was the response. "North of the ridgeline and east of the An-ny Oasis."

None of that meant anything to Tatsu. Even with knowledge of Joesar, he wouldn't have been able to place his location. The light-headedness made focusing on anything impossible. His thoughts fluttered in and out without settling on anything, and he pried his heavy eyelids open again. The woman standing over him had her body covered in wide-woven, layered fabrics, save for her face, which was dark brown in color. As she peered at him, the corners of her mouth pulled down in what appeared to be sympathy.

"Yudai?" he asked.

"Ah, your friend." Her lips twisted into a smile. "He is quite fine. Bossy, but fine."

Tatsu sighed as his muscles uncoiled, and his weight settled into the hazy waves of throbbing pain. His body wanted to drift because it was easier than dealing with the reality of the situation, but his mind struggled to stay aware. He was in an unknown area, surrounded by strangers, and his training screamed warnings at him. Walking into the wilds without knowing what manner of beast lurked within was suicide.

Still fighting against the war inside, he took another slow, shuddering breath before his body won out, and he fell into the embrace of darkness.

THE SECOND TIME he woke, his head felt clearer. The light still burned, but he pushed through the pain and opened his eyes to find Yudai seated next to him, hovering anxiously.

"You're awake," Yudai said. Tatsu couldn't tell if he was concerned or irritated, as Yudai's face betrayed nothing.

"You're alive," Tatsu replied, warmth rushing in his blood. Yudai seemed intact and in much better condition than Tatsu. "We both are."

Yudai's face clouded. "But only barely. And your hand..."

That alone was enough to jolt Tatsu out of the rest of his haze. Craning his neck to look at the appendage, he found himself staring at several layers of wrapped linens, crusted and solid as though they'd been thoroughly soaked and then left to dry in the heat. He tried to wiggle his fingers inside the wrapping but couldn't feel anything. Below his elbow, his senses disappeared completely.

His chest tightened, for he wasn't even sure his hand was still there.

"Is it...?" He couldn't finish.

"The toxins nearly killed you," Yudai said. He no longer sounded annoyed; instead, his voice had thickened with regret. "Nys said—"

"Nys?"

"The woman taking care of you. She's acting chief of the Cabaj-walkers. She gave you some kind of tonic to neutralize the poison and then drew it out with these big leaves I didn't recognize."

Tatsu stared down at the cloth covering his arm. "Is my hand still there?"

"Yes." The guilt hadn't left Yudai's tone, and wondering why made Tatsu's stomach heave. He turned away from his arm, trying to think about anything else.

Yudai leaned forward, dragging his hands slowly over his face before peering back down at Tatsu with a heavy expression. "Tatsu, I'm *sorry*."

"Why?"

"This shouldn't have happened. I should've been able to do something to stop this. If I had access to my magic, I could've *helped* you. I could've stopped the toxin."

"You can do that?"

"I can do *anything*," Yudai said, eyes blazing, and the absurdity of the claim made Tatsu smile. They sat for a few minutes in silence with the coolness of Yudai's hand on his good arm offering a small bit of solace in the bright, sunlit bleakness. Then the flap of the tent opened as Nys walked inside carrying a clay bowl in her hands.

"You are still here," she said to Yudai.

His face scrunched up at the edges, but he didn't say anything. Her statement implied something, but Tatsu was too woozy to puzzle it out.

"I heard that you saved my life," Tatsu said, and the skin around her eyes crinkled in a warm smile.

"That is the duty of the walkers." Nys shooed Yudai away from the side of the bed to take his place. "How are you feeling now?"

"Tired," Tatsu said, "but grateful."

He didn't mention his arm, because he didn't really want to know about it. In a perfect world, sidestepping the topic would cause it to disappear. But Nys reached for the hardened linens despite Tatsu's mental prayers to avoid it and began to pull them apart.

"Is he going to be all right?" Yudai asked from behind her shoulder. He inched around her to come near Tatsu's head, radiating a nervous energy that seemed to rattle the whole tent.

"He will live," Nys said. The statement offered no comfort.

The world stilled as Tatsu waited for her to finish unwrapping his hand, his heart sinking lower and lower with each piece removed. When Nys got to the end, he felt nothing—no sudden onslaught of emotion, no reaction from his arm. The skin of his arm wrinkled in pale, sickly dips, and long streaks of black bruised beneath his skin. Whatever the scorpion toxin was, the effects of it were still visible.

"Do something," Yudai ordered. "Wiggle your fingers."

"I'm trying," Tatsu admitted quietly.

And he was, only nothing happened. He couldn't tell if the commands to his hand were being received. There was no response, not even the barest shiver of movement. His hand might as well have been missing below his elbow for all he could perceive.

Tatsu raised his gaze to Nys's face, unsure what he was searching for. "I can't move them."

She stepped forward to grasp his bad hand. "Can you feel this?"

"No," Tatsu whispered.

Yudai stared at Tatsu's motionless hand with a thunderous expression before storming out of the tent without another word.

Nys sat back, and Tatsu tried to take some comfort in the fact that her expression hadn't changed. "The toxin has been removed. I believe the feeling will return in time, after your body has time to recover."

"And I'll be able to move it?"

"It is possible."

Tatsu's tongue stuck to the roof of his mouth, prohibiting him from saying more. He stared at the flap in the leather Yudai had disappeared through.

"Give him time," Nys said quietly as she smoothed the pelts beneath her knees. "He refused to leave this tent once we knew you had passed the critical phase and would live."

"What has he told you?"

Nys stood, her knees cracking in protest. "Enough. Your survival was more pressing than your background. The poison of the *enlusk* scorpion is quick."

"Why help us?"

"What danger were you to us?" she asked. "You were half-dead. I will bring you some food. It would be helpful for your blood if you got up and stretched your legs. The healing will progress faster if you are active."

It took an hour or two, plus a hearty meal of a grain-based stew, for Tatsu to feel strong enough to push himself up from the pelts and move around. Nys helped to set his lifeless arm in a linen sling held close to his chest. At first, merely a handful of steps prompted a long, winded rest, and his muscles shook from the period of disuse. But nothing was worse than the sensation of a dead limb attached to his body. Foreign and wrong, the object he didn't recognize had been grafted to his chest like the ghost of what he used to be.

Eventually, he made his way outside the tent. The falling sun provided his only notion of time in the desert, and the air had begun to cool. He didn't know how many days he'd been unconscious, which unsettled his thoughts, and he still didn't know where in the desert they were. As he stepped out to face the setting sun, he glimpsed no sign of mountain peaks on the horizon behind the leather dwellings.

Nys's band of Cabaj-walkers wasn't large. Tatsu counted only seven tents, plus a half tarp that appeared to be a makeshift stable for short, stocky horses. But all of the supplies looked sturdy and well worn, as though the entirety of the camp had weathered many seasons in the harsh desert. The leather had bleached almost the same color as the sand itself, and if viewed from afar, the tents would blend in with the dunes. It was a good camouflage, especially if one expected hostile outsiders. He didn't know the political situation within Joesar, but that aside, a good defense was a practical base for everything.

With the fading light, some of the walkers had set up torches in the sand, bathing the area in orange. The others milling nearby were dressed like Nys, with many light layers crisscrossed, likely to be taken off as the heat reached its peak during the day. Their heads were covered with loose hoods and their feet with tall boots that tied near the knees. Tatsu watched them move around the tents with practiced precision before he finally spotted Yudai near the far side of the camp, staring off into the distance. Moving around the sand took great effort, and his exhaustion didn't help matters.

He approached Yudai warily and stopped a few paces away.

"Nys says my hand might get better," he said. "The feeling should come back."

Tatsu had guessed Yudai was feeling guilty, but as the other man whirled on him, no signs of regret shone from his expression, only anger. Yudai was *sparking* with rage, eyebrows furrowed and lip curled so that he looked more like a feral cliffcat than a man.

"How can you do that?" Yudai growled. "How can you talk about this so calmly?"

"It's not the end of the world..."

"Look at you!" Yudai cried with a wide gesture of his arm toward Tatsu's sling, and the implication of it stung so badly Tatsu stumbled away. "Look at what's happened! Look at the consequences of what was done to me! And it's going to keep happening as long as I'm alive!"

A bubble of emotion lodged in Tatsu's throat. "It's not necessarily forever. My hand might get better—"

"And you're acting like *this*?" Yudai's voice boomed loud, too loud, his shouts carrying easily on the still air. "How are you not *angry*?!"

"Of course I'm angry!" Tatsu exclaimed. The dam burst free in a rush of fresh pain; his veins were on fire, and so were the tips of his ears, and every muscle in his body throbbed. "*Gods*, Yudai, I'm furious! Do you think I don't realize what this means? That I'll never shoot a bow again? That I'll have to relearn every skill I've ever been taught? I know what this means, and it could be a death sentence! Of *course* I'm angry. But I'm not angry at *you*."

There was a moment of perfect stillness before Yudai's expression collapsed.

"You should be." Yudai moaned, head sinking into his hands.

"This isn't your fault."

"Yes, it is." The words emerged muffled by the palms of his hands. "All of this is because of me. You did all this to try and save my life by basically giving up yours. I should've been able to *do* something."

He turned his back on Tatsu to face the sand and wiped at his face with his sleeve. Shoulders slumping, the loathing turned inward—likely frustrated and powerless, with nowhere to go but deeper within. Tatsu closed his eyes for a second, as if the blackness could erase all the time since they'd crossed into Joesar's borders. He took several deep breaths to settle himself and then cracked his eyes open again.

"I don't want to be mad at you," he said deliberately. "There's a lot to be angry at, but I don't... I don't really want one of those things to be you."

"Stop being such a hero," Yudai huffed.

"I'm sure you're going to kill me for this later," Tatsu said, "but I think you really need to work on managing your anger."

Yudai laughed, though it rattled harsh and stilted. "I *would* kill you if you were anyone else."

It felt good when his face loosened in happiness. If nothing else, the change in atmosphere turned Tatsu's attention away from the throbbing knot of grief in his chest. Yudai hadn't been wrong about the implications of the injury, but the idea of never being able to hunt on his own, if focused on, overpowered everything else. Tatsu couldn't afford to fall apart over the uncertainty of his own future. Ignoring the reality would work, at least for a little while, until they figured out what they needed to do—and what their new hosts were planning on doing with them.

Yudai twisted halfway around, and then his eyes flickered to something over Tatsu's shoulder. "That's Jotin, the man who found us."

Tatsu craned his head to see a young man with dark brown skin standing behind them. His hair, at least the part not shorn down to his scalp, was pulled back in a cord.

"Thank you," Tatsu said. "How did you...?"

A hawk flew low over the tents and landed on Jotin's hand, which was covered in a thick leather glove. The bird's intense gaze landed on both Tatsu and Yudai before the creature let out a short screech. As Tatsu stared at the raptor, his foggy thoughts struggled to catch up.

"It wasn't different hawks I was seeing, was it?" he asked, impressed despite himself. "Your bird was following us the whole time."

Jotin grinned. "Only fools wander into the desert without supplies. It is our duty to keep an eye on outsiders."

He motioned behind him toward the center of the camp where the bulk of the flickering torches stood. The sky had darkened considerably, and the flames illuminated the camp in several lopsided circles, elongating and stretching the shadows of the people standing about across the ground.

"You seem well enough to answer questions," Jotin said. "So, this is a good time for an explanation of why you are here in our sands. The chief is ready for you."

ALTHOUGH THEY'D ALREADY met the acting chief, Nys, standing in front of her and the others was still foreboding. Tatsu felt distinctly out of place as the walkers assembled in a semicircle around the lanterns, their layers of light-colored linens wrapped around their shoulders. Even when he'd knelt in front of the Queen of Chayd, he'd at least known what his role was. In Joesar, their position trembled, unstable as the sand beneath his boots.

Aside from Nys and Jotin, the other Cabaj-walkers stood in a blending of similarly dark skin and black hair, mostly pulled up and away from their necks. They formed an impassive wall, trained in survival and well versed in the desert layout, and they reminded Tatsu of the curved line of mages who had once stared down at him in the receiving room in Dradela's palace. Jotin, bringing up the far right, was the only one with an animal, his hawk now perched on a leather strap covering only one of Jotin's shoulders.

Tatsu wanted to shrink away from the line of walkers, but Yudai squared his shoulders and took a step forward.

"We thank you for your aid," he said. "And we wish no harm to you or your lands. Although our arrival is abrupt and unexpected, we hope you'll see fit to grant us passage through the sands to your capital city."

"So formal." Nys shortened the distance between them, languidly sliding forward, and the dancing light of the torches cast harsh shadows on the folds of her clothing. "You have not given an answer for why you are here to begin with. What outsiders would wander into our desert with no care for the trade routes?"

Yudai's jaw clenched, muscles twinging. "We seek information in Moswar from the alchemists."

"Ah," Nys said, as if she'd known the answer all along. "But why the avoidance of safe passage roads? They have been created to aid travelers with Moswar as their destination."

Yudai's gaze flitted to meet Tatsu's. Yudai took a deep breath but didn't say anything, and for several breaths, stillness hung sharp and heavy between them.

"We..."

Yudai seemed unable to continue.

"The routes aren't safe for us," Tatsu cut in. "We aren't exactly on good terms with our respective kingdoms. Encountering certain parties could be... detrimental."

Nys's face seemed to crinkle, but it could have been a trick of the light. "If you are wanted men, why do you think we would be willing to grant you passage through our lands?"

Another pause, and Tatsu's heart pounded out an erratic rhythm that echoed in his ears. Yudai's eyes met Tatsu's again as his expression hardened into resignation. When Yudai faced the semicircle of Cabaj-walkers once more, he drew himself up to his full height, raising his chin and balling his hands into tight fists at his sides.

"Because I am the heir to the throne of Runon," he said, "and I am invoking the aid-in-distress agreement for foreign rulers."

"You are not a ruler yet," Nys pointed out.

"I will be *king*," Yudai said.

Tatsu could have sworn Nys's mouth ghosted up into a smile. "We have no kings here, prince. Why must you go to Moswar?"

The visible tremble down Yudai's arms betrayed how poorly the conversation was going. His mouth thinned as he said, "Joesarian poisons were used to control my magic, and they have damaged my abilities. I need to know what these poisons were and how to reverse them."

The others remained quiet as Nys shifted her gaze away from Yudai and squared it on Tatsu. Her eyes held significant weight, and Tatsu winced, cradling his useless arm close to his chest.

"And you?" she asked.

"I'm only a guide," Tatsu said.

"Will you vouch for him?"

"Yes," Tatsu said without hesitation. Swallowing proved difficult, emotion choking him. "Yes, I will."

Nys turned her attention to the walkers behind her. The conversation, if it could be called such without sound, stretched over several tense moments. Whatever stirred between them did so almost indiscernably until one of the men on the farthest edge shook his head. Nys laced her fingers together and glanced at Yudai once more.

"Rest now," she said, more order than request. "Tomorrow morning, we will give you our decision."

"Tomorrow?" Yudai sputtered. "Why can't you tell us now?"

"Joesar is not governed by one person alone," Nys said, "and neither are we. We will convene and discuss your situation. When the sun returns to the sky, we will have a consensus."

Yudai seemed ready to say more, and whatever it was going to be, Tatsu knew the outburst would only make matters worse. He reached forward and grabbed Yudai with his good hand, hauling him back with all the strength left in his recovering muscles. His pull was at least enough to stall Yudai from immediately damaging their chances, though they both stumbled in the shifting sands.

"Thank you," Tatsu said to Nys and the Cabaj-walkers. Part of him wanted to apologize, but since he couldn't pin down an exact mistake to atone for, he didn't. Everything had already been said, and in truth, he was too exhausted to do much else.

Tatsu wished he knew Nys well enough to know if her expression really was bordering on amused. Their position with the Cabaj-walkers was unsteady, so assuming anything could lead to disaster.

"Thank you," he said again and tugged Yudai back a little more. "We'll take our leave now."

Chapter Four

REST CAME EASILY for his body but not his mind. By the time dawn broke and the desert heat began to rise, Tatsu had slept on and off fitfully enough to strengthen his body somewhat. He checked his left arm to find the streaks of black had disappeared, which was positive, though he still couldn't feel anything when he poked at it. The disappointment threatened to choke him, so he pushed himself up from the skins to take his mind off of it.

He expected the Cabaj camp to be quiet during the harsh daylight, but he was wrong. Outside the tent, activity still buzzed, though less hurried and more controlled—a careful dance of expending only energy necessary to perform essential tasks. Some of the men and women must have been at the meeting with Nys the night before, but all wore hoods to shadow their faces from the sun, so he couldn't recognize them.

Tatsu could think of no better way to avoid thinking about his hand than by exploring the grounds of the camp. He trudged slowly between tents and tried to keep himself out of the brunt of the sun as best he could. The tents sat positioned to shroud the important supplies in shadow, but the sun's orb blazed directly overhead, offering little relief. Tatsu allowed himself a short rest in a tent that smelled of incense and drying animal skins before heading back out again.

He arrived shortly at the makeshift stable, the half tent opening wide on the far side and curving down, puckering where iron darts pushed through the material into the sand. No signs of Yudai's presence lingered in the camp. The small horses within the shade carried with them an air of home, but less so after Tatsu pressed his hand to one of the animal's flanks. He expected the smooth hair of horses native to Chayd and was surprised when his fingers curled through coarse, almost wavy fur.

The horse shook its head, mane flying out from side to side, and Tatsu wondered if the animal was laughing at him.

As he waited with the desert mounts, a Cabaj-walker brought him a small, polished clay cup of strong-smelling water. A burst of sour at the end softened the bitter taste, neither of which Tatsu recognized. Likely, he'd drunk some sort of tonic—after all, the Joesarians were known for their skills in alchemy, though he'd yet to observe any of the Cabaj-walkers exercise the skill.

When Nys found him a while later, he inquired about it.

"There are no alchemists here," she said. "A few joined the Cabaj-walkers, but their assignments keep them elsewhere. The drink is simply a desert recipe for quenching thirst."

She made no move to leave again.

"Have you made a decision?" Tatsu asked.

"Yes," she replied. "Jotin is bringing your royal friend back now. He has the habit of wandering every few hours. Does he not sleep?"

Yudai must have been worried about the siphon, then. His reluctance to stay in one place for too long probably stemmed from his attempts to stop the effects.

Little existed within the desert ecosystem to drain, but if the siphon continued to grow stronger, perhaps he worried about it creeping into more living things than merely plants.

Tatsu gazed at the horse next to him, flicking its tail back and forth to scatter the large sandflies buzzing around its haunches, and rubbed the creature's neck again.

Instead of answering Nys directly, Tatsu said, "He's got a lot on his mind."

He hoped he didn't give too much away. If Nys read anything else into his statement, she didn't press the issue, and they sat in silence for a few minutes until Jotin and Yudai arrived.

"Good," Nys said, after they'd all assembled. "We have decided to give you passage to Moswar. Jotin will be your guide to the city."

"You won't be coming with us?" Tatsu asked.

"Our work is here in the sands, keeping them safe," she said. "We cannot spare the resources or time, but Jotin is a good choice. He will soon take his turn serving on the High Council in Moswar, and the chance to observe political dealings will serve him well."

Yudai's face betrayed nothing. He held still and subdued, chewing on the flesh inside his mouth.

"Thank you," Tatsu said to Nys. No matter what Yudai claimed, the Joesarians did not *have* to help them, and the aid was a welcome change.

"Yes." Yudai finally spoke, nodding once to Nys. "I appreciate your offer."

"Then Jotin will be your desert guide," she said, "and we will pray for your safe passage to the capital."

She left the open-air stable and disappeared into one of the nearby tents, leaving the three men alone.

"Get anything ready that you need," Jotin said. "Everyone here will be instructed to give you any provisions they can spare. We need waterskins, food, and a shelter, and we can divide the duties of carrying it between us."

Yudai raised one eyebrow at the man, though it didn't appear malicious. "You seem adept at giving orders."

"As I will need to be while serving on the High Council," Jotin said and mirrored Yudai's expression right back at him. "Leading you will be good practice. Now ready yourselves—we leave at dusk."

JOTIN, AND HIS hawk, led them away from the Cabaj camp after evening fell, loaded with supplies. Tatsu had handled far heavier things, but carrying the weight without two working hands provided a unique challenge. Jotin adopted a hard pace, clearly used to dealing with desert difficulties, and it took quite an effort to keep up. Even with the cool air of sundown settling around them, Tatsu's breath fled quickly, lungs burning. At least he didn't seem to be the only one struggling if Yudai's huffing behind him was anything to go by.

Near the middle of the night, Jotin sent his hawk off. As the bird took flight with several long flaps of its wings, Tatsu expected them to pause and wait, but, instead, Jotin urged them onwards.

"How will it find us later?" Tatsu asked.

"He always finds me again after an hour or two. Things are easier to see from the air, including us."

"And you've trained him to look for oddities?" Tatsu asked, one boot sinking deep into a particularly soft section of sand. "He reports back with his findings?"

Jotin smirked, though Tatsu couldn't tell if the expression was aimed at his questions or his struggles with the dune. "He alerts me if anything is strange or different."

"Is that how you found us?"

"Fools who wander into sandstorms certainly are strange. He was quite adamant after seeing you in the storm."

"And you understand him?" Yudai asked from behind Tatsu's bad side.

Jotin smiled fully then, his teeth blindingly white against his skin. "I do not use magic, if that is what you are asking. He uses bird sounds like normal. He simply won't land until I investigate."

He continued forward, and Yudai grumbled under his breath.

"I wasn't asking about magic. *Obviously*, the hawk uses bird sounds."

The hawk in question returned after an hour and landed without so much as a squawk, which somehow reassured Tatsu's nerves that things around them continued as they should. As the sun rose, they stopped and set up the borrowed leather tent. Yudai's face, resolutely turned away as they staked the leather upright, betrayed a hint of fear when Tatsu managed to catch a glimpse of it. Yudai didn't fight the sleeping arrangements, though if Tatsu had to guess, he likely wanted to. After all, he'd gone to great lengths to avoid the uncontrolled nighttime drain settling in around others. Sleeping three within the small space wouldn't be comfortable, but little about sleeping beneath the midday sun was conducive to any real sort of rest. Jotin woke with the setting of the sun as if trained to it and herded them off again as the sky darkened once more, no worse for the wear. As they began their trek anew, Yudai's shoulders sagged in what was probably relief.

The desert around them gradually began to change. Tatsu was beginning to think he and Yudai had chosen the wrong section of the sands to trudge through. Judging by the stars, they headed northwest, and as they crossed the space, the dunes evened out into a rockier, jagged landscape. Rather than pool atop itself in waving crests and lines, the sand grew heavier and clumped more along the ground, which was dotted with small stones and tough, mangy-looking weeds. Within the wide swatches of flat, packed sand, desert cacti stretched, massive and covered with spindles. Jotin pierced one with a sharp metal spigot and refilled their waterskins with a liquid carrying a sweet aftertaste.

It was much easier to walk without constantly fighting against the tumbling sands. On the far horizon to their right, the peaks of a large mountain range finally sharpened into focus. The air, while still uncomfortably and exhaustingly hot, stopped rubbing his cheeks raw as the atmosphere around them shifted.

Two nights of walking later, as dawn turned the sky pink, they came across a splash of bright color against the endless backdrop of beige—a small pond of sparkling, crystal clear water and several large palms. Tatsu blinked several times to make sure he wasn't imagining the whole thing in the wavering heat of the early morning.

"This is the An-ny Oasis," Jotin told them, leading them right to the water's edge. "A good place to stop if we keep a lookout for the *enlusk* scorpions."

Just the warning made Tatsu's skin crawl. As if on cue, his left shoulder started throbbing, though the painful sensation ended around his elbow. The last thing he wanted was another encounter with the arachnids, so he crept slowly to the edge of the blue pond and made sure the sand was clear of everything before he knelt forward to scoop water into his mouth with his working hand. Blissfully cool, the moisture shocked his parched tongue.

He wiped the back of his mouth with his sleeve as Jotin set down his pack and began to unload.

"We're staying here?" Yudai asked, mouth twisting down at the corners.

"The palms provide shade, which will help our tent stay cooler, and we will not have to worry about rationing our water until we leave." Jotin didn't look at Yudai but continued to pull out the tent and the carved wooden poles to tie the rope around.

Tatsu observed Yudai give the area a once-over, all the way up to the wide fronds of the trees waving overhead. "We can't stay here."

Jotin's brow furrowed, and he paused. "If you are worried about the *enlusk,* I was mostly joking. They keep to caves more than the oasis, but I can stand watch if you wish."

"No, we can't sleep here." Yudai thrust both hands out, fingers splayed. "We have to move away from the trees."

"Why would we move away from the shade?" It sounded as though Jotin were laughing at the absurdity of the suggestion.

"Because I'm going to *kill* it," Yudai said in a low hiss. "And as this is probably the only oasis like it for quite some time..."

"A few days in each direction, yes."

"Then unless you want all of these palms completely destroyed, you will set up our tent *away from the trees.*"

Jotin had stilled with one hand inside his pack. He straightened slowly, keeping his gaze on Yudai, and didn't respond immediately. His face betrayed nothing, but his fingers on the leather twitched. Overhead, his hawk turned lopsided circles in the sky.

"There is much you did not share with us," he said.

"I told you that I was damaged," Yudai replied through clenched teeth. "It was enough."

Jotin's expression hardened. "As the person willingly guiding you through lands that are not your own, I believe I should be the judge of what is 'enough.'"

"You're not in charge," Yudai shot back. "Nys—"

"My aunt."

"It doesn't matter. I'm not required to divulge personal facts to someone beneath my position—"

Jotin dropped the wooden stake he'd been holding. "*Beneath*?"

"As a foreign ruler, I'm worthy of all the respect and distance that comes with the position!"

"You're not a ruler yet," Jotin pointed out again, and Tatsu cringed, fighting the urge to bury his head in his hands. "And you are in *my* sands."

"Move us away from the trees!" Yudai cried. He threw his arms wide once more and then almost immediately pulled them back in, wrapping them around his chest. Without looking at either of them again, he stormed to the opposite side of the pond, where he nearly disappeared in the darkness of the shadows.

Tatsu started to follow him, but Jotin's hand against his chest stopped him.

"You," Jotin said. "You are Chaydese. You are aware of our kingdoms' long-standing animosity."

"What are you talking about?" Tatsu asked. He gulped, throat dry despite the drink he'd just had.

"Unless you want more of your kinsmen's blood spilt, I suggest you explain the situation. It is by courtesy alone that you are both being allowed to move through Joesar, and I am demanding all the information now."

With his eyes on Yudai's figure across the oasis pond, Tatsu tried his best to explain things—the siphon, Chayd's involvement with its sudden resurgence, and his own presence in the mess. He left out his connection to Nota, telling himself it was only because divulging the link didn't seem necessary. Telling the story felt surreal; their situation remained easier to deal with when he kept the entire thing at arm's reach, and dredging through the memories once more seemed to loosen all the bitterness. Regret sang through him until he wanted to be sick if only to expel the emotion.

Jotin sat motionless until Tatsu finished.

"What manner of hell did they create?" he murmured, eyes on Yudai across the water. "What monster did they unleash while our gaze was turned away?"

"They would have succeeded had we not been sent to steal him," Tatsu said. Then, feeling oddly bashful, he dropped his head to his useless, bandaged arm. "Even if the queen only wanted him for herself, in the end."

"Not him," Jotin corrected. "What sort of monster allows his own son to be abused and cornered like a beast?"

Tatsu started, looking up. Jotin looked more sad than angry when he sighed.

"That is why he fights so. He clings to his birthright, because it's the only remnant of his blood that doesn't pain him. It's the only thing that hasn't betrayed him."

Shame expanded like a slow-pooling puddle of spilled fire through his chest. Tatsu had been so wrapped up in his own grief and regret he'd failed to identify the most basic of Yudai's. To have a stranger point it out after so short a time made him feel no better than Yudai's father.

Tatsu was no better than his mother and her magical shackles.

Jotin seemed to sense some of the turmoil rolling through Tatsu's mind. He put a hand on Tatsu's good shoulder. "We will move the camp away from the trees."

"Thank you," Tatsu murmured.

"I do it for both of you. You worry so much about him that his struggle is reflected in your face."

Jotin began to erect the camp far enough away that Tatsu was sure the wild night drain would be kept away from anything unprotected. Jotin didn't ask if they were safe sharing the tent space with the siphon swirling beneath them, and Tatsu was glad because he didn't have an answer.

He decided to sleep in the middle, just in case.

Yudai didn't say anything after the argument with Jotin, and once the tent posed ready, he lay on the animal pelts without looking at either of them. Jotin seemed to slip into sleep as soon as his head fell, but Tatsu couldn't follow suit. He stared up at the leather above them, illuminated on the other side by the sun, and counted the rivulets of sweat rolling across his forehead to his ears.

After some time, Yudai shifted beside him with a sigh that might have been a muffled set of tears. Without really thinking, Tatsu reached with his good hand to find Yudai's. He laced their fingers together and squeezed hard.

There was a sharp intake of breath, a steadying gasp, and then Yudai's grip tightened in response. Even when his fingers threatened to cramp hours later, Tatsu kept their palms pressed together, pouring his unspoken apology between their skin with every hitching beat of his heart.

AS THEY JOURNEYED on the next night, the dunes fell away completely, and with less sand to whip above the ground, the acrid sting of the air faded into something softer. The land beneath their boots still rose and fell like gentle waves on the sea, but the sand, packed harder, offered less resistance to their hurried pace. The desert plants—cacti and withered brush—stood tall and sharply outlined against the sky when it progressively colored and brightened each morning.

The three of them didn't speak much as they walked, giving Tatsu too much time to slip inside his own thoughts. In his mind, darkness and grief loomed, and when he had nothing else to focus on, he feared he would get lost in the turmoil. Sometimes his memories jumbled up behind his eyes, replaying in the shadows haunting the desert night, and sometimes his thoughts consisted of a vision of the future—a future where he saw himself useless, unable to hunt or even clothe himself. When the silence between them stretched longer, punctuated only by the scuffling sound of their boots dragging across loose sand, it became impossible to ignore the call of his own fears.

The image of his father rose unbidden to his mind, but not the father he'd grown up knowing. Instead, he conjured his father during his last days, when the man was little more than a withered shell of what he'd once been, plague rattling in his lungs and fever scorching his skin. In his last lucid moments, his solid, resourceful father had been helpless and furious at his own ineptitude. Tatsu finally understood that feeling every time he shifted and his shoulder within the linen sling ached, all sensation ending at the elbow.

In the darkest hour of night, the time right before dawn when the shadows crowded together to fight against the light that would inevitably banish them, he lost himself completely to his own terrified imagination. This happened at the same time his vision pulsed the weakest, which was how he missed the ridges of solidified sand in front of him.

When the odd formation crunched under his heel, he stopped, mostly out of surprise. He thought he'd stepped on another scorpion and stumbled when the twisting in his gut threatened to steal his breath away.

A closer look showed no sign of any arachnids, only a ripple in the round-edged bumps, each circle larger than the last and radiating out like the sun's halo behind clouds.

"Tatsu?" Yudai asked from several paces away.

Tatsu leaned forward and squinted, trying to make out the epicenter of the rings in the darkness, and the ground shifted below his heels. Sand tilted forward, falling away where the middle of the circles sat, the granules skipping beneath him like a rockslide tumbling down a mountain. Tatsu threw his good arm out instinctively, but there was nothing to grab onto, and when he lost balance, he couldn't find a section of ground not sliding to the center.

"Tatsu!" Yudai cried, and he might have been running toward the avalanche, only Tatsu couldn't hear anything more in the clamor of shifting sand.

And then the epicenter of the rings opened up with a groan and a tarantula-like hiss, with four large pincers erupting out of the packed sand, curved around a gaping maw.

Tatsu grappled to find something, *anything*, to grab, and his fingers came away with only bits of sand and dirt. The sudden incline of the ground sent him flying closer to the pincer-lined mouth of the sand beast, and he tumbled over, smacking his forehead against the ground. As stars exploded in front of his vision, more of the ground caved as the creature's jaw opened wider in preparation for its meal.

When he threw his good hand out, hard clumps in the ground cut stinging lines into his palm.

"*Sayld*!" Jotin yelled as he skated across the chasm and down the scattering sands toward the pincers. Once near, he swiped at the closest one with two daggers. Tatsu never would have expected a direct assault to work, but the sand creature bellowed in pain, and all four of the mandibles curled in on themselves.

Then Yudai's hand reached for Tatsu's good one, and he tried to pull him up the slope.

"Come on!" Yudai shouted over the rumble of the ground and the trumpeting of the creature. "Tatsu, climb!"

It was hard to get any traction against the sand, but Tatsu tried his best anyway, running in place against the ground in a mostly vain effort to get back up. Over his shoulder, Jotin let out a fierce cry, more angry than pained, and another roar boomed from the sand creature.

The force of the noise reverberated through the ground and up Tatsu's legs, causing him to slide down the small bit he'd managed to climb.

The mandibles of the sand monster unfolded again. Either Tatsu's eyes were getting better in the dark, or his imagination was running wilder in panic, for the jaws seemed even larger the second time they reached out for him. Yudai still had ahold of his arm, but the exertion of putting all his weight on one limb summoned a dangerous ache in his shoulder. If the shoulder joint of his only good arm slipped out of place...

Tatsu kicked, succeeding only in pushing himself back as they all slid closer to the creature's waiting mouth.

"Come *on*!" Yudai cried.

The valley down to the mouth began to fall away farther, widening, and Tatsu's hip banged against the hardened sand with such impact it shook his bones all the way up to his neck and knocked his teeth together. Movement flashed, and Jotin's hands closed over his elbow, directly below Yudai's hold.

"Now would be a good time to use that magic of yours!" Jotin shouted.

"I *can't*!" Yudai exclaimed, half growl and half yell. "I can't control it!"

The deafening racket kept Tatsu from noticing the hawk swooping down until the bird was nearly upon him. The hawk's talons sank into his useless arm and pulled up in a move that surely would have been excruciating if he'd been able to feel it. Propelling him up, the sudden lift allowed both Yudai and Jotin to grab his shoulders and haul him the rest of the way with his boots flailing against the sand.

As soon as he was on stable ground, Jotin jerked him upright and forward, and they sprinted away from the sand creature as fast as their legs could carry them. Tatsu didn't know how long they ran, but he finally had to stop, lungs burning and body aching. The panicked fire within faded into an overwhelming exhaustion. He doubled over, heaving and struggling to catch his breath.

"What *was* that?" Yudai demanded.

"*Sayld,*" Jotin said, and Tatsu recognized the word from earlier, when the sand had first fallen away. "They are worm-like monsters that burrow beneath the sand to wait for prey. But I've never seen one out this far. This part of the desert holds little for them to devour. They usually cluster near the settlements and hope for strays to fall into their trap."

Yudai was staring at him, features twisted. "That's normal here? That *thing*?"

"What did you mean, you can't control your magic?" Jotin asked, ignoring the question.

"It's part of what they did to me." Yudai shrugged as his gaze fell to the ground. "I can't really use it."

"Why did you not go to your temple and get help?"

Yudai looked startled. "Temple? We don't have anything like that."

"Then where do your mages go?"

"They're there to serve the crown," Yudai said. "They do the king—or queen's—bidding. They aid the kingdom and its people."

Jotin shook his head. Part of his hair had come loose from the tie holding the strands back, and tendrils curled away from the shaved side of his head.

"That makes no sense. Mages in Joesar usually elect to join the temple, where they can learn and practice their craft. A few choose to remain out with the walkers and protect the desert, but it's not required. If they cannot train together, how are they to learn to use their gifts?"

Yudai didn't seem to have an answer to that, and he looked to Tatsu, perhaps hoping for support. Tatsu rotated his left shoulder up to try to readjust the bag on his back. The action dragged his shirtsleeve across the puncture wounds left by Jotin's hawk, and he winced at the sting.

Then he froze.

He'd *felt* that.

"It hurts," he said, gasping. Warmth bubbled up in his lungs, bursting free from his throat in a barking sort of laugh, and he stared at his arm and the spots of sticky blood soaking through both the sling and his shirt fabric. "It hurts!"

Jotin reached for his arm and poked at the skin. Tatsu couldn't feel all the pressure, though tiny pinpricks of pain shot up through his elbow when Jotin's fingers pressed against the injuries.

"The toxins have numbed your nerves," Jotin said. "But they are fading. I expect you will get full feeling back in your arm within a week's time. This is good news."

The word *good* didn't seem enough to cover Tatsu's light-headedness. He swayed a bit, overcome with gratitude, and had to put his good hand to his forehead to steady himself. For a long moment, it was difficult to breathe around the intoxicating pull.

The bloom of heat rocked him right to the core, and the visions of his useless future began to fade away.

"Thank the gods," Yudai murmured.

"Indeed," Jotin said, and he sounded much more sincere. "But it's nearly dawn, and we should get away from this place in case there are other *sayld* from the colony nearby."

Somehow, sleeping better during the relentless days became possible, but Tatsu didn't think his body would ever truly acclimate to the heat. By the next night, the atmosphere around them had settled into something far more comfortable. Jotin no longer acted aloof and, instead, radiated the calm sort of security of an ally.

The nights of travel blurred together. Tatsu's legs ached, the blisters on his toes healing and scabbing over. The dull throbbing in his shoulders from the pack never wholly went away, but he learned to ignore it. They picked their way around rocks, sidewinders, and at least one section of sand Jotin identified as a desert-mire, which he claimed would devour them whole, much like stepping onto rotten ice and falling straight through to the icy waters beneath.

As they walked, Jotin shared with them the old stories Joesarians told about the gods—the Five they thought ruled over the lands and determined each person's fate, old tales Tatsu had read snippets of growing up in his father's books. Chayd's tales of the old gods always ended with the men who had come after them and settled the lands in the gods' names, but Jotin never mentioned any ancient Joesarian heroes. The tales in the sands, it seemed, kept the deities at the full seats of power.

On the last day, as the sky brightened against the tan horizon, Tatsu could identify scents carried on the breeze. The air swept by with a tang of spice and the low note of animals held closely together in the sun—a sweaty, briny assault on his nose—so he knew they had to be close to Moswar. At the top of the next ridge, the city materialized into view, shimmering into existence as they grew closer to its gates. The loose, stretched sides of the farthest buildings blended in with the expanse of sand surrounding the city.

Moswar rose larger than Tatsu had expected. Seen from afar, the sand-block houses and tents clustered closer near the center, where the bulk of color was concentrated. No castle or palace stretched above the uneven roofs. Instead, a low, flat sort of mansion reached out into the gaps, sporting bright blue awnings that trickled into the rest of the city. In front of the manse was a large, square area filled with carts and tents and a few people milling around in the morning sunlight.

Jotin stopped on the ridge and pulled out two extra linen wraps that had been rolled into thick blocks.

"I cannot fully disguise you as Cabaj clan," he said as he handed each of them one of the fabrics. "But we can at least attempt to buy time before the others mark you as outsiders."

Yudai slung the wrap around his head and shoulders and then helped Tatsu with his.

"Whatever poisons were used on you were no doubt illegal," Jotin continued. "They are not easy to come across. You must talk to the right people, and they will not readily come clean about possession of such things. It may take several tries to find someone willing to talk."

He gave Tatsu a pointed look. "Coin loosens many a tongue."

"I don't have much," Tatsu said. "Just some Chaydese coppers and a few bronze *omn*."

"The traders will take them in exchange for Joesarian *miros*," Jotin said. "Traders are always good for that much."

"How will we know where to start looking?" Yudai asked.

"All of the alchemy adepts offer at least a selection of their wares at the *Raydrau.*" When Jotin received two blank looks in response, he clarified, "The night market."

Yudai sighed. "Then we have an entire day to wait before it begins. The sun's only now come up."

"Try to keep your heads down," Jotin warned. "I doubt we will find anyone so spoiling for a fight that they'd attack by virtue of your origins, but it's better to be safe. There are some foreigners in Moswar, though not enough to fully hide you."

Yudai sighed again and tugged his headscarf up. "Then let's go. That sun is merciless when it gets high."

With a fluttering in his belly, Tatsu followed the other two across the final hill of sand and into the capital.

Chapter Five

MOSWAR WAS BUILT into a flat horizon of beige, but once inside, the tan of the tightly clustered buildings pulled back to reveal a multitude of colors. Two large carved pillars in identical shapes—warrior figures, solemn and poised with swords ready—marked the entrance to the capital, and between them started the long, wide road of the city. On either side sat clusters of sandstone buildings with entryways sometimes draped in worn leather hides stretched out on spindly wooden poles. The resulting shadows offered relief even in the early morning hours. Already, sweat beaded along Tatsu's neck and ran down his back beneath his shirt and pack.

Most of the buildings near the entrance had open-air windows covered with wares and goods for sale. A small shop presented a spread of dyed linens, and another window displayed bread-like loaves created from a coarse, yellow grain. Strangest was the smell, enveloping them completely—the scent of burning incense mingling into a pungent fog, constantly cloying around their faces and making it impossible to discern a single note within. Sometimes, Tatsu thought he could detect bits of Chaydese spice within it, pulling up sweet-smelling memories, but as soon as he tried to focus on the nostalgia, the scent faded into something else he didn't recognize.

Jotin led them down the main road. Some of the people they passed were dressed similarly to Jotin with light, layered fabrics and high leather boots, and others had clothed themselves in leather vests with no sleeves, tied and fastened across their chests by thick cord. A woman pulling down a heavy awning had a headscarf around her hair, tresses piled up in impossible directions, ending with three loose tassels fluttering out from the top. As they walked, the steady hum of conversations surrounded them, for rather than opening for the day, the majority of the sellers were closing down. The Joesarians disappeared into their houses to avoid the unrelenting heat of the sun.

Overcome by the sights and the memories swelling in his chest, Tatsu slowed to drink it all in. To his right, a large opening had been cut into the stone of a building. Hanging beads, leather, and feathers filled it, creating a curtain that obscured the rest of the shop. Beside the store were two large crates piled high with broken pottery pieces, the remnants of sculpting too imperfect to sell. He was so caught up in the world around him that several moments later, he blinked back into awareness and found himself alone on the street.

He bit down the exclamation of either name; they couldn't keep much of a low profile if he caused a commotion by shouting. He had just started trudging forward again when the hair on the nape of his neck stood on end, and a familiar tingle shot down his good arm.

Tatsu froze and then snapped his head around to the space behind his right shoulder.

Behind him, a Joesarian man clad in very light linens patted down a worn-looking horse, and two Joesarian children hauled lopsided baskets back inside a building, their knobby knees knocking together with each step.

Still, Tatsu let his gaze linger. *Something* had triggered his instincts.

"What is it?" Yudai asked, reappearing in front of him. "Why did you stop? Jotin thought we'd lost you already."

"I had...I got the feeling I was being watched."

Yudai snorted ungracefully. "Of course you're being watched. At this point, we look like half-dead scraps the latest traders brought in from the desert. It'd be more suspicious if people *weren't* looking at us."

"I swear something's off." Tatsu frowned. Peering closer at the people on the road didn't reveal anything out of place. Everyone around them was preoccupied with their tasks, and most of them were moving wares from windowsills to close up for the day.

"You probably imagined it after days of being almost completely alone in the desert," Yudai said. "With this many people around again, my skin is crawling too."

Whatever had triggered the instinct faded. Tatsu's senses calmed, and he took a deep breath, inhaling more of the incense haze. It *had* been a long journey, and he was badly out of practice—even in Dradela, he'd often crumpled under scrutiny. Tatsu shrugged the pack back up his shoulder where it had begun to slip and shook his head.

"I'll keep my eyes open, just in case whatever it was comes back. It's probably nothing, but at least I'm paying attention now."

Yudai shot him one last look of disbelief before saying, "Let's go, then."

They walked until they met up with Jotin, who didn't say anything but did take a quick look at Tatsu's face, which had to be showing his apprehension openly. Tatsu's opinion of the man rose when, as they began to move together again, Jotin's right hand slid in to gently grasp the hilt of his sword. His fingers remained there until they'd passed the bulk of the storefronts.

The road was well worn and packed, though walking along it kicked up a fine layer of dust that settled on Tatsu's boots. The sky above the blocky horizon of square-molded buildings had begun to turn a clear, dazzling blue as the dawn colors melted away. Tatsu pulled the linen around his head and shoulders closer as Jotin took a left turn at the next small side street, which was narrower and less populated. Instead of large open windows to sell goods, the buildings along the new path had small slatted openings in groups of three.

"Where are you taking us?" Yudai asked.

"We should not remain in the streets during the day," Jotin replied. "I am taking us to the *sayen*, where we can rest and prepare for the *Raydrau* later this evening."

Tatsu wanted to ask what a *sayen* was, but never got the chance. Jotin turned into the round-arched opening in the high sandstone wall to their right that ran parallel to the street. Once through, the area opened up into a courtyard the likes of which Tatsu had never seen before. Dotting the entire area were tall palm trees and shoulder-height wooden posts, except in the center, where braided mats covered the ground. The rugs formed a circle around what looked to be a wooden barrel and an old, rusty iron well. Concentrated near the middle and radiating outward were hammocks strung between the palm trunks and the wooden posts, some containing the still bodies of those sleeping and others laden with bags and sacks.

"Travelers and traders who do not have their own carts stay here during the day to wait for the market,"

Jotin said while weaving them through the hammocks and posts to a single awning on the far left side. Tacked onto the inside of the wall, the fabric drooped to create a curved shadow along the ground. "The *sayen*-guide will be able to take your Chaydese coins and give you hammocks to rent."

"And we sleep here with everyone else?" Yudai asked.

"Sleep with one eye open," Jotin suggested, "just in case."

The *sayen*-guide turned out to be a woman wearing a wide, cape-like tunic that reached to her ankles and wrists and folded into thick bunches along her elbows. She took a handful of Tatsu's coins and produced three corded bundles of rope from a large basket at her feet. Jotin then motioned for them to follow, moving through the *sayen* until he found an area that seemed to suit him. Near one of the high white walls—one with only a few trees—Jotin's selection was well chosen. Tatsu was glad Jotin had thought to keep them away from most of the foliage. The other occupants, snoring in gently waving nets, remained far enough away to keep them out of potential harm's reach.

Setting up the hammocks by looping the rope between posts wasn't difficult, and it didn't take them long to prepare their resting areas. Once they'd finished, Jotin led them to the middle where the aged barrel and the well sat. When he pumped the well's handle a few times, flakes of rust drifted off the iron, but the water it produced ran clear and surprisingly cool.

After drinking their fill, Jotin pulled the warped and lopsided lid off of the barrel.

"*Ugh*," Yudai said, recoiling and putting a hand over his nose and mouth. "What is that?"

"A paste made of decomposing eggs and herbs to keep the insects away," Jotin said. As if unbothered by the smell, he dipped one hand in the barrel and came out with a blackish gel coating his fingers. "There are no nets at the *sayen,* so you will need to rub this on your skin."

Yudai's look of disgust intensified. "You want us to put *that* on our *skin*?"

"It is either this or be devoured by the midday mites," Jotin said with a shrug that seemed to say he didn't much care what Yudai did or didn't do.

Tatsu followed Jotin's lead and, wrinkling his nose at the assault, smeared the paste along his neck. The odor was so strong he worried he'd pass out, but after a few moments, the strength of it faded. Eventually, Yudai gave in and put the mixture on himself and, once done, helped Tatsu cover his good arm.

The *sayen* was relatively quiet save for the soft snoring from the hammock a few paces away and the wind rattling the palm fronds above their heads. Settling in against the ropes, the hammock certainly wasn't uncomfortable—looking up at the blue sky above the trees, the gentle swaying of his body from side to side soothed some of his nerves. Still, being so exposed left goose bumps on his skin, even with the wall surrounding the rest area, and his mind resisted the siren's call of sleep for a long time before he finally drifted off.

Tatsu dreamed of the desert and the never-ending yellow of the sand. Out in the dunes, the click of arachnids scurrying between shadows echoed as they, too, struggled to keep cool. The sun blazed directly overhead, but Tatsu couldn't feel the heat—except for on the skin of his damaged arm. The blood inside his useless appendage began to boil, as though the sun was evaporating his very essence right out of him.

His arm throbbed and burned as though on fire, and he clutched his fingers close to his chest. Falling onto his back, he started to roll, tumbling down to the valley between drifted sands. He was wildly afraid his entire body would burst into flames until a shadow drifted over him to block the worst of the sun's rays. Squinting up, the visage of the sky darkened, lost within long waves of hair tumbling over hunched shoulders.

"Ral?" he asked.

"Tatsu!" she said, and against the harsh glare of the sun, he could barely make out her mouth widening into a smile. "Wake up!"

He blinked, and he was in his hammock lying beneath the late afternoon sun. The fogginess of the dream clung to his mind in spiderwebs of lingering images, and getting his bearings took a moment. The shadow above him remained as it had been in the dream.

Tatsu's chest constricted, and he shot upright, nearly flipping the hammock entirely. "Ral?"

"Tatsu!" she repeated, flashing the same toothy grin. Tatsu was up and on his feet before he realized he was moving, pulling her into a one-armed hug. He pulled away to look her over, finding no evidence of trauma on her face or clothes. She seemed fine; her bronzed brown skin gleamed from the heat, and her dark hair hung loose and fluttering against her back. Under the neckline of her tunic, chunky beads of the *Oldirr* necklace created tiny folds.

"What are you doing here?" Tatsu asked. "How did you *get* here?"

Ral merely smiled again and turned to Yudai, greeting him with the same enthusiasm, which he returned with a somewhat dazed embrace. After she moved, a figure approaching from behind slid into focus, and things began to click into place.

"Alesh," he said, and she stopped a few paces in front of him.

"Tatsu." Her narrowed gaze fell to the linen sling curved around his shoulder. "What happened to your arm?"

AS EVENING FELL over the city and Moswar's citizens started to trickle through the streets again, the ragtag group swung split between the three hammocks. Ral and Alesh sat together, bowing the bottom of the ropes almost all the way to the sand-strewn ground, and Ral kicked her heels up, swaying the entire thing back and forth. Jotin, meanwhile, stayed against the wall, smoothing out one of his leather straps with a small knife while his eyes tracked between the rest of them.

"She was just so agitated," Alesh said with two fingers gently touching her sister's arm. "She wouldn't stop talking about you, and then she started running off without me until I had no choice but to give in."

"But how did she know we were heading here?" Tatsu asked. "*We* didn't even know until only a few weeks ago. We didn't head straight into the desert after leaving Chayd."

Alesh shrugged. "I don't know, but she was insistent. We went west into Rad-em and found a trader willing to give us passage in his cart."

"How did you pay for something like that?" Yudai asked. "That journey takes well over a week."

She didn't answer, but her face grew hard. After her gaze skipped over Yudai—with a flash of something Tatsu couldn't quite identify but wasn't sure he liked—it settled on Tatsu.

"Alesh," he said, his heart sinking. "Don't tell me—"

"Then I won't," she snapped. "I did what I had to. What else was I supposed to do, let Ral try to get here on her own? I couldn't convince her otherwise, and I couldn't *force* her to stay."

Ral's mouth puckered at the sides. "Tatsu here."

"You don't have to talk about her like she isn't sitting right next to you," Yudai said.

Alesh jerked her head to face him. "What would you know? Why do you think you have any right to tell me what I should be doing for my own family?"

"I know her too," Yudai shot back.

"Please," Tatsu said. A bone-deep weariness had already settled through his limbs. He pressed his fingers against his brow, wincing at the pang blossoming beneath the touch. "*Please*, let's not do this. We have so many other things that are more important."

"Such as the *Raydrau*," Jotin said. "It will be starting soon."

"We've visited the night market," Alesh offered.

Tatsu didn't want to ask the real question dangling in front of him—if they had visited the *Raydrau* with their trader-wagon that probably dealt in black-market wares. Instead, he waited for several breaths and said, "Actually, I'm glad you're here. You identified some of the poisons they used on Yudai in Runon, and Chayd likely tried the same toxins. We need to figure out which ones he was given and if there are any antidotes."

"Antidotes?" One of Alesh's eyebrows rose high.

"Or...reversals," Tatsu amended. "Someone in the market has to know a way to undo the damage the poisons did, but we don't think they'll be particularly forthcoming with the information."

Ral stood up then and crossed the space between the hammocks to put both hands on the sides of Yudai's face. It was probably surprise more than anything that kept him from pushing her away. He looked up at her with hooded eyes as she ran her fingertips across his forehead.

"Oh," she said, and the word weighed heavy. "Yudai, bad. Lots of pain?"

"No." Yudai sounded confused. "It never really hurts."

"No," Ral said. She dropped one hand to his chest and pressed against his ribs, on the right side above his heart. "Pain here."

Yudai sat back, breaking the connection between them. Tatsu thought maybe he'd reply, but nothing came out of his thinly pressed mouth. Yudai sank against the taut ropes and crossed his arms over his chest as Ral returned to Alesh's side.

"So, we need to find something to fix it," Alesh said.

"That's really all we can do," Tatsu agreed.

Alesh's eyes darted between Jotin and Tatsu, and then she nodded. "Well, since finding you seemed to be the reason Ral wanted to come out here, I suppose we'd better help you."

"We should go," Jotin said as he pushed off the wall. "I do not know how fruitful this endeavor will be."

As he watched Ral and Alesh stand to ready themselves, the buzzing beneath Tatsu's skin settled. The women were pieces of Chayd he felt much more comfortable having with him—bits of home that helped to make the unfamiliar buildings of Moswar less threatening. But as the group moved to leave, Yudai grabbed at Tatsu's arm and tugged him back.

"Are you sure this is a good idea?" Yudai asked.

"Why wouldn't it be? What's wrong with having them here? You know Ral; you know how she seems to just *know* things—"

"I'm not worried about Ral. It's her sister I don't trust."

Tatsu observed the other three make their way toward the arched entryway. "There's nothing to worry about. She came here to take care of Ral."

"She was more than willing to sell me out to the queen once in order to get her freedom. What makes you think anything has changed?"

"She didn't come here for the queen."

"But how do you *know* that?" Yudai asked. "You want to believe it was a coincidence."

The stars blinked overhead, and to his right, the sliver of moon arced over the flat tops of the Moswar buildings, stacked like blocks against the horizon.

"Look, Alesh is my friend," Tatsu started.

"I thought *I* was your friend. Or at least something like that."

Tatsu groaned. "Why are we doing this? I trust her."

"And what happens if you're wrong?" Yudai's fingers tightened around Tatsu's arm. "What happens if she's here to cart me off to Chayd because the queen has made another of those deals with her? What happens if she's only here for her own interests?"

"Then I'll figure out how to get us out of here. I'm not going to give you back to the Queen of Chayd; you know that."

Yudai stared for a long time, until the space between them became uncomfortable enough to rattle in Tatsu's bones. Then Yudai dropped both his hand and his gaze, sighing loudly.

"Fine. Let's go, then."

But as Yudai started up after the others, who'd paused just outside the archway to wait for them, Tatsu had a hard time dislodging the knot in his throat.

"THIS IS THE *Raydrau*," Jotin said as they stepped into a large open square very near to what likely was the center of Moswar. Despite the darkness, the night market pulsed, alive with energy and activity. Awnings stretched over the carts had lanterns of colored glass hanging from them. The mottled glow of overlapping baubles blended together across the ground, a painting of light extending well past the edge of the carts. The market was devoid of permanent buildings, consisting of only the awnings and tent stalls hitched up with small iron hooks sticking out of the ground. There were more people than Tatsu had ever seen in one place, and all of them seemed to have an agenda: buying, selling, or weaving with a strange sort of rhythm through those gathered in clusters around the cart latches.

The smell, thankfully, hung lighter than Tatsu remembered it being on the main streets, though he could still pick out the faint scent of burning incense. Only a few stalls sold food, most of it meant to be eaten on the go. Strips of smoked meat on spindly sticks and small bags of dried fruits sat on the side of several carts close to the entrance. The majority of the caravans and tents peddled other goods. As Tatsu leaned closer to the nearest one, dozens of woven animal figures inlaid with colorful stones sparkled in the multi-hued light.

"Perhaps we should split up," Jotin said. "Your friend here—"

"Alesh," Tatsu supplied.

"If she knows the poisons used, she may be able to pinpoint some of them, provided she can get past the initial negotiation."

Alesh looked slightly disgruntled. "What is the 'initial negotiation'?"

"The alchemists will not immediately show you black-market goods," Jotin said. "You must converse with them enough for them to trust you. If they believe you are a threat to turn them in, you will get nowhere."

"So, we argue?" Alesh asked.

"Only argue if you wish for them to test some of their more inventive wares on you," Jotin warned.

Alesh's gaze, when it met Tatsu's, seemed both annoyed and apprehensive. "So, I'm supposed to weasel into the good graces of Joesarian alchemists to find a possible antidote for the toxins without making them mad?"

"See what you can do, at least," Tatsu said.

"Fine." Alesh looped her arm through Ral's. "I'll take Ral with me. You three are on your own."

As the two women walked into the throng of people, the market goers shifted into place around them until they slowly disappeared from view.

Jotin turned to him, expression severe. "Let me handle the negotiations. And try not to make anyone mad."

He turned and moved toward one of the stalls on the outer border of the cluster of tents and carts. On Tatsu's right, Yudai coughed out a sound caught somewhere between a laugh and a sigh.

"It seems like all we really *do* is make people mad," he said.

Tatsu never got the chance to agree before they had to hurry to catch up with Jotin's retreating figure.

Chapter Six

AN OLD JOESARIAN woman with deep-set wrinkles across her weathered face operated the first stand Jotin made his way to. Strewn across the wooden table in front of the woman's fluttering robes were a wide assortment of bottles, the glass containers a multitude of colors and bulb-like shapes. A few others milled around the wares, occasionally picking up a bottle to peer at the cloudy liquid inside, and after a few minutes, Jotin pushed his way to the front of the crowd.

The conversation between the seller and Jotin was in one of the Joesarian dialects, so Tatsu hung back with nothing to contribute. Everything sounded civil enough, even if the language was beyond him, and if he had to guess, he'd say Jotin spent time inquiring about a few of the bottles sitting out on the table. Every so often, the woman would pick one up and point at it, explaining the contents, and Jotin would nod, moving on to the next one. Tatsu waited while trying to ignore the rising hairs on his arms, eyeing the other buyers milling about.

"He's working his way into the seller's good graces, isn't he." Yudai said, more statement than question. "If we have to do this each time, it's going to take forever to get through all the stands."

But Tatsu barely registered Yudai speaking, for his skin prickled with a too-familiar foreboding. He whipped his head to the side as he turned, but nothing jumped out.

There were too many people, and too much noise bombarded his senses from all directions. Closing his eyes, he reached out with his instincts; the excess of bodies and energy prohibited him from picking anything out, and the failure cramped his stomach.

"Tatsu!" Yudai repeated until Tatsu finally broke his focus on the crowd.

"Sorry."

Yudai frowned. "You're all jumpy and nervous again."

"Someone's watching us," Tatsu said, "and I don't like it."

The defensive sensation passed as the dread faded away, but he couldn't get his heart to calm down. Whatever toed at the edges of his faculties felt like the stalking of a cliffcat, perched high above him and out of sight, just waiting for the moment to pounce. Lurking in the shadows and tiring out its victim worked well for predators on the mountainsides, and the same thing in Moswar's crowds would spell a death sentence for them.

"Did you see anyone?" Yudai asked.

Tatsu shook his head. "No. It's only a feeling. But someone's there."

"That's not really very helpful," Yudai said, but he did seem a little less confident. He took a few seconds to steal glances at the nearby marketgoers. After checking the crowd for a time, Yudai put his hands to his head and ran his fingers through his hair. The roots, finally longer than his pinky finger, gleamed less uniform and more mottled. The top of his head might as well have had ink spilled over the crown, the black dripping down the bleached strands unevenly.

"This is silly," he said with a sigh. "If we can't see anyone following us, and we can't prove that anyone is there, what are we going to do about it?"

"I don't know."

"Who could even know we were here? We just got here, and we haven't announced our presence."

Still, Tatsu's chest wouldn't unclench, and the constrictive tightness of his arm sling wasn't helping matters. "Ral and Alesh were able to find us."

"That's different," Yudai said, scoffing. "Ral's *special.* I doubt anyone else has a tracker with her uncanny abilities leading them."

Jotin, at the alchemist's wares stand, appeared to be reaching the end of his conversation with the seller. He had nothing in his hands, and the tone of his voice rang resigned, even if Tatsu didn't know what was being said. He pushed himself up and away from the table full of bottles, shaking his head.

"Nothing," he said. "She refused to engage me with anything unlicensed."

"So now what?" Yudai asked.

"We try again with the next one and pray we have better luck there."

But the next one dragged out for even longer with the same results. Tatsu couldn't help at all when Jotin launched into his conversations with the sellers, and there was even less he could do when Jotin kept returning with nothing. Tatsu observed people walk away from other tents with small baubles, satchels of dried herbs, and totems carved from animal bones, but none of the alchemists they tried were willing to talk about their black-market poisons.

Stopping at one stall after another, they made their way on a zigzagged path through the *Raydrau*, until the sun peeked up over the horizon and Tatsu's eyelids threatened to sink closed. No further instances of being watched prickled his instincts, nor had they made any progress toward stopping Yudai's uncontrollable siphon.

Morning's arrival stung. Tatsu was exhausted from keeping such a focused guard all night, and Yudai was cranky from defeat.

"So that's it?" Yudai asked as the last stand they visited began packing up the glass bottles to store during the day. "We have no options?"

"We did not talk to everyone," Jotin said. "There is still a chance that someone here will know something."

"Yeah, but not even one person agreed to show you their poisons."

Jotin looked haggard; he'd done all the talking throughout the night, and no doubt his throat pounded from the repercussions of it.

"Sometimes, approaching the merchant several times shows your resolve and determination. It is possible that repeated visits will convince the alchemists we are serious about our questions."

"Then we need to come back again," Tatsu said.

Yudai hissed out his frustration. "This system is *useless*. How did these poisons ever make their way to Runon if this is the process to get them?"

Tatsu's stomach twisted. He tried not to think of Alesh and her jobs back in Chayd, but the thoughts came unbidden anyway.

"Smugglers," he said. "We're approaching the source rather than the network. All of these alchemists already have people they trust running their products out, and we aren't part of them."

Jotin nodded, though being correct summoned no joy within Tatsu.

"The alchemists in the market have little to gain by talking to us," Jotin agreed, "and everything to lose. We are not trusted or known here; why would they want to help us?"

Through a break in the thinning crowd, Tatsu saw Alesh and Ral walking toward them. Ral held a small beaded trinket, but Alesh's hands were empty, and any hope Tatsu had of success disappeared with the stars overhead.

"Sorry," Alesh said, crossing her arms over her chest. "People here *really* didn't want to talk to me. Not even my old connections helped. I'm doubtful many of them even had what I was asking for."

As Ral played with her prize, beads strung on several thick leather cords, Yudai shrank inward on himself. In light of their dismal night of work, his face had lost its edge—instead of the haughty chin tilt that was always more endearing than snobbish, he seemed lost and alone. His heavily curved shoulders made him appear smaller, and curled up on himself, he didn't look much like a prince at all.

The sight of him sent a shock of something unsettling through Tatsu.

"Hey," he said and reached for Yudai's arm. "We'll find something, I promise. We'll sort this out."

"Let's go back to the *sayen*." Yudai wouldn't meet Tatsu's eyes. "I'd like to move our hammocks to make sure I don't kill any trees."

Despite his prodding, Tatsu couldn't get Yudai to talk to him any more as they returned to the *sayen* under the pinking dawn sky. They walked in silence, bodies sagging with the crushing weight of disappointment.

AFTER A RESTLESS day of sleep, they went back to the *Raydrau* to try again. The second night was just as bustling as the first had been, except, somehow, the magic from the multicolored rings of light spreading across the ground seemed dimmer. The hanging lanterns and shadowy tents held less promise and fewer rewards, and the optimism Tatsu had first felt dissipated, leaving him empty. He tried to engage Yudai but got few real responses. Yudai acted as though hope was gone, burned out of him with the soaring heat of the desert sun.

"It's only been one night," Tatsu tried again as they gathered near the edge of the night market where the buildings gave way to the flat, sand-packed square. "We'll find something to help tonight."

"If this doesn't work, what do we do?" Yudai asked. "Move every day so I can't drain an entire city? Hide away from the world forever?"

"We'll...we'll figure something out. We'll find the smugglers who move the toxins across Rad-em and into Chayd. We'll sail across the Oldal Sea to find a new antidote entirely. There's always something else we can do."

But his heart wasn't completely in the words, and from the set of Yudai's jaw, he knew it too. Tatsu was useless with only one arm, his dead limb strapped close to his chest in a linen sling. He didn't have the knowledge of the desert fauna or the art of alchemy to do anything himself, and returning across the mountains promised only more of the same pain they'd already escaped from. Tatsu tried to come up with another possibility, but the options got stuck in his throat. His whole body reverberated, hammering the same message out with each shuddering beat: *this was the last option to save Yudai.*

Jotin, for his part, didn't appear downtrodden.

"We can hit several stands again to prove our resolve," he said. "And I can go to more that Alesh visited yesterday. I may have better luck as someone from within the dominions."

He turned to wade his way into the crowd. Tatsu froze, and he called out, "Wait. We should stay together."

Jotin raised both eyebrows. "That will halve our ability to reach all the alchemists."

"Stay together," Tatsu insisted and ran his tongue over his dry lips as he rubbed at the hair standing up on his arms. "And keep your eyes open."

The feeling of being watched continued as they moved together to the first stand. Ral delightedly traced her fingers over the colored glass bottles holding a variety of tonics. Tatsu shifted so the bulk of his attention spread out behind them, longing for his woods where he knew the risks. Before, the creeping feeling had faded within minutes, but rather than disappear, his hackles intensified. A bitter taste burst in the back of his throat, and for a moment, his mind flashed back to when his father had first fallen ill over ten years ago. The lurking danger held something dark, something Tatsu didn't think he would be able to fight—it was the sinking, aching feeling of inescapable inevitability.

His whole body trembled on high alert as they waited for Jotin to finish his conversation, but Tatsu never saw anything out of the ordinary in the people milling throughout the market. Minute by minute, the fire flickered into nothing, leaving him tired and rattled.

Jotin had no luck with the first merchant or the second, but the third took more time than any others so far. Milling about and waiting for it to conclude, whether the outcome was good or bad, seemed to make all of them anxious. Alesh moved between several closer stalls to crane her head in and see what they were selling, and Yudai crossed his arms over his chest, an immovable weight. Tatsu tried to close his eyes several times and will his body to relax, but he didn't have much success with it.

"Where's Ral?" he asked after he opened his eyes the second time and couldn't find her in the crowd.

"She found a fortune-teller a few stalls back," Alesh said. She turned to point to the tent in question. "I told her she could stay there and wait for us. I think she was getting bored."

"I'm going to go check on her."

Alesh frowned. "She'll be fine in the tent. We're still nearby. Is something wrong?"

"No," Tatsu said but didn't wholly believe it. "Stay here in case Jotin needs you to identify something used."

On his journey to the stall Alesh had identified, he almost ran into a Joesarian man wearing corded leather, and then he *did* run into a woman wearing a long cape-like dress that curved up and over her head. The smell of meat cooking over coals invaded his senses for a moment, distracting him.

It didn't take long to get to where he was going. The steeply pitched tent was made of silks so thin Tatsu could see partway through them, the material shimmering in the flickering candlelight. A ring of mounted wax surrounded the opening, and Tatsu ducked beneath the candles and pushed the silks aside to slip in.

Inside sat a small, old Joesarian woman with long black hair falling in sheets over her linen-wrapped shoulders. Ral knelt in front of her, and she turned with a wide smile when Tatsu entered.

"Tatsu!"

"Ah, you have come," the Joesarian woman said in Common. "I have been waiting for you."

"How did you know I was coming?" Tatsu asked. The tent boasted no wares on display, which seemed odd in a marketplace devoted to moving goods. "What exactly are you peddling here?"

"My sight," the woman told him with a smile.

Tatsu felt out of place as he fidgeted, glancing about the sheer tent and wishing he could see more of what was going on outside.

"I sell secrets of the future," she continued. "My name is Soom, and I have been waiting for your arrival for many seasons."

"Tatsu, sit!" Ral said.

There didn't seem to be anything else to do, and against his better judgment, Tatsu was drawn to Soom. He took a wide step and then sank beside Ral while keeping his gaze on the fortune-teller in front of him.

"You see the future?" he asked.

Soom leveled him with a gaze that saw too much. In lieu of an answer, she held out her hands palms up on the wooden table, clearly expecting him to follow.

Tatsu, unable to stop himself, put his good hand on top of hers.

"I see everything." Soom's fingertips poked at Tatsu's palm, and the air inside the tent quieted, growing heavy. The material separating them from the rest of the *Raydrau* wasn't thick, but somehow it muffled the constant sounds from outside. Seated within the too-warm circle, it seemed as though they'd been transported somewhere else entirely.

After a while, Soom looked up again. "You have much fear inside you."

"Is that bad?" Tatsu asked.

"Not always. And not all of it is for you."

Tatsu tried to pull his hand away, but her gnarled fingers gripped it tighter.

"You carry your past with you. You should learn to let it go—it only holds you back from your way forward."

"What's my way forward?"

Soom's face broke out into a wide smile, creases pulling at her brown skin. "My dear, you already have it. Have you not realized yet?"

Finally, Tatsu succeeded in getting his hand back. She hadn't done anything to him, but still, his skin stung. He balled his fingers into a fist close to his shirt.

"Well, this has been wonderful and all, but we should go," he said. "The others are waiting for us."

"Tatsu came," Ral said.

Soom looked to Ral with a kind expression. "Yes, my child, he did. Your arrival means the winds of change have finally begun."

"How did Ral know to come find you here?" Tatsu asked.

"She is like me. Surely you must have figured that out by now. She can see things before they happen."

"But that's magic," Tatsu said, feeling uneasy. It had been a while since he worried about Ral's abilities—if anyone else knew, she'd become a target.

"No," Soom said, frowning, "and yes. It is a different sort of magic, older than the sand itself. It is not like those who control the life of this world."

"Magic," Ral repeated. She put both hands up, palms toward the sky, and stared at them for a second before lifting her gaze to Soom. "Help. Help magic. Help Tatsu."

Soom closed her fingers around Ral's again. "Yes, child. We are helping him."

"Stop," Tatsu pleaded, rubbing his hand across his brow. "If Ral has magic, are people going to go after her?"

"No," Soom said.

Ral's smile returned, softer somehow. "Tatsu worries."

"What did you mean you're helping?" Tatsu said. "Do you know who we need to talk to in order to get the tonics? Do you know how to fix Yudai's magic?"

"No."

Tatsu looked from side to side as his blood started to heat. "You sell the future. You said you sell your sight. Couldn't you see where we need to get the antidotes?"

"There are no antidotes for your prince here."

Time stopped as Tatsu froze. It was one thing to think those thoughts at the darkest part of the night, but another to hear them from someone else. As he wrestled with the aches blooming through his limbs, Soom's expression softened across the table.

"I am sorry. That was not what you wished to hear."

"I...we came here to find something." Tatsu's lips stumbled around the words. "And...if we can't, if there's nothing..."

He pressed both hands against his eyes as though he could block everything out. He'd known, deep down, but hadn't wanted to believe it. He'd known they wouldn't find anything in the Moswar markets.

"Will he die?" he choked out and couldn't look at her, afraid of what he'd see on her face.

"That is your fear," she said. "You are more afraid of losing your prince than anything else."

"He's not my prince."

He let his hands fall away from his face and found Soom smiling at him. "Isn't he?"

Laughter, acidic and angry, forced Tatsu's mouth open. "What help are you? You can't even answer my question. We came here to heal him!"

"Yudai pain," Ral said to Soom, and the old woman rubbed her weathered fingers over the back of Ral's hands. "Bad pain."

"You did not come here to heal him." Soom's gaze stayed on Ral's kneeling form in front of her. "You came here for your next step."

"What is that if it's not to *fix* him?"

Soom's expression shifted—her eyes lowered, and her mouth puckered. After a moment, she started to languidly shake her head from side to side. She looked infinitely old. "I know you want answers, but I cannot give them to you. It is not my role."

"Then what *is* your role? What are you doing?"

As the woman held his gaze, the world slowed again. Several seconds of nothing ticked by before the weight of everything crashed against his senses, and then, in a snap, the rush of the world came roaring back. Tatsu's whole body began to shake, all the way down through his useless arm. He knew what she was doing. She was distracting him.

She was *distracting* him.

"No," Tatsu whispered. His legs propelled him up and forward, away from Soom and her vague predictions offered across the low table, away from the reality he'd been so desperate to ignore.

He stumbled out of the sheer tent into the mass of people, disoriented and unable to fill his lungs with enough air. As he stood there, spinning, he wasn't sure where he was or the direction he'd initially taken. He didn't know where Jotin had moved on to, or where Yudai and Alesh were. The breath he sucked in rattled through his ribs, burning in hot flashes. Wild terror overpowered the sour-sick feeling of being betrayed.

And then he saw the flash of shadow, darting low between slow-walking bodies in the *Raydrau*. He leapt after it immediately, his good shoulder bumping into nearly every person he tried to push his way through.

Tatsu tripped twice and somehow managed to keep himself upright as he ran after the figure. The shadow had the advantage of surprise, but Tatsu had spent his life chasing after game in his father's woods, and he knew how to keep pace. When the dashing figure took a wide turn around a small cluster of people, Tatsu slipped through two of the stalls to cut it off. He caught a skinny arm just as they reached the stand Jotin and Alesh idled in front of.

With a savage cry, Tatsu jerked the person he'd captured backward and was caught off guard when there was much less resistance than he'd expected. Tatsu found himself staring at a crumpled mess of thin limbs and wide, startled eyes.

"What?" Tatsu said, and beneath his grasp, the Joesarian child shivered. He couldn't have been more than eight years old and looked like he'd never seen a full meal in his life. No weapons hung from his worn clothing; in fact, nothing about him betrayed any sort of danger.

"A street urchin?" Jotin asked, moving up beside Tatsu and his catch. "He was following us?"

"No, that doesn't make sense," Tatsu said. The child began to squirm and kick his leather-clad feet against the dirt. "I *knew* someone was watching us, but the fortune-teller said—"

"The fortune-teller?" Alesh interrupted. "Is Ral still there? Why isn't she with you?"

Jotin leaned in, pushing his face close to the child's. "What are you doing here? Why were you following us?"

"Please," the child cried, and two fat tears fell from his dark eyes to run down his cheeks, leaving shimmering tracks behind them. "Please."

"This can't be what she was talking about," Tatsu continued, aware that he was babbling nonsense. The receding fear left him light-headed, lungs burning. The sounds of the night market grew louder and louder, drowning out everything except the thundering echo of his heartbeat. "This can't have been it."

"Please," the child said again, with more tears pooling in the corners of his eyes. "He said—"

"Who is *he*?" Jotin cut him off, and that was when it all clicked into place.

Tatsu spun, still dizzy, and it took moments too long to locate Yudai, standing behind them near one of the other carts. He was still hunched over in a miserable ball, his arms wrapped across his chest, but his back faced Tatsu as he looked over the meat pies in a nearby trade stall.

"Yudai!" Tatsu cried, and Yudai turned to the sound of Tatsu's voice right as the thick-cloaked man beside him sprang forward. There was only enough time for Tatsu to see the glint of a knife held in his hand and to suck in a pained lungful of air before the man struck—a wide arc that would have done much more damage had he managed to hit Yudai's back.

A sharp cry of pain sounded, and then the world exploded as Yudai's magic *erupted*.

The force of it blew Tatsu off his feet. His good shoulder hit the ground before the rest of his weight, sending shocks of pain through his back. For a moment, his ears registered nothing but a heart-wrenching silence, and then all the sound in the market was replaced with the barrage of winds whipping about his head. He scrambled to his feet as the intensity of Yudai's magic ripped through carts and tents alike. Torn apart, the debris caught in the wind and began to swirl above their heads.

"Yudai!" he tried to yell, but the wind stole his voice too. With his good arm held in front of his face, Tatsu took a step toward Yudai's kneeling form and was nearly impaled by a splintered tent pole hurled through the air like a javelin. On the ground to his left, Alesh lay on her stomach with both hands curled around the back of her neck.

Tatsu could see Yudai's outline against the beige of the ground, but his figure was so obscured and warped by the winds and the swirling market debris that the image blinked in and out of existence. Staring into the wind, Tatsu's eyes watered and burned; tears leaked out as he dropped his gaze and pushed forward, praying that nothing hit him.

The leather of a tent pulled free and snapped through the air to wrap about a cart, rocking it back and forth with the magical pull. Tatsu sidestepped, falling more than walking, to get himself safely by the whole of a wooden tabletop. Deafening, the sound of the wind screamed against his ears, but he battled through it, hurling his weight toward Yudai.

And then, all of a sudden, the magic stopped, and the debris held aloft by the wind dropped to the ground with a series of echoing, earth-shattering crashes.

Tatsu stumbled forward and barely managed to stay upright when the resistance he fought against disappeared. The loss of the roar against his ears shook worse than the actual sound had—he took a shuddering breath, and then another, as a wail started up somewhere to his left behind a smashed-in cart. The screams that started up, a cacophony of misery, froze Tatsu completely. People were hurt. *People were dead.*

"Yudai," he said, gasping, and somehow he got his feet to carry him to the man kneeling on the dirt. He moved to grab Yudai's arm and paused when he saw Yudai's shoulders shaking. Holding his right arm, palm facing the sky, Yudai's layered clothes were splashed with darkness.

It took Tatsu a moment to realize the stain was Yudai's own blood splattered on the linen. It wasn't red at all—the sticky residue was black, like the midnight sky, ink still wet and glittering.

Yudai raised his eyes, wide and betrayed, to Tatsu's.

"What is this?" he whispered, both voice and body trembling. "What have they done to me?"

Chapter Seven

TATSU KNELT IN front of Yudai and tried to ignore the shouts and cries rising in anguish. He reached out to brush against the still-wet blood, but his fingers came away black. As he stared at the streaky liquid languidly running toward his palm for a few seconds, fiery acid burst hot on the back of his tongue. Above their heads, the sky was lightening—morning had filtered through the clouds once again, bringing with it the slow-building heat of the day.

"Don't panic," Tatsu said instinctively and then leaned in to inspect the wound. The assassin had gotten a good amount of skin with his knife, but Yudai's movement had kept the majority of the injury superficial. The long cut across his forearm continued to his torso, where the blade had sliced through both layers of cloth, leaving a harsh line across Yudai's abdomen. Tatsu focused on the arm wound, where the bulk of the blood seemed to seep from. After pushing shreds of fabric aside, he pressed his hand against it to stop the flow. The hope that the blackness stemmed from the knife rather than Yudai seemed the only thing his mind could latch onto; he hoped so fiercely each lungful of air burned.

When he removed his hand again, more of the black bubbled up from the cut.

"Gods," Yudai gasped, and his expression crumpled. "*Gods*, this is going to kill me. I'm going to die. They've poisoned me, and I'm going to die."

"You're not going to die," Tatsu said. But even as he moved in to cover the cut with his hand once more, his thoughts swirled. How had they gone so long without seeing the aftereffect of the toxins? It was either luck or doom that'd kept such a terrible repercussion hidden from them both. His mind whirled with thoughts of Yudai withering and dying before his very eyes, consumed from within as his own poisoned blood betrayed and devoured his body.

The man in front of him was still very much alive, though terrified and in a fair amount of pain. Focusing on the reality took considerable effort.

"It's not bleeding too bad," Tatsu said and was surprised at how steady his voice sounded. Was his courage for himself or Yudai? "If we wrap it, the wound will clot and seal itself within the next ten minutes or so."

Yudai stared at him, breathing hard, looking as if he'd given up entirely. It seemed wrapping the injury with one arm would prove too difficult. As though summoned, Alesh moved in and pulled off her linen headscarf. She wound the fabric around Yudai's elbow to stop most of the blood flow and then swept it down and across the injured flesh. The cut continuing along his belly had already stopped bleeding. Tatsu checked it again, but he was satisfied it would heal on its own. However, the blood-blackened clothes, heavy with the tacky remains, were a lost cause.

Only after standing, content Yudai was not in any immediate danger of dying, did Tatsu have the courage to look at the *Raydrau*—or at least what was left of it.

Very little of the market near them had been spared. Ripped away, the nearest tents had left behind broken splinters of poles still sticking up from the ground. Most of the carts had been smashed, two of them toppled and flipped completely with all their wares strewn across the dirt. Each step taken produced a wince-inducing shatter of glass due to the bottles and vials littering the pathway in pieces, their tonics long soaked into the ground.

Since the force of the magic wind had pushed everything aside, the blast radius immediately around them was cleared except for one thing: the assassin's body hanging from a half-flattened stall, kept aloft by the wooden beam protruding through his chest. The blood spread in a bright red arc about the man's body, and the sight of it made Tatsu's stomach churn.

Tatsu stumbled away, but Jotin moved toward the corpse with purpose and pulled back the brown cloak. He tore free the leather glove covering the man's left hand, revealing a shimmering silver tattoo tracing across and up the brown skin of the assassin's knuckles.

"Mercenary," Jotin said, voice thick with disgust. "A hired man from Rad-em."

"Someone paid mercenaries to come and kill Yudai?" Tatsu asked. "How did they even know we were here?"

Jotin shook his head. "I do not know. But whoever ordered the hit likely sent that urchin boy to track our movements through the city."

Tatsu stared at the dead man's face, half covered with a thick cloth that looped across his shoulders. He tried to ignore the thoughts crawling up, menacing to devour him whole. *My mother might have done this.*

Wrenching his eyes away, he turned from the body and knelt in front of Yudai. All the words got stuck in his throat, so he said nothing and, instead, clasped his black-stained fingers over Yudai's shoulder. Yudai's silver eyes glistened with unshed tears, and the lines of his face betrayed the struggle to fight them back. Through heaving breaths, Yudai opened his mouth.

"You are under arrest," came a booming voice behind them, out of Tatsu's line of sight. "By order of the *Daos* Guard of the capital city of Moswar, you are to come with us to the High Council where you will be charged with the destruction of the *Raydrau* and the murder of at least three citizens."

"It wasn't his fault!" Alesh cried.

Yudai's face went slack for a moment, and then he wrenched to the left. His body shook beneath Tatsu's touch, but it didn't take Yudai long to school his features into a hard sort of acceptance. When the lines of his face smoothed out, something snagged in Tatsu's chest, and he would have sworn his ribs contracted as if barring his lungs in an iron cage.

"Don't," Tatsu whispered.

"I understand," Yudai said, ignoring Tatsu and pushing himself up to his feet.

"Wait, what?" Alesh asked. One of the guards had his fingers wrapped around her arm, and she was fighting against the strength of it. Several long strands of hair fell loose from her black braid and hung down the middle of her face, waving from side to side with her movements. "You can't go with them! This wasn't his fault, that man tried to *kill* him—"

"And conveniently, he is dead," one of the guards said. "Which means you are all to come with us as witnesses and possible accomplices for the sentencing."

"You can't take me," Alesh said. "I can't leave my sister."

But as if on cue, Ral appeared behind the cluster of leather-clad guards, unharmed and no worse for wear. Alesh made a noise that seemed torn between relief and exasperation, but at least she stopped pushing against the guard's hold.

Tatsu's chest ached. His body reverberated with exhaustion, reeling from the aftermath of the attack, and, in truth, he couldn't have fought if he wanted to. Nothing remained, not after the fire fled and left him bereft of air.

Yudai balled his hands into fists at his sides as he turned to face the guards with his shoulders squared. The black stain splattered across his clothes matched the streak of blood on the bottom of his chin.

"Take me to the High Council," he demanded.

THE WALK THROUGH Moswar's streets reminded Tatsu of the similar spectacle in Dradela when Alesh had been by his side, both of them in heavy handcuffs. The *Daos* Guard elected not to use the same iron on their current party, but the heavy feeling of being punished was much the same. Alesh, perhaps having flashbacks to the first time, had immediately grabbed hold of Ral's hand and didn't seem keen to let go. Ral, for her part, didn't make any move to run off, and her contentment with marching beside the others helped ease the tension in Tatsu's shoulders.

Chasing her footprints into the desert could only end badly.

"What are we walking into?" Tatsu asked, slowing to walk beside Jotin. His boots kicked up small clouds of dust as they moved along the roads, the packed dirt brightening as the sun rose overhead.

"The High Council is made up of one representative from each Joesarian dominion," Jotin said. "There are twelve dominions that make up our kingdom. These twelve representatives serve for two years before they are replaced."

"And your father—?"

"Is part of the current High Council. The council members remain in Moswar during their service to negotiate trade agreements, navigate international politics, and hear cases deemed important enough to be brought before them."

"I'm not sure if it's better or worse to be facing twelve leaders, rather than just one." Tatsu sighed. "We don't exactly have the best record."

"The council members return to their lives after their service is up," Jotin said. "I think you will find that they retain much of their sense of how the world outside Moswar works."

"That's not really what I'm afraid of," Tatsu replied and kept his eyes on Yudai's long strides in front of them as he was held firmly between two of the *Daos* Guards moving in tandem. Yudai's shoulders squared straight and high, but Tatsu wondered when exactly he'd become able to see through the confident mask Yudai wore—there were cracks in the façade, revealed in the tiny tremors rippling all the way down Yudai's back.

When Tatsu glanced back at Alesh, her face was set in a similar fashion. He wanted to tell her everything would be fine, except the lie rang wrong. With nothing to offer, he fell back into the uncomfortable silence.

The skin of his bad arm itched, and despite his initial joy at feeling anything in his fingers, the return of sensation didn't seem positive. Each step closer to the Joesarian High Council made the trembling worse, until it was so overpowering he could barely focus on the finely carved openings decorating the buildings to either side of him. The rhythmic thuds of their footsteps echoed his dread back at him. Over and over, his thoughts kept twisting toward Nota, and the knowledge that his mother was responsible for everything pounded against his ears.

He stared at the angles of Yudai's shoulders and whispered for forgiveness for the traitorous blood within and the misfortune of being born to a woman so cold.

"This wasn't your fault," he said to Alesh as their group turned a wide corner and started in the direction of a sprawling single-story building made from sand so worn from wind it sparkled beneath the dawn. "I'll find a way to get you and Ral out of this."

"I think we're guilty by association." Alesh's voice sounded grim, and her lips were set in a hard, thin line.

Tatsu looked to Ral, who gazed back at him with the barest hint of a smile.

"Still," he said, "if there's any way to get you away from this, I'll do it."

The *Daos* Guard led them inside the sprawling central mansion to a spacious room with wide, high ceilings propped up with bare beams of wood. Covered with small shards of brightly colored glass, the walls rang out of place after so much time spent on the beige-hazed streets. Within the fragments were images, abstract in nature with free-flowing lines and curves pulsing with life and energy. The room started deep and narrowed as it lengthened, so that the aft section was half the size of the entrance. A sizeable crowd milled by the doorway. Most were Joesarians, dressed in leather and light-colored scarves, and all were gathered in front of a long, dark table.

Twelve figures sat motionless—the High Council of Joesar.

With so many bodies, the end of the room created a bottleneck that threatened to close in even as the guards pushed the spectators aside to make space.

"Esteemed Council," one guard said, and his voice boomed jarringly loud. "We bring you the man responsible for the destruction at the *Raydrau* and his accomplices."

One of the councilwomen, seated near the middle of the table, waved them closer with a flick of her fingers, and the guards shoved Yudai forward with so much force he stumbled.

"It was not an intentional destruction," Yudai started, with a dark look over his shoulder at the guards. "I was attacked while in the night market—"

"Why would someone attack you in the *Raydrau,* stranger?" one of the councilmembers asked.

"Are you blaming our citizens for this?" said another.

"No, it was a mercenary," Yudai said. "Our Cabaj guide identified him as a hired man from Rad-em, and when he tried to kill me, my magic—"

"You blew up nearly half the market," a member interrupted.

"I didn't mean to."

"And yet here you are," said the first woman, spreading her hands wide in front of her. "And your magic has destroyed part of our city."

"We could see the mess from the windows here," another said.

Yudai looked over his shoulder at Tatsu, his eyes glistening for such a quick moment Tatsu doubted the sight. Yudai turned to the table. "I don't have control over my magic right now. The attack on my life...prompted the explosion."

"Which brings us back to the original question," said a man of the council who wore layered linens, much like the ones Yudai and Tatsu had been temporarily gifted. "Why would someone attempt to kill you in Moswar?"

Yudai's chin lifted. "Because I'm the Crown Prince of Runon."

A beat of silence, with tension thick enough to taste, and then the farthest woman at the table asked, "How do we know you are telling us the truth?"

"Father," Jotin said, stepping forward. "I have traveled with him since we found them in the Cabaj-dominion. His words are true."

The man with the familiar clothing raised both eyebrows—his features were so similar to Jotin's that Tatsu should have deduced earlier he was Jotin's father. "And you have proof of this?"

"Nys believed his word," Jotin said, frowning.

"Nys is not a member of the High Council anymore. And with no proof of this claim to royal lineage, the Council must seek to find the truth of the matter."

When Jotin stepped back, deep-set lines crossed his forehead. At the rear of their group, Alesh and Ral were holding hands. Tatsu's gut fluttered, an unsettled butterfly beating against the sides of his stomach and tickling up his throat.

"If none of you hold an official capacity to prove the claim..." Jotin's father said.

"I do," said a voice from behind them, and the crowd parted to reveal a woman with a deep, heavy blue hood pulled up over her head. The thrum of recognition echoed all the way down Tatsu's fingers, even through his bad arm.

Leil marched, halving the space between them before dipping into a shallow half bow, one knee audibly creaking beneath her. "I hold the official capacity, as an ambassador from the court of Chayd, to verify this man's identity. He is who he claims."

The High Council fell silent.

"Very well," the first councilwoman said. "In respect for the royal kin of our neighboring lands, we will clear the room for a private audience with Prince..."

"Yudai," Leil supplied.

"...to get to the bottom of the destruction of our market and the deaths of our citizens."

The guards began to clear the spectators immediately, but Tatsu darted forward to press his fingers against the crook of Yudai's elbow.

"I can try to stay if you want," he said.

But Yudai's face was set, and he shook his head. "This is my duty. I'll be fine."

"I'll wait for you, then," Tatsu promised, and one of the guards pulled him away with heavy hands on his shoulders. Yudai gave no answer or reply. He faced the twelve seated solemnly in front of the apse of the room without any emotion marring his face.

"Jotin, we will keep your new friends here for the day," Jotin's father said from his place behind the table. "See that they are given whatever they may need and are put into the second guest wing."

Tatsu was surprised when even Leil was ushered out of the council chambers with them. Once all of the bystanders had been removed, the doors to the chamber banged shut, making Tatsu wince. Ral laughed, bright and happy, and threw a hand over her mouth to muffle the sound.

"What are you doing here?" Alesh asked Leil, an edge to her voice. She shuffled closer to Ral again as though creating a human shield.

"I came here after Yudai...escaped," Leil said. Her eyes darted to Tatsu's as the words tumbled out, and her throat bobbed beneath the shadows of her hood falling over her face. "I wanted to know what we'd done. We'd used so many poisons from Joesar, and I...wanted answers."

"And your official capacity?" Tatsu asked.

Leil's gaze dropped to her feet. "As a mage, I'm part of the royal court. I hold a status that's respected. It's why they accepted my reassurance of Yudai's identity."

"You are part of what did this to him," Alesh said, a low hiss. "In fact, it's partly your fault the *Raydrau* was blown up! If he had control of his magic—"

"Please, Alesh," Tatsu said. Leil's eyes glinted heavy with guilt, the same guilt Tatsu had seen on her face when he freed Yudai from under their noses. He knew the ashy, bitter taste of the emotion. Lingering beneath his tongue, regret often flared to life to remind him of his own hand in the situation. From the pursing of Leil's mouth, she clearly felt the same thing.

"Gods," Alesh said, sighing. She glared at Tatsu, and her fingers on Ral's arm clenched tighter. "This is her mess, and I don't trust her."

"I came for answers," Leil said. "I only wanted to help—"

"Little late for that, isn't it?" Alesh shot back. "Look what's already happened."

Before the tension could blow completely out of hand, Ral tugged on Alesh's head covering. "Hungry now."

Alesh didn't completely relax, though she did deflate.

"All right." She gave Leil one last distrustful look.

"I will take you to the kitchens," Jotin said. "And after that to your rooms for the day. I suspect the Council's dealings with your royal friend will take some time."

As the three of them started down the hallway, Tatsu tried to project sympathy toward Leil, which she mostly ignored. She curled her arms around her chest as though trying to disappear completely into the floor. The dark hue of her robes made such a contrast to the white stones that it was almost impossible to look anywhere else.

"What have you learned about the poisons you used?" Tatsu asked quietly.

Leil shook her head. "Very little so far. They are highly illegal, so no one wants to risk talking about them."

It didn't surprise him she'd suffered the same barrier they had. Tatsu thought back to the black of Yudai's blood and had to squeeze his eyes shut for a moment to drive the image away. Even then, the ghost of it hung just beyond his vision, out of reach.

"I'm sorry." Leil's eyes glimmered. "We didn't know what would happen."

"I don't think anyone did," Tatsu said. "Not even my—not even Nota. Maybe that's why Yudai's father allowed him to be used like that."

"His father?" Leil straightened. "The king? He must have known."

"Why do you think that?"

Leil shrugged halfheartedly, refusing to meet Tatsu's eyes. "He was going to benefit the most from it, wasn't he?"

"What do you mean?"

"You didn't know?" Leil bit her bottom lip, rolling it beneath her teeth. "The siphon didn't only affect the land, it affected *him* too. It would have extended his own life far beyond his gods-given years. He could've ruled for centuries."

The world went black at the edges. Tatsu's lungs constricted painfully. He was only dimly aware of his back hitting the wall behind him, until he slid to the ground, stone digging into his flesh with sharp flares of pain. Choking enough to gag, he pressed his palm to his mouth to keep his stomach contents in place.

"I didn't—" He couldn't finish for several wheezing breaths. "I didn't know."

"Then Yudai must not know either."

Tatsu buried his face in his hand. "I can't be in this position again. I can't tell him—but now I know, and I can't *not* tell him. This will *kill* him. I can't do this."

Leil seemed uncomfortable standing above him. She crossed her arms over her chest and looked down at his boots. "Maybe he doesn't need to know."

Tatsu's shoulders shook against the wall behind him.

"This is the sort of secret that ruins people, and I'm already a mess. How am I supposed to keep him together when I can barely do it for myself?"

"You don't have to," Leil suggested. But that wasn't true. She couldn't feel the pounding of Tatsu's heart against his bones, demanding that he do everything he could, commanding him with every step to keep one hand outstretched to the man next to him.

She leaned closer, frowning again. "Tatsu, you don't have to do this."

He did. He could taste it in the acid scalding the back of his tongue, and he could hear it through the ringing in his ears. Compulsion wormed its way through his thoughts and memories, blossoming as though the desire had always been there, an acorn erupting into a mighty oak tree. His eyes pricked with hot tears, more of a reflex action than anything else, and he wasn't sure which emotion had prompted the sting.

Sighing, he dropped his fingers from his mouth and then smothered as much of his terror as he could. "Yes, I do."

"Why?"

Tatsu shook his head. "You should go and find the others. I told him I'd wait for him, but you don't need to."

Leil didn't say anything else, but she did cast one last curious glance at Tatsu's crumpled form before she disappeared off to where Jotin had taken Alesh and Ral. Alone in the hall, Tatsu stared up at the seam where the walls met the ceiling, wondering if clawing out his betrayer of a heart would help. Maybe the only solution was holding the wretched organ in his hands. Maybe watching his feelings drip down his fingers in red sobs would rid him of the ache curling up from the pit of his stomach.

He pressed his fingers against his brow, wanting to laugh and cry at the same time. He wasn't sure whether the trembling in his fingers was from the overwhelming reality facing them all or from the truth whispering out from his long-shadowed yearning.

You're a fool, his mind screamed, raw and desperate, *and this is going to kill you both.*

Chapter Eight

AFTER WHAT HAD to be at least an hour, Tatsu's knees began to cramp and his stomach started to growl. He shakily extracted himself from his huddled position and made his way down the hall. The others had long since left the kitchen, but several palace servants still worked inside, and they quickly served him a bowl of a steaming half-mashed grain mixture with reedy vegetable roots. As he sat eating, trying to blend in with the wall behind him, he watched the Joesarian servants glide through the kitchen in their practiced waltz and wondered what they'd been told, if anything, about their unexpected visitors.

When he finished, Yudai still hadn't come out of the council chambers, and Tatsu wasn't entirely sure what to do. Jotin had been instructed to take them to their rooms for the day, but Tatsu hadn't paid attention to where they were. He found himself in the center of the hallway, looking from door to door and feeling quite lost until Ral appeared seemingly out of nowhere to stand in front of him. Maybe she'd heard his footsteps and come to investigate, expecting a game.

She cocked her head at him, waves of dark hair falling over her shoulders. "Tired?"

"All the time," Tatsu said with surprising honesty. "I can't remember the last time I *didn't* feel exhausted."

Ral gave him a small, sad sort of smile and took his good hand. "Tatsu, come."

She led him down the hall into a narrow wing that ended abruptly and contained only three doors. The sun had come up during Tatsu's time spent on the ground. High windows, little more than slits in the stone, reached up the walls to touch the seam of the ceiling, and the sunlight spilling in painted the opposite stones with impossibly bright rectangles of yellow. The temperature had gone up, but the height of the openings kept the interior relatively cool by allowing the hot air to slip out the windows as it rose.

Ral opened one of the smooth wooden doors and gestured for Tatsu to enter. On one side of the comfortably shabby room sat a table and single chair, both made of well-worn wood, and a light-colored linen hammock hung to the other side, tied up with thick, bleached ropes.

Tatsu sank into the chair and let his head fall into his palm.

"Ral, what're we going to do? Everything is falling apart."

"Tatsu fine," Ral replied. She knelt in front of him and pressed her palms into her thighs.

"But it's not about me."

Her face softened a bit as she nodded. "Bad things."

"Every time I think we might finally be able to fix something, there's another problem thrown at us. And we can't keep up, because we never get the chance to solve any of them before dealing with the new one. We're barely staying afloat as it is, and now this?"

Ral moved forward to grab Tatsu's hand, her fingers warm and smooth.

"Leaving was supposed to solve the problems," Tatsu whispered. "It was supposed to be our escape, and look what it's turned into."

"Needs you," Ral told him. "Be strong."

"I don't know if I can." Guilt was thick on his tongue, left over by the runny dinner he'd choked down without really tasting.

Ral's fingers tightened around his as she leaned in. "Tatsu strong. Chosen for strong."

Tatsu barked out a laugh. "What a joke that turned out to be. Life chose me for something I'm ill-equipped to deal with."

"Not life," Ral said, voice soft. "Not life, Tatsu."

Tatsu stared at her for a long moment. Her skin was the color of the bronze Chaydese *omn* in the bits of daylight filtering inside the room, and the sunbeams shining on her hair created a backdrop behind her head, illuminating her shoulders. She'd always carried with her an aura of calm, and even in a strange building in a faraway land, that remained the same—with her, Tatsu's body wanted to soften in relaxation. He squeezed her hand, partly for additional reassurance and partly to convey his gratitude for her empathy.

"Do I tell him?" he asked.

When Ral looked at him with an enigmatic expression, Tatsu let his eyes dart across the room.

"This is Yudai's room, isn't it? You brought me to Yudai's room."

She stood up but kept her hand in Tatsu's, and Tatsu wanted to cling to her and her certainty. It had to be a burden to know too much, to see too far. Ral was a mystery he wasn't sure he'd ever truly understand, but he appreciated how often she used her gifts to help him when it was never her job to do so.

"Thank you," he murmured and hoped she understood the rest of the words stuck behind his teeth.

"Tatsu fine," she said, and a smile crinkled across her face. "Tatsu be fine."

Tatsu looked down at their entwined fingers. "You know too much, don't you? That's what the fortune-teller said. You see everything that'll happen down the path, and you have to walk it anyway."

Strands of her halo-like hair fell over her shoulders as her smile stretched wider.

"Is it hard, knowing what will come to pass?" Tatsu asked.

"No. Life moves."

"Yes, it does. Alesh assumed her whole life she had to take care of you, but I'm starting to think it was always the other way around."

Ral's only response was a breathy little giggle as she let go of Tatsu's hand. She took several steps toward the door, and after surveying Tatsu sitting on the chair, she nodded. She seemed content with the situation, and, somehow, her certainty helped settle the rest of Tatsu's nerves too.

"Be strong," she repeated.

"Sleep well," he said. And then she slipped out the door, leaving him alone.

HE DIDN'T END up waiting very long. With only the sunlight on the wall to gauge time by, Tatsu guessed he'd been in the room for only twenty minutes or so before he heard footsteps and voices outside the door.

"—will go after nightfall. Thank you for taking me here," Yudai said, muffled on the other side before the door was opened. It took a moment for Yudai to notice Tatsu seated within, but when he did, his whole body seemed to unwind, a visible sigh traveling through his limbs.

"This will be fine," he continued to the unknown figure next to him, without taking his eyes off Tatsu. "Thank you."

Yudai stepped inside and closed the door behind him, and in the light of the sun, the dark circles beneath his eyes stood out like rings of coal streaked across his skin. At some point, he'd washed off the remnants of the black blood from his face, though the stains on his shirt remained.

"Is it all right that I'm here?" Tatsu asked. "I probably shouldn't have presumed it would be."

"Yes." Yudai's fingers fell free of the wooden handle. "I'm glad you're here."

As Yudai crossed the room to sink his weight into the hammock, Tatsu asked, "You were in there for a long time. What did they say?"

"A lot." Yudai sighed and ran his hands slowly over his face. "I explained my situation to the High Council and gave them the background on Nota and Zakio, and the incident in Dradela."

"And?" Tatsu's throat closed in apprehension.

"They aren't arresting me."

Relief sang, and Tatsu sat back, even more weary than he'd been before. "Good. That's...quite good."

"I have to meet the representative from the temple tonight and see what she has to offer about my situation."

Sorting through his memories took a moment, but Tatsu slowly pieced together what he'd been told en route to the city. "The temple is where mages go in Joesar?"

"Yes, but it's not here in Moswar. There's always a representative here to work with the High Council and hear their requests, but the mages themselves reside far out in the desert."

There was too much talk of mages. The morning's events tugged on Tatsu's mind.

"What happened at the market wasn't your fault."

When Yudai turned to meet his gaze, his eyes were hooded. "It still happened at my hand."

"My mother..." Tatsu shook his head. The words felt too intimate to describe someone he'd never met, so he corrected himself. "Nota did this. She sent people to kill you—"

Yudai laughed, and the sound wasn't happy. "She'll never stop trying. She's lost me as her pawn. Now I'm a threat again, and she won't rest until she sees me killed."

"You think they'll keep coming?"

"I think anyone who hired mercenary assassins to off me will accept nothing less than success," Yudai said darkly, glaring at a spot on the wall shrouded in shadow. "I doubt they were cheap."

A knot had taken up residence in Tatsu's belly, and it pulsed angrily in time with his heartbeat. He didn't want to think about his own flesh and blood being cruel enough to send hired men just to guarantee a death. He searched for something, anything, to take his mind off the darkness weaving webs behind his eyes, and the distraction he settled on offered no relief.

"Yudai," he started, searching for the right words, "I was talking with Leil..."

"Ah." Yudai's sigh seemed to know too much.

"She said your father was...benefitting from the drain. And it was going to unnaturally extend his life, so he could rule for hundreds of years. I think that was part of why the Queen of Chayd wanted to use you."

Yudai's face disappeared into his palms, and for several moments, nothing in the room dared to move, not even the winking sunlight on the opposite wall. Then Yudai sucked in a deep, hissing breath that caught between his lips, and he slid his hands down his neck.

"I think I knew," he said, voice low. "I think part of me always knew."

"Yudai, I'm so sorry."

"It's another piece to the puzzle, right?" Although Yudai flashed a smile, the expression appeared very forced.

Tatsu rose, propelled toward the hammock for reasons he wasn't brave enough to name, and sat next to Yudai's hunched figure. "This doesn't change anything about you. Don't let this dictate who you are. You're better than that."

"I'm not sure my father ever really cared about me as a person," Yudai said down to his fingers, eyes focused on nothing. "Certainly never as a son."

"Well, as life would have it, it seems I sort of know how you feel."

Yudai laughed again, bitter but genuine. "I suppose you do."

"There are people who care about you," Tatsu said after a pause stretched thin. Yudai tilted his head to meet Tatsu's gaze, and so much in his expression defied definition.

"I know."

Tatsu's heartbeat was pounding so furiously it seemed to echo down his bad arm, and recognizing the sensation, foreign in the worst ways, came later than he'd have liked to admit. When the meaning finally sank in, he gasped, wrenching his eyes away to stare at the linen sling covering his hand. He still couldn't move his fingers, but his elbow throbbed, pain radiating to his wrist.

"How's your arm?" Yudai asked.

"I think it's getting better."

By the time Tatsu glanced up again, Yudai's face had closed off somewhat, his smile slightly strained. The abrupt change in atmosphere threw Tatsu, and he stumbled over what to say in the sudden shift.

"It would probably help if you got some sleep." Yudai's expression had gone maddeningly blank.

Tatsu wanted to get some kind of hint from him, even if it was anger, but nothing bobbed to the surface. He ignored the pang blossoming from his stomach when he tried to move, muscles cramping from too much time in one position. "And we meet with the temple representative tonight?"

"Yeah."

Tatsu stood, feeling light-headed. "Then we'll see what she says. Maybe she can detect something we can't."

Yudai didn't say anything more as Tatsu left.

The room across the hall was empty when Tatsu tried the handle. He sank into the linen hammock, the gentle rocking of the bed more distracting than soothing. Staring up at the ceiling, he willed the world to slow down, but even after the room settled into warm peace, Tatsu couldn't quite seem to drift off.

EYES GRITTY AS though full of Joesarian sand, Tatsu rose early into the evening, giving up completely on the idea of rest. At dusk, the sun lit the hall with a soft rosy glow, and devoid of other people, the calm serenity of the corridor alleviated some of his worry. A single servant passed Tatsu and pointed him down a second, wider hallway with the promise of a rejuvenating bath. He followed the instructions to a set of reinforced double doors.

Moswar's not-palace expanded into twin baths, larger in size than some of the shops in Dradela and fully surrounded by high walls. The space between the gender-divided pools was piled with mottled stones and a few palm trees casting oscillating shadows across the water. Tatsu wasn't sure how pleasing a hot bath would be in the desert, but after he'd stripped and waded in, sinking into the water proved glorious.

He'd risen early enough to be alone, so he lazily lapped the pool a few times to wake up his muscles. Near the back of the bath and built into the wall sat a stone basin which held several bottles half-full of milky liquids. Pouring some into the palm of his hand revealed the offerings to be various types of soaps, and he ran one that smelled of jasmine through his hair. A thinner liquid carrying hints of cinnamon he slathered over his body. It'd been quite some time since he'd been able to clean himself with anything besides river water—in fact, he couldn't remember the last time he'd had a warm bath at all. Despite the day's shimmering heat, the bath's warmth soothed the irritation on his skin, the red welts left from days in the wind and sun.

Tatsu stayed until his fingers wrinkled and then got out to dry off with one of the folded towels near the entryway. Once clothed, he made his way to the large kitchens he'd visited that morning and found a few servants already there working on dinner, as well as Alesh, sitting by herself behind the notched tabletop.

Tatsu sat across from her. The familiar sight of her long braid hanging over her shoulder and brushing across the top of the wood was nice. Her wet hair indicated she'd also been to the baths at some point in the afternoon.

"Can't sleep?" she asked with a wan smile.

"Too much in my head."

One of the kitchen workers brought him a small bowl of spiced vegetables swimming in a thick broth, along with a handful of roasted nuts and a mug of slightly sweet water. He and Alesh ate in companionable silence until Tatsu's spoon scraped the bottom of his bowl.

"Why are you here?" Tatsu asked quietly. "Why did you come?"

"I told you; I had to come with Ral."

Tatsu glared at the remnants of soup stuck to the underside of his spoon. "But that's not why you came, not all the way out here to a kingdom you've never been to."

Around them, the swell of the kitchen workers' movement bubbled up as fires blazed and iron pots clanged against one another.

"I think you did the right thing in Dradela," she said. Her fingers played with her braid, the bottom end curling slightly around them. "I don't think anyone should be used like Yudai was. Honestly, the more I thought about the way we found him strapped to the chair, the angrier I got. When Ral began itching to go after you, it wasn't much of a decision."

"Thank you," Tatsu said but wasn't entirely sure why he'd said it.

Alesh shrugged. "You don't have to thank me."

"But not everyone would do that. Think of how many people would be willing to let it happen because it didn't concern them."

"I don't think the number is that high." She frowned. "Many people would try to stop something horrible like that, even if it took them a little time to get there, like with me. You always think the worst of people."

Tatsu didn't answer.

"Remember when we were kids? You thought the worst about everyone in Dradela too."

"But people always whispered about me behind my back."

"Is that why you cut yourself off from the city so much?" Alesh asked. She leaned in over the table onto her elbows, and her braid narrowly missed falling into the uneaten remains of her dinner. "Do you really think that *everyone* in Dradela thought of you as an outsider?"

"People told me that to my face," Tatsu said.

Alesh reached for his hand. "There are always a few bad eggs in the bunch, Tatsu, but you can't honestly think *everyone* felt that way. What about Hesch? You remember what a good friend he was to your father. What about me and Ral?"

"My father used to tell me..." Tatsu couldn't find the right words. "He used to say that he would hear people talking when they thought he wasn't listening—about me and my mother's influence. He said, eventually, he couldn't deal with it anymore."

"Your father told you people did that?" Alesh looked horrified, eyes widening.

The hot swell of shame forced Tatsu's gaze to the table once more. "Didn't they?"

"No." Alesh's voice was very soft. "No, I never heard anyone speak badly about you."

"And your parents never...?" Tatsu's jaw snapped shut as he realized the implied insult, cheeks flaming, but

Alesh didn't seem upset by it. She shook her head and squeezed his fingers hard enough to sting.

Tatsu put a hand over his eyes, wishing he could take back everything. He couldn't tell if the emotion choking his throat was relief or anger—maybe it was both, coiled up with the increasingly tarnished memory of his father. The knowledge keeping him happily alone for the past ten years had been so solid. He'd been so sure that closing himself off in his father's cottage in the woods was necessary.

Even now, already knowing he'd been wrong, discovering another piece of the puzzle stung.

Alesh stood and rounded the table to throw her arms around Tatsu's neck and pressed her face in the groove where it met his shoulder.

"Tatsu, I'm *sorry*. Her breath tickled at the corner of his jaw. "I didn't know that was why you kept away in the woods. I thought you didn't like crowds and people."

Tatsu tangled their fingers together again, just to feel the heat of her skin, but he couldn't coax any words past his lips.

"Be careful," she whispered. "Be careful with Yudai."

"Why?"

"He's a prince. That comes first and foremost, and I'm afraid you'll get hurt."

Tatsu's mouth went dry as his tongue expanded to clumsily stick to the roof of his mouth. He nodded once in a sharp jerk and then again to soften the action, though he didn't quite succeed. Footsteps sounded in the corridor behind them, and Alesh pulled back, patting both of Tatsu's shoulders lightly.

"Oh, here you both are," Leil said as she pushed the door aside and stuck her head into the kitchen. "I've been sent to get you. We're going to the temple to meet the priestess."

Chapter Nine

THE MAGES IN Moswar inhabited a small, cozy building—a representative outpost made of sand blocks alternating in hue. In the elongated shadow of the council palace, the mages' temple looked deceptively small, like a wing they'd forgotten to add until too late. All the windows sat high along the walls, narrow and staggered, as though to allow nothing more than arrows to slip between the edges. No ornaments decorated the outside to proclaim the building's use, but behind the first set of walls, the top curve of a thickly leaved tree was visible through the roof, protruding from within the building; the temple, it seemed, had been constructed around it.

There was no door, only an arch of blocks that gave way to the widening interior, so their group entered without so much as a knock. The space inside radiated serenity and smelled faintly of both burning incense sticks and wet leaves, and Tatsu's thoughts quieted, lulled by the calm. Just studying the trunk of the central tree whose roots dug deep beneath the uneven floor made him feel more like himself again. The tree's widespread branches summoned a desperate ache in his chest as he flashed back to his woods, but the sensation faded when a woman wearing simple, light-colored robes approached them, bringing with her an air of comfortable ease.

"Welcome, Prince Yudai," she said and bowed slightly at the waist, which seemed to surprise Yudai. He fumbled before recovering enough to return the gesture. "The High Council informed me of your visit and the purpose behind it."

"Thank you for meeting with us," Yudai replied stiffly, his shoulders square and tense.

"My name is Tiran. I am the current temple representative to Moswar. If you and your friends would follow me, we can begin the tests without delay."

Yudai started forward without so much as a glance at the others, leaving them no choice but to follow.

"What sort of test is this?" Tatsu asked under his breath to Jotin, whose face was a hard mask of stone. He didn't voice the rest of his question—*Is it dangerous?*— but Jotin seemed to pick up on the unspoken currents anyway.

"I doubt the High Council would send us here to be in further peril. However, I do not know what the priestess will do."

"Is it possible that the Council would..." Tatsu's voice trailed off as his cheeks burned with an aching heat. "I'm sorry. I shouldn't have— Your father is on the Council. I didn't mean to insult him."

One of Jotin's eyebrows rose, but his mouth stayed in a neutral line. "Yet you did anyway. Perhaps you are not wrong to question it. These are strange times. To find mercenaries within Moswar is troubling."

"Do you think someone in Moswar knew of the hired men?"

"A week ago, I would have sworn that no one did." Jotin looked grim. "Now, I am not so sure. To have infiltrated the city so thoroughly that a child could track our movements...well, it might be possible after all."

Tatsu let his gaze wander to the stones beneath their feet. "When do you begin your time on the Council?"

"A few months from now. I may be able to find out more at that time."

In a few months' time, anything Jotin learned would be useless, but the sentiment was nice to cling to.

They followed Tiran to a small, mostly enclosed enclave in the back of the building, which was lined with the same high, narrow windows as the main chamber. Two leather chairs faced each other in the middle of the floor, and a low, worn bench stretched across the back wall. A waist-high table held a single burning candle and a small potted plant with bright yellow blossoms and waxy leaves. Tatsu took a seat on the bench, and the others followed suit as Yudai took one of the chairs. Nothing about the room or the building was threatening, but even the most dangerous of situations could present a veneer of peace.

The midnight quiet, while serene, also hid the greatest threats.

Tiran pulled out a linen cloth from the miniature table and leaned over Yudai to wipe at his left hand.

"I will need to take a sample of your blood," she said. "Once I have that, I can attempt to analyze the properties within and locate the corruption."

"Corruption?" Yudai echoed.

Tiran smiled, though the expression appeared forced. "We will learn more soon."

She produced a hallowed bone case from the pocket of her robes. Held within it was a small needle. She leaned in again. "This may hurt, but please stay still."

Yudai's gaze flickered to Tatsu's and stayed there, filled with apprehension. Their eyes held through Tiran's finger prick and blood drawing, but after, Tatsu couldn't stop himself from looking down at the small glass vial of what appeared to be cloudy ink. Even though he expected it, all the air left his lungs in a harsh rush at the sight of the black blood. His chest throbbed as though he'd been struck. The ink-like liquid ran hot through Yudai's veins, yet no shadows of its malignant nature had ever bled through to his skin.

Yudai, Tatsu noticed, did *not* look down at the vial.

"Now what?" Yudai asked through clenched teeth.

"Perhaps you would like your companions to wait in the main chamber?" Tiran offered, holding the vial between her hands while studying it. "The results—"

"It's fine." Yudai's gaze met Tatsu's briefly again and then wrenched violently away. "I—they can stay."

"Then I will perform the analysis," Tiran said. "Try to remain quiet; noise may disrupt my spell charting."

Tatsu had seen only a few mages actually work magic: Yudai, of course, and both Zakio and Leil. Even though he knew nothing of how magic was worked, all three mages were distinct in their casting. Leil always hesitated before she began anything, afraid, somehow, of her own abilities. From what Tatsu had seen, Zakio flaunted his expertise in grand, showy climaxes. And Yudai's ability, when it slipped back within his grasp, was an extension of himself, something he commanded with ease.

In his lap, Tatsu let his hand rest palm up. He clenched his fingers a few times, wondering what others would notice about him if he'd inherited the ability.

Tiran's was different still. Her magic began so subtly he almost missed it, until the air vibrated softly with energy and hummed just beyond his thoughts. She moved with controlled, fluid waves of her hands blending seamlessly together between one motion and the next. Then her fingers curved around the vial, and it pulsed a warm, yellow light.

The air in the room stood motionless. With a bright flash, the vial trembled in Tiran's hands, and beside Tatsu, Leil released a lungful of air in a half gasp. The light faded as Tiran sat back with beads of sweat glistening on her forehead. Only a moment, and she looked exhausted. Was that the price magic demanded of its gifted users?

"Well?" Yudai asked, his voice sharp and nervous.

Tiran didn't answer right away. Her shoulders sagged before she shook her head.

"The analysis was...inconclusive. It is possible I am simply not adept enough to fully uncover the changes made. However, there are still effects of the poisons lingering within your blood, and I may be able to identify what they came from with the help of an alchemist."

As she stood, frustration flashed across Yudai's features, pinching his eyes and twisting his mouth.

"I will send a messenger to retrieve one of our trusted mixers," she continued. "We may be able to decipher which poisons were used. If you would excuse me for a moment..."

It was clearly more a polite statement than a request. Tiran left the small alcove for the larger room, her robes swirling as she took the sharp turn. Yudai sank in the leather seat, so lost within himself Tatsu turned to Leil beside him, instead.

"What did you feel in her magic?" he asked.

"I wish I had more time to study it." Leil stared at the glass vial Tiran had left behind, still swirling with black. "The way the Joesarians weave magic is different from ours, but it feels the same at the base. I would enjoy getting a chance to watch a slower, drawn-out spell, to see if I could replicate the way they push through the fabric of energy."

"But you couldn't feel anything else in Yudai's blood?"

Leil shot him a sympathetic look. "Sorry. Without having cast the magic myself or knowing what I was looking for, I won't be much help."

As the minutes ticked by, Ral got antsy. She stood, walked the length of the room, and looked at the walls. Once she was finished with that, she migrated to the exit to peek around the corner. Alesh smiled thinly at Tatsu.

"Maybe we'll take a walk." She touched a hand to Ral's elbow and guided her to the large chamber they had entered through. "We won't be gone long."

"Do you want someone to go with you?" Tatsu asked.

"No." Alesh glanced at Yudai's slumped figure. "You should stay here. Besides, it's never been us the mercenaries were hunting."

After they left, Tatsu crept to Yudai's side. "Are you all right?"

"I feel like I'm on display," Yudai mumbled toward his clasped hands. "Like I'm some sort of experiment the scholars are conducting. This is exactly how it felt when my father would throw those celebrations to try and entice me a bride—like I'm some kind of prize to be bartered over."

"I don't think Tiran thinks of you like that."

Yudai didn't answer. His eyes were focused on the wall, or something far beyond it, glazed over in memory. When he finally came back to the present, he did so with a deep breath and one hand dragged punishingly over his face. His nails left behind furious red welts that lingered, swelling and pinking under Tatsu's gaze.

"It makes sense now," Yudai said, but it seemed to be for himself. "I've been thinking about what you told me. About my father, and the benefit of...of using me. Once it became an option, I think my father decided there was no further need for me. He stopped the bride-search celebrations a year before my eighteenth birthday. At the time, I thought he'd actually listened to me for once and respected my wishes. But looking back..."

He turned away, refusing to meet Tatsu's eyes. "I was happy to stop the endless parades to the nobles and their daughters. Now, I'd give anything for that to still be the worst of it."

"Instead, Nota went to him with her plan to harness your magic."

"It must have seemed a far better option for a king with a stubborn, disagreeable son," Yudai agreed.

"You're not *always* disagreeable."

He got a strained smile in response as Yudai met his gaze again. "That's because you're not trying to marry me off against my will."

Something angry and bitter hardened in Tatsu's stomach, throbbing and pulsing against the bottom of his ribs. Unable to come up with anything to say in reply, he looked at the bench where Leil and Jotin still sat and found Leil watching them both with undisguised interest. Her stare sent a shiver down his spine.

Tatsu stood at the sound of footsteps, slightly muted beneath soft-soled sandals.

"Tiran is coming back," he said and returned to the bench.

Tiran reentered with a fresh wave of incense following her. "I have sent the messenger. He should be here within the hour."

"So we wait," Yudai said with finality.

RAL AND ALESH returned before the alchemist arrived. The mixer walked in about thirty minutes later, wearing some of the most brightly colored clothes Tatsu had yet seen in Moswar. A deep-blue robe with splashes of green dye spreading out like uneven flower petals fell past his knees. His hands, clasped in front of his body, were stained with a black coating to the ends of his fingertips that appeared more like ink etched into his skin.

His demeanor was calm and polite, but there was something in his air Tatsu didn't wholly trust. Perhaps it was the knowledge he brewed poisons powerful enough to change the very makeup of a man's body that gave Tatsu pause.

Tiran gave him the vial of Yudai's blackened blood, and the alchemist took several minutes to inspect it before opening the top and pouring a few droplets into the palm of his hand. When he leaned in to smell the congealed bits, Tatsu pulled his gaze away, stomach turning.

"And you do not know which poisons were used?" the alchemist asked.

"*Itur*," Alesh volunteered from the bench. "And *umet*. At least those were the two I could identify. There were more I didn't know; those were just the ones they had nearby."

Tatsu stared at Leil until the woman began to fidget, twisting her fingers together in her lap.

"I can confirm those were used more than once," she said quietly. "They also dosed him with both *iyera* and *aoyma* together."

Alesh shot Leil a startled look that sharpened, though she said nothing.

"Then it is no wonder," the alchemist said and wiped the black from his hand with a grimace. The weathered lines of his face deepened as his features twisted.

"No wonder what?" Alesh asked.

The man raised his chin as he replaced the stopper on the blood vial with care. "He has been fed more toxins than any normal human should realistically be able to endure, and at extended lengths. The corruption in his blood is not from the poisons. It's from the magic trying to combat them."

"Are you saying that my own magic did this?" Yudai's eyes flashed.

"It certainly would never have happened without the poisons," the alchemist replied. "But the only way your body could protect itself was to neutralize the toxins in your bloodstream. By altering the base of your blood, it kept your heart from recognizing what the poisons were. I believe this kept you alive, but the consequence was that those toxins were allowed to then remain where they were, festering and slowly corrupting your blood from within."

Yudai's hands shook against his thighs. "Are you saying this will kill me?"

"I cannot say." The alchemist sighed. "Perhaps an adept mage could attempt to reverse what has transpired within you, but I can do nothing. The toxins in your blood are long gone; only magic can hope to reverse the effects now."

Yudai's face turned to stone, his rage so palpable Tatsu thought he could swipe his hands through it if he reached out.

"It would have killed you far sooner had you been without your magic," Tiran said. "And all is not yet lost."

"And how do you figure that?" Yudai asked through clenched teeth.

"The matter with your blood is unrelated to the matter of your blocked magic. If you seek out the high priest at the mages' temple, he may be able to do more for you. Your abilities are being held from you by a magic wall within, and I'm afraid I am not skilled enough to break it."

"And the drain?"

"Also a matter for the high priest," Tiran said. "What was done to you was quite advanced—I have not the ability to sort through the threads."

Yudai drooped, a puppet with its strings abruptly cut. "Where is the mages' temple?"

"South," Tiran said, "through two dominions located on the edge of the Dar-Itusk Basin."

Yudai's lips pursed and then flattened into a thin line before he looked at Tatsu. In the space between them, the incense coiled into a fog. "Can you give us a minute, please? I need to discuss the plan of action with my companions."

"Of course." Tiran disappeared into the sanctuary with the alchemist beside her. After their footsteps faded away, Yudai sighed, heavy and weary.

"This temple..."

"It would be quite a journey," Jotin finished. "The Dar-Itusk Basin is near the southern bounds of Joesar and runs in a line across our sands, dividing the desert from the coast."

"But we can't stay here," Tatsu said. "Not with the mercenaries after us. I assume no one would bother hiring only one."

"Which means there will be more," Alesh said and crossed her arms over her chest defensively. "Here, in a city inhabited by thousands of people."

Yudai's expression went dark. "And I'm a threat to everyone should they find me again. I doubt the council would even let me stay after the incident at the *Raydrau*."

"So, it appears the mage's temple is our only real choice," Tatsu said.

"I suppose we might find some answers anyway," Yudai agreed, but his tone didn't sound optimistic about the prospect.

"I would continue with you to the temple," Jotin said. When Tatsu's head snapped toward him in question, he shrugged, the barest hint of a smile playing at the corners of his mouth. "Somehow, I would like to see this through."

"Somehow?" Alesh repeated.

The smile on Jotin's face grew more pronounced. "I'm intrigued. And you'll need a guide."

"I'm glad my situation amuses you," Yudai said with bite. Tatsu glared at him, and Yudai's eyes rolled a bit before his shoulders hunched over again. "Sorry. It's been a rough day."

"Then we'll head to the mage's temple?" Tatsu asked Alesh, who sat on the edge of the bench, poised and seeming ready to bolt upright. Next to her, Ral watched, hands folded demurely in her lap. "Are you both coming with?"

"I don't see any way around it," Alesh replied. "Ral clearly wants to go with you; there's not much use in me trying to stop her."

"I'm glad to have you," Tatsu said, and he didn't miss the way Yudai's face twisted into a brief grimace.

"I'm accompanying you as well," Leil said.

"No," Yudai replied immediately. "Why would you want to?"

Her fingers, held together in front of her body, began to knit together in erratic movements. "This is partly my fault—"

"*Yes*," Yudai interjected.

"—and I want to help, as much as I can."

"All right," Tatsu told her, just as Yudai repeated his earlier answer of "No!"

Silence settled over the group. Yudai stared at Tatsu for several breaths, his jaw tightly clenched. Then, as the tension began to buzz like an agitated hornet against Tatsu's ears, Yudai said, "Tatsu, can I talk to you for a minute?"

He didn't even wait for Tatsu to agree before stalking out of the room and into the sanctuary. The sharp twinge of pain in Tatsu's temple rippled across his forehead.

"We'll be right back," he said and followed Yudai out to where he waited near the thick-trunked tree that reached up into and beyond the wooden rafters.

Yudai whirled before Tatsu had even stopped walking. "What are you doing?"

"Look, I know why you are upset right now—"

"Tatsu! Alesh I can deal with, even though I don't trust her not to decide she'd rather take whatever the Queen of Chayd is offering for my return, but you want the *mage* to come as well?"

"She's offering to help."

"She," Yudai hissed, "was one of the people holding my *mouth* open so they could pour these poisons down my throat."

"And I was the one to haul you out of Runon's castle for the queen." Tatsu stuck his good arm out to the side with his palm facing the sky. "We've all made mistakes. And I think we need all the help we can get right now."

Yudai turned away, frowning deeply. "I don't trust them."

"We need them. We need people on our side."

"It was easy when it was just us." Yudai sighed, his eyes flickering up to the ceiling.

"Well, I also got stung by scorpions and almost died when it was just us," Tatsu pointed out. "So maybe this way is better."

Yudai barked out a short laugh. "That's not what I meant."

He fell silent, and more than anything else, Tatsu wanted to reach out and trace his fingers across Yudai's bare skin. The desire surprised him, and fumbling for anything that might help distract him, he asked, "What *did* you mean?"

"I only...I liked it when it was just us." Yudai's eyes, shining and hooded, seemed to roam over Tatsu's face, searching for something.

So did I. But the words got caught between Tatsu's teeth, and he couldn't stammer them free. Despite the inherent dangers they'd thrown themselves headfirst into, part of him longed for the slow days atop the mountains before they'd stepped foot on the desert sands. He rarely felt comfortable with others, but on the peaks with Yudai, there had been a sense of familiarity and peace.

Things were different. *They* were different. Now that they knew of everything happening in Yudai's blood, they had no choice but to chase down any possible answers.

Yudai's shoulders seemed to relax, the tension and solitude of his royal persona falling away. "You—"

Tiran appeared in a doorway at the edge of Tatsu's vision, to the side of the sanctuary, and Yudai's mouth snapped shut. His arms crossed over his chest as if to deflect a physical assault.

"We'll need directions to the mage's temple," Yudai said, loud enough that she could hear. "Apparently, we're *all* going."

Chapter Ten

THEY SPENT THE next nights preparing their supplies for the journey, save for Yudai, who was confined by council orders to the palace grounds in hopes of avoiding any further incidents. Jotin volunteered to go to the *Raydrau*, and Tatsu was glad for it. He didn't care to return to the space where the magic had erupted; he had enough nightmares without needing to add any more.

On the third evening, after they woke from their daytime rest, Tatsu was packing up his allotted weight into his bag when Alesh rapped her knuckles against his door and slipped inside, her plaited braid swinging over one shoulder.

"Listen, I wanted to talk to you." She shut the door behind her. "I've been thinking about the other day, when Leil talked about the Joesarian poisons they used on Yudai."

She curled her arms across her chest. "Remember when I left Ral to stay with you, the day that started this whole thing—when that job went bad? Remember how I...how I said I could hear bottles clanking in the crates?"

"Yes," Tatsu said, unsure where the conversation was going.

"We had an anonymous buyer and drop-off point, but I don't think they were ever supposed to get there." Her eyes flashed when she leveled a stare at him. "I think it was all going to the palace."

Tatsu paused halfway through folding his leather gloves into a small triangle. "That was well before anything with Yudai began. The queen wouldn't have had any use for the toxins at that point."

"This whole time, I've been thinking that I did this to you," Alesh said. "That I dragged you into this by getting you involved. It wasn't until you got back with Yudai and started talking about your mother and the magic barrier that I realized it was the other way around."

"What do you mean?"

Alesh tightened her arms. "We were jumped halfway to the drop-off point by the guards, but I think it'd always been planned. And most of the others were either killed or arrested—I think I was the only one who got away. They *let me go*, Tatsu. They let me go because they knew I'd lead them straight to you."

"Alesh." Tatsu's mouth had gone very dry.

"It was always about you. They knew I'd go to you when I was injured and it'd give them cause to arrest you. They never wanted me."

"If that's true..."

"The queen was playing a very long game," Alesh said, "with both of us."

Tatsu's bad wrist ached, sympathetic to his heart. "Why are you telling me this? You know it doesn't change anything."

"I'm giving you something to think about when it comes to dealing with royalty. These are the games they play with those they consider pawns."

Telling her Yudai was different rang useless. Tatsu would only be wasting his breath if he tried, so he stayed quiet and stared at his half-finished pack, resentment building.

"I spent some time with Tiran," Alesh said, changing the subject as she stared at the far wall. "She had some suggestions for our journey."

"What kind of suggestions?"

"She was concerned that the residual drain is increasing in frequency and gave me some ideas on how to keep the rest of us safe from it."

Keeping his tone as neutral as possible, Tatsu asked, "And what did she have to say about it?"

"Don't look at me like that. I'm trying to keep my sister safe. The drain is *dangerous*."

"I never said it wasn't," Tatsu replied. "But I'm also not going to keep Yudai at arm's length out of fear of something that isn't his fault."

Alesh sighed. Her eyes slid to the right, to the closed door and then back over the clean swept tiles beneath her boots. "Tiran suggested setting up two camps at night, to avoid any possible complications with the drain's magic."

"No," Tatsu said and returned to his work of readying his pack with only one hand.

"Will you hear me out, please? I'm only making sure the rest of us don't get killed by this thing—"

"He's not a thing, he's a *person*."

He looked over his shoulder long enough to catch Alesh leveling him with a stony glare.

"I wasn't talking about Yudai," she said. "I was talking about the drain."

"Which is part of him. So, actually, they're pretty much one and the same."

She fell quiet and then huffed under her breath. Within the room, the air had cooled significantly as the sun dropped, yet the atmosphere still choked Tatsu. He was glad they'd be heading out into the open sands. Being cooped up within the palace unsettled his thoughts and left pinpricks of frustration beneath his skin.

"I know Yudai doesn't like me," Alesh began.

"Yudai doesn't *trust* you," Tatsu said. "And when you come up with things like this, it's not all that hard to understand why."

"Being cautious doesn't make me a bad person."

The fight left Tatsu, his muscles crumpling all at once. "No, it doesn't. But it's not easy being in the middle of you two. I feel like I'm constantly betraying someone."

"This isn't a fight, Tatsu. We're going to the temple together. You don't have to choose a side."

It felt an awful lot like he did, but Tatsu bit his tongue to keep the thought inside.

"The drain is only affecting plants," he said. "It hasn't touched living people yet."

"Yet," Alesh repeated, eyebrows rising. "But I'm not going to let my sister be the first, even if it means making decisions people don't like."

She left Tatsu's sleeping quarters, and Tatsu had to temper his irritation as he finished getting the supplies into his pack before leaving to join the others.

JOTIN LED THEM out of Moswar and into the moonlit dunes beyond the city limits, turning them south shortly after they passed through the gates. Near the settlement, the sand remained packed and hard, with a well-worn path, and they had to step among the scraggly clumps of desert weeds to avoid the sticky leaves catching on their clothing. The flashback to the *sayld* and its monstrous pincers pushed Tatsu to take greater care as they walked, but there were no rings on the ground to indicate that any creatures lay in wait for an evening meal.

They were a motley group altogether. Jotin led the pack with his hawk alternating between a perch on his shoulder and the clear night sky. He moved with such quiet confidence atop the sands the crunching beneath his boots sometimes faded completely. Leil was next, with her dark hood and the gold bracelets hidden beneath her robe, and behind her, Alesh and Ral kept pace in the middle.

Tatsu missed relying on his bow with a fierce, sweeping ache, but even without it, he stayed in the back with Yudai, who seemed hesitant to quicken his steps to join the others. For Tatsu, being out of the city offered a chance to breathe freely and stretch his legs, even if it meant returning to the relative unknown dangers of the Joesarian desert. Yudai, however, looked more glum with each of his halfhearted steps.

"We'll find some answers," Tatsu said when Yudai's morose gait grew too much to bear. "The high priest will be able to do far more than Tiran could."

"Maybe."

"When there's nowhere else to try, that's when there are no other options. And even then, we'd find something."

"We?" Yudai parroted. When he raised his head, his expression was full of scorn. "Do you think all these people will stay when the options start falling away, one by one? Do you think the others will be willing to bleed and die for something that may never be fixed? Something that may *kill* them?"

Tatsu stared at the overlapping footprints in the sand from the group ahead of them. "I know you're scared, but people aren't going to desert you like that. Pushing people away who are trying to help isn't going to encourage them to stay longer."

He expected a snapped remark from Yudai and was a little impressed when nothing of the sort came.

"Yeah." Yudai sighed instead and ran a hand through his unruly hair. "You're right. I'm just...more used to people turning on me than the opposite."

"I know."

Yudai laughed a little, and he bit down on his bottom lip before glancing at Tatsu. "This may come as a shock to you, but I don't particularly enjoy feeling vulnerable."

"No." Tatsu raised his hand to his chest in mock surprise. "I had no idea."

Yudai sidestepped to bump against Tatsu with his shoulder, and the smile stayed on his face. "When the vultures come, I'm offering them you first."

They continued along behind the others, a good number of paces back, as the stars winked overhead.

"Thank you," Yudai said softly some time later. "I don't really think I say it enough, but I mean it. What you're doing for me..."

"I know." Tatsu smiled.

Yudai glanced sideways, though his tangled hair obscured most of his eyes. "I couldn't do this, any of it, without you. I wouldn't even *be* here if it weren't for you."

Instead of answering, Tatsu reached over and squeezed Yudai's wrist, and the silence between them sighed, infinitely lighter.

ALESH STAYED TRUE to her word when she and Ral set up their camp several paces away from the others. She offered no further explanation, and Yudai pointedly ignored the entire process. Eventually, Leil joined them, splitting the group three and three.

Yudai didn't comment on the arrangements, but the next evening, as they blearily pulled themselves out of fitful sleep in the sweltering heat, a ring of decay had wilted the spindly weeds around the tent he'd used.

Tatsu didn't touch the withered remains. Yudai, however, showed no hesitation in pulling up a clump of them. He watched the leaves disintegrate in his hand.

"Alesh was right," he said, voice low. Tatsu didn't think she could hear him as they repacked their own supplies across the clumped sand. "It's getting worse."

He raised his chin to stare at Tatsu. "It might be dangerous for you to be near me."

"That doesn't mean it's affecting *us*. The only indication that it affects people at all was—"

"—the *Oldirr* elder and her tribe," Yudai finished, his expression dark. "And you saw what it did to them! It drained every last bit of life they had, killing everyone in its wake."

He fell silent, and Tatsu could think of nothing to say in response.

"I'm not letting that happen again." Yudai's voice held an edge of steel. "Not to you. Not after everything."

"It won't," Tatsu said. But a web of doubt had started to spin itself around his insides. He'd woken already tired and assumed the blame lay with the high desert temperatures. He pressed three fingers against his forehead and closed his eyes, focusing on the blackness behind his eyelids. Perhaps the exhaustion *had* come from the drain, but there was no way to know for sure without a physical sign.

"We don't have any indication that it's draining us," he said.

Yudai turned to Jotin, who was rolling up the leather skin to wrap several thin cords across the bundle. "Tomorrow, you should sleep in the other tent."

Jotin stilled next to them; he'd clearly heard the concerns. His gaze moved between them for several moments. "All right."

"You too," Yudai ordered Tatsu.

"Don't be ridiculous," Tatsu said.

"I'm not. And I'm not asking either. I'm not going to be held responsible for hurting you."

Tatsu rose and kicked a bit at one of the dead weeds as though the crumbling leaves were the true source of his problems. "When it comes to that, I'll move. But until that time—"

"*Tatsu.*"

"Stop arguing," Tatsu said and tossed Yudai his pack. "If your magic is draining the world all night, you might need to save your strength."

BY THE MIDDLE of the third day, they'd made their way into a strange section of the desert bombarded by erratic strong winds that caught the granules, lifting them into the air in a dance. Making good time through the gusts turned out to be monumentally difficult, and their collective shuffling through the sands sharply slashed their morale.

"I assume we're in a new dominion," Yudai said to Jotin. Even his hawk was having trouble getting up above to the warm thermals and seemed content to spend most of its time on the leather strap curved across Jotin's shoulder. "Shouldn't we be meeting some of the walkers by now?"

"We should." Jotin put a hand in front of his face, but his fingers did little to stop the barrage of sand. "Perhaps the winds have kept them in camp. That would be the smarter thing to do."

No one seemed eager to ask why they didn't follow suit if the idea had so much merit.

"They have likely set up their tents near the southern border, where the hills are," Jotin continued. He'd been following some internal compass, but to Tatsu, all the dunes looked exactly the same when painted by moonlight.

"And that's where we're headed, I imagine," Alesh said. Then she turned to Ral beside her and asked, "What do you think?"

Ral smiled, the skin at the sides of her mouth crinkling. "Go south."

"Is that a suggestion or...?"

"Go south," Ral repeated, and when she met Tatsu's gaze, her grin stretched further. "South to the stones."

"Did she speak with Tiran about the mages' temple before we left?" Jotin asked.

"No," Alesh said. "I did, but Ral wasn't really paying attention, and Tiran didn't say anything about stones."

Jotin continued to stare at Ral with furrowed brows, the shadow of a frown passing over his features.

"Is something wrong?" Tatsu asked.

"The temple was established within the Myvar Ruins," Jotin said. "An old palace built on bedrock in the Dar-Itusk Basin. The temple is made almost entirely of stones, including the large pillars sitting out in front acting as defensive watchtowers. How would she know that?"

"I've given up on understanding why Ral knows these things," Yudai said.

"She's not magic," Alesh said, defensive and prickling, with a sidelong glance at Leil that wasn't nearly as subtle as she likely wanted it to be. "She just *knows* things sometimes."

Leil, for her part, merely shrugged. "I already knew she wasn't magical. I'm not going to steal her away to the palace if that's what you are afraid of."

Alesh didn't answer, but Tatsu knew very well that had been exactly her fear.

"That means we're headed to the right place, at least," Tatsu said. "Ral's usually correct with guiding us to our next step."

"Yeah, next steps which included me getting stabbed in the market," Yudai pointed out. "*And* the fight with Zakio in the mountains. At this point, I'm not expecting any warm welcomes at this temple we're headed to."

"You probably shouldn't expect a warm welcome anywhere," Alesh said pointedly.

"Oh, certainly not with *you*," Yudai shot back.

Alesh rolled her eyes. "There's no need to be snippy. I wasn't being cruel. But the person who was—and still is—behind the siphon, whether intentional or not, is likely going to be seen as a threat. We're lucky we were allowed to stay in Moswar for so long."

Yudai stared at her for a moment, and then his mouth puckered into something sour. He grumbled over his shoulder at Tatsu, "She isn't wrong."

"Well, that's progress, at least," Alesh said.

Jotin's hawk startled them all with a loud shriek, taking flight from its perch on Jotin's shoulder despite the winds still working against its wings. As the bird took to the stars, now obscured by clouds, Jotin adjusted his weight into a crouching stance and pulled his sword free from its sheath.

"What is it?" Leil asked. "What's happening?"

"Get ready," Jotin said, his voice grim. "We are no longer alone."

Four of them padded out from the cloud of dust settling around the dunes like fog, paws slinking across the sands and pointed ears twitching. In his mind, Tatsu returned to the Weeping Forest, facing off against the drained wolf. A wall of sound roared against his ears as he tried to reorient himself, and the memories dissipated as the animals stalked toward them.

"Scavengers," Jotin said.

"We're too far in the dunes for a pack to be here!" Yudai said, but he was edging away as the wild dogs closed in.

Yudai wasn't wrong, but it didn't matter as the dogs' pace quickened. The matted fur of their sides stuck low to individual ribs; they were starving, perhaps after chasing game too far from their territory. Tatsu couldn't think of any other reason a small pack of dogs would consider a group of six adult humans easy prey.

Starving animals were desperate. Starving animals were dangerous.

He reached for his bow, only to remember halfway that using it one-handed would be a waste of energy.

"Ral and Tatsu to the center," Jotin ordered.

Tatsu bristled. "I'm not—"

"Stop arguing!" Yudai cut him off, and anything else was drowned out in the shriek of Jotin's hawk, streaking down with outstretched talons aimed directly at the pack leader's face.

As the hawk's claws found their mark, the rest of the pack leapt forward. One of them aimed for Alesh and found her knife waiting. A second dove around the rear of their cluster, and Leil lifted a wave of sand from the ground to throw at the creature's snout. Tatsu stepped to the middle, trying to shield Ral as much as he could, though the feeling of uselessness stung. Once, he'd have been able to take down half the pack before their forelegs propelled them close enough to strike.

The canine that had tried for Alesh went down hard, and she whirled away from its corpse to help Leil with the next. That left Jotin with the third, as he tried to keep the animal in front of him—and Yudai behind him—as much as possible. Sharp teeth and powerful jaws snapped on the edge of Jotin's topmost layer of clothes and ripped away tendrils of the linen. As the dueling pair rotated about each other, they came far too close to the middle of the circle for Tatsu's liking. He threw an arm in front of Ral and urged her backward, doing his best to keep them both from tripping over the one matted body already on the ground.

"Leil!" Jotin yelled as he took another slash at the animal and missed by a wide margin. Leil spun and pushed both hands out in front of her chest, sending with them a powerful burst of sand and dirt. The force of it hurled the creature several paces away, and Jotin darted after it.

Recovering from the hawk's attack, the pack leader struggled to its feet, and even with specks of crimson across its muzzle, the animal lunged forward with a snarl. Tatsu pushed Ral down with a shove and propelled himself in the opposite direction, but he landed badly on his injured shoulder. The resulting pang reverberated through his upper body, turning his vision red. He tried to find the breath stolen from his lungs as the sounds of struggle faded into a low din.

By the time his awareness cleared, the animal was stalking toward Ral's kneeling figure.

"No!" Yudai cried and jumped in front of her with his hands in front of his face just as the canine howled a warning and leapt.

They met somewhere in the middle and thrashed each other upon landing, rolling across the sand. When the dust settled, the animal crouched over Yudai with flecks of foam spraying from its snout with each growl. Yudai's hands curled around the creature's neck, holding it at arm's length, but it was barely enough—droplets of the animal's saliva caught on his cheeks as his arms shook. The animal growled in frustration, unable to reach him with each snap of its jaws.

A strangled, terrified cry ripped out of Yudai's throat as he managed to push the creature away from his face. For a second, the force seemed to be enough, until the wolf bucked up, breaking Yudai's hold on its neck and slammed down with both front paws. There was a crack that made Tatsu wince, and then Yudai's exclamation mutated into one of pain. He rolled, likely out of instinct, but the move left his back completely open.

Tatsu yelled Yudai's name but wasn't sure if Yudai could even hear him above the howl of the animal as it prepared to leap. The chance never materialized; a surge of warm, crackling energy flared up as Yudai's magic surged into a protective cocoon. A second later, Alesh darted in, utilizing the blind spot and the canine's preoccupation to slice in deep with her knife. As her arm arced toward the front, she twisted her wrist, and the animal fell to one side with a splatter of red across the sand. Then everything went very, very still. The burst of magic quickly fizzled into nothing more than raised goose bumps along Tatsu's arms.

Yudai heaved a sigh of relief, falling flat against the ground, and the contact thudded solidly.

"That was close," he said, sounding tired.

Tatsu pushed himself up while trying to ignore the throbbing pain in his shoulder and held out a hand to Ral. The few seconds of pause weren't nearly enough to rid his body of the spike in nervous energy, and, dizzy and light-headed, he didn't have energy for anything more. He watched Alesh as she stared down at Yudai with an inscrutable expression on her face.

"You saved my sister," she said.

Yudai opened one eye to look up at her. "Anyone would have done the same."

He seemed unprepared when Alesh offered her hand to him and pulled him onto his feet with impressive force. Yudai stumbled a bit, and Alesh didn't let go. Instead, her hand slid up to grasp his forearm—a solid, meaningful grip as she tugged him to her.

"You protected her with your life," she said, and Yudai looked distinctly embarrassed. "You were willing to die for her."

"I didn't—"

"Whatever you need, it's yours. I'll be here for you." Judging by the way Yudai's mouth parted, Alesh must have tightened her fingers. "There's a debt to repay here."

Yudai appeared ready to argue, and then his teeth snapped shut. He regarded her for a long moment before nodding once, the action sharp and short.

"Very well. I accept your pledge."

Alesh let go of his arm and turned away to check on Ral. Tatsu passed Jotin, who was wiping clean the smears of blood from his blade, to approach Yudai. He was still breathing hard, bent over as though his chest ached from the earlier impact.

"Are you all right?" Tatsu asked. When Yudai's eyes closed, his shoulders sagging, Tatsu reached forward without conscious thought to touch the side of Yudai's face.

Yudai's eyes opened, wide at first, and then they darkened and narrowed in what could be read as distinctly content.

"Yeah," he murmured. His face tilted to settle further against Tatsu's palm. The contact caused Tatsu's entire arm to tremble as warmth bloomed through his chest. Tatsu swallowed hard, finding little to dampen the sensation.

He darted his tongue out to wet his lips, and that was when Tatsu realized how he stood in the middle of the others, surrounded by the Joesarian desert, cupping Yudai's face in a manner too gentle to be misconstrued. He dropped his hand to his side, wiggling his fingers—which tingled in response—his face hot despite the cool night air.

Yudai unflinchingly held his gaze until the discomfort forced Tatsu to tear his eyes away.

"Thank you." Tatsu wished he could slow his own breathing, but it remained beyond his control. "For saving Ral, I mean—that was brave. And Alesh..."

"I misjudged her," Yudai said. When Tatsu finally glanced back at his face, Yudai's eyes were tracking Alesh's movements over Tatsu's shoulder. "I thought she was lacking in honor, and that was why she was willing to sell me out to the queen. But it was never a question of honor—it was about loyalty. And her loyalty wasn't to me."

Tatsu's mumble in reply was as noncommittal as he could make it, but Yudai picked up on the undercurrents anyway.

"You've experienced being at the losing end of that loyalty before."

"We had different priorities," Tatsu said by way of explanation and gazed out at the beige dunes stretching beyond them. "We've always had different priorities."

"She's not a bad person to have as an ally."

"No." It was Tatsu's turn to sigh. "She's certainly not."

Jotin finished cleaning his sword and resheathed the blade. "We should go. If the creatures have moved outside of their hunting territory, it means something has shifted their paths. We should be cautious as we continue south."

"You mean we'll encounter more of them?" Leil asked.

"I doubt they were redirected from anything native to the desert."

"Ah," Yudai said, and his features fell a bit. "The mercenaries."

Alesh put one arm around Ral, who at least hadn't been injured in the commotion. "If we're going to run into more of them, we should probably start taking watch during the day as we sleep."

"That's not a bad idea," Tatsu said. "We've been assuming all this time that any enemies would sleep at the same time."

"Or that we'd wake up if anything approached," Alesh added. "It's not the safest plan."

Jotin moved away from the bodies of the animals. They would likely begin to fester in the morning heat as the sun rose and draw in any other scavengers lingering nearby.

"Later," he said. "We need to put distance between us before the sun rises. We can discuss the arrangements for watch then."

Tatsu gave one last look at the bloodied carcasses on the sand before they continued south.

Chapter Eleven

A DAY LATER, they encountered an Oasa-walker who agreed to escort them to the full campsite. It took three more days to reach the camp, situated at the bottom of a large dune that shielded the tents from the worst of the winds. They arrived in the early part of the day, just as the heat was beginning to rise and the walkers within were slowing their routines.

Skins had been lifted onto wooden poles with bundles of cord-tied leather suspended between them, forming the tents. The skins were different from those the Cabaj-walkers had used—rubbed thinner and translucent in spotty patches—and matched the clothing of the walkers. Tatsu recognized the walkers clothing as a style he'd seen at the *Raydrau.*

Spead out, the Oasa camp left pockets of space between the structures, likely used to encourage increased windflow. The camp also boasted several thin horse-like creatures with coarse, closely trimmed fur, which Jotin called *tith.*

"They make better time across the sands," Jotin said. He left the group standing near one of the animals while he accompanied the Oasa-walker to their acting chief. Tatsu held out his hand to the *tith*, and the creature's velvety nostrils against his skin felt just like a horse's would. If he closed his eyes and blocked out the abnormally large floppy ears, he could imagine they were back outside of Dradela where the traders kept their mounts secured.

Ral's fingers curled into the fur of the animal's hide as she laughed.

"Dirty," she said, and she wasn't wrong. Tatsu's hand came away covered with a layer of grime.

"What are we now, halfway?" Alesh asked.

"I don't know," Tatsu said and wiped his hand on his pants. "But at least we found the walkers. That's got to be a good sign, right?"

"Tatsu ride?" Ral asked, with her head cocked toward the *tith*.

"I don't think so, but maybe Jotin can get you some food for it later."

The idea seemed to cheer her, and she continued to pat the creature's flank as they waited. "Want one."

"Have you ever met the Joesarian mages?" Alesh asked Leil, who was standing a few paces behind them with her arms crossed over her chest as though the animals were discomforting.

"Never. They've never come to the court in Dradela."

Tatsu's mind transported him to the woods on the edge of Chayd's borders, where they'd sat on opposite sides of a fire at the beginning of their journey and spoke of magic. "So you don't know what the mages can do or how powerful they are?"

"No." Leil met his gaze, unwavering.

"I don't love the idea of showing up unannounced to a temple full of mages we have no information on," Alesh said.

"It's likely they'll know we're coming before we get there," Leil said. "Mages can feel others' magic, especially as we near the location. The closer the magic, the easier it is to accurately track."

Something in the back of Tatsu's mind stirred, a twinge of knowledge he couldn't put his finger on. But within a moment, the sensation faded, and he was left none the wiser.

"Knowing we're coming and expecting us as allies are two different things," Alesh said, and Leil spread her hands out to either side in response, shaking her head.

Tatsu gave the *tith* one final pat and turned to look for Yudai. Eventually, he spotted him past several tents with his back to the group and the animals, and Tatsu set out across the packed sand to join him.

"You don't like the *tith*?" Tatsu asked when he reached Yudai's side.

"I thought it was wiser if I wasn't near anything else...living." Yudai grimaced.

"Leil said that the mages in the temple will know when we approach."

Yudai shrugged. "It's likely, at least if we're using any magic en route. They'll sense it."

"Can you?" Tatsu asked. "Sense other magic, I mean."

The air around them shimmered as Yudai's face fell. "No. I can't feel anything being used near me anymore. Not since they—not since the siphon began."

Tatsu wiped at his forehead with his good arm. Already, the desert sizzled, and the sweat beads trickling across his skin sent shivers down his spine. Yudai's gaze shifted to somewhere over Tatsu's shoulder.

"Jotin's returned," he said and then fell quiet as the other man approached.

"The acting chief has agreed to lend us a walker to take us to the next dominion," Jotin said. For perhaps the first time, he looked uncomfortable in the harsh sunlight. So many days spent traveling during the night had left them all ill-equipped to traversing beneath the harsh sun when long shadows cast across the sand were shortened. "He has also agreed to let us remain here for the day to rest. We will depart as the sun sets this evening."

"Fast turnaround," Yudai said, though his voice was neutral.

Jotin looked apologetic. "I think he wishes us out of his territory."

If Jotin was going to say more, he never got the chance. Yudai waved him silent with his fingers extended toward the horizon. "It's fine. I get it."

"We should urge the group to get as much rest as possible," Jotin said to Tatsu. "As we near the Dar-Itusk Basin, the terrain grows far more difficult to cross."

The Oasa acting chief's charity extended to two of the thin-skinned tents and a generous helping of water, stored in large clay jugs. It also included a quick dinner of salted meat and a strange, tart fruit that grew on trees near the desert's oases. Without prompting, Yudai chose the tent farthest from the *tith* and their pen, and they split between the two.

Even beneath the cooler shadows of the leather, Tatsu couldn't relax enough to drift off. When it became obvious he was only going to hinder his tent-mates' rest with his tossing and turning, he got up and wandered outside. The sun, directly overhead, threatened to overheat him within minutes, so he slipped into one of the tents housing the *tith* supplies. He meandered around piles of worn leather saddles, tangles of thin cord reins, and threadbare blankets designed to keep the animals' backs from chafing.

Jotin joined him a minute or two later, and, somehow, Tatsu wasn't surprised.

"Can't sleep?" Jotin asked.

"Too much on my mind." Tatsu ran his fingers over one of the nearby saddles. His bad arm ached, and he pressed at it unconsciously, prodding the skin until the pain subsided. Jotin hadn't moved by the time Tatsu raised his chin. "It's a lot of responsibility. Do you ever feel overwhelmed?"

"By this?" Jotin asked, and then his lips pinched together. "No. But I am not the one who has altered the course of a prince's life."

Tatsu ducked his head. "I didn't—that's not what I was trying to do."

"You were doing what you thought was right, and through that decision, you have changed the future. What would have happened to Yudai had you not taken him from his homeland?"

"The world would have been devoured. Of course, I couldn't let that happen."

"Not merely the world." Jotin moved deeper into the tent, staring up at the curve of the skin stretched above their heads. "I know little of magic, but I suspect the prince would not have lived through the ordeal. At the very least, he would have been significantly changed."

Tatsu shook his head. "But I wasn't trying to save the world. I was just...reacting."

"And now? You are trying to restore the prince to his throne."

"I—no." Tatsu fumbled for the words. "I'm only trying to keep him alive."

"Either way, the end result is the same. You have altered the future, both his and your own."

Tatsu glared at the jumble of leather cords at his feet, so tangled he couldn't pinpoint the start of it. "That's worse, somehow. I didn't mean to do any of this. I was there at the right time, in the right place, nothing more."

"Many people would say that was fate."

"I don't know if I believe in fate," Tatsu scoffed. "Do you?"

To his surprise, Jotin laughed, and the rare sound caught Tatsu off guard. "You ask all the right questions, I think. I do not know what I believe. But I believe I am on the right path, and that is enough."

The smell of the leather, oiled and thick, swelled stronger in the heat of the day. It conjured up old memories Tatsu had long since pushed aside, and the resulting ache within his ribs unsettled him. Too much was happening around him, and all of it important. His own feelings were lost within the storm of the journey, which carried them to their next destination as though they had no choice in the matter. In the past, he might not have cared, but things had changed.

Tatsu pressed his fingers against his sternum, wincing. "I wish I had your confidence."

"Do you not?" Jotin's eyebrows rose. "I thought you were following your heart."

Tatsu barked out a laugh, the sound cutting off unfinished. "I don't know if I can trust my heart."

Then he ran his tongue over the dry flesh of his lips. "Have you ever been in love?"

"Yes," Jotin said.

"What happened?"

"She died."

Feeling like a fool for bringing up something that had ended so badly, Tatsu shrank away, his bad arm trembling. "I'm sorry, I didn't mean to make you relive things."

But Jotin merely shrugged. "We were very young, and not yet adults. We knew the risks the sands carried when we went out with the walkers. We were headstrong and confident, and we were wrong. I regret that she died, but I do not regret the love we shared."

"How can you talk about this with such a clear head?"

"Time. It has been years, and that time has given me a much better perspective on things. Though I suspect this is not the answer you were hoping for."

Tatsu's heart beat so loudly he could have sworn it must have sounded through the tent. He tempered his next plea—*tell me how to deal with this*—and instead asked, "Have you been with the Cabaj-walkers all this time?"

"Except for the times I was dispatched to Moswar, yes."

"And after this, you'll join the High Council."

"A different kind of responsibility," Jotin replied, "but necessary all the same."

"Will you miss the freedom of the desert?"

When Jotin smiled again, his expression was gentler. "I think we always miss that which we can no longer have."

Tatsu thought of his father and the simple, easy days of hunting together in the woods before the complications of the siphon and its wreckage had woven their way into his life, and agreed.

AFTER THE LONG, hot midday, the idea of leaving as the sun fell was daunting, but Tatsu pulled his supplies together anyway and readied himself to go. The others seemed to be faring better; at least they appeared to have slept, which was more than Tatsu could claim. Ral bounced in high spirits, and Leil's shoulders squared straighter, though Alesh's forehead was lined with sweat from the still-soaring temperatures.

"We should pack extra water," Jotin said. "As we get closer to the southern coastline, the heat will remain through the night more and more."

"Wonderful," Yudai grumbled.

Their new Oasa guide led them away from the camp and, for the most part, stayed well ahead of them. Tatsu wouldn't have been surprised if the walker thought of them as merely a short diversion from her main task. She didn't engage them in conversation during rests and urged a relentless pace across the packed sands. The dunes, which had at one point seemed to tower as high as small mountains, began to flatten out until there were few rolling hills left at all, and the plains of the desert they made their way through became more dirt than sand, mixed together. More and more plants found their way up through the clay-like soil, and the foliage gradually expanded to include large bushes, thick-trunked trees, and spotty blossoms with rounded petals and dark pink centers.

Near the middle of the night, the Oasa-walker called for another break near a small grove of trees, and Tatsu was grateful for it—his feet were aching. Kicking his boots off would reveal skin rubbed raw in red blisters.

Leil sat down and immediately put her head into her hands as their guide picked a spot several paces away with a good view of each direction, unimpeded by the trees or their wide, curving leaves. Ral seemed more interested in the tree trunks themselves. Alesh, looking somewhat pale even in the blue-tinged moonlight, collapsed into a slumped seated position.

"Is your hand getting any better?" Yudai asked, settling into the dry sand-dirt ground next to Tatsu.

"A bit." More and more of the pangs in his shoulders made their way down to his left elbow as the nerves registered small sparks of sensation again.

Yudai gestured at Tatsu's arm as though wishing to inspect the limb, and Tatsu complied. When Yudai's fingers brushed aside the linen and made contact, they were cool against Tatsu's skin.

"You can feel that?" Yudai asked. "Your hand flinched when I touched it."

"It's muted, if that makes any sense. I can feel the touch, but it's a second late and far away."

Yudai slowly dragged his hand lower, to Tatsu's wrist. Near Tatsu's hand, the nerves responded less, but still, he could sense the ghost of Yudai's touch as he ran his fingers in smooth, straight lines. Tatsu's stomach twinged, his mind growing foggy. He closed his eyes, letting himself sink into the whispers of contact emerging from the haze.

"And this?" Yudai asked, voice soft. He might only have been touching the back of Tatsu's hand with the very tips of his fingers, light and soft like a butterfly's wings. The hair on Tatsu's arms stood on end as his skin buzzed.

He opened his eyes to find Yudai's fingers pressed firmly down into his flesh, and though the first sweeping wave of cold was that of disappointment—he should have been able to feel far more with so much pressure—a part of him didn't want the ministrations to stop.

"Should I—" Yudai started.

"Don't." As the air left Tatsu's lungs, the fingers of his bad hand twitched, a vibration starting in his shoulder and echoing through his tips. "Don't stop."

Yudai lifted his hand, and Tatsu worried he'd said something wrong, that he'd crossed the invisible line they'd always toed. Then Yudai returned his fingers to inch the short edges of his nails down the inside of Tatsu's forearm. *That* was much more of a response from the damaged nerves; the pull against his skin pooled in his spine and pulsed, flickering flames causing Tatsu to suck in a quick hiss of air. His fingers jumped sharply again.

Yudai's eyes flashed, reflecting the moonlight when he glanced up, sending a wave of tremors through Tatsu's muscles. Yudai looked like he was going to say something, lips parted as he leaned forward.

"Tatsu!" Ral called out, and the fear in her voice caused Yudai to drop Tatsu's arm. "Tatsu, help!"

Tatsu was up on his feet faster than he would have thought possible with the exhaustion weighing down his limbs. He spun to face Ral, who was kneeling by Alesh's side, and Alesh—

Alesh's eyes were closed, her face very pale as she gasped out quick, labored lungfuls of air.

Tatsu darted in to press his right hand against the side of her face. Her skin burned blisteringly hot, far too much to be discomfort from the heat.

"*Shit*," Tatsu said and tried to rouse her. "Alesh. Alesh!"

The only response he got was the fluttering of her eyelids, which, after a second, squeezed shut again.

"What's happening?" Leil asked. "What's wrong with her?"

Ral pulled at the loose strands of her hair hanging past her shoulders and peered at Tatsu with a crumpling expression. Tatsu wanted to say something reassuring, but he could think of nothing. Any possible words died on his tongue as Jotin sprinted over and skidded to a stop on his knees, leaving indentations on the ground behind him.

"How long has she been like this?" he demanded.

"Just now," Tatsu said. "But I thought she looked pale earlier."

"And this morning, she seemed very hot," Leil added.

Jotin put a hand to Alesh's forehead. "Sun sickness. She needs rest and water, but we cannot get more of those until we reach the next dominion."

"How far?" Yudai asked.

"Two days." Jotin glanced over his shoulder at the Oasa-walker to confirm his estimation. "Perhaps less, but we will not be able to make good time with her condition like this."

"Will she be all right?" Tatsu asked. He tried to keep his voice low, but Ral seemed to hear anyway. She let out a low, keening sort of whine and pressed her hands against her face.

Jotin pulled Alesh up into a seated position, but her body sank, limp. He could only get her to stay by holding her upright. "She should recover if we can get her to the camp as quickly as possible, provided..."

"We don't run into anything else in the desert that wants us dead," Yudai said, "or eaten."

As Jotin dragged Alesh to her feet, she groaned, but the sound was pitifully weak. Tatsu stood and then reached for Ral's arm.

"Ral, did you see this?" he asked. "Was this supposed to happen?"

"Sick," Ral said with a sad whimper that tore at Tatsu's chest. "Help."

"We will, I promise. But I need you to tell me—did you see this happening? Was this something you saw in our future?"

Ral stared at him for a long moment, her cheeks streaked with tear tracks glistening in the starlight, and then shook her head.

"If Ral didn't see this coming, are we doing something wrong?" Yudai asked.

"I hope not," Tatsu said.

Yudai leaned in, though his eyes stayed on Alesh's sagging figure with its one arm slung over Jotin's shoulders. "What do you think it means?"

"I think it means that we're on our own," Tatsu said and gave Ral a small smile while patting her shoulder.

ALESH WOKE INTERMITTENTLY, but never with very much coherence. Sometimes she would try to speak, but the words never made very much sense. To keep up their pace, two of them had to half carry, half pull her across the sand, alternating to avoid succumbing to exhaustion themselves. The air congealed, tense and strained; they were on the brink of something none of them could see the end of, and fear of the unknown seemed to make everyone nervous.

When he wasn't helping to move Alesh through the desert, Tatsu tried to stick close to Ral, who stayed quiet as they made their way farther south.

"Alesh'll be all right," Tatsu said, and Ral burrowed into his chest, perhaps to hide from the world. "We'll take care of her, I promise."

"Still sick," Ral said.

"I know. Can you see anything else? Once we get to the camp?"

With her face mashed against his shirt, Tatsu couldn't see her expression, but she shook her head sharply from side to side. "All dark now."

"Dark is bad?" he asked.

"Sometimes. Sometimes, just new."

Tatsu put his arm around her shoulder. Jotin and Yudai were hauling Alesh in front of the party, and the toes of her boots left long, erratic lines in the dirt. "When you see things that are coming, what do they look like?"

"People shapes. Night shapes."

"Shadows?"

Ral shrugged. "Sometimes scary."

"I bet." Tatsu sighed. "Like seeing ghosts all the time."

After the words left his mouth, a thought floated up into the forefront of his mind: if Ral could see forward, could she also see backward? Perhaps he was more right about the ghosts than he thought. Perhaps they all had ghosts trailing behind them as they continued on, memories from lost hours and forgotten decisions. He wondered if she could see their mournful, faded faces.

He didn't ask, unsure if he was more concerned with frightening Ral or himself.

They continued in silence for perhaps ten minutes before Leil let out a shriek of alarm. A second later, a wall of dirt and sand shot up from the ground in front of her with a blast of force and noise, causing Jotin and Yudai to stop so suddenly they nearly dropped Alesh's body. As Leil held the mixture aloft with trembling hands, Tatsu caught a glimpse of a snake slithering away, covered in mottled brown scales.

The sand fell to the ground after the creature had skidded out of sight, and Leil pressed a shaky hand to her chest.

"I'm sorry," she said, glancing between them. "I reacted, and I thought with Alesh..."

"It does not carry poison," Jotin said.

Flinching, Leil shrank back into herself. "I'm sorry. I didn't know."

"It's fine," Tatsu told her, but as they continued walking again, he looked to where the dirt and sand had fallen after floating through Leil's magic control.

A shudder ran through Ral's body, still pressed against Tatsu's side. "Dark again."

"Yeah," Tatsu agreed and couldn't quite get a handle on the uneasiness in his gut. "We need to take care of one another."

THE RIST-WALKER camp didn't resemble the others they'd seen; instead, the structures were made of mud and fire-burned clay, clearly built to be permanent rather than mobile. The benefits of keeping the camp in one spot showed in the large herd of sheep-like animals kept in wood-walled pens and the sprawling gardens filled with desert flora. At the edge of the Dar-Itusk Basin, the ground was strewn with reedy, thin-stemmed plants growing tall with fat leaves and small white blossoms. The weeds seemed to be the food staple of the sheep meandering through the paddocks on black hooves. Even with the sun rising overhead, the desert air thinned into a less oppressive stickiness—with the winds of the gorge rising up to meet them, the heat lost much of its bite.

The village appeared much more like a lookout than anything else. When they took Alesh to one of the thatched-roof huts, the Rist-walkers who met them didn't ask questions before taking her into the darkness and the cooler temperature the structure offered. Tatsu was glad for the sense of priority, even if the subsequent meeting between their Oasa guide, Jotin, and the Rist-walker acting chief didn't include the rest of them. His presence certainly wouldn't help the arrangements, and they would work faster without having to translate everything said.

With nothing else to do, Tatsu left Ral kneeling next to Alesh in the healing hut and made his way to the edge of the camp where the Dar-Itusk Basin began. Whatever Tatsu had thought the landmark was, he'd been wrong. At first glance, the true sight of the sprawling gorge carved into the land overwhelmed, stretching far to the horizon in both directions. Its sides, first smooth and then jagged, were littered with small, rocky outcroppings. Sharp-angled rock, at first tinted orange like the clay huts, darkened with the descending shadows until there was nothing but blackness as far down as Tatsu could see. Gouged into bedrock and the very bones of the land, the basin was a scar, gaping and sighing up at the souls perched along the top of it.

Tatsu stumbled as he stared down into the abyss terrifyingly close to the Rist-walker camp, and his boots kicked over a small pebble. Bouncing against the sides on its way down, the rock clanked noisily and disappeared into the shadows. Ten seconds later, after he'd nearly given up on hearing its final strike, the sound of stone hitting stone reverberated in rippling echoes up through the cavern. The basin seemed to shift, yawning, and Tatsu stared down, wondering what manner of beasts lurked at the farthest reaches from the sunlight.

"I never thought I'd see this," came Yudai's voice from behind him, and Tatsu jerked away in surprise toward the ledge again. "Amazing, isn't it?"

Yudai sounded reverent, but Tatsu's arms were covered in gooseflesh. Looking down into the nothingness was eerie—even staring out at the siphon-drained mountains past his woods hadn't been quite this off-putting. Tatsu couldn't imagine living there on the edge of the world, day in and day out.

He said as much to Yudai, who looked amused. "I didn't figure you to be scared by a hole in the ground."

"It's not just a hole. It's as if the land has teeth."

"A natural sinkhole." Yudai leaned in dangerously close to the precipice, seemingly unconcerned by the drop down. After a moment, he pulled back and glanced at Tatsu with a wide grin. "What do you think is at the bottom?"

"Nothing good." Tatsu tried to suppress the shivers threatening to take control of both his arms, even with the lingering numbness in his left fingers.

They stood side by side for a while as the wind caught in the hooked land curving over the basin's entrance and whipped up past them, threatening to take their linen coverings with it. It felt good to stand beneath the sun without fearing the repercussions of the sweltering heat, and for a moment, when he closed his eyes, Tatsu understood why the Rist-walkers had chosen to establish their base there. Then he pried his eyelids apart once more to see the desert's gaping mouth lying in wait at his feet and shook his head.

"The sooner we get away from this place, the happier I'll be," he said.

"I have bad news for you, then." Yudai's eyes crinkled in just enough sympathy to be noticeable. "Jotin says we're to follow the ridgeline of the Dar-Itusk Basin until we reach the farthest edge of it, where the corners meet. The ruins are there among the shallower depths."

"That figures," Tatsu mumbled. He took two steps away from the side of the sheer downturn and his chest immediately loosened. The abyss rumbled beneath his boots, and he watched several loose rocks rattle against the ground at his feet before he found his breath again. He half expected something monstrous to jump out of the blackness, with teeth and claws. When nothing did, he clutched at his shirt with his good hand, struggling to determine the cause of the shaking.

"What—" he began, and that was when he realized the vibrations weren't coming from the basin at all, but from behind, near the Rist-walker camp. He whirled to see a cloud of dust approaching the clay structures, particles held aloft by the pounding of hooves.

Hooves. *Riders*.

"No," Yudai said, as though his will alone could push the riders away. "How?"

"They followed us." A burst of scorching acid hit Tatsu's stomach, and bile rose in his throat. "They followed us here."

Within the camp, shouts rose as the walkers undoubtedly came to the same conclusion. Yudai grabbed at Tatsu's bad arm, yanked Tatsu to him, and hissed in warning, "Ral!"

"Alesh," Tatsu echoed, heart dropping.

He turned back to the camp and launched himself forward with all the strength he still had left, right as a thundering, terrible splintering noise sounded from the far side of the settlement. A wave of sand and dust barreled toward them, and Tatsu threw his arm over his face to shield himself from the sting of the granules.

There were more shouts and several screams, the kind that curdled his blood. As the ring of steel pierced the air and shrieked against his ears, he knew they'd led the mercenaries straight to the Rist-walker campsite. All the following carnage would fall squarely on their shoulders.

Still fighting the blast of sand clogging his nose and throat, Tatsu fell forward and smacked his head against something that hadn't been there only moments earlier: the broken slats of a wooden animal pen, now a cage encircling them to keep them contained.

Chapter Twelve

"NO." TATSU SPUN in a circle to take in the entirety of the pen surrounding them both. "No!"

He slammed his good shoulder against the broken boards separating him from the camp, but the enclosure didn't budge, held aloft by magic more powerful than anything he had inside him. Outside their cage came a cacophony of shouts, screams, and the clanging of swords, all muted beneath the thundering roar of the mercenaries' desert mounts. He and Yudai were sitting ducks, and they could do nothing to reach the others still within the huts.

Ral was in one of those structures, and Alesh, too sick to fight. Tatsu threw his weight against the wall again. "Ral! No!"

A throbbing pain in his shoulder was all he had to show for his efforts. He banged the splintered boards with his palm as he tried to find a weakness in them. "Jotin! Leil!"

Where *was* Leil? As the only one who'd be able to counter the magic holding them prisoners, she had to be trying to help, unless she'd been incapacitated. She would have been an easy mark in her deep-blue Chaydese court robes. Tatsu had no hope of identifying her voice among the shrieks blurred together, nor Ral's—

"No, no!" Tatsu shouted, and panic rose in his throat. Just as he took a step back to try ramming the cage again, Yudai grabbed his wrist to stop him.

"Together!" Yudai exclaimed. "On three!"

At the end of the count, they both threw their weight against the boards, but only ended up falling backward and over each other in the center of the cage. With the wood blocking them in, Tatsu couldn't see anything happening outside. He couldn't identify the mage keeping them encaged nor the identities of those laying siege upon the Rist-walker camp, but every scream cut off by a gurgling moan seized upon Tatsu's heart and squeezed it with fiery regret.

They were imprisoned within the magically held field because the mercenaries *knew*—they knew if they attacked Yudai directly, they'd trigger his magic, and they knew that without such an event, he wouldn't be able to combat them. Their enemy had learned of the explosion in the *Raydrau* and what caused it, and had adjusted accordingly, as—

"Cowards!" Tatsu cried, ramming his shoulder into the cage once again, even though he knew continuing to push wouldn't do him any good. An exclamation of pain sounded very near to their location, and Tatsu smacked his palm against the nearest board hovering by his head.

"Tatsu!" Yudai yelled, and when Tatsu whirled on him, Yudai's features were hard and set. "You have to hit me!"

Yudai had followed the same thought process, only to a far more extreme conclusion. Tatsu opened his mouth to protest but never got the chance.

"It's the only way!" Yudai said. "You know it's the only way!"

"I can't—"

But Yudai stilled in the center of the makeshift cage with his hands clenched into fists at his sides, his eyes tightly shut. "You have to mean it; it's the only way it'll work!"

The pounding hooves were nearing them, and Tatsu assumed once the Rist-walkers were dealt with, it would be their turn. Ral, and Alesh, vulnerable in the camp, and Jotin and Leil—

"Tatsu!" Yudai urged with his eyes still closed, body braced for impact.

A thousand words caught behind Tatsu's teeth, a thousand words lay dormant on the tip of his tongue, waiting to be awoken, but he couldn't get any of them out. With a shaky breath, he tucked the fingers of his good hand into a fist. He'd be useless if he splintered the thumb in his only working arm.

If he aimed for Yudai's cheek, he was unlikely to break any bones, but would it be enough?

"I'm so sorry," he said and swung his fist forward with all the power he could muster.

He made solid contact; the force of the impact rattled all the way up through his shoulder, and for a second, all he could focus on was the tremor in his bones. Then Yudai's magic exploded with so much intensity Tatsu flew up in the air, blown back with the remains of the broken corral posts. He hit the ground rolling and landed on one of the boards, twisting his knee in a sharp jerk of pain, but the pressure in his chest ached far worse. He couldn't breathe—the harsh fall had knocked the air out of his lungs, and he gasped, desperate to find his breath again.

Clawing at the sand and dirt, he struggled to stay conscious. Without air, his vision wavered and darkened at the edges. He couldn't see, couldn't get his eyes to remain on anything, and his mind went blank. Around him, a mix of noises clamored, sounds he couldn't distinguish and shouts he couldn't understand. It wasn't until he rolled over, coughing up grains of sand and clumps of dirt, that he managed to gasp in a painful, trembling breath. He repeated the action again and again, until the color of the world surged back into being.

He flipped over, wincing as his bad shoulder throbbed beneath his weight, and pushed himself up with his good hand and his bad elbow. His vision might have returned to normal, but his ears still weren't able to register any specifics. Only through severe squinting was he able to see Yudai barreling in the direction of the encampment with the wind on his heels, leaving a trail of red in his wake.

Tatsu crawled toward the closest pool of crimson, which had only partially soaked into the earth. Two eyes stared back at him—a severed head, lips still parted in surprise, the body nowhere near enough to see.

"Yudai," Tatsu whispered to the unseeing features, now still and ashy gray. Then he pushed himself to his knees with all the shaking power he had left, stumbling once and narrowly avoiding falling into the spread of crimson. "Yudai!"

He'd lost precious seconds knocked loopy from the blast, and Yudai had moved out of sight behind several clay buildings. The screams, however, were easy to track. Tatsu surged closer to them just in time to see one of the mercenaries flying out of the inky shadows, a fence post wedged deep in the man's chest. When his body hit the ground face-first, the rest of the stump pushed through with a blood-curdling snap.

Lying against the reddening sand, the mercenary's open mouth was a warning, a testament to the power they'd declared war against.

Tatsu stumbled, light-headed and still dazed, until he rounded the nearest structure to find two Rist-walkers standing with wooden spears held ready. Both men were stained with red and dirt but still on their feet. In front of them, Yudai hovered above the sand. He threw his hand out toward one of the remaining mercenary riders, and a splintered post caught the man through the stomach, protruding out of his back as he fell off his horse and collapsed onto the ground.

A second later, another mercenary ducked out from the shadows of one of the huts, aiming for the Rist-walkers rather than Yudai. Both walkers turned a fraction too slowly, and Tatsu hadn't the time to yell out a warning. The mercenary had almost completed the length of his jump when the force of Yudai's power threw him backward. The stolen spear, spiraling in midair, impaled him cleanly.

He was dead by the time his body hit the dirt.

"Yudai!" Tatsu cried.

Yudai spun to face him and then reached, his palm out and fingers wide. Tatsu scarcely had time to register the movement before the magic rushed past him. When he looked to his left, the surprise at seeing another mercenary so close to him, blade on its downward arc, propelled him back unconsciously.

Just stopping the man's sword thrust would have been enough, but Yudai's magic control twisted the man's head all the way around in a sickening crunch of bone, and his listless body slumped onto the dirt.

Tatsu slapped a hand over his mouth, unsure if it was to stop his scream or his stomach's terrified revolt.

In the horrified moments that followed, he tracked his location, taking in the bodies littering the ground. At least ten, probably more, and those were only the ones he could see. To his left, a man sprawled with his mount's reins knotted around his throat, and past that, a figure lay splayed with both arms ripped clean. Every corner of the camp bore bloody remnants of the fight—though it hadn't really been a fight, not really, at least not after Yudai's control had been activated. A few Rist-walkers lay among the wreckage, but the majority of the bodies were garbed in black, faces and heads covered with dark cloth.

Tatsu had always known what Yudai could do; after all, he'd witnessed it, in Dradela and then again in Moswar. But this... Those other times had been self-defense, a wished-for escape. This was an all-out assault. This was a *massacre.*

There were no mercenaries left to target with the magic wind still whirling over their heads.

"Yudai," Tatsu tried again and put his hands out, fingers spread to show they were empty. "Yudai, it's over. It's fine; we're all fine. You can stop."

Yudai stared at him, and Tatsu was suddenly afraid something else had taken control of him, something grim and unreachable. But then the winds disappeared, Yudai's soles hit the ground in a dull thud, and Tatsu let out the breath he hadn't realized he'd been holding. Part of him wanted to go to Yudai, but another part of him, the part that ultimately won out, hesitated. Yudai knew it. He stared at Tatsu and refused to look away, his eyes demanding all the answers Tatsu wasn't ready to give.

"Gods," someone next to Tatsu moaned. "What *was* that?"

"Me," Yudai answered and held Tatsu's gaze with a ferocity that bordered on taunting as he stalked past him to disappear into the shadows of the buildings. As much as Tatsu wanted to go after him immediately, there were more pressing matters.

He made his way quickly to the healing hut where they'd dropped Alesh off, and his panic dissipated when he found her unharmed but still feverish. Next to her, Ral sat on her knees holding her sister's fingers with one hand and her *Oldirr* necklace with the other.

"You're not hurt?" Tatsu asked.

Ral shook her head, eyes wide. "Tatsu?"

"No, I'm fine," he said.

"Yudai?"

Tatsu hesitated, his gaze pausing on the quick rise and fall of Alesh's chest. "Yudai...took care of the mercenaries who were after us. They won't bother us again. At least..."

He let his sentence trail off, uncomfortable with finishing it: *At least* these *mercenaries won't bother us again.*

Ral seemed to understand. The lines of her face softened. "Not bad."

"I know." Tatsu pressed his good hand against the warm side of the structure. Leave it to Ral to cut right to the heart of the matter. "He's not bad. Stay here, all right? I'm going to find the others."

He left the building and nearly ran into Leil, who was holding the side of her head as though in pain.

"You're alive," she said, fingers gingerly pressing at the side of her dark hood. "I wasn't sure after—"

"You weren't in the fight?"

She pulled her hand away from her head, inspecting it as if she expected to see blood on her fingers. "They hit me with something to knock me out. I'll have a lump the size of a fist here tomorrow."

"Have you seen Jotin?"

Leil shook her head. "I haven't seen anyone. There's carnage everywhere—what happened?"

"Yudai," Tatsu said, and guilt throbbed bitter on the back of his tongue.

"He killed *all* of them?"

"It was us or them." He shouldn't have let Yudai walk away. "He did what he had to do to keep us all alive. They came to kill him."

"I know." Leil looked away, fingers still playing with the edge of her hood. "It's...difficult to look at."

"Then close your eyes," Tatsu snapped. "And thank Yudai for allowing you the option."

He walked away knowing full well he'd crossed the line, and even though his conscience was urging him to go back and apologize, he kept walking. The disdain in her tone had only pulled up all the things he should have said to Yudai instead. He winced as he wove through the huts. Finding Jotin was paramount; then he could go after Yudai to make sure he was all right. With all the blood pooling under his boots, he didn't have time to soothe Leil's feelings.

And there *was* blood, everywhere. So much that Tatsu couldn't pick his way around it to keep his soles clean. He didn't dare look behind him at the red tracks he left on the packed dirt. In the sandstone-packed streets of Dradela, Yudai's power had manifested as a shield rather than a sword. The difference in the tactics was strewn at Tatsu's feet, and it was all he could do not to gag.

The Rist-walkers were up and moving, which made finding Jotin all the more difficult. Each time one of the walkers knelt near a comrade's form, Tatsu had to look away. He blocked out the sights of trembling fingers closing eyelids, but he couldn't completely ignore the sounds—soft sobs and shuddering breaths muted against shaking palms. As his search began to feel fruitless, Tatsu let his gaze drift to the faces of the bodies on the ground, praying not to find Jotin's features among them.

A sharp cry sounded overhead, and Tatsu whipped his head up to see Jotin's hawk slowly circling the camp in wide loops.

"Tatsu!" came the second cry.

Tatsu breathed deeply. "You're alive."

Jotin's face sported a streak of red that didn't seem to be his own, and he was either unaware or unworried about it. "When the men arrived, we weren't sure where you were. I feared they found you first—"

"They did," Tatsu said. "But I was with Yudai, and they trapped us to keep him from interfering."

"How did they find us?" Jotin's mouth pursed into frustrated puckers of skin. "We should have had days before the nearest scout could have reported back on our whereabouts, especially in the Joesarian dominions."

"One of the Rist-walkers? Or our Oasa guide?"

A second too late, Tatsu realized the implications of what he had suggested, but the copper smell of blood was too pungent for the full weight of regret to settle into his bones. He shrugged when Jotin's sharp gaze met his own.

"I'm just trying to figure out what went wrong," Tatsu said in the only apology he could manage with his heart still hammering in his chest.

"You are not wrong to question." Jotin sighed and leaned forward to pick up a discarded spear, clearly one of the Rist-walkers' judging by the intricately carved wood and the swatch of blue-dyed fabric wrapped around the shaft. "I wish I could speak for my kinsmen, but these are troubled times, and I fear you may be correct in your misgivings."

"Yudai isn't one of them. Would you be surprised if loyalty to their lives won out over keeping him a secret?"

Jotin shook his head. "In the past, I would have said yes. But this..."

He gestured wide from side to side. For a long while, they stood amongst the wreckage and the bodies, and the pause did nothing to help Tatsu's still-singing blood.

"Will there be more?" Tatsu asked.

"If there are, we should no longer impose on the dominion walkers or else face the same scenario in the future."

"We're lucky we all made it out alive."

Jotin looked up to his hawk, still circling the carnage. "And that very well may be the only luck we find on our side."

"So we go alone to the ruins?" Tatsu asked.

"As soon as Alesh is well enough to travel." With force, Jotin stuck the spear into the ground, and the hilt sank into the sand enough to keep the weapon upright. His expression was a tangled web that Tatsu couldn't find the end of to unravel. "We will find no further goodwill here."

"How long?"

"She will recover with rest, shade, and water within a day more." Jotin looked to Tatsu again with that same knowing gaze, eyes burning with something that might have been fury. "Find your prince—we should leave at dawn tomorrow. Our departure is the only kindness we can offer the Rist-walkers now."

YUDAI WAS SITTING on the edge of the Dar-Itusk Basin when Tatsu finally found him again, his legs dangling over the cliff ledge. Tatsu approached the sharp fall with care and stopped after Yudai glanced over his shoulder.

"You don't have to explain the look on your face," Yudai said, voice soft and surprisingly neutral. "I know that look."

"It doesn't mean anything."

"You were afraid of me."

There seemed to be little point in denying it, so Tatsu didn't bother. "Only for a second."

"But I'm not wrong." Yudai craned his head behind him once more. His silver eyes, gleaming even in the shadows of the basin, held too much Tatsu couldn't read—or didn't dare to. Tatsu let the quiet stretch between them before he took a deep breath and crossed the remaining space. He scuffed his boots in the dirt, acutely aware of how close he was to tumbling down into the never-ending darkness.

"It's all right," Yudai said, staring off at the horizon where the other side of the basin had to be, lost in the setting sun and the gold reflecting from far-off sands. "I'm not mad. Sometimes, I'm afraid of me too."

"This doesn't have to change anything."

"Doesn't it?"

Despite the lingering heat, Tatsu shivered above the shadows of the gorge. "It's just...part of you, like everything else is."

"A part that scares the only people who care about me."

"Everyone has things that scare people."

There was a moment of strange, stilted silence between them before Yudai said, voice much lower, "I killed those people."

"Yeah," Tatsu agreed, and the word stuck on his tongue, too dry and half-swollen. "But they would have killed us, all of us."

"I know," Yudai whispered. He sounded very small, far away and untouchable. "Does that make it better?"

"It has to. It has to be the reason. Otherwise, it's..."

He was at a loss for how to finish until Yudai finished for him. "Murder."

"You're not a murderer."

"I'm not? These weren't the first people I've killed. Look at what the siphon did to the Shyreld and the forests."

"That wasn't *you*, that was the siphon—and you were being controlled."

"But not here," Yudai said. "This was me, all me."

"That—" Frustrated, Tatsu shook his head to try to clear his thoughts, which did nothing. "You're twisting my words now. The point is—"

"The point is I killed those people." Yudai held his hands up to stare at his palms. "Me, with my own power and control."

"It was self-defense."

Yudai let his hands drop, staring off at the basin once more. "When does that stop being an excuse? When am I simply a killer?"

"Never," Tatsu said without pause. "You're not a bad person."

"Then you're the only one of us who believes that."

Tatsu sucked in a deep breath, and the sound whistled between his teeth. "Then I'll have to believe enough for both of us."

"Can you do that?"

"Yes," Tatsu said again, and it came out very soft.

Yudai stared down at his palms again. Maybe he could see the blood there, invisible to Tatsu's eyes. Maybe it burned in the middle of the night when he couldn't wash the memories away, like a branding stain he'd carry his whole life. Tatsu ached to remember the blots already there—Yudai's howls at the Shyreld still haunted his darker thoughts. He couldn't imagine how heavy the burden had to be on Yudai's shoulders.

"The others?" Yudai finally asked.

"Alive. A few bumps and bruises, but you saved their lives."

Yudai's fingers curled in. He breathed deeply enough that Tatsu could see the ripple of the action through his torso. Finally, he tore his gaze away from his hands to look back up.

"You're wrong, you know," he said.

"About what?"

Yudai shuddered. "This *has* changed me. This has changed *everything*. I'm not the person I was before they...used me."

"There's nothing wrong with the person you are now."

"No," Yudai replied. "I don't think you would have liked the person I was before."

Tatsu stared out over the black shadows stretching down into the gorge's foreboding emptiness. "Would you have cared about that, before the siphon?"

"Yes," Yudai said, and his eyes were sharp, taking in too much—he was always seeing much more than Tatsu wanted him to. "I think I would have cared very much."

Tatsu should have asked him to explain. Later, when he was staring up at the hastily patched roof of the narrow hut and trying in vain to sleep, the question burned hot in his throat without any answer to satiate his curiosity.

Chapter Thirteen

ALESH'S SYMPTOMS WERE significantly reduced the next morning, and the group left the Rist-walker camp before dawn had completely broken over the horizon. The only send-off they received were three stony-faced members of the camp watching them depart in silence before returning to the duties of preparing the dead for their final rites.

Tatsu had expected nothing more.

Jotin led them along the side of the basin where the ground crumbled and cracked beneath the thudding of their boots, on a path far enough away from the edge none of them could accidentally fall in. But it was still far too close. Tatsu could peer over the edge if he craned his neck, and even that was too much. He stayed to the right side of the path as much as he could manage as they trekked across the dirt and sand.

After the events at the camp, none of them seemed inclined to chat, even Alesh, who had gotten most of the events secondhand once her fever had broken. But Leil stuck close to Tatsu as they walked, and after a few glances at her over his bad shoulder, Tatsu finally said, "I'm sorry about my bluntness yesterday. I was rude to you."

"You were anxious." Her mouth twisted to the side. "We all were."

"Still, I shouldn't have snapped at you."

"And I shouldn't have questioned Yudai's actions with such..." When she trailed off and didn't finish, Tatsu thought he could probably fill in the blank: disgust, perhaps, or horror. He snuck a glance at Yudai, walking a few paces ahead, who didn't appear to be listening to the conversation.

"Sometimes the right choices are also the worst ones," Leil said, lowering her voice as though following Tatsu's line of sight.

The statement rang startlingly true. Tatsu thought back to his father's cabin in the woods and the seclusion offered there, wondering if his father, too, would have believed his actions correct in the grand scheme of things.

"Maybe you're right," Tatsu said when the silence stretched too long and he felt he had to say something.

"Do you trust him?" Leil asked.

Tatsu stared at the back of Yudai's head where his hair waved long and unruly, the colorless ends brushing against his collar. "With my life."

"I wish I had that kind of conviction." Leil was twisting her hands again, and Tatsu tried not to stare at her fingers knotting together and apart. "I wish I could believe as you do that things will work themselves out."

"You're here, aren't you? So, you must believe in something."

Leil's expression darkened, but she said nothing further.

Perhaps an hour before dusk, Ral broke out into a run toward the edge of the Dar-Itusk Basin, sending Tatsu's heart plummeting. He shouted her name as a warning, though he needn't have—she skidded to a stop at the side of the sheer brown cliffs and stared down at the gaping maw.

The others joined her at the edge and peered into the nothingness.

"What is it?" Alesh asked. "What do you see?"

"There's nothing," Yudai said.

Tatsu's stomach flipped as he stared into the abyss where the shadows cut off the rock in sharp angles so they eventually completely disappeared. They stood motionless until Ral bent over, her hands curved over the joints of her knees.

"Look," she whispered, as though they weren't already doing so.

As if in response, a noise echoed up through the caverns, a low and feral sound reverberating up through the rock. Almost a moan, a mournful note from the land itself, enveloping them all and sending shivers down Tatsu's spine.

"What's in there?" he asked Ral quietly, afraid raising his voice would invite another reply from the deep.

Her eyes were wide and clear when she looked back at him. "The dead."

Tatsu stepped back involuntarily, putting distance between himself and the drop, vindicated when the others looked similarly ill at ease.

"These ruins," Alesh said, voice thick, "they're in the basin? Inside that place?"

"At the far edge, where the land meets the cliffs," Jotin said. "The location is not within the basin as you are thinking, but rather on the corner of it."

"But you're leading us alongside it," Alesh said.

Jotin put his hands up in surrender. "I did not choose the location of the mage quarters. I can only lead us there."

"Who decides to live in a place like this?" Alesh hugged herself.

"There's a power here." Yudai sounded almost reverent again as he bent forward to scrape his fingertips against a portion of the smooth rock. "It's not exactly magic, but there's something to it."

Lingering old magic would certainly explain Ral's fascination with the basin, but it did nothing to soothe Tatsu's nerves. "We shouldn't linger," he said.

It took some time before the others heeded his warning, and in the stretch as they slowly peeled themselves away from the cavern, Tatsu could have sworn he heard several more ominous sounds from within the blackness. Whatever was down there, whether it be the winds howling through the crevices or something worse lurking in the depths, it wasn't something Tatsu was eager to familiarize himself with.

"We should keep going," he said to prod them again. Finally, the others pulled away from the edge to start along Jotin's path once more. But Tatsu couldn't shake the chills settling just beneath his skin.

SETTING UP CAMP along the basin was even worse, though Yudai seemed cheered by not having to worry about the siphon's drain, since nothing grew along the cliff's edge save for a handful of scraggly weeds. Jotin suggested keeping watch in shifts, and though the idea was innocent enough, Tatsu wondered if Jotin also worried about the things waiting in the darkness. Perhaps he was overreacting because of his own fear. Perhaps Jotin simply wanted to make sure they wouldn't be taken by surprise by any other mercenaries tracking them through the sands.

Or, perhaps Ral's cryptic remarks about the basin had rattled all of them.

Tatsu drew first watch. He waited by the small fire Jotin had started as the others crawled into their sleeping rolls, the air stilling in the moonlight. Only Yudai stayed awake with him, seated to the left and staring at the flames.

"You should sleep too," Tatsu said.

"I'm fine." Yudai set his chin on his knuckles. "It's not a bad night."

While they sat in companionable quiet, Tatsu's nerves were on high alert for any further noises escaping the basin at their backs.

"Leil thinks I'm a monster," Yudai said, breaking the silence.

"So you heard our earlier conversation."

One of Yudai's eyebrows quirked upward. The bruise swelling along his cheek and eye, courtesy of Tatsu's blow the day before, shone purple in the firelight. "No, but thank you for confirming I'm right. I could just tell."

When Tatsu turned to him for clarification, Yudai lifted his shoulders in a halfhearted shrug. "It's the way she holds herself around me now. She won't look me in the eyes."

"She's confused," Tatsu said, though the statement could apply to more than simply Leil.

Yudai shook his head. "She was never with us because she believed in me, not like you. I think she feels guilty about the way the mages treated me in Dradela."

Tatsu let the comment go without a response and, instead, let himself get swept up in the crackling of the fire. The familiar, soothing sound drowned out the rest of his old memories. In the darkest part of the night, the ones he wasn't proud of had a tendency to rise up often.

"Don't," Yudai said, jolting Tatsu from his reverie.

"Don't what?"

Yudai gave him a knowing look. "Don't start feeling guilty about delivering me to the queen again. You already apologized for that."

"Get out of my head," Tatsu said, but he smiled despite himself. "There's enough rattling around in here already."

"You're remarkably easy to read."

Tatsu had never had much practice at keeping his emotions to himself—there'd seldom been enough people nearby for it to matter, and of the ones remaining, all knew him already. He wondered if it should have bothered him to be deciphered with such ease, but his heart hummed out a slow, light rhythm of acceptance.

"How much farther do you think the ruins are?" Tatsu asked to change the subject.

"Jotin said two days, maybe, if we make good time."

Tatsu sighed. "The sooner we can move away from the deep part of the basin, the better I'll feel."

Then he looked sideways at the man seated next to him, evaluating Yudai's relaxed posture. "Why are you avoiding sleep? You aren't worried about what lies in the basin."

"No, but *you* are," Yudai replied with a soft sort of smile.

Tatsu ducked his head, hoping the shadows hid his embarrassment. "Are you going to stay up with me through my entire watch?"

"Yes."

The warm feeling in Tatsu's belly remained until the maw behind them groaned again, a deep, bone-trembling noise coupled with shaking that started at his toes and echoed up through his limbs. Tatsu's throat tightened as he tried to ignore the implication that something was alive—and monitoring them—at the bottom.

"How's your arm?" Without waiting for an answer, Yudai reached for Tatsu's hand. His fingers were warm when they wrapped around Tatsu's. It was an accomplishment that Tatsu could loosely squeeze back, the most control he'd had over the arm since the scorpions' stings.

Yudai said nothing more but kept his hand where it was in perhaps the kindest sort of quiet acknowledgment of Tatsu's fear he could've given.

"If something attacks us, I'll be useless to stop it without my bow arm," Tatsu said.

"Well," Yudai replied and smiled again, "then I suppose you'll have to hit me again and give me another black eye so I can save us both."

"Promise?"

Yudai's fingers tightened again. "I promise."

BY MIDDAY TWO days later, the basin to their left narrowed enough to allow Tatsu to see across the ravine to the other side, and he took the change to mean they were getting closer to their destination.

Tatsu quickened his pace to draw even with Jotin at the front of their group, finally asking the question he should have voiced days earlier. "What do Joesarians believe about the basin?"

"There is a reason the mages live here," Jotin said, picking around a bit of loose rock and sending it skittering down the side of the cliff. "The basin is the resting place of Ilaka, the god of the afterlife and the keeper of souls."

"Then Ral was correct with what she said. The dead *are* within the depths."

"Physically, no," Jotin said. "The Joesarian death rites are performed so that the souls may cross through to the afterlife stripped of their sins. The Dar-Itusk Basin is merely the gateway, where Ilaka can grant them safe passage to the beyond."

In the Rist-walker camp, the rites underway before they left were largely removing the organs and anointing the bodies with preservative oils, and Tatsu had assumed pyres were the next step.

"Why would anyone construct their settlement on the site of a holy place?" Tatsu asked.

Jotin laughed. "You Chaydese and your ideas of holiness—land is meant to be used, whatever its significance may be. Living off the side of the basin does not diminish its importance in other aspects."

When Tatsu didn't respond, Jotin continued, "Our beliefs state there are gods all around us. We could not possibly avoid all spaces for fear of disrupting them. They exist on a different plane that we cannot touch. Our actions do not impede theirs."

"I'd never thought of it like that," Tatsu admitted.

"Are you not spiritual?"

"I never really believed in much. Chayd doesn't keep to the old ways anymore."

Jotin was silent for a moment. "I find the 'old ways' to be comforting in the end, and perhaps that is the entire point."

"If you don't believe the dead are truly down there, then what do you think is making those noises?"

"There are some mysteries I cannot answer," Jotin said. "Perhaps we will never know."

A few moments into the silence between them, Jotin's mouth curved into a smirking smile. "Or perhaps it's merely the wind whistling through the rock, eroded by time and water."

It was the second time Tatsu had been overcome with the heat of feeling foolish in less than a day, and he huffed out a frustrated grunt while trying to ignore Jotin's soft laughter.

"I apologize," Jotin said after a few moments. "It's been a long time since I had someone I could tease—I have not seen my sister in over a year."

"Where is she?"

"Studying alchemy in Moswar. And once she's completed her apprenticeship, she will join the Cabaj-walkers in my place when I begin my time on the High Council."

"Are you close?"

Jotin's smile softened into something very fond. "Yes. She is a clever, witty conversationalist, and we grew up pushing each other to be better."

"Then I'm glad to hear it," Tatsu said.

"Do you have siblings?"

Tatsu thought of Zakio's blood splattered across the white snow and, forcing his tone into what he hoped was neutral, said, "No, I don't," to end the conversation.

THE MYVAR RUINS sat perched on the edge of the Dar-Itusk Basin where the crevice's narrow corner met the dusty, sand-strewn ground of the desert. Their crumbling rock walls stood out starkly gray against the beige. Looming over the rocks and casting long shadows across the dirt, the impressive building was adorned with several tall towers and an open archway at the entrance, the sight of which provided Tatsu with both relief and a jolt of nervous energy. The ruins reminded him too much of Aughwor Prison and its cold loneliness within. He looked back at Alesh and could have sworn he saw the ghost of the same remembrance across her features.

"That's our destination?" Alesh asked, sounding dubious.

"They may not be expecting us," Jotin said, "so we should proceed with great care."

Tatsu rather thought their greatest care was in making their way across the rocky terrain to the ruins—many boulders towered over them, and around them smaller rocks impeded movement. Several times, they had to slow to a crawl to pull themselves with grappling hands over the obstructions. And even though, at the far edge of the basin, the sloping bottom could finally be seen, Tatsu still feared tumbling into it. Getting to the stone archway of the towering castle, the only structure still in one piece, took far more time than anticipated.

He kept a sharp eye on Ral's progress, but she didn't seem to have much trouble climbing over the stones.

"They wouldn't have sent a messenger?" Leil asked as they paused beneath the archway to take in the rest of the looming building. Dotted with flickering candles, the windows loomed, and the pathway leading inside was so worn and broken in parts it mirrored the jagged rocks of the approach.

"They may have," Jotin said. "But whether or not the messenger arrived or got here before us, I cannot say."

"What happens if they think we're enemies?" Tatsu asked.

Jotin's eyes narrowed. "We should all pray they do not make that mistake."

The warning wasn't reassuring, particularly since they'd been sent to the ruins on purpose with a task, but Tatsu banished the remainder of his apprehension. He looked first at Yudai, who had squared his shoulders again and donned the stony expression of a royal heir, and then at Alesh, who shrugged helplessly.

"Let's go," she said. "We might as well get it over with."

They walked into the wide, airy entrance hall.

The ceiling was lined with wooden beams running parallel to one another and covered with vines that hung down and moved with the breeze. While the walls remained starkly undecorated and bare, small square indentations had been carved into the stone and contained candles set in brass. Despite the lack of decor and the absence of color, the ruins were warm and inviting—comfortable, even—something Tatsu hadn't encountered since he'd left his cottage in the woods. As their boots sent echoes reverberating through the chamber, Tatsu made a full circle staring up at the ceiling and the stillness there with the fingers of his good hand involuntarily splayed out at his side.

The building seemed familiar; no, the ruins felt like *home*.

None of them dared to move or breathe until a door at the end of the chamber opened, and the sweet smell of floral incense drifted toward them. Locked between the impassive stone walls and the high roof, the scent filled Tatsu's head, sending a haze through his thoughts. His muscles relaxed, slouching as all the remaining fight left his body, and he feared, somewhat foggily, he might collapse onto the floor in a boneless heap.

Focusing on anything eluded him, impossible and fleeting. A warning sounded in the back of his mind, too far away to reach. He couldn't quite grasp the sensation buzzing behind his thoughts, even after he breathed in another deep lungful of the incense, letting it warm like an ember through his chest until all his blood was alive with it. Memories rose unbidden of his father's cooking, wafting through their small house, and the chirping of night insects in the darkness. Tatsu's temples ached. He was tired, so tired and weary from the journey he could barely contain his desire to submit to the sweet siren's call of sleep, surrounded by comfort and peace.

"Tatsu," Yudai's voice sounded to his right, but that, too, was murky. In Tatsu's mind, Yudai joined his father in the cabin, laughing over a rabbit stew that smelled so good Tatsu's mouth watered. He wondered if he should do or say something. He was vaguely aware of reaching for Yudai's fingers, which was followed by another soft laugh, the kind of gentle, easy emotion he'd rarely seen Yudai express.

Spring, and the smell of flowers, and Tatsu gave in; he went down on his knees, pressed against stone tiles that were a moment later the wet, rich soil of the forest. Then he fell to his stomach, and the warmth of fingers held in his hand was the only clue he had there was anyone else still with him. He was aware of bright blooms, the sound of the breeze rolling through the leaves, and Yudai's little sigh of contentment threatening to lull Tatsu's eyes closed completely.

Home.

He took one last deep breath and felt nothing more.

"Rise," a voice commanded, cutting through the woods that had wrapped itself around Tatsu's very being. With that simple word, everything was gone.

The sudden absence of the sensations burst cold against his face, the sting of winter's chill after sitting too long by the fire. Tatsu gasped like a man drowning and fighting for life. The flowers and stew and forest breeze disappeared, until the stones beneath his body and the cool stillness above his head were the only things that remained.

Yudai's fingers slipped away as he struggled to his feet.

"What was that?" Yudai asked, brittle and furious, and it took Tatsu much longer to climb back into a standing position. "What did you do to us?"

A man stood near the middle of the entrance hall holding his palm out, flames leaping out from his grasp as the sickly-sweet incense faded away. "A compound designed to soothe into complacency. I apologize for the tactics, but we had to be sure you meant us no harm."

"Effective," Jotin mumbled. "I thought I was dozing in the desert beneath the stars."

"The desert?" Alesh's eyebrows shot up to her hairline. "It was the mountains and a warm afternoon with no one else around."

Tatsu looked to Yudai, who pointedly ignored him and said nothing. Speaking of that sense of comfort and home would be like giving the memory away, and even if the images had been artificially produced, Tatsu wished to keep them.

"A technique designed to spare bloodshed," the newcomer said. He was dressed in a long gray robe that looked like Leil's but seemed to be made of something far lighter, with a wide hood and even wider sleeves. "I am Hysus, high priest of Joesar."

"We come seeking aid," Jotin said, stepping forward. "Tiran in Moswar sent us to ask for your help. Yudai—"

"Ah, yes." Hysus focused his sharp eyes on Yudai. "The Crown Prince of Runon is finally at our doorstep."

"You knew I was coming?" Yudai asked.

"Then there *was* a messenger," Leil said.

Hysus shook his head. "I merely guessed you would one day arrive. The waste in Runon's wake was too great to ignore, and the implications far too dangerous. Knowing you would be unable to stay within the borders of that which bound you meant it was only a matter of time before the breath of the gods brought you here."

He advanced, gliding toward them as the flames in his hand dissipated abruptly with a snap of wind. "It is an honor to greet you, Your Highness. And I welcome you to the Myvar Ruins."

Chapter Fourteen

HYSUS LED THEM into a smaller chamber connected to the entrance hall where the air was cleaner, and the last vestiges of the incense-induced images cleared from Tatsu's mind. Being bereft of the all-encompassing sensations left him reeling, disoriented, but his focus shifted as they made their way to the narrow room where several other mages wearing similar robes stood waiting.

"If you knew I'd be coming, then you know what's happened to me," Yudai said.

"I do not know specifics," Hysus replied. "Only the aftermath ravaging the land."

"Then what do you think you can do to help?"

Hysus gestured at the mages gathered quietly around him with hoods pooling down their backs and faces tinted orange from the candlelight. "We shall see what we can find in your blood, and from there, we will discover what we can do."

One of the female mages was put in charge of performing a blood drawing very similar to what Tiran had already done, and Yudai's jaw remained tightly clenched even after she'd finished. Hysus's test—whatever it entailed, as all Tatsu could sense was the faint buzz of magical energy being used—took much less time than Tiran's had. When it was complete, Hysus sat down in a rickety-looking wooden chair and stroked his graying, closely trimmed beard.

"Well?" Yudai asked when his patience seemed to wear out.

"Had all the effects of the poisons been intended, I would be impressed," Hysus said. "But I do not believe they were. There are too many things at work, activated by a toxin outside the original formula, to be purposeful."

"Explain," Yudai demanded.

Hysus spread his hands to either side. "Where to start?"

"My blood," Yudai decided after a moment's hesitation. "Start with my blood. The alchemist said the poison corrupted it, and that my magic was fighting the effects."

"One of the unintended consequences of the toxins," Hysus said. "The effect is permanent. You will retain the corruption for as long as you live, as it has fundamentally changed the very base of your blood. It no longer feels the same as untainted blood, and my magic cannot penetrate the damage. A particularly cruel consequence is that it would undoubtedly cause the death of any offspring you might produce."

Yudai deflated, the breath leaving his lungs in a sputter. "What?"

"Your family line will end with you."

In the stunned silence that followed, Leil turned her face to the ground, and Alesh pressed a hand to her lips. Tatsu watched Yudai, his own gut twisting as Yudai fought to regain control over his expression. It took only a few seconds, faster than Tatsu would have thought possible.

"And the siphon?" Yudai continued, his voice wavering ever so slightly.

"Yes," Hysus said, sighing. "That is the main concern, and fortunately, the one I believe we can do something about."

He stood and pushed his long sleeves to his elbows, although the slippery fabric almost immediately fluttered back down.

"The magic used to activate the siphon is untouchable, for it has been coded with the mage's blood who designed it. But the siphon itself was developed through starving your body until the magic responded in kind, like a feral animal lashing out. We may be able to reverse that by simulating a similar experience to 'trick' the siphon into retreating."

"Which means the siphon would be gone?" Yudai's forehead creased.

Hysus smiled, a slow, wide grin that crinkled across his brown skin. "It means you will have control over the siphon as you do your natural abilities and will be able to turn it on and off whenever you please."

"How?" Yudai leaned forward, fingers trembling with anticipation. "What do you need to do?"

"It is not going to be easy," Hysus said. "I will need to think on the best method to replicate the grueling conditions that initially triggered the drain. From there, my adept mages and I will manipulate the siphon's energy back into your body until it is enough to overload the drain and push it into dormancy."

"That's it?" Alesh asked.

Without looking away from Yudai, Hysus added, "The siphon was created through torture, and to reverse it, we must do the same. Your body may not survive. It will be...excruciatingly painful as your already damaged core struggles to accept the onslaught of what we will force upon you."

"He might die?" Alesh recoiled, eyes wide. "And that's the only option?"

"But it would stop the siphon," Leil said.

"We didn't come here to let him *die*," Alesh snapped.

Yudai's gaze flitted over to meet Tatsu's. "We didn't come here to walk away without a solution either."

The world spun, and Tatsu couldn't quite catch up. He took a deep breath in hopes of steadying himself, which did nothing to help. Staring at Yudai, all he could think of was the possibility of watching his death, and even the imagined picture of it was too much to bear. He couldn't find his footing as the stones slipped out from beneath him.

Around him, the voices muted into a low roar, individual words indecipherable.

"Tatsu?"

He started and turned his head to find both Alesh and Leil focused on him expectantly. "I'm sorry?"

"Well, what do you think we should do?" Alesh asked, clearly frustrated.

"We?" Tatsu echoed.

"Should we go through with this or not?"

Tatsu took in Yudai's rigid shoulders, his posture a hardened piece of armor. "I don't think we have any say in the matter at all. It's Yudai's body and Yudai's magic. It's Yudai's choice."

"But we came all this way to fix things," Leil said. "If left the way it is, the siphon's only going to get worse, with no possible—"

"It doesn't matter," Tatsu said. Yudai's face was carved from stone, but his eyes shone with gratitude. "It's not our decision."

Alesh looked to Yudai, and then Leil followed suit. The quiet that descended on the room cooled eerie and heavy. The atmosphere congealed enough to mimic the incense-hallucination all over again, a lull balanced on the edge of the basin outside, teetering and ready to fall, dislodging them all from the footing they thought they had.

Yudai closed his eyes, his mouth parting in a shallow exhale. When his eyes opened once more, the vulnerability had disappeared. "What do you require in payment if you help me?"

Hysus's eyebrows raised. "I ask for nothing, prince, but for the relief of knowing the siphon's wrath will be contained and controlled from the world."

"No one asks for nothing. There has to be something; you owe me no loyalty."

"Do not presume that we do not honor foreign royalty's claims," Hysus said. "Even if you were not bloodbound to the crown, actions taken for the good of the world benefit us all."

Yudai nodded once, curt and short. "Then I'll do it. Get your mages ready."

"We will prepare for the reversal tomorrow," Hysus said. "My mages will show you to the guest quarters. I suggest you get a good night's sleep. Your body will need all the strength it has left to survive the ordeal."

IT SEEMED THE ruins didn't see too many visitors by the layer of dust coating each of the rooms they were led to. Though narrow, with a single slit of a window facing the outside and a heavy wooden door connecting to the hall, each space was functional and comfortable. The weariness in Tatsu's bones seemed to hit all at once as he took in the wood-framed bed, and he longed to collapse into it and fight away his gnawing fear.

Once they were all deposited in their rooms, several robed mages brought up simple dinners of soup, a flat, starchy bread, and ale. Tatsu picked at the food while wishing his appetite would return. The next group of mages brought in lukewarm water for the metal bath bins, which Tatsu thought might have been a subtle hint to the state of their group after days in the sand. He washed his hair three times in his efforts to get all the grime out, and his skin tingled for a long time after.

Tatsu sat on the bed beneath his window flexing and unflexing the fingers on his bad hand as best he could. Outside, the setting sun turned the sky into a brilliant display of reds and oranges.

Thinking too hard about what would happen the next morning summoned too many dark thoughts, but lingering in the dusk glow, gradually fading into purple and blue, he found himself unable to focus on anything else.

A knock on the wooden door startled him, and when it was opened without him answering, he knew who it had to be.

"You're not sleeping," Yudai said. Once he was inside the room, he leaned against the door to shut it, the iron of the latch clicking behind his back.

"I don't know if I will. Why are you awake?"

"It might be my last night," Yudai said, but both his tone and smile were forced. "I'm not sure I want to spend it alone."

He let go of the door handle and took one step into the room, his fingers knotted together in front of him—a nervous habit he didn't often display.

"Coming here was my choice, you know." Yudai's gaze lifted to the ceiling, to the stones above their heads. "I wanted answers."

When he didn't seem ready to continue, Tatsu prompted, "And now?"

"I wasn't raised to do this." The hushed words sounded as though they caught in his throat. "I was raised to believe I held all the answers and all the power. I wasn't supposed to need anyone else."

"It's not a weakness. That's not a bad thing."

Yudai stared at him across the space, mouth pursed, and then shook his head as he bit down on his bottom lip, puckering the flesh. "Tell me what to do."

"I told you, it's your decision."

"Please," Yudai said, and all the earlier fortitude in his tone had fled. He was wrecked, panicked, and desperate, and the high-pitched lilt at the end of the word threatened to be Tatsu's undoing as his heart stammered out an empathic staccato beat. "*Please*, Tatsu—tell me what I should do."

"I *can't*." His own voice cracked at the end, useless, betraying everything he was keeping inside. "I don't know what to do or what the right answer is. I'm terrified to see you...I can't do this. I can't *watch* that. I can't tell you what to do because I don't *know* what to do."

Yudai's face crumpled.

"I don't want to die," he whispered, and when he heaved a breath a moment later, it hitched with a constrained sob. "Tatsu, I don't want to die."

Tatsu didn't know which of them moved first, but he was crossing the room before he willed himself to do so. They met somewhere in the middle, and Tatsu's mind blanked. He wasn't thinking or planning when he reached for Yudai to pull him in; he was just feeling, aching with a kind of terror he'd never felt before and trembling with the implications of what the morning would bring. The only thing he could see was Yudai, the bossy, spoiled, beautiful person putting his life on the line to stop the siphon he'd never wanted, and Tatsu worried his ribs were no longer strong enough to keep his heart encaged.

His aim was terrible when he leaned down. Their teeth clanked together with a pang that rippled through his jaw. But then Yudai gasped, half a sob, and Tatsu pressed their mouths together to kiss him with everything he had inside.

Yudai's hands tangled in his hair, tugging with a needy, still-desperate frenzy. Tatsu wrapped his arm around Yudai to get him closer, tug him nearer, as though he could eliminate all the space between their bodies. Gods, he was drowning. Moments stretched into the span of a lifetime. Yudai's mouth opened beneath his to suck in a breath, and Tatsu took the opportunity to delve inside, reaching up to cup Yudai's face. He didn't know why he'd fought it for so long—against his skin, Yudai felt like he belonged, like he was always meant to be there.

Tatsu flipped them back against the wall as one of Yudai's legs encircled his thighs. He couldn't decipher which way was up or down, because Yudai kissed just like he lived, demanding more, commanding control, and asserting his authority.

Then he felt the tug of Yudai's magic against his lips, pulling the very life from him, and Tatsu stumbled back with so much strength he nearly fell.

He pressed two fingers to his lips—the tingling aftermath of the siphon's hunger.

"It's okay," Tatsu stammered, mostly in response to the crushed expression on Yudai's face. "I'm okay."

"Tatsu, I..." Yudai's chest heaved as he trailed off. His red lips had already swelled, and his hair was a mess, sticking out at the sides. But Tatsu had never wanted anything as badly as he wanted Yudai in that moment. Something—the situation or Tatsu himself—hardened Yudai's features, and he ran his tongue over his bottom lip. "I'm going to live tomorrow. I'm going to live through this."

It seemed more a promise than a declaration, and when Tatsu gathered Yudai in a tight embrace, Yudai melted against his chest.

"I need you," Yudai said, muffled against Tatsu's shoulder. His fingers clutched at the back of Tatsu's shirt, the only lifeline he seemed to have left. "Tatsu—"

"I'll be there, through everything."

Tatsu wondered if Yudai could feel the hollow howl of the rest of the pledge, left unspoken: *even if it means I have to watch you die.*

TATSU WOKE THE next morning to impatient knocking against his door, but it took too long to orient himself in the midst of his fuzzy, post-dream thoughts.

"Tatsu?" Alesh's voice called from behind the wood. "Are you awake?"

"No." He only belatedly worried his answer wasn't loud enough for her to hear.

A pause, and then Alesh's voice dropped lower. "Is Yudai with you?"

Tatsu looked down to Yudai's mussed head, tucked against his shoulder. Yudai's weight angled heavily on his bad arm, yet Tatsu was grateful he could feel the pinpricks of numbness from it, even if the sensation was uncomfortable.

"Yes. Give us ten minutes?"

Alesh mumbled something Tatsu couldn't catch before her footsteps moved away from the door. Yudai lifted his head to gaze up at Tatsu with bleary eyes.

"Did you sleep much?" Tatsu asked.

"More than I expected. I didn't think I'd be able to relax enough."

Tatsu wanted to say something encouraging, but a heavy stone had settled in his gut. Yudai shifted a bit, curling in closer, and he pressed his cheek against Tatsu's chest again.

"I wondered last night if I was making the right choice," he said, softly and muffled against Tatsu's shirt. "But I can't go through life without control over this *thing* inside me, not being able to...well. I can't go through life like that. Even if it kills me."

"I know." The lump in Tatsu's throat made it difficult to swallow.

Yudai's fingers fisted in the shirt linen. "I used to wish for death when I was in Runon under Nota's control. I used to pray it would come for me, and when you showed up to steal me away, I thought it finally had. I welcomed it."

Tatsu didn't know what to say, but he threaded his fingers through the featherlight strands of Yudai's hair.

"I'm not ready for it now," Yudai whispered. "I thought I was, but the truth is, I'm terrified."

"Yudai, I—"

"Don't." Yudai pushed himself up onto one elbow. "Don't say good-bye. I don't think I can handle it."

But Tatsu knew if he never got another chance, he'd regret all the words threatening to die on the tip of his tongue. "I don't regret—"

"*No.*" Yudai bolted upright. "I'm serious, Tatsu, *don't.* I won't be able to go through with it if you say..."

When he didn't finish right away, something inside Tatsu's chest wished he would, fire pulsing through his veins.

"Please don't make this harder than it already is," Yudai said.

Tatsu sat up and pulled Yudai in to touch their foreheads together—the closest he dared to get while the siphon remained, lying in wait beneath Yudai's emotions. He cupped the back of Yudai's neck.

"I won't say anything," Tatsu said.

"Thank you." Yudai's eyelids fluttered closed. "For everything."

Tatsu tightened his fingers and, somehow, against all the nerves in his body trembling not to break the moment, said, "We should go; the others are waiting."

HYSUS AND THE others were waiting for them as they sluggishly made their way down to the small receiving chamber just off the expansive entrance hall. The Joesarian mages, clothed in layers of loose fabric floating with every breeze around the angles of their bodies, stood straight and tall, their robes lending them a distinctly ethereal image. Tatsu would have thought the vision impressive, but with the aching in his gut, the effect simply rattled into place, another puzzle piece threatening to shake down his worldview.

"Have you changed your mind?" Hysus asked Yudai when they stopped near the middle of the room.

"No." Yudai's voice was steady enough, but his hands at his sides curled into tight fists and trembled.

Hysus gazed at the tremors but didn't comment on them. He folded his own hands in front of him and laced his fingers together, the dark brown of his skin a striking contrast against his white linen robes. "Then I ask you to follow me, for we have prepared for the process."

Tatsu was glad they weren't offered any food—his stomach wouldn't have been able to handle breakfast on top of everything else. They followed Hysus to the end of the receiving hall and from there through a narrow set of staircases that seemed to go on forever. By the time they reached the caverns at the bottom, the air had cooled significantly, a far cry from the unrelenting heat of the desert. The basin's winds howled, amplified by the rock, and the slow dripping of water echoed as they made their way through the cavern by ducking beneath low-hanging stone.

Only a minute or two later, the rock opened into a wide, sprawling underground cave, the smell of fresh water carrying on the breeze before the steady twinkling sound of it. Two outlets, like waterfalls against the dark walls, emptied down into a large pool carved from the rock with the bluest, clearest water Tatsu had ever seen. There were no openings to allow for natural light, and the lanterns had oxidized in the strange sphere of underground moisture. The impact of the scene appeared to hit them all at the same time as they fell eerily quiet, overcome by the bright blue of the pool contrasting with the orange of the rock-clay walls and the high ceiling reaching down with erratic stalactites.

"An underground spring," Leil murmured.

"Created by the depths of the basin itself," Hysus said, his voice echoing as it bounced across the stone.

The sight was more beautiful than almost anything else Tatsu had seen in Joesar—but his mind was functioning too slowly to connect the pieces laid out in front of him. He failed to grasp the significance of the location choice until Yudai shifted and turned to Hysus.

"Water," he said, voice flat. "You're going to put me in water."

"The only thing that contains no living energy for the siphon to devour," Hysus agreed.

Yudai opened his mouth as though planning to continue, but no sound came out.

"You're going to drown him," Alesh said, very softly.

"The only way to trigger a similar effect with the siphon is to subject the prince to the same extreme that begat its creation in the first place."

Tatsu's chest ached.

"Walk me through it," Yudai ordered.

"We will prepare your body for the ritual. Then, one of my mages will then hold you beneath the water," Hysus said. "As your body begins to panic, it will undoubtedly trigger the siphon's desperate grasp. The drain will search once again for something to keep you alive. With the water surrounding you, the energy will be drawn to a single place."

"The person holding me down."

Hysus raised one eyebrow. "From there, the adept mages will manipulate the siphon's energy and turn it back to your own form."

"You can do that?" Leil asked.

"The siphon is merely another form of energy," Hysus said. "Corrupt and dangerous, but energy all the same. How else do you think the mages in Runon were able to direct the drain to only target lands outside of Runon itself?"

"You must have powerful mages for that." Alesh crossed her arms over her chest and glanced quickly at Ral, who seemed more entranced with the cave than the conversation.

"Then in Chayd—" Leil began, and then her jaw snapped shut. But Tatsu knew where her thoughts had gone. Her thoughts mirrored the ones he'd let gnaw him inside out back in the woods outside his father's cottage, staring out at the mountains and hills ravaged by the siphon. Chayd had no mages strong enough to control the drain, which Leil herself had once admitted.

Had the queen succeeded in using Yudai, Dradela would have been destroyed.

Somehow, in the midst of everything else unfolding, the image of what might have occurred had Tatsu not intervened swelled to overshadow his reality. He shook his head to rid it of the thoughts. Yudai glanced at him, but there was nothing in his expression to show he'd made a similar connection. His features were ashy-white and drawn, and against the paleness of his cheekbones, his lashes fluttered inky black.

"When I'm under the water," he started, hesitantly, as though drawing out the question would delay his own torture, "my body will be dying."

"Yes," Hysus said. "Once the siphon has been reverted, we will pull you from the pool and remove the water from your lungs, but..."

"You don't know if it will be fast enough to save me."

"You can't be serious about doing this," Alesh said. "This is too much to even consider. They're going to kill you."

Yudai looked to Tatsu again, and Tatsu froze. Every nerve in his body screamed for Yudai to reconsider, to walk away whole, and yet he knew Yudai was looking to him for strength, not compassion. All he could manage was a single curt nod, and he hoped it was enough—it would have to be. He couldn't force his teeth apart for the words to fall free, and even if he'd been able to, who knew what the words might have been.

"This is it," Yudai said quietly. "One way or another, this will decide things."

"Yudai," Alesh began.

Yudai cut her off with a wave of his hand. "No good-byes. No one says anything or else—just don't."

He turned to Hysus. "I'll do it. I'm ready."

"And so are we." Hysus gestured toward the pool's shimmering edge. "Please, let us prepare you for the ritual."

In preparation, he was stripped to the bottom layer of his linens and then clothed in a long white robe that draped across the cool rock of the cave floor. Adorned with blue thread woven into the designs, curves and stripes and unknown symbols blossomed across the sleeves and the back as if enveloping Yudai in their grasp, a bramblebush of support.

"What is this?" Tatsu asked Jotin, who hung back near the entrance of the cave rather than venturing farther. Tatsu got the impression he didn't feel comfortable with a mountain of rock sitting above their heads. "What are they doing?"

"The death rites," Jotin said. "At least the rites as are known to the mages."

"They're different?"

They watched as two of the mages anointed Yudai's hair with sweet-smelling oil and then waved a burning incense stick around his shoulders. The patterns their hands and arms made were clearly a practiced art.

Jotin's lips thinned. "Mages have their own beliefs. They are more connected to the gods and the land, and they send off their departed with more specific instructions."

"You said Ilaka resides in the basin to transport souls to the other side?"

"Yes."

"Then tell him to wait longer for this one." Tatsu's voice was much harsher than he intended. Observing Yudai stand with his arms outstretched, preparing *not* to return, was sandpaper scraping against the inside of his throat. "The gods can't have him today."

"He is ready," Hysus said. "Luia, please prepare to hold him."

A woman with hair coiled in a large bun at the back of her head moved to the side of the pool and knelt on the stone. Though a mage, her arms were covered in thick leather gloves—a deterrent, perhaps, worn in hopes of keeping the siphon's corrupt fingers from her skin a second longer.

Tatsu wondered if the rest of them were also at risk, standing near where the drain would be prompted into a frenzy. He'd seen the extent of Yudai's power, and he'd seen the siphon's aftermath. Even with the water's crushing weight, the pool alone might not be enough to stop the magic; the mages could lack the ability to control it. He thought briefly of telling the others to leave and then decided against it. Jotin already looked close to bolting for the tunnels again—the others likely knew the risks and had already made their choice to be present.

Hysus led Yudai to where Luia was kneeling and then prompted him into the water. Yudai gasped a little when he waded in, signaling how cold the water must have been, coming directly from between the rocks. The pool was a little more than waist deep by the time he'd reached the center, water hitting the middle of his chest. Luia followed and stood behind him with her hands on his shoulders.

Her body trembled, visible even across the hollowed space.

"He's going to fight," Tatsu said quietly. "His body will fight on instinct."

"They're giving him *iyera*," Leil said.

The name rang vaguely familiar, though Tatsu couldn't place it. "What is that?"

"A compound that causes people to become quite docile," Jotin said. "It's often used by healers when their patient is badly injured, giving the mind a cloudy haze."

"For mages, the confusion is enough to cut them off from their abilities," Leil whispered.

An image rose unbidden in Tatsu's mind of standing before Tiran back in Moswar as she held the vial of Yudai's blood. *Iyera* had come up then as having been used before, which made much more sense; *something* had to have removed Yudai's magic from his grasp, for Tatsu had never known Yudai with full control.

"They will remove his connection to his magic so he doesn't lash out with it," Leil continued.

Yudai had once said being without his abilities made him feel as though he were missing part of himself—to subject himself willingly to feeling it again, even for the short time prior to being pushed beneath the water, had to be a horrible decision. Tatsu stared at Yudai's wavering figure within the pool, but Yudai steadfastly refused to look in Tatsu's direction. Luia curled one hand around the back of Yudai's head, tipping his jaw up, and Hysus moved forward from the side of the pool to pour a noxious-looking substance between his teeth.

"It begins soon," Leil said. To her right, Alesh slung an arm over Ral's shoulders and tugged her closer.

"Yudai," Ral called out. Tatsu wasn't even sure it was loud enough for Yudai to hear until his gaze snapped to her. "No more pain, Yudai."

But the *iyera* was already taking effect. Yudai's shoulders loosened as his body sagged backward against Luia, and any response he might have given was lost. Everything in the cave stopped, including Tatsu's breathing, until Yudai finally, *finally*, met his eyes. Fear glinted in the molten silver. The terror shone brighter than anything else as Luia put her hands on Yudai's shoulders again.

"Gods," Tatsu breathed. "This is wrong."

Yudai's lips parted, a little, just enough, and that was when Tatsu moved forward with the intention of stopping the entire thing. He couldn't watch it play out—he couldn't watch Yudai die. They had rendered him listless and were going to shove him beneath the water. Somewhere inside Yudai's thoughts, he *had* to know what was going on. To be complicit in one's own death was a kind of horror Tatsu had never known. He couldn't let Yudai dangle himself so close to the edge.

"Yudai!" he cried. As he began to take the second step leading to the pool's edge, prepared to drag the man out of the water with his own two hands, Jotin's fingers clamped firmly around Tatsu's good wrist.

"Tatsu, no!" Jotin pulled back.

"Stop this! Stop them! Yudai!"

Jotin's arm encircled his middle, and Leil stepped in front of him with her arms outstretched as though to tackle him. The curve of her bicep nearly obscured Yudai's outline within the shimmering pool as Luia's arms pushed him down.

"No!" Tatsu shouted.

"Tatsu, stop! He made his choice!" Leil pleaded.

Tatsu struggled against Jotin's hold, but the other man's strength was too much, his grip too tight.

"Yudai!" he cried.

Luia submerged Yudai completely, and Yudai's head disappeared within the crystalline pool.

Chapter Fifteen

TATSU'S BLOOD SANG, palms clammy, while in the middle of the pool, Yudai's fingers and hair slipped beneath the surface of the water without any fight. Seeing him so limp, a rag doll lacking fight as air bubbled up briefly, stole Tatsu's breath away. He angrily shrugged off Leil's hands but couldn't dislodge Jotin's arm as all the air left his lungs.

"No," he said, a half gasp. "Yudai, no."

The water stilled to a placid calm, and within its clarity, Yudai's robes floated up around his body. The moment caught in time, a pause more in line with a sucker punch. They might as well have thrown him over the edge of the basin—the featherlight spread of his hair and clothes would have been the same.

Then Yudai began to thrash.

His movement disrupted the pool with whitecapped waves and splashes, but on the edge, Hysus remained visible, leaning forward with both hands outstretched to the water flung in all directions. He yelled something Tatsu didn't understand, and Luia's expression twisted into a grimace.

"The siphon has started," Jotin said. When Tatsu tried again to jerk away, Jotin dug his forearm painfully into his belly. "If you run now, you disrupt the process, and we all die. They need to control the siphon, or everything fails."

A thousand words threatened to tumble over his tongue, but none chattered free. They never should have gone through with such a terrible ritual. The mages were going to lose control despite their good intentions, and Yudai's magic was a spring-loaded box waiting to be opened. As the scene unfolded, Yudai's thrashing intensified, and the expression on Luia's face morphed into something much more like panic. Tatsu could have sworn his heart stopped entirely.

A noise sounded to his right, the ping of metal against stone, and then half the water rose up from the pool in uneven plumes reaching toward the ceiling. Tatsu couldn't tell if it was Yudai's magic or the siphon, and maybe it didn't matter; the mess of the two had long since tangled up too badly to be separated, and the whole situation spun furiously, reacting to the exertion of control. Three other mages joined Hysus's side to mirror his stance, palms spread out toward Yudai and the spires of water.

Hysus shouted something else, and most of his words were lost in the thunder of the churning pool. Energy pulsed beneath Tatsu's skin, not a buzzing in his veins as usual, but a vibration working all the way up from his toes to shake his entire being. He stumbled as the sensation threw him off-balance, and the fall provided enough to dislodge him from Jotin's hold as both of them tumbled backward. Tatsu hit the rocks just in time to feel the ground shift and move beneath his fingers. An earthquake.

Yudai was going to bring the whole cave down around their heads.

"Ral!" Alesh was yelling, and they scrambled on all fours to find a stable position with the clanging and rattling of the cave. In front of Tatsu, Leil already lay on the ground, rolled into a ball with her hands covering her face. Tatsu tried to catch sight of the mages between the ground quaking and the water erupting up out of the pool, but he couldn't make anything out through the spray.

The tremors shaking his body began to pull at him, claws digging into the flesh of his back and frantically, desperately tugging him closer. It was the same tugging sensation he'd felt on his lips only the night before—*the siphon.* As Tatsu gulped in all the air his lungs could handle and pushed against the pull across slick stones, everything stilled.

For a moment, the pause was literal. The plumes of water making contact with the ceiling froze in their upward trajectory and held there, sculptures solidified by a power greater than anything Tatsu would ever know. Hysus and the other mages snapped into view, but they too had been caught in mid-action. One of them floated in the air, lifted clean off her feet, and another had started to topple forward into what water remained in the pool. They hung motionless, suspended on nothing, as time within the cave quivered with the taut anticipation of a bowstring ready to snap.

Tatsu opened his mouth to yell, and time rushed back to fill the sudden void with a small popping noise.

The crash of the water falling back down into the pool—and the sides, and the cave walls—overpowered everything else before the splash of the mage, completing his arc into the pool, echoed. The water that hit Tatsu and Jotin was nothing compared to the wave cresting a few paces away, drenching Alesh and Ral. Tatsu scrambled to his feet, boots slipping across the surface of the rocks, and took three steps before he jumped into the pool.

Luia was already pulling Yudai's limp body out of the water by the time Tatsu reached them. Tatsu threw his good arm around Yudai and echoed the movement with his bad arm as best he could, and the two of them hauled Yudai's body to the side where Hysus was waiting to assist. When Yudai's back hit the rocks with a splat, not even his fingertips twitched. His lips were parted and slightly blue, the halo of his half-black hair a stark contrast to the too-white sheen of his skin.

"He's not breathing," Tatsu said and didn't bother to pull himself out of the pool before reaching, muscles seizing with fear, to find a pulse he knew wasn't there. "He's not breathing!"

"Turn his head to the side," Hysus ordered.

Tatsu did as directed, and Hysus must have been using magic for the buzzing returned to Tatsu's limbs, a tingle rippling within. Tatsu kept his hand on the back of Yudai's head as he waited a moment and then another, before Hysus pulled the water free from Yudai's lungs out through his mouth.

Tatsu put his head against Yudai's chest. His heart hammered out a frantic beat as he listened, willing Yudai's lungs to move with everything he had in him.

When they finally did—a sputtering, hitching rhythm, shallow but blessedly there—Tatsu gasped, his muscles slackening.

"He's alive." He shifted back, legs shaking within the pool, unwilling to unwind his hand from Yudai's neck. He looked up at Hysus. "Will he wake up?"

"We wait and see," Hysus replied. "Nothing is certain."

"What if he doesn't?"

Hysus shook his head and turned to aid his mages climbing out of the pool while Tatsu stayed where he was, half lying against the rock with his soaked shirt sticking to his skin. He stared down at Yudai's face, at his closed eyes and parted lips, and willed him to stir, over and over, until Hysus announced it was time to carry Yudai back into the ruins.

THEY LAID YUDAI on a small straw cot in the receiving room, and, one by one, the mages vanished into the corridors until only one remained. Hysus put a weathered hand to Yudai's face, checking the temperature of his skin and the pulse in his neck, and his expression betrayed nothing.

"We knew this could happen," Hysus said. "His body could have been devoid of air for too long. For someone already ravaged by poisons and the drain, we always knew it was possible the ritual could prove to be simply too much."

"No." Tatsu moved forward to take Yudai's still fingers in his own. "There's still a chance he'll wake up."

"You should find something to distract yourself," Hysus said gently. "The first day is the most critical period, but if he does not wake up by morning tomorrow—"

"He will." The corners of Tatsu's eyes pricked with hot tears, and he forced them away because letting it out meant accepting the offered reality. "He'll wake up."

Hysus touched Tatsu's shoulder and squeezed briefly, just enough to offer what reassurance he could, and then he too was gone, disappearing into the corridors to tend to his mages.

Jotin and Leil had left with the others, but Alesh and Ral lingered. Not wishing to see the concerned expressions and sympathetic eyes, Tatsu refused to turn; seeing the pity would have proved too much. He rolled the shoulder of his bad arm, and even though shocks of sensation rippled all the way down through his wrist, the gratitude failed to register.

"Tatsu..." Alesh began.

"He'll wake up."

"I'm sorry. I didn't want this to happen. I never wanted this to happen."

Tatsu ran his tongue over his chapped lips. "I would have followed him to the end, you know."

"I know."

"Ral?" Tatsu asked, and behind him came the shuffling of her boots as she drew nearer. "What can you see? What will happen?"

"Dark, Tatsu. All dark."

"Will he wake up?"

Silence descended, and Tatsu risked a glance over his shoulder to see her shoulders hunch helplessly.

"Tatsu," she started to say, and sound roared against his ears. He couldn't let her finish.

"Don't. Please...don't. Don't say it. There's still a chance he'll wake up."

"Yeah," Alesh agreed, but it lacked conviction.

"Can I—can I be alone with him?" Tatsu asked. "I'll stay here. You should both find something to eat."

"Don't do this to yourself." Alesh's fingers pressed lightly between Tatsu's slouched shoulders in support before she led Ral out of the room and into the hallways.

He'd thought it would feel better once alone, but instead, the stillness felt far worse. The weight of the situation came barreling down on him, threatening to push him into the floor and swallow him whole. There was nowhere to run to escape Yudai's lifeless body in front of him, and when Tatsu tried to take his next breath, his lungs rebelled against it, choking the action with a painful sob.

"I'm sorry it took me so long to get here," Tatsu whispered as he tightened his grip on Yudai's fingers and raised Yudai's hand to his face. "I'm sorry I didn't try to stop you from doing this. We could have worked around the siphon. This wasn't the only way."

Tatsu squeezed his eyes shut and dug his fingers into the straw of the cot. One of the pieces dug hard into his thumb, and he pressed down harder just to feel the ache jump up to his elbow—anything to try to distract his thoughts.

"Wake up, Yudai," he mumbled against Yudai's palm. "Wake up."

There was no response. Tatsu stayed, curled over the cot, until the sun made an arc overhead and the light streaming in through the windows waxed long across the stone floor.

THE NEXT MORNING, the lack of change soured Tatsu's tongue. Yudai hadn't opened his eyes, and though his breathing was steady, if a bit shallow, their time was running out. It physically hurt to pull himself away from the side of the mattress, but Tatsu managed it when Hysus brought in a few of the mages, carrying a small silver bowl between his cupped hands.

"We can attempt to stimulate his body into waking." Hysus leaned over Yudai's body with the bowl, which sported a smooth lid that rang softly when pulled free. "This is a compound used for injuries when the mind is unable to return to consciousness."

"What if it doesn't help?" Tatsu asked.

Hysus's gaze, when it landed on Tatsu, was sharp. "Then the gods have made their decision."

He took a pinch of the dried herbs from within the silver and waved them before Yudai's nose. When his action failed to produce the desired effect, he passed the bowl to one of the other mages and moved in closer. He then pulled down on Yudai's jaw before placing the mixture on his tongue. When Yudai's teeth snapped around the herbs—an awful sound rattling the stone walls—Hysus kept his grip firmly around Yudai's chin as though expecting a backlash.

For too long, nothing happened, and Tatsu's eyes stung.

Then Yudai's head jerked to the side, eyes squeezing shut tighter before blearily opening as if the bits of morning sunlight were already too much. Hysus released his fingers just as Yudai's mouth opened to cough the herbs up onto the side of the mattress.

Yudai's eyes darted across the room as his breathing quickened in a panicked sort of disorientation that made Tatsu afraid some part of Yudai's mind and memories had been stolen by both water and darkness. Yudai gulped in air before his eyes found Tatsu's face and stayed there. He took one wheezing, rattling breath, and then another before his fingers curled against the straw one by one.

"I'm alive?" Yudai asked, his voice hoarse and cracking at the end. One of the mages moved forward with a small glass of water Yudai gulped down in less time than Tatsu thought possible.

"It would appear so," Hysus replied.

"Did it work?"

"We will not know for sure until you are well enough to test it," Hysus said.

Yudai began trying to push himself up by his elbows, and Tatsu sprang forward to press a hand against his shoulder.

"Not immediately," Tatsu said as Yudai struggled against the pressure. "You've been out for almost a full day. You can't—"

"I'm not wasting any more time." Yudai shook, exertion draining all the color from his face, and the tremors in his arms vibrated the whole cot.

"We weren't sure you'd ever wake up," Tatsu said, more quietly, which seemed to work. Yudai's gaze flickered in his direction, and his scowl softened somewhat. He stopped fighting, letting Tatsu help to reposition his weight.

It took perhaps a full minute for Yudai to sit up and move his legs to dangle off the side of the mattress. Drained and exhausted, the dark circles under his eyes resembled inkpots despite the rest he'd just awoken from. Still, he ran a shaky hand through his hair to untangle it.

"What should I do?" he asked Hysus, who had refolded his fingers with a deliberate sort of care and was standing off to the side, watching shrewdly.

"Reversing the siphon into your energy should have given you control over it," Hysus said. "And it should have helped to crack the shields keeping you from your abilities."

"So I try to use my magic," Yudai said in a way deliberately not a question. He didn't wait for the answer before raising one shaking hand in front of his body, which swayed erratically from side to side. Then he looked to Tatsu, sucked in a deep breath, and his arm stilled.

"It does little good to delay," Hysus said.

Yudai's tongue flicked out, darting over his lips. Just as he stretched his fingers wide, Tatsu's ears popped. The sudden spark of the magic was swift, a smack against Tatsu's back threatening to knock the air out of his lungs. The vortex of wind that appeared in Yudai's palm started small but pulsed powerfully, tipping over one of the smaller tables at the side of the room and scattering several empty vials, which clattered to the floor. A second later, the manipulation of energy vanished so quickly the absence of its ghostly fingerprints echoed.

Ral made a happy little noise behind the row of mages, but Yudai collapsed against the cot.

"I lost it," he mumbled, staring down at his empty palm. "I couldn't hold on to it."

"In order to access the full extent of your abilities, you will need to counter the shields preventing you from accessing them at will," Hysus said. "Without the blood that created it, we cannot completely erase the corruption of your magic—the siphon. The siphon must be satiated entirely to restore the balance."

Yudai continued to stare at his fingers as he closed them unhurriedly. "You're saying I need to use the siphon to break the rest of the shields. That I need to drain the person who put their blood as a code into...me."

"Yes. I believe that would satisfy the siphon and activate the remainder of your abilities."

"How would she have done this?" Yudai's expression twisted into a grimace. "How could she have controlled the siphon through her blood without..."

"I believe she mixed her blood into the toxins they fed you," Hysus said.

"Gods," Alesh said, recoiling, standing behind Ral. She'd snuck in while Tatsu's attention was elsewhere. "She fed him her own blood?"

"It would have been the only way to ensure the siphon reacted to her magic control when it was created," Hysus replied and then looked at Yudai sharply. "It also served the purpose of keeping you from fighting back once she robbed you of your abilities."

Yudai opened his mouth to say something but never got the chance. A young mage barrelled through the door in a whirlwind of frenetic motion and almost tripped over his own feet. He stumbled to the center of the room and then, as though remembering the protocol several moments too late, fell into a jerky half bow.

"High Priest, sir," the mage said. "There is an urgent messenger from the capital. He was told to wait while Yu—the prince was unavailable, and they said he's woken."

"From the capital?" Hysus asked. "Then, by all means, send him in."

The young mage complied without delay and tumbled back out the doors. A few seconds later, a Joesarian messenger appeared, clad in white linen layers and knee-high, well-worn leather boots striped with the dusty remains of his desert path. He bowed with far more grace than the mage had and pulled a paper free from the inside of his tunic.

"This letter arrived by hired courier a week ago in Moswar," he said. "It was delivered to the High Council after your departure and then sent out after you. I apologize for the delay, but tracking your progress through the sands was made more difficult with the attack in the Rist dominion."

He passed the letter to Hysus, who inspected the wax seal. His brow furrowed. "It bears the Runonian seal."

"It's for the prince," the messenger said. "It has not been opened."

Still frowning, Hysus handed the folded parchment to Yudai, who took it gingerly. He inspected the parchment for a long time, holding its corners with the tips of his fingers before he tugged the edges free from the wax.

"'A life for a life,'" he read and then looked up. "That's all it says."

"It came with news, though not from the same man," the messenger said. "Reports have reached the Council's ears from Runon that High Mage Nota has taken control through a coup."

He paused, taking a deep, audible breath before facing Yudai directly and squaring his shoulders. The sharpness of his posture and the lines on his face all blurred together into the figure of someone delivering the worst news he could think of. Tatsu braced himself for what he knew was coming before the messenger opened his mouth again.

"The King of Runon is dead."

The chamber constricted, air whistling to a halt, with Yudai at the head, looking as though he scarcely dared to breathe. His expression was caught somewhere between disbelief and horror, his lips parting to gasp out an exclamation never fully summoned or formed. He stared at the messenger, and then at Hysus, and then back to the letter in his hands, the gruesome meaning a dark, crushing revelation painted over his features. Sucking in a ragged lungful of air, he stared at his future held between trembling fingers.

By the time his wide eyes met Tatsu's again, the space between them had elongated into an impassable gorge, the twin to the basin outside the rocky slopes of the ruins and just as terrifyingly black and deep. The King of Runon was dead, and so was the man who'd allowed his only son to be broken for his own gain. His blood heir stood at the apex of the receiving room and shook like a leaf in a storm, holding the crumbling parchment that had forever altered his world.

It'd taken a long time for Tatsu to think of Yudai as a prince. He'd always been one, of course, but he'd been a victim first, and a bargaining tool second. After that, he'd simply been Yudai, with his bloodline binding invisible cords around his wrists, out of sight and out of mind. The longer Tatsu stared at him, the heavier the realization he no longer looked at a prince.

Tatsu wanted to reach for him and found he couldn't. His body shook, a desperate, mournful rattle starting in his gut and echoing through his fingertips.

A gasp rang out behind him. Tatsu wasn't sure what it was directed at until he noticed his body moving unbidden, sliding to the ground until one knee smacked against the stones. At the edge of his awareness, he barely registered the others in the room doing the same.

Yudai's expression had twisted into unhappy shock, and his eyes in the morning sunlight glinted silver with what might have been betrayal—a knife severing all the things he'd been feverishly clinging to.

"Long live the king," Tatsu whispered, and even with the louder echo of the others around him, the words still tasted of ash.

Chapter Sixteen

YUDAI'S EYES ON him burned unbearably heavy for a long time, until the others in the room stood back up, and Tatsu let his gaze drop to the floor.

"Thank you," Yudai said, and it took a moment for Tatsu to realize he was addressing the messenger still standing in front of the wooden door, "for bringing this message. You're dismissed."

Visible only from the far corner of Tatsu's gaze, the man bowed and disappeared from the receiving room.

"Hysus, I thank you as well for reversing what you could." Yudai's tone was iron and interlaced with layers of molten ore. Commanding—the voice of a man who knew others would obey, and it sounded so little like the Yudai Tatsu had been with last night the shift physically hurt.

The certainty, once solid and warm within the deepest recesses of his thoughts, had faded. In its place sat an empty space, the kind he only noticed after it'd been filled and was suddenly lacking. At that moment, it was fragile and still raw at the edges, expanding until the emptiness consumed everything inside him and replaced his memories with ice. The sharp pain in his chest reminded him of returning to his house in the woods, after all the things he'd thought he'd known about his father had fallen apart, an absence far sharper than a knife and pulsing with anger.

"I think I need some time," Yudai said, "to rest and gather my thoughts."

It was another dismissal, though far less direct. Hysus, for his part, seemed unaffected by the implications. Instead, he bowed, his long sleeves bunching and folding.

"Your strength will return with time," Hysus said. "Right now, your body is still trying to process the trauma it was exposed to."

"I need some time alone," Yudai repeated.

He stared at the crumpled paper in his hand. It'd been so long since Tatsu had been included in the command he'd nearly forgotten what the orders felt like. Hysus and the mages left immediately, Leil and Jotin on their heels, but Ral hesitated a second longer with Alesh beside her.

"Yudai scared," Ral said, so quietly Yudai almost couldn't hear.

The barest flicker of movement in Yudai's eyes darted in Ral's direction, but he said nothing. He sat on the cot they'd kept him on for the past day with his hands—and the message—resting in his lap. Bowed, he appeared more tired than he ever had before, with the weight of the world heavy on his shoulders.

"Come on." Alesh tapped Ral's forearm with one finger. "Let's go. He wants to be alone."

The quick look Alesh sent Tatsu was enough for him to understand he was meant to follow, but doing so was difficult. Yudai wouldn't look up, either at him or at anything else in the room, and Tatsu knew falling to his knee had muddied everything that'd transpired between them. *Them*, the singular, heavy word bursting across his tongue was suddenly more memory than reality.

"Tatsu," Alesh prompted from the doorway.

Tatsu could still feel the heat of Yudai pressed against him, could still hear the hitch in Yudai's throat from when Tatsu had dragged his mouth across slightly parted lips. But nothing remained of that memory in Yudai's slumped form, only the dipped chin of the man who would be king, destined to bear the crown alone.

A man who had seen the throne torn away from his fingers and then returned through the actions of the same person it'd been stolen by.

"Coming," Tatsu called, or tried to, for the words came out far too low.

Yudai didn't look at him as Tatsu made his way out of the room.

HE DIDN'T CALL any of them back until nearly sundown, after most of the day had slipped away into the hazy sun outside.

"If you don't mind, I need some time with my... friends," Yudai said to Hysus, who had come with them after the summons. He remained seated as though he hadn't moved, on the side of the cot, but something in his posture had shifted. He looked in control once more, having reined in his emotions. "We need to discuss our next move and act accordingly. Clearly, the situation has changed."

Hysus tilted his head to the side, clasped his hands, and bowed forward slightly at the waist. "Your Majesty. Should you require anything else, you have but to ask." He glided out the opposite door.

Silence, charged and sparking, settled upon Tatsu's shoulders, as Yudai's too-straight posture remained a rigid line against the far walls. Then, Yudai sighed, slumping, and in that moment, he was himself again.

"Gods," he murmured and covered his face briefly with both hands before sliding his palms across his head to smooth the errant hairs away, which did little to tame the unruly strands. "This has been a lot to take in."

"Your Majesty," Jotin began, and Yudai's head snapped up, eyes flashing.

"Don't do that. That's not..."

He trailed off, words somehow failing.

"You may not be crowned," Jotin continued more gently, with one hand slightly raised in front of him. "But the throne is rightfully yours, no matter who has stolen it in the meantime. Protocol should be followed."

Yudai's hands paused at the sides of his head as he opened his mouth to object and then closed it again. He shook his head. "Let's just...focus on what we need to do. Nota has killed my father and taken over Runon."

"No one will oppose her?" Alesh asked.

"No one can." Yudai pursed his lips together. "There's no one strong enough."

"Before you, there still wasn't," Alesh pointed out. As an afterthought, she added, "Your Majesty. So what kept the mages from rebelling all this time?"

"Fear," Leil said, voice low. "They always had something to lose."

All heads in the room turned toward her. She twisted her hands in front of her robes and dropped her eyes to the sand-dusted stones.

"There's a reason mages are kept at the castle to be commanded by the king or queen," Leil said. "There are records of where each mage came from—the family left behind. And there are always others within the ranks who would suffer. The retribution for a mage who even thinks of opposition would be swift. Nobles would eliminate the mage's remaining non-magic family and likely arrest the other mages who'd allowed it to happen."

Her breath caught in the back of her throat, a choking half sob. "What Nota has done has ensured everyone connected to her will die, and that all other mages within the kingdom are similarly punished. It will not merely be her to suffer."

"She has nothing to lose, right?" Alesh asked. "Her family must be gone already for her to risk it."

Yudai's eyes met Tatsu's for one blistering moment. "I don't think that's an issue here."

"Then she had help," Jotin said. "Within the nobles, she had support. If what you said is true, then someone has pledged to protect her."

"And the only way I can get control back over my magic is by draining her. Which means I *have* to go back to confront her."

"But you don't have the power to actually win, Your Majesty," Leil said.

Ral, who had been silent and largely uninterested during the conversation, straightened. "Yudai, careful. Bad power."

Yudai frowned, contemplating, and then looked to Tatsu. "So what do we do?"

"I'll go where you command, Your Majesty," Tatsu said before lowering his head.

Yudai stared at him, frozen, before turning to the small semicircle of others with his mouth stretched into a half smile, half grimace, teeth bared and blinding. "Would you give us a moment, please?"

They left with leaden steps, and Tatsu tried to ignore Alesh's knowing look as she grabbed Ral's hand and walked out the doorway.

Only the two of them remained, along with the abyss stretched wide between their boots. Yudai threw his arms out to either side before Tatsu focused his gaze on his leather laces.

"What are you doing? What *is* this?"

"I'll do whatever you order," Tatsu said.

"That's not what I'm asking for," Yudai snapped. "That's not what I want. Why are you treating me like this...like this person you don't know?"

Tatsu shook his head. "It's your decision, and I'll follow—"

"*Stop*. You won't even—why won't you *look* at me?"

Tatsu slowly raised his eyes, even though he knew what he'd see. Yudai sparked with anger and coiled frustration.

"Why are you acting like nothing happened last night?" Yudai asked.

"We can't continue," Tatsu whispered. His throat had gone dry, with his tongue sticking to the roof of his mouth. "It's different now."

"Nothing is different."

Yudai moved, perhaps out of instinct, and Tatsu put a hand up to stop him while taking a step back.

"You're the rightful king," Tatsu told him.

"I'm still *me*!" Yudai cried, hands smacking against his own chest. "I'm still the person I used to be!"

"You're not!" The weight of the divide was crushing, a burden Tatsu hadn't been prepared to bear. He'd been a fool, a blind fool, for failing to see the end of the path he'd been walking. The eventual result had always been there, and he'd willfully turned away from its light. That realization was perhaps the most embarrassing of all—he'd walked straight into the ravine and only noticed the drop after he'd fallen over the side. "You're *not* the same person. You're a *king* now."

Yudai fell silent, his jaw snapping shut with such force Tatsu could hear his teeth knock together. Neither spoke as the sun sparkled outside, and Yudai's eyes, distant with the wall slammed down between them, never left Tatsu's face.

"You're wrong," Yudai said, his voice low but not soft. There was an edge of something there that Tatsu hadn't heard in many months, a deliberate shield separating them. "I was a king last night when you kissed me. You just didn't know it yet."

They stood like that for a very long time, unable to cross the widening space, until Yudai drew in a slow breath.

"So this is it now? This is how we're going to be?"

Tatsu shook his head again.

Yudai caught his bottom lip between his teeth and held the chapped skin there, eyes turned to the ceiling, the safest place to look. The cords in his neck rippled and stretched before he released his lip to run his tongue across the flesh.

"Call them back in," he said, and nothing remained: no emotion, no glimmer, no softness. Yudai was hard edges and thick barriers again, the man Tatsu had carried out of the palace walls, the man he didn't know. Something caught and pulled within Tatsu's lungs, an ache howling to rip him in two.

Yudai was a king, and Tatsu was the son of the woman who'd spilled the blood to make him one.

"Your Majesty," Tatsu said and bowed with mostly his shoulders before going to the far door. Only Alesh stood on the other side, propped against the wall with her arms crossed over her chest.

"We weren't sure you'd come back out for us," she said as she stepped into the middle of the corridor. "The others went to talk to Hysus."

"Ral?"

"She's fine. Jotin is looking out for her. I think she likes the mages."

Alesh followed Tatsu into the receiving room. Yudai refused to look at Tatsu, but his eyes did settle on Alesh's face briefly.

"What's the plan?" she asked.

"We go after Nota," Yudai said, fingers twitching at his sides. "She's the end of it all, no matter which issue we focus on first. I have to confront her to drain her. It's the only way I get my magic back."

Alesh nodded before her expression changed. She stared at the window beyond the both of them before she tilted her head to the left and narrowed her eyes. "The letter she sent would have been several weeks behind us."

"What do you mean?" Yudai asked.

"The letter came after you, but the messenger indicated it was sent direct. That means Nota tracked you well enough to know exactly where you'd gone. Instead of going after you, she sent a letter with a message only you would read." Her forehead furrowed. "Why would she bother with that if she thought the mercenaries had killed you?"

Wrinkles bunched further around her eyebrows as she glared at the crease where the wall met the floor. "Why would she—"

Her teeth clacked together as her eyes widened, and she stalked out of the room without another word, leaving Yudai and Tatsu in her wake. Yudai turned to Tatsu with confusion settling across his features.

"What is she talking about? Where did she go?"

But Tatsu stared at the open doorway left swinging behind her swift departure as things began to take shape in his mind. He'd ignored it—he'd ignored everything he should have been able to see all along. But Alesh had caught the thread of the web he'd inadvertently let them fall right into.

"Nota had been planning a coup," Tatsu said. "She'd been forging alliances and figuring out how to assassinate your father. *That* was her plan. 'A life for a life.' She'd never been trying to take yours."

"She didn't hire the mercenaries." Yudai's eyes widened. "Then who—?"

"No," Tatsu breathed, and he took off into the hallway Alesh disappeared down without conscious thought. Oh, he'd been the fool indeed. He'd been so wrapped up in Yudai and his own feelings that he'd failed to see what'd been right in front of his face. The Joesarian walkers had never given away their position or sold them out.

"Alesh!" Even with the burst of speed fear and panic supplied him, Tatsu couldn't catch her, and he didn't know where the others were. He skidded to a stop at a junction of corridors lined with polished stone and flickering candles. Heart pounding, he spun, trying to gauge which way to go. A door slammed at the end of the hallway to his right, so he took the path, praying to whichever Joesarian god might be nearby it was the right one. "Alesh!"

Behind him, Yudai's steps followed. "Tatsu, what's going on?"

Tatsu couldn't find extra air for a reply. He kept running, trying to get to the end before Alesh did, but deep down, he already knew he was going to be too late. She'd put the pieces together before he did.

He took a corner far too close and banged his elbow against the stone. Grimacing, he tucked his good arm against his side and continued to where the corridor ended in wide double doors that announced the dining room. The others stood inside, visible through the narrow opening in the swinging doors left banging behind the banner of Alesh's braid.

"Alesh, don't!" he exclaimed.

Leil turned at the sound of his voice and found Alesh's knife waiting for her. Tatsu tumbled to an ungraceful stop, his legs refusing to obey commands, as Leil's lips parted in a silent circle of pain. Alesh pulled the weapon free and leaned in near Leil's ear.

"You put my sister in danger, you traitorous snake."

"Alesh," Tatsu pleaded.

Alesh grabbed for the back of Leil's hood, spun the woman around, and dragged her blade deep across Leil's throat. The blood hit the floor before Leil's body did, and after the echo of the thud subsided, there was nothing but their ragged breathing and the stunned silence of the others in the room.

"What have you done?" Tatsu asked.

"What had to be done." The look Alesh spared him lasted for only a second, too quick for him to pinpoint anything of substance. "She'd been revealing our position the entire time."

"You can't prove that." Tatsu shook his head. "Alesh, you can't prove that!"

"You know it just as well as I do! All those times she was using magic—Tatsu, she was showing them where we were! That was the only reason she came with us!"

Beneath Leil's crumpled, unmoving form, the gold bracelets on her wrists glinted in the candlelight, and

Tatsu's stomach roiled. He'd wanted so badly to believe in her, in her desire to make things right again. She'd talked of her family as a cherished thing she missed, but her actions had always been for the queen who controlled her. Though Alesh was probably right, the betrayal stinging deep in his bones wasn't aimed at Leil. It'd never been her fault. She'd only been the pawn.

Behind him, Yudai burst through the doors and abruptly stopped. Though Tatsu couldn't see over his shoulder, he knew Yudai had to have recoiled from the sight. There was a sharp intake of breath and then, "*Gods.*"

"Tatsu, you have to understand," Alesh said.

"You can't just *kill* people you think are guilty," Tatsu replied, voice rising. "You can't— Alesh, now you have no proof, and her blood on your hands!"

"How long before she brought more mercenaries to us? How long before she put my sister's life at risk again, or all of ours? She was a traitor, Tatsu."

On the far side of the room, Jotin moved forward. He knelt by Leil's body, ignoring the pool of red expanding beneath her dark robes to put a finger to her wrist. Tatsu wasn't sure why the man checked to see if she was still alive. Alesh had gone deep with her knife, and there was nothing of Leil's throat left to salvage.

"I did what I had to do to protect us all," Alesh said, sparking and angry.

"You can't just do things on your own!" Tatsu cried. "She was still a *person*, Alesh, and she deserved the dignity of explaining herself!"

Alesh's faced twisted. "Are you angry that I took matters into my own hands without asking your permission? Or are you angry because I did what you knew you'd never have the strength to do?"

"We never questioned why you came with us." Tatsu took a step back, toward Yudai and the doors.

"You don't have to. I'm here to help!"

"That's what Leil led us to believe as well." Tatsu took in her crumpled body once more, and a final pang fluttered in his chest. She'd risked everything by showing up in Moswar, even if the Queen of Chayd had sent her. And even though all the pieces made sense together, it hurt to see the final end of things. The Queen of Chayd had every reason to want Yudai gone, for the crown on his head would see her own actions brought to light. But looking at Leil's blood on the stones felt wrong, a step too far in the other direction.

He'd thought her a friend—he'd thought Alesh a friend as well. With a sinking feeling, he realized he could have been wrong about all of them.

He stumbled another shaky pace back.

"Tatsu," Alesh tried, reaching for him.

"Don't," he said. "Please don't. We're leaving."

Tatsu turned for the doors, aching for air, since none remained in the dining hall.

"What do you mean?" Yudai asked, insistent. "*We're* leaving?"

"She was a traitor under our noses the entire time," Tatsu said. "Do you trust *anyone* anymore? Every person here could be desperate enough to give away our position. So who here are you going to trust?"

Yudai's jaw clenched visibly before he said, voice low, "You."

"Then let's go." Tatsu's fury left behind an odd, empty sort of nothingness. After such a long assault of his emotions, the clarity was welcome. "I'll get you to your throne."

They made it out of the doors and back into the hallway before Yudai's hand found Tatsu's forearm to stop him.

"Are you sure you want to do this?"

Tatsu pulled away from the touch, which had started to burn—only in his mind, no doubt, but still just as jarring. "I'll do what I need to do, Your Majesty. We leave before the sun disappears."

Chapter Seventeen

THEY WERE VERY quiet as they made their way on the dusty sand, beneath the soft light of the moon. Tatsu wasn't sure which of them was responsible for the silence. It wasn't as though he had nothing to say, for truly, the opposite was true; Tatsu's mind spun full of too many thoughts and words wishing to fly free from his tongue. But Yudai said nothing, and so, in turn, Tatsu kept his mouth shut as well. The quiet grew thunderous and deafening between them, as loud as a shouting match would've been.

Tatsu longed to return to the time when they would have quarreled. With a verbal spar, he knew he could have read the barbs for the trust they truly represented. Instead, Yudai's face had been lined with carved stone, and the sudden emptiness between them was a far keener sort of pain after knowing what it had once been filled with: promise and possibilities and *them*, a tangle of lonely sighs and longing smiles.

The stars provided easy navigation with the lack of cloud cover. Going over the mountains the way they'd originally come would take far too much time, but the Arani Pass had been reopened before Tatsu had even left Chayd. Knowing Nota had not been responsible for the assassins and that her method of discovering their location was gone made the choice an easy one. They would head northeast until they reached the valley connecting Joesar and Runon, a path carved deep between towering peaks.

When Tatsu shared his plan with Yudai, he received very little by way of a response.

"Is there something else you wish to do instead?" he asked.

"No," Yudai said, but his tone contained something Tatsu couldn't read, and he no longer felt comfortable enough to press at the mismatched edges. "We need to get to Nota, and that's the fastest route."

They walked until dawn's first rays began to peak over the horizon. Yudai's pace had slowed considerably. Fighting against the exhausting and lingering effects of the reversal on his body, he moved sluggishly, and while he never said anything aloud, pain etched lines on his face.

"You need to rest," Tatsu said. "We stop here for now."

It wasn't until after he'd prepared the tent against the rising sun that Yudai spoke again. "Why do you think she did it?"

"Alesh?" Tatsu asked.

"Leil."

Of all questions, he'd hit the right one, but also the worst. Tatsu had been thinking of little else, save Yudai, the whole time they'd been trudging beneath the stars. He'd tried so hard to summon righteous anger and fury against Leil's actions, but no matter what, the end result remained merely a detached sort of sadness.

"I think she was a prisoner," Tatsu said and thought of the gold bracelets on her wrists, thick and wide like jailer's shackles. "I think the queen could command her to do whatever she wanted, and Leil had no choice but to obey."

"You mean all those things she said in the temple."

Tatsu busied himself with retying the stretch of old, oiled leather as their makeshift tent. "Was she right?"

Yudai looked at him in question, so Tatsu clarified, "About the mages in Runon. Is it true, what she said?"

"Yes. I suppose."

"You told me"—Tatsu tongued each word deliberately—"a long time ago, the mages were afraid of you being royal. Because you had magic *and* the throne, and they would no longer be needed if that were the case."

"Yes." Yudai raised his eyes to meet Tatsu's gaze without flinching.

Tatsu swallowed hard. "You need to be better."

One of Yudai's eyebrows rose to his hairline before Tatsu could shake his head and explain. "You need to be a better ruler. You need to...you need to fix that. You need to *change* those things. Mages are people too— Look at you. They have families and hopes and dreams, and they shouldn't be shackled to the whim of the royal family like that."

Yudai was watching him with an unreadable expression, and Tatsu ducked his head, cheeks heating. "You need to be better than that."

"I will," Yudai said. "I will be."

It was the sort of promise that, only two days ago, Tatsu would have accepted by reaching his hand out and taking hold of Yudai's fingers. His arm still itched to go through with the action, even as he tried to temper the feeling, and across from him, Yudai's expression reflected the same internal struggle.

After a long moment, Yudai wrenched away with a frown. His tongue darted out to wet his lips as his mouth twisted into a sour grimace.

"If I ever *am* king anyway."

"You will be," Tatsu said.

"I have to drain Nota to take the throne."

As if Tatsu could have forgotten.

If Yudai was waiting for Tatsu to try to convince him otherwise, he'd be waiting for a long time. Tatsu said nothing. His mother's death—the death of the strange, faceless apparition, the woman who'd birthed him—was an acceptable end to the whole of their story. He wondered somewhere in the back of his mind if his father would have agreed with him, but then pushed the thought away.

"You should rest," he said instead and dropped onto the skins near Yudai's position. With the siphon under control, the life around them should be at no further risk while they slept.

Yudai's gaze was soft and open for a second. It looked like he wanted to say something, but then the moment passed, and he was a king once more, untouchable and unreachable.

"All right." He lay down without argument.

Even so, it was a long time before Tatsu slept, haunted by the ghost of a kiss he ached to reclaim.

PROGRESS WITH ONLY the two of them traveling proved quicker than Tatsu'd imagined, even with the inevitable drag accompanying Yudai's recent ordeal. They stuck close to the Dar-Itusk Basin for a few days until Tatsu felt confident they neared the Rist-walker camp. Instead of revisiting the walkers who wouldn't welcome them, Tatsu veered their path north by the light of the stars.

Their biggest problem remained not knowing where the dominion settlements were. Tatsu suspected Jotin had deliberately steered them around the various villages to avoid any issues, both with the uncontrolled siphon and their suspicious origins. At the time, such tactics had been smart, but the settlements had to exist. After all, Moswar was not the only city in Joesar, and the dominions all had to boast their own modest towns to have any autonomy. They needed to find clusters of people in order to restock their food supplies and fill their skins with water, but Tatsu was unsure where the settlements might be on the mind-map of the desert he'd been trying to create.

As they moved away from the basin's clumped, weedy dirt, they found themselves back in the larger, rolling dunes of the mid-desert, which made locating both food and water a more difficult task.

Traveling with Yudai, with the air stretched thin and awkward, rattled his skin. The unfamiliarity reminded Tatsu of the Shyreld and the slow ascent into the hooded peaks there, when he hadn't even known Yudai's name, and the prince's distrust of him had been so palpable and thick he could've run his fingers through it. They'd gone backward, and the worst part was the knot of regret sitting heavy in Tatsu's belly. He'd been at fault for changing their relationship; his actions had made Yudai a stranger again.

Sometimes when they slept, fitful and sticky beneath the sun, Tatsu couldn't get his body to relax enough to drift off. On those days, he'd turn and stare at the curve of Yudai's shoulder and the unruly hair on the back of his head, yearning to reach out and touch it again.

On the fourth day, after they'd long left sight of the cliffsides and were down to their last scraps of dry, salted meats, a settlement gleamed on the horizon. The low-standing structures weren't nearly as impressive as Moswar; the buildings, built smaller, barely changed the horizon until they drew much closer to them. Tatsu didn't know which dominion of Joesar they were in nor whether the village would welcome them, but a permanent structure usually meant an intersection with trade routes. He assumed there'd be enough traffic to merit some kind of a market.

He was right. They found a small trade outpost erected just outside the white city walls, well worn and beaten from desert windstorms. They were able to trade half of the weathered coins Jotin had given them earlier for food and water, plus a small jar of the sticky paste they'd used in Moswar to keep the insects away.

"This still stinks," Yudai said, lip curling in disgust as he palmed the vial.

"It's worth using if the smell keeps you from being eaten alive," Tatsu said.

"We don't have much more, do we?" When Tatsu raised his eyebrows in confusion, Yudai clarified: "Money. We're almost out. I saw you trying to disguise how few coins were in that pouch, but you're terribly unsubtle. We're not close enough to the pass to make it without more."

"If we get to a place I can hunt, we'll be fine."

Yudai's mouth twisted down further. "And if we don't?"

"If you're trying to tell me you think it was a bad idea for us to come alone, it's a little late," Tatsu replied, snapping more than he intended to, only because he'd come to the same conclusion two days earlier.

"I didn't say that."

"Thank the gods for small favors, then." Tatsu was suddenly eager to get away from the traders and their undisguised interest as they watched the two of them snip without bothering to pretend to be busy with something else. The desert might be a boiling wasteland beneath even the early morning rays, but Tatsu still preferred the heat to the stares.

"You're frustrated with me." Yudai sounded more amused than anything else. "I don't think that you of all people get to be frustrated right now. After all, you're the one who chose this."

This seemed to imply more than just their ill-advised trek through Joesar's expansive borders. Tatsu ignored the comment in favor of checking the sun's beginning arc, gauging which direction they'd want to take before setting up camp outside the settlement's line of sight.

A few minutes later, Yudai sighed, clearly exasperated. "Tatsu, come on. This is ridiculous—*talk* to me."

"I thought you said this was the way it has to be now."

"Don't you know me?" Yudai huffed. "You know very well why I said that. I was *angry*. I just wanted things to be like they were before."

Again, Tatsu said nothing, biting down on his tongue to keep his thoughts from escaping. The pain surging between his teeth was the only thing keeping him silent.

"I miss you," Yudai said, voice low.

If Tatsu stopped walking then, it was only because he'd decided they were far enough away from the village to set up camp for the day. He shrugged his pack off, knelt next to it, and pulled out the small posts and rolled leather.

"Tatsu," Yudai tried again.

All of it burned, hotter than the sun, but Tatsu handed him one of the stakes and said, “It would help if you could get these pushed into the ground.”

TWO DAYS LATER, as they picked their way across the rolling dunes, it began to rain.

The clouds formed quickly—too quickly to do much about when there was nothing nearby but the sand. Coming down in sheets, the rain worsened quickly and didn’t let up, pelting their skin even through the layers of linen they’d wrapped around themselves. For a long stretch of time, they cowered beneath the thin leather, which provided no protection against the pooling water at their feet, as the rain mixed with small balls of hail, falling like marbles. The baubles wobbled around against the puddles and the hardened ground, unused to being assaulted by the moisture.

Rainstorms and flash floods weren’t unheard of in the desert, but they were uncommon enough that Tatsu hadn’t planned for them. Sitting in the torrential downpour, his foolish, naïve oversight loomed as the thing to doom them.

The only positive was that they were able to refill their waterskins until they nearly burst, and Tatsu’s thirst was fully sated for the first time in what felt like weeks.

“We have to keep going,” Tatsu yelled over the thrum of the rain against the sand. “We need to get to higher ground.”

Yudai’s eyes tracked to the water gathering beneath their feet, rushing across the top of his boots in strong waves.

"The flooding will concentrate in the natural valleys," Tatsu said.

Yudai nodded sharply and allowed Tatsu to lead them farther up one of the slick, treacherous dunes. With the clouds pouring rain on them, Tatsu couldn't see the sky. He led them as far away as he dared without knowing the direction they moved in, and then no farther to avoid having to double back over their own footprints once the cloud cover cleared.

His boots—not intended to be worn while sloshing through mid-shin standing water—quickly soaked through. The water, a river forming before their eyes, was difficult to walk against as it pulled between the dunes. More than once, Tatsu slipped on the overwhelmed sands. He feared falling forward, afraid the sudden jolt of his full weight would reinjure the nerves in his hand as it sluggishly regained the range he used to have.

Near the top of a dune, his heel slipped, catching in a dip in the hardened sands. His foot shifted, and then, as the rushing water swept down the dune's side and across his boots, his whole body fell with it. He scrambled to grab hold of something, but found nothing—only the shocking cool rain beneath his palms. His last thought as the barrage overtook him was that drowning in the desert seemed a very ironic way to die.

As the water pulled him under, he spun, toppling from the sand dune to the rain-river formed between the hills, angry and furious and fed by all the surrounding ridges. He hit his head against the water-hardened sand, and his vision went momentarily black, coming back with dark spots circling at the sides.

The rain and wind stopped as Tatsu's terrified and aching lungs gave a last sputter of panic that he'd finally reached the end. He'd die in a rainstorm, and his body would float back to the Dar-Itusk Basin. Then, as his breath hitched, it became apparent the world actually *had* paused, at least the surrounding water. The stillness bubbled, slowly expanding, until the rainwater exploded both out and up, propelling Tatsu's body toward the top of the dune he'd just been washed from.

He ended up kneeling there, sputtering and gasping as the rain continued to belt against his face. As he struggled to catch his breath, a look over his shoulder revealed Yudai's hands raised and outstretched.

"Thanks," Tatsu managed to grit out, with another bout of coughing quickly following.

"Are you hurt?" Yudai leaned in, and the control he had over his abilities fizzled out with a snap. The remaining water fell back into the rush. Yudai clicked his tongue against the back of his teeth with a *tsk* of disappointment and frustration. "I lost it again."

"You had it when it mattered." Tatsu pushed himself up to his feet. The rain didn't seem to be letting up any, but his body was shaking with gratitude for Yudai regaining control over his magic, even if the abilities weren't complete. "Thank you for saving me."

"Did you think I was going to let you die?" Yudai asked, frowning. The creases near his mouth deepened after a second. "I'd hoped you thought better of me, no matter what's going on between us."

Tatsu wanted to get them out of the rain, but the only way to go was back down, and it seemed too soon to tempt fate by wading into the bulk of the water again. "That wasn't what I meant. I never thought you'd let me die."

"We're stuck up here, aren't we?" Yudai gestured with his arms. "We can't go into the water or risk drowning again, and until the rains stop—"

"—we stay here," Tatsu finished. "You're right. If I'd known the storm was coming, I wouldn't even have left the village. Coming out in this was the most dangerous decision we could've made."

"And now we're soaking wet."

Tatsu couldn't suppress the shiver working its way up his spine.

"We've been through worse," he pointed out, thinking of the snowstorm spent holed up in a cave.

"I'm not sure that's the thing we really want to be aspiring to."

Tatsu sat down on the sands. The dune, steep and angled, kept the water from pooling at the top, so as long as he didn't let the rush sweep him backward, it was the driest place they'd get. He stared up at the gray cloud cover for a while hoping to see a crack, though he never found one.

Yudai settled next to him. Strands of his hair stuck flat to his forehead. "Maybe it's an omen."

"You don't believe in that sort of thing."

Yudai shrugged. "The Joesarians do. Maybe that's enough. After everything, it certainly seems like I'm cursed, doesn't it?"

"You're not cursed." Tatsu sighed.

"How do you know? You're hardly an expert in the subject."

"If you were cursed, I wouldn't feel—" was as far as Tatsu got before he clanked his teeth together hard enough to send a ring of pain through his jaw.

When he failed to start again, Yudai leaned closer. "You wouldn't feel *what*, Tatsu?"

"There's been so much going on. You're just scared. Once the rain lets up, you'll feel better about it.

Remember, you got some control back, and now the siphon isn't draining wildly anymore—those are all positives. If you were cursed, I doubt things would go well enough for that."

Yudai clicked his tongue again, pushing his sopping hair out of his eyes. "Quit changing the subject. You're awful at dancing around things."

Even if it was true, it didn't matter. The only defense Tatsu could cling to was silence. If he didn't say the words out loud, he could pretend they weren't true. The air of denial provided him with a shield, albeit a crude one. He sat very still as Yudai stared at his palms beneath the sheets of rain in the sky's deluge.

"I ruin everything I touch," Yudai said softly, his words almost stolen by the storm.

"No, you don't." Tatsu reached over without thinking and grabbed Yudai's hand, mostly to try to stem the man's self-loathing.

"I ruined you, didn't I?" Yudai said. "Or at least I ruined *us*."

"No." Tatsu squeezed Yudai's fingers. "That part was all me."

"We can be that again, you know. *Us*. I'm not—I'm not angry anymore."

Tatsu peered at him through the rain, and Yudai tilted his head a little to the side before adding, "I sort of understand why you panicked."

"I didn't panic."

"Yes, you did," Yudai said with an airy sort of half laugh. "But I get it. The crown is...a heavy burden to bear."

They sat like that for some time, letting the sky fall around them as the waterlogged sands shifted only slightly beneath their weight.

"I'm sorry," Tatsu whispered, afraid the words came out too quietly for Yudai to hear, "for pushing you away."

Yudai regarded him for a very long time with an unreadable expression. "I'm still the same person I always was, you know. I'm still...me."

"I know, but it feels different."

"Technically, I'm not even king yet. And due to losing my throne in a coup, I suppose I'm not even royalty at the moment. If you want to really get down to it, since your mother stole my crown and declared herself queen, by virtue of your bloodline, you're closer to the throne than I am right now."

"I hadn't actually thought of that." Tatsu wasn't sure whether he wanted to laugh or not. Above them, the storm seemed to be letting up, shifting to a lighter, breezier shower that stung less.

Tatsu glanced at Yudai with his hair matted against his ears and stuck in looping curls to his cheekbones. Yudai's expression was both hopeful and cautious, the strange sort of marriage that somehow always seemed to work on him and look regal despite its vulnerability. Tatsu wondered how many moments he'd lost simply watching Yudai and cataloguing the lines of his face and the curve of his mouth, especially at times when no one was paying him enough attention to notice. Yudai was hauntingly beautiful, all hard angles and bristling pride.

Tatsu hadn't realized he was leaning forward until Yudai's palm pressed against his chest to stop him.

"Don't," Yudai said, voice hoarse and low. "Don't do this unless you mean it. Don't do this unless I can keep it—"

Tatsu closed the gap between them and muffled any words meant to follow. There was none of the desperation from their first kiss; after all, they'd both been pushed to the limits of their own courage, afraid to look over the edge for fear of falling completely away. The rain pooled where their lips joined and ran rivulets to Tatsu's chin as they kissed, an unhurried exploration that sent a barrage of flutters down to Tatsu's toes and then up again. Yudai's lips were warm and soft, pliable as they parted with a soft sigh, and Tatsu pressed his fingers against Yudai's cheek to let his thumb caress the skin there.

Slightly breathless, Tatsu pulled away to wipe at the rain gathered on his eyelashes, and Yudai tilted in to press their foreheads together.

"I was never sure," he said quietly. "I thought maybe I was reading all the signs wrong, and then I was terrified you'd push me away completely, so I was never willing to step over the line. I just knew...I just knew I'd rather have you with me, even if I couldn't have you the way I wanted to."

There was so little that Yudai ever conceded—it made the confession ping that much harder against Tatsu's ribs. He curled his hand at Yudai's cheek around his ear, lost in the soppy strands of hair.

"When have you ever refused to take something you wanted?" Tatsu asked, trying for a joke and deflating a bit when Yudai's features hardened into a distressed sort of unhappiness.

"Not with you," Yudai whispered. "Not with this."

Unsure of how to deal with the warmth washing over him, Tatsu simply leaned in again and hoped Yudai could feel his agreement against his lips, over and over.

Chapter Eighteen

THEIR PROGRESS QUICKENED after the rainstorm due to an unspoken concern settling sticky over both of them. Stretched thin, the days limped to their shortest lengths, allowing more hours of darkness in every day. The desert shimmered with heat, but back home, Tatsu knew his woods would be covered each morning in a white frost. Winter made the Arani Pass all the more treacherous, and going through the mountains would be impossible. Their trajectory, already shaky and foreboding, was dictated by the weather, and the notion was unsettling.

Failing to have a backup option could force them into far more dangerous situations.

Tatsu's thoughts grew heavier with each thud of his boot soles. The danger awaiting them once they left the desert would be nothing compared to the confrontation Yudai was willingly walking himself into. When the sun broke over the dune-strewn horizon at dawn, the discomfort in Tatsu's stomach grew more pronounced. The truth of what was waiting for them rattled in his fingers. Yudai wasn't going to be able to defeat Nota without full control of his magic.

He feared saying it aloud, as though giving the words sound made them all the more real, but from the shadows on Yudai's face, Tatsu thought maybe Yudai knew anyway.

They found one more trade outpost as they neared the jagged, snow-covered peaks of the Turend Mountains. Tatsu used the remainder of their Joesarian money, though the coin only half-filled their packs and waterskins. He traded away most of their desert garments for thicker leathers to keep them warm in the mountains. Despite Yudai's newfound control of the siphon, Tatsu still felt more comfortable sleeping beyond the village limits, near the wooden pens where the traders kept their mounts.

Three days later, they stood at the edge of the sands, staring at the grains mixed in with clumps of weeds. Beyond their boots, the rocky mountainsides sloped up and away in sharp swatches of dark gray, the color harsh when all they'd seen for weeks was the yellow-orange of the sand. They were right back where they'd started. Staring across the horizon, Tatsu forced back the rising nausea and tried not to think about the fact that, once they crossed into the mountains, they were on both Chayd and Runon's doorsteps as unwelcome, hunted guests.

"Do you think the queen still has the mercenaries after us?" Yudai asked as Tatsu continued to hesitate. "Or have they lost their tracker and given up without Leil to tip them off?"

"I don't know. But I hope..."

He couldn't find enough energy to finish the thought.

"They may not expect us to have come straight back to Runon."

"Or maybe that's exactly what they thought we'd do," Tatsu said.

They certainly were quite the sight. Despite Tatsu's attempts to keep them out of the brunt of the desert sun, weeks spent in the desert were painted across their skin.

Tatsu's wrists and hands were a mild brown faded beneath the layers of cloth on his forearms, and Yudai's normally light-olive face bore a darker tan, making the white ends of his hair stand out even more. Tatsu's limbs carried a perpetual heaviness from too little water rationed for far too long, but at least the snowcaps to either side of them promised respite from the thirst plaguing his throat. They were exhausted, both of them, the sort of weariness even standing on the brink of inevitability couldn't chase away.

Tatsu hadn't been sure he'd ever be back, and yet... He rubbed absentmindedly at his bicep, wincing at the slight pinch elicited.

Yudai raised his eyebrows, amused, it seemed, by Tatsu's staring. "Are you worried?"

"Aren't you?"

"I don't know." The honesty rang genuine. "I can't predict what's going to happen when we get there."

I can. Visions of Yudai's body, broken and twisted by the overwhelming force of Nota's magic, flashed before Tatsu's eyes. The wild imagining proved almost enough to make him stall further—only one more day of sleeping through the desert sun, as if they could avoid the whole thing by keeping it at arm's length.

"What's wrong?" Yudai asked.

"Nothing."

Yudai snorted ungracefully. "Gods, you're so bad with emotions."

"Well, sorry my father raised me in the *woods*," Tatsu said.

"Oh, don't blame that. You're the one who stayed there after he died."

"Shut up," Tatsu said.

He'd meant it as a joke, but Yudai went quiet. Afraid that he'd managed to break whatever was between them, Tatsu turned to find Yudai studying him.

"Do you regret leaving?" Yudai asked. "Coming out here for me, was it the right choice?"

"Yes. I mean, it was the right thing to do."

Yudai frowned. "But you lost everything."

"That wasn't..." Tatsu struggled to find the words. "I wasn't really living in the woods. It was more like... surviving. I thought if I just stayed by myself, the world would pass by around me and everything would simply... keep going."

"So you're saying I brought you to life?"

Tatsu groaned with more force than necessary. "This is a great conversation to continue down if you want another black eye."

"I'm joking," Yudai said with a warming laugh.

Tatsu reached over to take Yudai's hand and was calmed, somewhat, by the reassuring squeeze of his fingers. "How long will it take to get through the pass?"

"Four days, perhaps. A week, maybe."

Then there were between four and seven days before Tatsu's worst nightmare came true. He could only hope Yudai would be able to activate the siphon before he was overpowered—and then, when the drain grabbed hold of what it needed, Nota would be unable to continue fighting. The siphon's cure was Nota's blood.

The siphon's cure was *his mother's* blood.

Something in Tatsu's chest twisted sharply, beneath his sternum, and he rubbed at the offending spot unconsciously.

"You're frowning again," Yudai said.

"Never mind that." Tatsu dropped his hand to his side. "Let's go. In the pass, we'll need to move during the day again."

"It's a trade route that recently reopened. There are going to be others there, and we can't avoid detection forever."

"But we *can* avoid being recognized. Keep the Joesarian linen wrapped over your head and hope no one was in Runon years ago to remember your face."

Switching to a daytime routine was difficult only because by the end of the afternoon, having trudged through sand that grew sparser beneath their boots, Tatsu could barely keep his eyes open. The air cooled almost immediately and congealed, heavy with moisture from the snowcapped mountains to either side of them. The Arani Pass rose up gradually from the desert banks, into the higher altitudes of Runon's colder climate. Tatsu was thankful they didn't see any others moving across the roads during the first part of the day.

Returning to Runon was strange. Given the last time he'd been there, he never thought he'd return. His actions in stealing Yudai out of the castle made him an enemy to both the former king and the current queen. He wasn't sure which was worse: Yudai's father's wrath or his own mother's indifferent attention.

Either way, he knew he wouldn't be welcome within the capital.

"Can we rest?" Yudai asked, his voice strained as the sun at their backs began to fall behind the peaks.

Tatsu had pushed them too hard while lost in his reverie. He stopped urging them forward and spent some time searching for the best place to make camp, far enough away from the road so their tent was unlikely to be seen in the dark. The change in clothing helped immensely—his exposed skin prickled cool, but not yet cold, and the thicker weaves they'd donned in the last settlement were already worth the smaller portions of food.

It felt strange to be sleeping under the stars again after so long in the desert sun. After getting their tent ready, Tatsu lay down on the skins with only a second of delay before Yudai slid in beside him and curled up at Tatsu's side with his head on Tatsu's chest.

"Warmer this way," Yudai murmured, and Tatsu didn't mind the lie. Wrapping his arm across Yudai's shoulders gave him a spark of hope he'd be able to keep Yudai at the end of things, even knowing what lay before them. When he'd first pulled Yudai out of the chair in Yuse's castle, the man had been little more than skin and bones; Tatsu was glad Yudai's muscles had grown and recovered, his biceps softly rounding. If Tatsu let his fingertips hesitate too long against Yudai's joints, at least Yudai had the good sense not to point it out.

"What does the siphon feel like now?" Tatsu asked.

"Mm?" From the pause, it seemed Yudai had already drifted off. "The siphon? Like...I'm hungry, but I'm not. It's a bit like a pulling inside that wants to be let out."

"Does it hurt?"

Yudai shook his head, bumping his forehead against Tatsu's chin. "No. It's just...strange."

Perhaps something simmering within the siphon's malignant desire knew they grew ever closer to the goal. Tatsu's arms tightened around Yudai.

In less than a week, he would finally meet his mother, the woman he'd dreamed about and imagined his whole life. In less than a week, Yudai would try to use the siphon to drain her energy and leave her a husk, gasping for life.

The siphon's cure was his mother's blood.

Against his shoulder, Yudai began to snore lightly. Tatsu held up his recovering hand, and even though he couldn't see the outline in the darkness of the tent, he knew the lines of his palm and the curve of his fingers—the callouses on the sides from years of hunting and skinning, and the way the skin of his knuckles folded over itself. Nota's blood ran hot through him. Hysus had said the siphon needed the blood coded into it in order to break the rest of the barriers.

Yudai couldn't win without full control of his abilities, and the answer to his problem was thudding against Tatsu's eardrums.

Tatsu closed his fingers into a tight fist and brought his hand against his chest, squeezing his eyes shut. Perhaps Yudai hadn't realized it. Or, perhaps he'd already arrived at the same conclusion and dismissed it because of his feelings. But the only way Yudai would win was with all of his magic, the same magic denied because of the siphon billowing up through his bones and pressing against his flesh.

In less than a week, either Yudai would die at Nota's hand, or he would drain her dry, and the only way to ensure the latter happened was to break the siphon's barrier to his magic.

Tatsu's heart hammered out a terrified, angry rhythm against his lungs, knowing his choice would be to ensure that Yudai lived, even if it meant leaving his own corpse, brittle and desiccated, to rot in the Turend Mountains.

THEY PASSED A small caravan of traders the next day who gave them brief, uninterested glances before continuing on. The second group they encountered seemed more intrigued, perhaps because Tatsu and Yudai were the only ones on the road walking toward Runon instead of away from it. Neither group asked any questions, and Tatsu watched them both roll out of sight on squeaking wagon wheels just to be sure no lingering suspicions urged the traders to turn back.

Yudai quieted as they drew closer to Runon.

Hunting grew more productive once they'd returned to the trees and the mountains, although the winter wind had already driven off most of the prey. Tatsu did manage to get a white-coated hare, which he skinned and cooked with care to save all the meaty pieces he could, the first fresh food they'd had in at least a week.

By nightfall on the third day, no time remained, for Tatsu could see roofs nestled against the mountainsides in the distance signaling their arrival at Runon's border. Instead of finding a small alcove tucked away from the road, Tatsu spent the better part of an hour moving up the mountains, picking his way across jagged outcroppings. He'd paid a good deal of attention to the markings they'd already come across, and several tracks indicated a bear and her cubs had spent their summer in the area before moving on. A cave had to be nearby, and from the look of the old prints, it would have been long since empty. His instincts were right; above the road, he found an abandoned den, one wall covered with long scratch marks and a curtain of cobwebs hanging from the entrance.

Yudai inspected the cave with tightly knotted eyebrows. "Are you worried about someone finding us? I know we're close, but this is quite the hike up from the road. I doubt anyone else'll be able to find a place like this."

"You can never be too careful," Tatsu said, but the lie came out weak. He turned away to busy himself with making a fire in case Yudai had caught it.

Outside the cave were several bushes sporting thick branches they could eat, provided they boiled and softened the bark, along with a few handfuls of bright red berries. Together, they made a thin but filling stew.

"You're planning something," Yudai said after they'd finished eating. "Why did you bring us to this cave? The side of the road would have been fine, and you know it. No one has given us a second glance."

Tatsu poked at the fire embers with a stick while chewing on his bottom lip, until Yudai, visibly frustrated with the silence, jabbed him in the arm with his index finger.

"What's going on?" Yudai asked.

"You're not going to be able to defeat Nota without the full use of your magic."

Yudai's expression darkened, but he said nothing.

"You're walking into your death," Tatsu said.

"I'm not. I can win even if I don't have all my abilities."

"How?"

Yudai's mouth twisted into a scowl, and he ducked his head to pick at the bits of dirt and rock left by the summer bears.

"There's a way that you can get your magic back—"

"No," Yudai cut him off, head snapping back up. "That's not an option."

Then Yudai *had* already reached the same conclusion. Tatsu twisted his mouth into a rueful smile despite himself.

"Seems like an obvious solution, doesn't it?"

"It doesn't seem like anything other than a horrible idea."

"The siphon needs Nota's blood."

Yudai stood suddenly, nearly tripping into the side of the fire, and put his hands over his ears as though he could block the whole thing out. "Stop it. I'm not listening to this. This is *stupid*."

"Yudai, you know this is the only way you'll be able to win."

Yudai stalked to the mouth of the cave and stared out at the darkness. He shifted one hand from his ear to his mouth, fingers tracing his jaw as he stood motionless for several long, tense moments.

"You brought us here to this cave because you planned this," he said, breaking the silence. He turned to face Tatsu. "You brought me here to *drain* you."

"It's the only way."

"How long?" Yudai demanded. "How long have you been planning this? How long has this been your end goal? Is this why you came with me?"

"Yudai." Tatsu put his hands out, palms up in surrender. "Don't do this. It's only been since we made it to the pass that I knew what I had to do—"

"What *I* had to do!"

Tatsu sighed. "It's the only way."

"No," Yudai said, but all the fight seemed to go out of him. His shoulders dropped, hunching in on themselves as his face fell to the cradle of his hands. "Please don't ask me to do this. Please don't ask me to kill you."

"You won't," Tatsu said. "You don't have to take everything."

"Tatsu, I *can't*. I can't do this to you. You're the only person I've..." He didn't finish, biting down on his bottom lip.

"Don't you think there's a reason I ended up here with you? Out of all the things that might have happened, it ended up being this?"

Yudai rubbed his face, dragging his fingers down his cheeks and leaving angry red marks trailing behind. "Don't say that. We didn't happen for this. I refuse to believe that."

"I don't want to watch you die," Tatsu said.

"And I don't want to watch *you* die."

Yudai rolled his teeth over his bottom lip until the flesh was swollen and torn. In front of Tatsu's boots, the fire crackled and popped and blackened the still-green branches he'd fed it.

"I trust you," Tatsu said as gently as he could.

Yudai shook his head. "I need time to...process this. Give me time to think."

"We don't have that much time."

"A day," Yudai insisted and wouldn't meet Tatsu's gaze. "Give me a day to make a decision."

They fell asleep on separate sides of the fire, and the empty space at Tatsu's sides ached a keen, pulsing loss. He slept restlessly, waking with every noise floating in from the trees outside, and if he focused too hard on what he'd asked Yudai to do, his entire body seized in terror. Staring up at the ceiling of the cave as night trickled back into day, he willed his heart to slow and the panic to ease, but none of his internal pleading seemed to matter.

Finally, Yudai got up and rounded the fire, crossing the space between them to slide to the ground at Tatsu's side. The tightness in Tatsu's chest lessened then. If it was to be his last night, it'd be an acceptable way to go—curled around Yudai's warmth with his face nuzzled into the curve of his shoulder.

TATSU SPENT THE next day combing the sides of the cliffs and dipping into the trees to hunt. In the end, he was able to catch only a small ground squirrel in his makeshift snare. Cleaning and smoking the few bits of meat gleaned from the creature, he worked in silence with no sign of Yudai in the cave. Tatsu didn't worry until after he'd finished, when the sun was beginning to set, and then he set out past the jagged den entrance. Instead of going toward the thicker, still-green trees lining the road, he went up through a small path of mostly deep-wedged boulders sturdy enough to hold weight. He picked across them until he came to a larger, wider outcropping curving around the side of the mountain.

He found Yudai perched on the ledge with his legs dangling in the air, a precarious seat that looked wildly unsteady.

"The sun will be setting soon," Tatsu said, pausing a few paces behind where Yudai was sitting. "Are you going to come back inside?"

"Maybe."

Tatsu shifted against the smoother slope of the rock face behind him, farther away from the drop Yudai seemed unconcerned about.

"You're probably right to be angry with me," Tatsu said. "I suppose I'm not leaving you much of a choice."

"No" was Yudai's answer, though Tatsu was unsure if it was agreement or not.

"I didn't expect this to happen."

Yudai sighed then, long and deep and infinitely weary. "I know. I'm just..."

Tatsu waited for him to continue and after a few moments prompted, "Just what?"

"I'm tired of this happening. I'm tired of these being my choices. I know it's stupid to complain about it being unfair, but there's really no other way to describe it. I only...I only want to live without these shadows hanging over my head."

"You're a king. I'm not sure you *can* live like that."

He expected an argument, but Yudai merely sighed again. "Maybe you're right."

When Yudai still made no effort to move, Tatsu asked, "What are you going to do?"

"I hate you for suggesting this." Yudai's voice was hoarse and low. "I hate you for *wanting* me to do this. But most of all, I hate you for being right. This is the only way I can beat Nota."

"She'll kill you otherwise."

"Yes," Yudai agreed. "She will."

Despite the entire situation being of his own design, Tatsu's fingers froze stiff. He thought he'd been prepared to face his potential end. He thought he'd been at peace with his choices. But faced with the reality of his demise, the feeling bubbling within was far different than he'd expected, a desperate fear he could neither predict nor control.

"I trust you," Tatsu said, because it bore repeating. "You won't hurt me if you can control it."

Yudai pushed himself up to his feet, toes hanging off the edge of the cliffside entirely before he took two steps back onto more solid rock. He closed his eyes, breathing deeply as his throat bobbed, and then opened them again. When he met Tatsu's eyes, his gaze was piercing.

"Why are you offering me this?"

"You know why." Tatsu reached his hand out. "Come inside."

Yudai didn't fight against Tatsu leading him back into the cave, as though he'd lost his will to argue further. The fire was still crackling with the new branches, and Tatsu sat on the far side of it. As far as location went, the den would have to do. What effects would the siphon bring? What lingering aftermath might consume him? Perhaps there would be nothing, or perhaps...

Tatsu stretched out on the ground as though preparing to sleep.

"Tatsu," Yudai whispered, a gasp for air.

"Take what you need and then stop it," Tatsu said. "I don't know if my blood will have the same power as Nota's, but some part of it must work. I could open the magical barrier around you. When Nota coded the drain, Zakio was able to control it as well."

"This is *terrible.*"

His fingers scrambled across the rock to find Tatsu's, and Tatsu gave them a reassuring squeeze he didn't wholly believe. Yudai surged forward to kiss him, hard and angry, though Tatsu wasn't sure where the rage was directed.

"I didn't ask for this," Yudai said, his breath warm against Tatsu's cheek.

"That's why I'm offering." Tatsu sucked in a deep lungful of air. "You can do this."

Yudai's hand fell away as he sat back on his heels.

"Only enough to break through some of the barrier," he said, a promise that curdled in Tatsu's stomach, "and then I'm done."

"Only enough," Tatsu agreed.

Yudai closed his eyes and put his hands against Tatsu's arm, trying to anchor himself. The air within the den stilled and thickened, until Tatsu feared losing his ability to breathe completely in the noxious tension. When the siphon began, there inside Tatsu's lungs, inside his heart, the magic pressed against his ribs and threatened to split him in two. He might not possess any magic, but his mother's blood was singing beneath his skin, and it had to be enough to satiate the drain. Bits of the magic hummed against his ears, remnants and whispers of what he could've been if the ability had been passed along.

Pinpricks rose up along the bare skin of his neck and face when the siphon slid into his bones; the magic was hot, a fire blazing up from within. And then the pain started. Every one of his nerves began to ache and throb as the drain demanded and took, carving out the parts that had once belonged to him and himself alone. His body fought on instinct, spine arching, and when the pain reached a frenzied peak, he thought it'd be over.

Then the siphon flared out, expanding in a hot rush that might have been burning the flesh clean from his body. Whatever control Yudai had been exercising was gone. There was an awful scream that only belatedly registered as his own, an inhuman noise of misery wrenched free from his throat as the drain overtook him entirely. Only anguish remained. Even the ground beneath his back and Yudai's hands on his arm were gone. Nothing registered but the bursting sensation of his muscles being cleaved from his bones, a spasm so strong that the brunt of it, had he been coherent, would've caused him to vomit.

Dimly, he registered Yudai crying out his name. Then the white heat overwhelmed his senses, and there was nothing.

Chapter Nineteen

THE TALL TOWERS of Runon's castle stretched up toward the sky. Behind the white stones, the moon winked in and out as clouds passed in front of it, and beneath the soft flickering glow, black shadows lined the ground. He couldn't recall exactly what the palace looked like, but it was there, solid and commanding, just as one of the doors creaked open to welcome him inside.

A quick look back showed a wooden cart, though the horse had been let go. The cart rested at a sharp angle against the ground, the rear raised so high the boxes held within had fallen to the front in an ungraceful heap. Behind the wagon stood a broad-shouldered man, and at first glance, it seemed he was securing the wheels. A second look at his hunched position revealed him to be hiding instead, and after a second of stillness, he raised his head up to peek around.

Seeing his face was a physical blow—it was his father. His father without the gray that had peppered through his hair, without the deep lines set in his face from years of worry and isolation. His father as he might have looked twenty-five years ago when he was still young and open, before Tatsu was born. Crouched behind the cart, his father waited for a long time until footsteps sounded, quick and light, from inside the open door to the castle halls. A figure darted out.

A woman with a high-coiled circle of hair and dark-colored robes flew into his father's embrace in a flurry of sighs.

His father's arms wrapped her tightly, drawing her in so her face ended up completely hidden in the folds of his shirt.

"You shouldn't be here," she whispered, her words clipped and accented, as if her tongue was unused to the sounds and struggling to produce them. "You *can't* be here."

"Before we leave, I had to come back." His father stroked the skin of her cheek. She pulled away slightly just as the clouds overhead cleared, and the moonlight fell unobstructed against her face.

She was Runonian. After a single thud so hard it throbbed, Tatsu's heart threatened to stop entirely—she was his *mother*.

"There are rumors about the king," his father said, and his voice dropped low, as though he suddenly remembered the castle door in the shadows, still ajar. "They say he's gone mad."

His mother shook her head. "He is not well."

"If he's gone mad, then come with me." His father leaned forward, pressed with urgency. "I can't leave you here—"

"I can't go." Her fingers dug tight into the fabric of his sleeves and tugged it into harsh creases. "I can't leave."

"You can't stay. It's not safe."

His mother sighed. "I'll never be safe."

"Nota."

She let go and put distance between them, curling her arms around herself. "You have to go where it's safe."

"Please reconsider," his father pleaded.

His mother shook her head and took another shaky step away. Her shoulders heaved in the darkening shadows. Beneath the magic and the somber robes, she was only a young woman, barely older than twenty, and it hurt to see so many of his own features reflected at him. She lifted a trembling hand to her mouth.

"Please," his father tried one last time, but it was a lost cause. His mother continued to take fumbling steps to the creaking door, and the shadows slid over her face until she was shrouded completely.

"Just go," she whispered. Then she disappeared into the castle, and the scene faded away as Tatsu's reality roared back into being with heavy, painful pangs.

SOMEHOW, DESPITE IT all, he managed to open his eyes, though not enough to register anything more than a crease of bright orange glow, which burned and prompted him to squeeze his eyes shut again. He teetered wildly on the precipice of unconsciousness with the surge of pain filling every crevice and only just managed to keep his awareness. Dimly, the events came flooding back, jumbled and fuzzy until Tatsu could piece together why every nerve in his body was throbbing.

Yudai had used the siphon on him.

He tried to open his mouth and move, and neither really worked. All that came out was a low, ragged-sounding moan. The second time he opened his eyes, he was prepared for the onslaught of light and squinted against it until shapes materialized in front of him—dark, wide eyes and wisps of wavy black hair.

"Hey," Alesh said. Her tone held so much tenderness Tatsu didn't trust his own senses telling him she was really there. The last time they'd spoken had been in anger, and she could have been another dream. One of her hands was on his forehead, fingers gently running through his hair, and the sensation was more grounding than anything else. "You're finally awake."

What happened? Tatsu attempted. The words came out a blurred string of unintelligible syllables, but she seemed to understand anyway.

"You've been out for a week. We weren't sure...well, when we found you again, we weren't sure you'd even last another night."

"How...?" Tatsu asked.

"We'd been following your trail, with Jotin, since you left the mages," Alesh told him. Then her expression shifted, the corners of her mouth curving down. "After we got to the pass, you weren't hard to find."

Her tone dipped dark at the end, but Tatsu's head was spinning too much to press the topic further. His stomach ached—the pangs of a body gone far too long without food—and the nauseating hunger verified Alesh's claim. He'd been unconscious for quite some time, long enough that trying to move even just his fingers and toes was an impossible feat. The strange dream he'd had of his parents remained at the forefront of his thoughts, even as the rest of the sleepy cobwebs faded.

"Yudai...?" The absence of Yudai next to him jittered his bones. The other man should have been there in Alesh's position, spine hunched with anxious exhaustion as he kept watch.

"He's here," Alesh said and then rolled her eyes as she looked away from Tatsu and across the room. "Your boyfriend is having some trouble with his guilt and thinks you're angry with him."

There was a miserable sputter from somewhere beyond Tatsu's line of sight. He tried to move his limbs again, and the second attempt stirred twinges in his muscles, a promising sign that, with time, his body would reconnect the threads.

"Not..." he began.

"I know." Alesh smiled briefly down at him before stilling her hand in the mussed strands of his hair. Another shadow moved at the corner of his sight, rounding the fire.

After some hesitation, Yudai called, soft and tentative, "Tatsu?"

Tatsu's fingers twitched in response. Alesh stood and moved out of the way so Yudai could slide into her vacated spot.

"Gods," Yudai whispered, voice wavering. "I'm so sorry, Tatsu—I'm so, *so* sorry."

Tatsu wanted to tell him it wasn't his fault. It'd never been his idea to begin with, and Tatsu had always known the risks. Another burst of pain flared in his chest, aching so fiercely that the outline of Yudai's head blurred, and Tatsu struggled against another wave of dizziness. In the end, all he could do was jerk his fingers sharply. At least Yudai understood that. He grabbed Tatsu's hand and squeezed.

"I shouldn't have agreed to this," he said. "I hurt you because I was selfish enough to think my life was more important."

Tatsu couldn't summon the energy to disagree, so he hoped his sigh was enough. Yudai leaned in over Tatsu's face and traced his fingers over the line of Tatsu's cheek.

"I'm so sorry. I thought...I thought you were dead."

His voice dropped to little more than an angry breath as he continued, "Gods, I thought I'd killed you."

Weariness overtook Tatsu as his body sank into an aching need for further rest. His eyelids fluttered closed against his will, even though he fought against the heaviness. He was still aware of Yudai's warmth beside him and fingers against his skin, and both caused his heart to thrum in contentment.

Stay, he wanted to say, but he couldn't get the plea out.

Yudai clutched Tatsu's fingers tighter. "Sleep. I'll be here when you wake up—I promise."

THE NEXT TIME Tatsu woke, he felt better. With his head clearing, his memories had fallen back in order. Opening his eyes and blinking at the fire took markedly less energy, even with the dull ache in his temples. With Yudai and Alesh's help, he was able to sit up and lean against the cave wall, and the small action sang like triumph.

When his eyes landed on Ral seated by the edge of the flames, she grinned widely at him.

"Better," she said.

"Where's Jotin?" Tatsu asked.

"He's out trying to find some food," Alesh said. "It's been taking him quite some time to get out past—well, to find anything we can eat. He'll be back before nightfall if all goes well."

Yudai's arm against Tatsu's was trembling, and Tatsu turned, slow and stiff, to look at him.

"I should have asked you to practice with the siphon before you used it on me," he said.

Yudai smiled, but it didn't quite reach his eyes.

"That was a *phenomenally* stupid idea you two came up with on your own," Alesh said. "But you should eat something. We've got a few pieces of meat left."

It took him longer than he liked to get the food down, but after, his stomach ceased its moaning. His arms and legs began to feel more like his limbs again and less like strange, foreign objects attached to his body. A few experiments in bending his elbows and knees proved he still had all his mobility, even the sensations in his bad hand he'd only recently gotten back.

Yudai stuck close by his side without saying much.

"Did it work?" Tatsu asked the question that'd been languishing on the tip of his tongue for too long.

"I'm sorry." Regret shadowed Yudai's face. "I couldn't control it, and I—I lost any hold I had on it."

It stung, knowing all the pain had been for nothing, and the bitterness made Tatsu feel queasy. He tried to keep the emotions off his face, but from the way Yudai's eyes dropped, he wasn't sure he succeeded.

"Don't," Tatsu said. "Don't put this on yourself. We tried."

"And look where that got us."

"I'm going to be fine."

Yudai shook his head. "I'm not talking about you."

Tatsu's eyes slid to Alesh, who was standing near the fire with her arms crossed over her chest, watching them both with undisguised interest. She shrugged, the action pulling at the fabric of her shirt.

"You said we were easy to find," Tatsu said carefully. When he looked to Yudai again, the other man wouldn't meet his gaze, his chin falling all the way to rest on his knees as he picked at a bit of dirt on the floor of the cave. "What did you mean?"

"You should see it for yourself," Alesh replied. "Can you stand?"

He could, but only with her assistance. As Alesh helped him hobble to the cave entrance, he turned back to find Yudai still crouched on the floor and miserable. He made no move to follow them out. As they departed, his fingernails scraped harshly against the rock.

Ral, however, scrambled to her feet and slipped out of the cave with them.

The truth was, Tatsu had been prepared for what lay before him. He'd known it was coming as he struggled to stand, piecing together what had happened after he'd succumbed to the siphon and the darkness. But seeing the remnants spread out in front of him felt much different than the gnawing worry churning in his gut.

Dead trees lined the sloping mountainside—brown and gnarled, curled into withered stalks of skeletal fingers reaching for a second chance at life.

The siphon's grotesque aftermath, months after Tatsu'd thought he'd never have to see such an expansive swath of it again.

Tatsu inhaled deeply and let the air go with a low, slow hiss.

"This is how we found you once you'd started into the pass," Alesh said softly. Perhaps she didn't want her words to travel back to Yudai, hunched around himself in the cave.

"How far?"

"About halfway," Alesh replied, "and spread out like the points of a star."

"Sad." Ral bent to brush her fingers over the dead grass nearest to her boots. "All sad now."

"This is why it didn't work," Tatsu said. "He lost control of it, and it kind of...exploded."

Alesh eyed him warily. "I understand what you were trying to do, but going into this without any help or support—"

"I know. I didn't think you'd follow us."

"I can't believe you left *without* us," Alesh shot back.

Tatsu's legs trembled beneath his weight, feeling like jelly. "I'm sorry. I was angry, and I just reacted. I shouldn't have left you behind—it was wrong."

He paused, doing another sweep of the ruined landscape before he said, "And you were right about Leil."

"Gone now," Ral said. "No more red. No more black."

Alesh didn't look particularly happy to be correct; instead, her face softened as she shifted beneath Tatsu's arm slung heavily over her shoulders.

"The Joesarian mages were furious," Alesh admitted. "I shouldn't have taken matters into my own hands. Hysus almost didn't allow us to leave."

"Why did he?"

Alesh held up her right arm and shook the limb until her sleeve fluttered down near her elbow, revealing a thick iron shackle wrapped snug around her wrist. Tatsu stared at the cuff clearly marking her as a criminal, and in response, Alesh grimaced.

"Hysus said the only way to get it off is with magic," Alesh said. "He told us the mages don't have the authority to judge others for crimes, but that someone needed to do it. I guess Yudai felt like the best choice. He's a ruler, or at least he will be, anyway."

After everything they'd been through, Alesh had ended up right back in chains. Tatsu's eyes pricked hot, but he drove the heat back.

"Alesh..."

"It's fitting, I suppose."

Tatsu focused on the wilted plants around them to find something steadier to cling to. "What did Yudai say about Hysus's decision?"

"He'll judge me when the crown is on his head. Says he needs me too much right now."

Tatsu smiled despite the heaviness dragging his body down. "At least he's smart enough to realize that. We made a mess of things by ourselves. Look what's happened because of it."

"Ah." Alesh squinted into the distance, past the black, twisted branches curving down around the rocks and thickening near the road, a beige snake against the brown. "I see Jotin coming back. That's earlier than I expected."

"Again!" Ral cried with an insistent tug at Tatsu's sleeve. "Again, Tatsu."

Her fingers slid to circle Tatsu's wrist.

"The worst happened again," Tatsu agreed. But Ral frowned and pulled at him, trying to corral him back into the shadowy den.

"Yudai again," Ral said. "Do *again*."

"Yudai? You...you want Yudai to use the siphon again?"

Ral beamed her slow, wide smile at him.

"Ral, no," Alesh said. "It's dangerous, and look what already happened! There's no telling what further damage the magic could cause."

Tatsu let Ral tug him back into the cave. Yudai was crouched in the same position they'd left him in, but he must have been listening to at least the last part of their conversation because he was watching them with suspicious eyes as they came in.

"Yudai, again," Ral repeated.

"You can't be serious," Yudai said. "There's not a chance I'll—"

His words trailed off when Ral moved to stand in front of him and pulled the heavy *Oldirr* necklace out from under her blouse. She didn't hesitate before leaning forward to drop the beads into Yudai's hand.

Yudai stared at them, motionless, before sluggishly running his thumb over the largest of the baubles.

"She's been carrying this around since the Shyreld," Yudai said.

"I forgot she had it," Alesh said. "She wouldn't take it off, even when we were back in Dradela. She fought me when I tried to take it once."

Ral laughed, cheeks a dark orange in the firelight. "Sorry."

"What *is* it?" Tatsu asked.

Yudai hummed a low note of surprise and turned the necklace over once to inspect the back. His fingers slid over the beads a few times. "How did she know?"

"Who?" Tatsu asked.

At the same time, Alesh asked, "What are you talking about?"

Yudai looked up at Ral with a shrewd gaze while his fingers continued their ministrations on the accessory. "How could she have known this was going to happen?"

"Ral?" Alesh said.

"The elder," Yudai replied, but his voice was distant, his thoughts clearly elsewhere.

"Is it magic?" Tatsu asked.

Jotin stepped through the entrance of the cave with his knife held tightly in one hand. He didn't appear surprised to see Tatsu awake and moving about, and while his eyes held for several seconds on the necklace in Yudai's palm, he didn't ask any questions.

"No, it's not magic," Yudai said. "At least, not exactly. The pendant is made of lodestone."

"That's a natural magnet," Jotin said. "They are sometimes used as guides in the absence of stars."

"I don't understand why that has anything to do with our situation," Alesh confessed.

Ral dipped her head so that loose waves of her hair tumbled over her shoulders, her hands clasped together. "Use, Yudai."

"You can use it?" Tatsu asked.

"I...might be able to. Lodestone can be a focusing device for mages."

That got everyone's attention, and all eyes swerved to Yudai's seated figure.

"Are you saying that Ral's had that this whole time, and we just *now* figured it out?" Alesh asked.

Tatsu's stomach twisted for a much different reason as he leaned forward. "Could you have used this before you got the siphon under control?"

"No," Yudai said, and the tension in Tatsu's abdomen receded. "No, it wouldn't have done anything. But now..."

"You aren't really considering using the siphon again, are you?" Alesh asked, incredulous.

Yudai hesitated. He met Tatsu's eyes, heavy with a thousand things he'd likely never say out loud. When he finally found his voice, he said, "I don't...know."

"Look at what happened!" Alesh said.

"But if the necklace acts as a focusing device, wouldn't that prevent the same sort of catastrophe?" Jotin asked.

"Tatsu almost *died*," Alesh said, and the reminder brought Tatsu's attention back to the dull ache taking up residence in his bones.

"I suspect that it's not really our decision to make." Jotin's tone was light, but the hard line of his shoulders, square and rigid, as he sat down was anything but; he was nervous.

Throughout the conversation, Yudai had neglected to pull his gaze away from Tatsu's, and when both Alesh and Jotin lapsed into a strained silence, he sucked in a breath that whistled through his teeth.

"I nearly killed you," he said, just loud enough for Tatsu to pick out the words. "I can't do that again."

"It's still the only way to ensure you don't get killed later," Tatsu replied.

"Nothing can ensure that."

Tatsu winced. "This is your best chance. I lived through the first time."

"That's no guarantee you'll live through the second, and I *can't* be responsible for your death. I *can't*, I'd—"

He shut his mouth with a snap of clanging teeth, the statement hanging unfinished.

"This necklace might change things," Tatsu told him as gently as he could. "Right?"

Yudai said nothing.

"Test it first," Jotin said from across the fire. "Test it first and then decide."

THEY WALKED OUT past the drained foliage until they found a tree left alive—a still-green conifer dotted with pinecones—and formed a semicircle around the trunk. Yudai turned the necklace over in his hands in an anxious gesture before biting his lip and taking a step forward.

"What if it doesn't work?" he asked, voice low.

"What if it does?" Tatsu returned.

Yudai looked annoyed, but his nerves seemed to keep him from replying. He waited as several more seconds ticked by before exhaling loudly.

"Focus on the tree," Jotin said. "That lodestone has got to be the answer."

Tatsu agreed. The *Oldirr* elder, with all her foresight, wouldn't have given them something they wouldn't eventually need. Still, the remnants of memory from the first time they tried rose up in his mind, clouding his thoughts with small spikes of fear, and he struggled to tamp them down.

Alesh moved back as well, taking Ral with her, clearly feeling the same apprehension.

"Right," Yudai said to himself and then held the necklace out in front of his chest with both hands covering the bulk of the beads. When the siphon flared into life, Tatsu's ears rang. The energy bubbled up in front of Yudai, swirling so thick Tatsu could almost see it, and then, with a snap like a bowstring, the drain's magic enshrouded the pine tree. Needles bled from green to brown in the blink of an eye, too quickly for Tatsu to see anything but the aftermath. Withered and shriveled, the pinecones melted into the branches in grotesquely misshapen lumps.

It all happened so fast. Yudai's whole body stiffened as his arms went out to either side, and all of the life held within the siphon's deathly touch sparked in the air before he inhaled it. Then his shoulders slumped forward as he gasped, one hand flying to grapple at his throat.

Only the tree was touched—the decay didn't extend past the deep-dug roots.

"It worked," Alesh said from behind Tatsu's shoulders. "I can't believe that worked."

From the look on Yudai's face, he couldn't believe it either. He turned to face them with the necklace held gingerly in one hand.

"I can control it," he said. "I can *direct* it."

"Then that's what you needed all along," Tatsu said.

Alesh crossed the space to join them. "You'll try again? With Tatsu, I mean."

Yudai sucked in a long, hissing breath. "If Tatsu agrees—"

"Yes." Tatsu nodded to reaffirm in case there was any question of his sincerity. "I agree."

Yudai's expression softened into something very fond that warmed Tatsu. "All right. Let's try again."

It didn't seem like a good idea to mess with powerful magic outside where they were exposed and vulnerable, so they returned to the cave. The agony the siphon had wrought the first time was not easily forgotten, and the bile rising up in the back of his throat was his body's knee-jerk reaction to facing the entirety of it again. But, somehow, he got himself to the side of the fire, sat, and straightened his clothes as if it would matter should the worst occur once more. If he failed to survive a second time, he hoped they'd have the good sense to burn his body anyway.

"Are you afraid?" Yudai asked, quietly enough to be between only the two of them. "You've gone quite gray."

Tatsu thought about lying, but there didn't seem to be much of a point if his fear lay etched into his features. "It's not exactly a pleasant sensation."

"Tatsu, you don't have to do this if—"

"Stop." He tried to be gentle as he cut Yudai off, but his gut was churning. "I want to. I want to help you."

Yudai pursed his lips and nodded. "I know. Don't you dare die, you hear me?"

"I won't," Tatsu said and hoped the promise would hold true.

He lay down slowly and wriggled to move the small pebbles embedding themselves in his back. Taking in a deep breath, he closed his eyes and tried to center himself. It helped when he focused far beyond the cave and what they were doing, to the world beyond the drained husks on the mountainside, but only so much. His thoughts spiraled back to the fear lodged like a stone in his throat.

Yudai's fingers closed around Tatsu's.

"Everything will be fine," Yudai whispered.

Tatsu took one final, deep breath, and then the siphon slammed against his chest to knock all the air loose.

The sensation was much different the second time; rather than the magic pulling at his skin, the energy centered on his chest. From his shoulders to his thighs, his body began to warm, hotter and hotter, until Tatsu was sure he was emitting a blaze of light. His fingers and toes remained motionless even when he tried to jerk them away from the fire blazing up from his abdomen. Through it all, strangest was the absence of pain; the whole thing whispered at his thoughts, the siphon asking permission and waiting to get a reply. The pull was insistent and firm but holding steady without forcing anything further.

Tatsu honed in on the bubbling warmth and, with a soft sigh, gave in. *Take what you need.*

The effect was instantaneous. Heat flared throughout his body, right down to his fingertips, and then even further outward, past the confines of his skin. Beside him, Yudai squeaked, not quite pleasure and not quite pain, and for a short while, they floated in nothing, joined by the magic arcing between them. Tatsu could *feel* Yudai—Yudai's breath a staccato rhythm that didn't line up quite right, his heartbeat an echo in Tatsu's ribcage. And then Tatsu reached out with his awareness to the necklace's lodestone center, an insect with fangs that sank into his flesh and *drank*.

For a few beats, the connection merely shimmered, but in the next moment, lit up with bright blossoms of pain.

Tatsu thought he cried out, though he wasn't sure. His awareness faded as he clung to the sensations, hoping they'd keep him awake, and when his attempt threatened to fail, his arms jerked enough to smack against Yudai's leg.

The siphon cut off with a pop reverberating in Tatsu's ears as the cave, fire, and reality snapped back around him.

He gulped in air, wondering if, somehow, he'd failed to breathe for the duration of the drain's ghastly touch. But he was conscious, and the ache in his body was already calming, and that was certainly more than he could say of the previous try. Wrenching his eyes open took time. When he did, the fire was painting the walls orange.

"Did it work?" he rasped, his tongue swollen and stuck to the roof of his mouth.

"You're awake." Yudai leaned over and pressed the back of his hand to Tatsu's cheek.

"Wasn't I always?"

Yudai shook his head, though Tatsu felt the action more than saw it. "You were out for a while—ten minutes or so, maybe."

It hadn't felt like everything had gone dark for so much time, but Tatsu's lips were very dry when he ran his tongue over them. He spent some time bending his knees and elbows until there was no pause between his command and the movement.

"Did it work?" he asked again.

Wind rose up, encircling his arms and legs and lifting him off the floor. He floated there, confused and breathless, until the miniature cyclone deposited him gently back onto the rock. He swiveled around to meet Yudai's eyes, sparkling in mirth.

"It worked."

Chapter Twenty

FOUR DAYS LATER, Tatsu stood on a ridge looking out on the slanting tile roofs of Runon's capital of Yuse. The close-set buildings filling the horizon in front of them prompted a heavy apprehension, and the thought of returning to the city was more palpable than his weariness, which lingered after the siphon's energy drain. But if seeing the settlement again was strange for him, it had to be even more conflicting for Yudai.

A glance in Yudai's direction told him he'd been right, since Yudai's features were twisted with too many emotions to name.

"Breathe," Tatsu said softly. The last thing they needed was Yudai succumbing to thoughts of old trauma. The torture he'd suffered within Yuse's palace walls had been beyond cruel, but they needed him in control if they were to have any chance of getting out of Runon alive.

Tatsu's directive seemed to help. Yudai's shoulders rose with a deep inhale and relaxed on the exhale.

"How are we going to get into the castle?" Alesh asked. "We had help last time."

Yudai narrowed his eyes as if filing that tidbit of information away for future use. "We walk in. Nota will be expecting us."

"A lot can go wrong between here and the front gates." Alesh flattened her lips into a thin line. Perhaps she'd wanted to add something more and had thought better of it.

Tatsu didn't need to be reminded of the dangers, and, honestly, neither did Yudai. They paused on the rocky hill that stretched out gray and narrow from the high peaks of the Grand Mountains on the north edge of Runon's border. It was some time before Yudai seemed to shake off his misgivings enough to move forward. The path curving down into Yuse's outer boundary was well worn but empty, and Tatsu wasn't sure what that could imply. Their footsteps were the only sound as their soles scuffed against loose rock and dirt hardened by winter's lack of rain. They picked their way along the ridgeline and into the basin that flattened out into the city proper.

Since the drain, Tatsu's muscles ached from when he woke to the time he fell asleep, but the pain twinged familiar enough to forget about as long as he was focused on something else. The worst was the odd sort of buzzing left behind—an empty, agitated noise that tended to get louder as the world around him did. He wished he could ignore the disquiet as well as he could the exhaustion in his limbs. The lodestone necklace was hanging safely from Ral's neck, and Tatsu didn't particularly want to come in contact with it again.

When they grew nearer to the wooden buildings on the outskirts of the city, Tatsu expected to hear the sounds of the slums. He should have been able to pick out the constant shuffle of too many bodies too close together, especially in the bite of the winter chill, but his ears registered nothing. The silence was worse than the uncomfortable din would have been, as the absence of noise continued even after they made their way past the first of the shambling houses.

"I don't understand," Alesh said. "Where are all the people?"

A loud clang from within one of the shacks took away any chance to answer. Tatsu stumbled back in surprise as the door, hanging precariously on one rusted hinge, swung open and allowed a figure to tumble out. The stranger, hunched within layers of thin linen that couldn't possibly do much against the cold, paid no notice to them as he trudged onto the lane and shambled farther into the city. Tatsu stared at the retreating lump of fabric as the shuffling footsteps gradually faded away.

"Follow him," Jotin said quietly.

Alesh looked surprised. "What? Why?"

"Something's not right here."

They did as directed, keeping a safe distance between themselves and the stranger until they arrived at a square where the road widened and opened into one of Yuse's many market hubs. The trade carts and stalls remained, some nestled into the paneled buildings and the rest propped up with spindly poles. Tatsu let the wave of nostalgia roll over him. The last time he'd seen one of the market squares, it had been well past nightfall, and most citizens had been in bed. The timeworn signs of constant use were far more visible in the daylight.

Jotin stopped them at the edge of the closest building with a hand in the air as the stranger they'd followed approached one of the carts with the same sluggish gait. The man reached toward the merchant with his outstretched hand, palm up with a silver coin flashing against his skin.

Tatsu wasn't sure what exactly Jotin was staring at, but whatever it was had to be the cause of his creasing eyebrows. Few others milled about the open square, and Jotin's eyes jumped between them until he dropped his hand back to his side.

"What is it?" Tatsu asked.

"The man we followed is wearing a ruby-inlaid signet ring," Jotin said, "and all three of the people here have hands smooth and free of calluses."

"A ruby ring?" Alesh asked. "To afford that, he'd have to be a—"

"Noble," Yudai said as he stared at the scene playing out in front of them, even as one of the people caught sight of them and stared right back.

Alesh looked confused. "But that man came from a house in the slums. Why would he be there, dressed like that, if he were a noble?"

Instead of answering, Yudai strode into the square toward the nearest figure. With far more force than necessary, he grabbed the woman's hand and studied it, peering down with narrowed eyes even as she squawked in indignation and tried to snatch her fingers away.

When she finally succeeded in freeing her hand from his grasp, Yudai straightened and said something in Runonian. What followed was a quick exchange Tatsu couldn't understand, until the woman covered her face with both hands and let out a small, piercing wail almost immediately muffled. She ran off in the opposite direction, and Yudai returned to their group with an unreadable expression.

"They *are* nobles," he said. "They were...punished for failing to support Nota's position on the throne. She stripped them of their homes and property."

"Can she do that?" Alesh wrinkled her nose.

Yudai shrugged. "She must have enough other support—either through fear or genuine belief—that others within the court backed her decision."

"At least this tells us there is dissent within the castle over her rule," Jotin said.

"But is there enough?" Alesh looked at Ral, who smiled at the rest of them.

Yudai fell quiet, so Tatsu leaned in. "How many do you think are on her side because of the fear of retribution?"

"I don't know. But if I had to guess, more than half—I don't think many nobles would willingly support a belligerent mage usurping the throne, no matter how bad things became. My father's house has ruled for centuries, giving the nobility favorable conditions to flourish. And if this is what she's doing to her enemies..."

"What happened to their property?" Jotin asked.

"It was given to the poor, the ones who lived in the slums," Yudai said. "Likely, it would be to those who had family within the mage ranks in the castle, or maybe those who worked as servants there. Perhaps even mages' families."

Tatsu didn't want to look at Alesh, because he knew what he would see, but his eyes shifted unbidden to her features anyway. Silent agreement glimmered there, a sudden sweep of admiration for what Nota had done. He couldn't fault her for the feeling—Alesh knew better than most how easy it was to fall to the bottom of society, and how hard it was, once fallen, to climb back out. Her mouth stayed shut, but he knew she wanted to comment. It was a mercy she refrained.

Jotin cleared his throat as if to disperse the tension webbing between them. "We should continue. Our goal is the palace?"

"Maybe," Yudai said, and all of a sudden, his courage seemed to fail him. "Or we could find somewhere to wait for tomorrow."

"It's not a bad idea to get some rest before facing her," Tatsu said.

Yudai didn't reply to that. Instead, he turned to Ral. "What do you see?"

Ral shook her head, which Tatsu thought was answer enough.

"Listen," Alesh began, and Tatsu's relief at her silence was proven short-lived. "I know Nota's done some awful things, like killing your father and using you for...well, using you. But turning out the nobles and giving their property to the poor isn't one of them."

"Don't." Tatsu's snap was harsher than he'd intended, though still too late to stop her.

Alesh's eyes flashed. "I'm telling him what he needs to hear. The concept of nobility is a system that keeps people in poverty for the benefit of the rich."

"Nobles aren't only found in Runon."

She rolled her eyes. "I'm not saying they are! I'm saying the plight of the poor is always ignored by kings and queens, and—"

"That's not the issue at hand here," Tatsu interrupted.

"Isn't it? From where I stand, it seems like it's the basis for everything. It's the rich thinking they're more important than everyone else and taking what they can accordingly, and Yudai needs to be better than that."

"How can I believe that the nobles are better than others when the worst betrayal I've ever suffered was at the hand of my own father who wore the crown?" Yudai's voice was low and dangerous.

His tone seemed enough to give Alesh pause before she kept going. "Then you see how unfair it is to keep some people down to elevate others."

Yudai didn't answer right away, though his eyes tightened.

"Remember the people who've helped you," she said, more subdued than before.

"I do," Yudai said curtly, "and I will."

"None of this really has anything to do with confronting Nota," Tatsu said.

Yudai sighed. "No, she's right. It has everything to do with Runon and the throne itself. But even if you agree with the decision, I'm not going to go any easier on the woman who killed my father."

"I'm not asking you to," Alesh told him. "Just be a better king."

Tatsu had asked the same of Yudai weeks ago in the desert sun, but whatever doubt he'd had that Yudai would fail to meet his expectations had disappeared. He knew Yudai would be better—Yudai already *was* better, in every way a person could be. Tatsu could promise that without ever having known the man Yudai had been before the siphon.

Silence stretched long and tense, setting Tatsu's teeth on edge.

"The closer we get to the castle, the more obvious we become," Jotin reminded them. "We are not inconspicuous here."

"No," Yudai agreed. "We're lucky people are too swept up in their own problems to notice."

Except they weren't, not with the clacking footsteps sounding several roads down, thundering despite the ringing the siphon had deposited in Tatsu's ears. The noise was too loud to be that of the few defeated figures milling about the area. It was the remembered clatter from the first time he'd been in Yuse—the sound of soldiers' iron-studded boots across cobblestones. A moment later, the sound blurred into a thudding of weight as it merged from the stone-lined path onto the dirt lane, and it was too late. They'd been found.

The guards rounded the corner before Tatsu could summon words to warn the others. With swords raised, they advanced on his group in a sweeping formation, filling the road and blocking their escape. Even running in the other direction would be useless, for they needed to go into the city and not out.

"You were saying?" Alesh grumbled and pulled Ral closer to her side.

The guard in front said something in Runonian that Yudai countered with a growled response. Tatsu, however, put his hands into the air. By this point, he'd grown used to being taken in by guards, and there was little point in arguing. The guards—and likely Nota as well—knew who they were and why they were in the city. Escaping would prove impossible.

"Hands out," the first guard said in Common, and Tatsu stuck both hands forward in compliance. The shackles clamped around his arms were heavy and thick, uncomfortably tight, and rusted where the binding met the linked chains.

Only two pairs of soldiers escorted them, with the rest remaining, and it became clear how they'd been found once the group began moving down a wider cobbled lane. The fallen noblewoman Yudai had spoken to in the square was cowering near one of the shop buildings, and the guard in front stopped to hand her a small piece of silver.

"Don't blame her," Yudai said before Alesh could comment on the transaction. "She's probably desperate to get back into Nota's good graces if she thinks it'll restore the life she used to lead."

As they were pushed forward, Tatsu twisted to watch the nameless woman curl in further, and he felt only emptiness.

The march to the palace took less time than Tatsu had thought it would. Perhaps his memory of Yuse's size was wrong, or maybe staying within the city for days before they'd snuck into the castle had skewed his recollections. If anything, he thought he'd remember how long it took to drag Yudai's limp form out of the city and into the hills, but that too seemed hazy with time and distance, another lifetime ago. Trudging after the guards, hands clasped together with iron, echoed in finality as the last chapter in a journey he'd never meant to start.

Yudai's crown was at the end of their path, but so was Nota, and with her were the answers to all the questions swirling inside him.

Knowing the two were in the same place, within the same person, was hard to justify. The soldiers led them through the palace's double doors carved deep with a relief showing a man holding a shining rod atop a jagged mountain. Previously, they'd bypassed this main entrance when sneaking in through the servants' quarters.

"When this starts," Yudai said over his shoulder, "get out of here."

It seemed to be aimed at all of them, but Yudai was a fool if he thought Tatsu would join the others in their escape.

"Get Ral out," Yudai ordered again. Something Alesh would be all too happy to obey.

There was barely time to process more than that before the guards shoved them through a second set of majestic-looking doors carved with reliefs and into a wide, high-raftered receiving chamber.

Tatsu trailed a step behind Yudai, but even glancing over his shoulders, the scene within the castle wasn't what he'd expected. He'd thought the interior would resemble the gathering in Dradela with nobles lined before the queen and the court mages arced at the back of the throne. But the chamber was nearly empty, and as the soldiers marched them down the center to the apex, he shivered with cold.

Only one figure sat within, on an intricately carved chair dotted with translucent crystal and flaking bits of dark paint, held aloft on a dais.

The soldiers stopped, and the one in charge stepped forward to announce them in Runonian. There really was no need for it—Nota rose immediately from the throne. She knew Yudai. She knew the lines and curves of Yudai's face better than Tatsu did.

Yudai's shoulders squared into an impressively straight line from tip to tip.

"Welcome home, Prince Yudai," Nota said in Common, perhaps for the good of them all. As she moved into view, Tatsu shifted to the right, getting his first look at the woman who'd been shadowing them from the very beginning. She was shorter and smaller than he'd imagined, with hair just beginning to gray at the temples, swept into a high bun. Her silver eyes, rimmed with dark kohl and the same teardrop shape as Tatsu's, narrowed at the group of them. Her remorseless visage chilled him to his toes. He pinpointed so much of his own face mirrored back at him, from the curve of her cheekbones to the long point of her nose.

"You knew I'd come," Yudai said. "You baited me with that letter. Did you think I'd let you get away with murdering the king? Murdering my *father*?"

Nota ignored him, her gaze sliding instead across the contingent of guards and their prey bound in shackles. "You didn't come alone, I see. Have you managed to pick up some strays?"

Yudai visibly bristled, but Tatsu stepped forward past the soldiers flanking them.

"That depends on your definition of the word 'stray,'" he said.

Her eyes sparkled as the truth dawned on her, though her expression, pinched at the edges, didn't show surprise.

"Hello, Mother."

Chapter Twenty-One

"COVER YOUR FACE," Yudai said under his breath, and that was all the warning they got before the windows of the chamber lining the walls above the wood reliefs exploded in a shower of colored glass.

A few shards nicked Tatsu's arms, held up as a shield in front of his eyes, but the majority of the glass was blown away with the burst of magic-conjured wind. When the magic tunneled through the chamber, it took the guards with it, their armor clanking noisily across the stone floor as they flew clean through the doors. Keeping the wind from affecting his friends while targeting the others was an impressive show of power on Yudai's part. Though Tatsu couldn't see his mother's expression, he wondered if she'd registered the same.

She had to have—she knew what Yudai was capable of. Knowing the full extent of his abilities had been the driving force behind her decision to turn him into a weapon.

As Tatsu lowered his arms, the shackles on his wrists began to glow. Heat pulsed against his skin for a split second before the iron fell away with a loud clang, echoed by the same thing happening to the restraints on the others.

On the dais, Nota raised her hands.

"Alesh!" Yudai snapped, and she needed no further encouragement.

Alesh grabbed Ral's arm and took off through the still-open doors with Jotin speeding behind her. Tatsu, for his part, pulled his bow free from the leather strap across his back. He might not have full use and movement of his left arm, but he had enough to hold the bow steady, and there was no way he was letting Yudai face Nota alone.

The buzzing in his ears roared loud and insistent as Yudai and Nota's magic flared in the space between them.

Yudai surged forward first with an angry cry and a surge of air moving so quickly around his hands licks of fire sparked out to either side. He dashed toward Nota, pushing the flames out to reach for her. But the fire only got as far as the front step of the elevated floor as it was extinguished by a gust of wind. All of it happened so quickly Tatsu could barely follow; they were summoning and adjusting their hold on their respective magic too fast for his eyes to properly focus.

Yudai turned at the last second and twisted, the wind at his fingertips grabbing the shards of glass still littering the floor and pulling them up into multi-hued clouds. As he continued along the edge of the room, the trail of stained glass floated in circles about him, first a tail and then hugging close like a vest. Nota cried out in a wordless exclamation as she started toward him with her fingers curled into claws.

They met behind the throne and slipped briefly out of view. Tatsu took the respite to ready an arrow, notching it against the bowstring just as they spilled out from behind the chair. The gap between them had closed somewhat. When Yudai shoved his palms toward Nota, bringing another burst of wind, she picked up the rest of the glass shards and held them in front of her as a block against the onslaught. Tatsu crept along the periphery of the room with his fingers tight around the fletching of his arrow, hoping to be ignored. Their movements, too fast, prevented him from getting a clear shot.

Nota gained on Yudai until she was very near to him before he shifted his focus and threw his arms out wide. He scooped them down low in front of him, and when he raised them back up, Nota flew up with them. She hung precariously balanced on the cyclone wave of air—and then the throne broke free from its place nailed to the floor and thudded against Yudai's left side.

Yudai fell, and so did Nota, though she managed to use her magic to catch herself before hitting the ground. She was quicker than Yudai as he struggled to get back onto his feet, and the glass soared toward him in a barrage of sharp edges and reflected light.

Tatsu let his arrow fly.

At the last second, she noticed it coming and spun, gesturing at it with her hand to redirect the arrow's course into the nearest wall. But Tatsu had only ever needed his attack to be a distraction, and in the time she'd lost protecting herself, Yudai righted himself. Hands outstretched at his sides, he manipulated the air into flames again.

When it hit her, the fire burned away half of her coiled hair, leaving behind angry red stubble. She shrieked as she fell to her knees and rolled away, but even with the agony the flames had left behind, she didn't yield. A snap against Tatsu's ears, and her magic flared stronger than before, perhaps from the pain feeding it.

Nota summoned so much wind that one of the brightly painted banners near the door ripped free from the stones. The brunt of it slammed Yudai against the opposite wall, high enough to keep his toes several handspans above the floor. He struggled, writhing against the hold, as Nota shakily stood back up.

"You stole my life," she seethed. Burn marks extended down her cheek and had taken off half of her right eyebrow. Already, the exposed part of her scalp was blistering. "Simply by being born, you stole the future I was going to make my own. Instead, I remained a slave to someone else's whims."

"And then you gave me that punishment too," Yudai said.

As she moved toward him with purpose, Tatsu also began to slink around the broken stone where the throne had been lifted away. The whirl of colliding magic overpowered the soft sound of his soles against the tiles. Nota seemed to have forgotten Tatsu was there—at least her eyes never left Yudai's face as she advanced. Fitting, perhaps, given how long she'd spent ignoring Tatsu's very existence.

"You deserved it," Nota said. Her fingers curled down into her palms. "You were a bossy, arrogant child who thought the world would be given to him on a silver platter, never noticing the misery of others. Did you ever think to look at the miners toiling in the mountain? Or the farmers barely putting food on the table?"

"I was a child!" Yudai exclaimed. His magic sputtered against hers, as though ire at her words quickened him, but then his movements faded and his arms flattened against the wall once more.

"A child who would be king and was never taught to care for anything but himself. You and your greedy father stole the riches of this kingdom off the backs of the men and women you work as animals!"

"You stole my crown," Yudai said, more growl than anything as he clawed and pushed again at the magic holding him against the wall.

"It should have been mine! Mine and my son's—"

The opening felt too fitting to be ignored. Tatsu slammed his boot into the back of her knee, and she crumpled into a heap, crying out when the burned side of her head hit the floor. Her hold on Yudai collapsed as well, and he tumbled down. Yudai managed to catch himself and propelled a few steps forward while Nota recovered more quickly than should have been possible. Tatsu hadn't even turned to check on Yudai before he was lifted up and shot across the room toward the broken windows.

His mother's magic push had so much force he had to grab hold of the wooden pane to keep from flying completely out the window. Leftover bits of glass embedded themselves in his palm as he dangled, helpless and vulnerable. He'd re-announced his presence by involving himself in the fight, and now, his thoughts jumped wildly as he tried to find a course of action that wouldn't result in breaking his legs on the drop back down. Relief came when Yudai's magic surrounded him in a protective cocoon and floated him toward the floor.

He'd gotten only halfway down before Nota slammed her fist into Yudai's face.

Maybe it was surprise she was still up and moving after everything, or perhaps shock she'd resort to something as base as a fistfight. Whatever it was, the blow caught Yudai so off guard he toppled backward head over heels. The magic dispelled beneath Tatsu and dumped him unceremoniously onto the tiles. Pain flared up in both knees, throbbing slightly out of time with the ache from the glass in his hand.

Nota lunged at Yudai, and all about her, bits of the floor tiles rose, spraying clumps of mortar and rock, called to action through her will.

Yudai was weakening; Tatsu could feel it. Yudai was still there, beneath his skin, the magic and the bond forged by the siphon a cold wave in his blood. There hadn't been enough time for Yudai to regain the control he'd once had, and his magic, in the aftereffects of everything, was a disobedient child sluggish to respond to his commands.

The siphon tugged at Tatsu's awareness, a silent question, and Tatsu sighed out the answer. *Take what you need.*

The bond flared to life once more. The siphon, which felt more like a bridge than a sword, curled its way through Tatsu's limbs and up into his chest. After a moment of resistance, it burst free, blurring Tatsu's vision and sending a fog over his thoughts. He fell forward onto his elbows to avoid pushing the glass further into his palms and sucked in a dizzying lungful of air just in time to see Yudai's abilities erupt in a beautiful explosion of light and color.

Red fire and gray tiles encircled his head, and as the wind and flames swirled around Yudai, a rainbow of light filled the chamber. At first, Tatsu thought he was imagining the hues from some kind of strange siphon-related effect before realizing the stained glass had been caught in the magic release too.

Tatsu was so entranced by the sight he almost missed how the cloud of magic and color and raw power overtook Nota's body until her outline disappeared. By the time her figure was visible again, she was lying crushed and limp on the floor, and the fight was over. The siphon's bond released its hold within Tatsu, fading out like the cloud of magic itself, until the chamber held nothing but the three of them and Nota's ragged breaths.

Tatsu's heart was hammering against his ribs when he stood, and he winced at the soreness in his knees pulsing up with each step. Yudai stood over Nota's form, though he turned to look at Tatsu with a blank expression when he approached.

"I thought you might like a word before I kill her," Yudai said. *Drain her*, Tatsu's mind supplied, and he kept the addition to himself.

He knelt next to his mother's broken body. There wasn't much left—the fire had burned away more of her skin, and several tiles must have hit her legs, for one of the bones was splintered so badly it stuck out of her flesh. In less time than it took to track a deer, he'd both met and lost the image of his mother he'd wished for his whole life. He mourned that he'd only remember her as she looked at the end, with tiny cuts littering what remained of her skin, but even that seemed morbidly fitting.

She stared up at him with glinting silver eyes as her fingers jerked uselessly at her sides.

"I knew it would be you," she said in a rasping voice. A trickle of blood had worked its way down her chin from the split in her bottom lip. "I knew letting you live would one day come back to haunt me."

Tatsu frowned. "Then why did you?"

"I couldn't kill you." She coughed, a wet sound that echoed. "In the end, I couldn't do it."

Perhaps the words should have meant more, as though her admission might have changed his outlook and memories. The truth might have fluttered quietly between them and forged some kind of connection, but Tatsu felt nothing, and the absence of emotion rattled him more than his mother's ruined face.

"I would have died for him," he said quietly, though he knew Yudai could probably still hear. "So, I suppose it's fitting you will instead."

He stood, and only then realized he'd never reached for her hand. The only thing they shared was blood, and that was all it ever would be. By taking a step back, his body felt lighter than it once had. He'd expected a monumental confrontation, but the entirety of his time with his mother would end with an uncomfortable nothingness as her blood silently stained the chamber floor.

"Do it," Tatsu said to Yudai. "I have nothing else to say to her."

Yudai regarded him with another unreadable expression but said nothing more and eventually turned back to Nota's body. Tatsu looked away when the siphon bubbled up, despite it buzzing against his ears as the magic sizzled in the air around them. When he finally craned to peer over his shoulder, the body on the floor looked nothing like the woman Yudai had been fighting. Nota's corpse resembled the *Oldirr* elder on the snowy mountainside of the Shyreld, a desiccated mummy with leathery skin and too-thin appendages.

His body shuddered out a pang of regret, but it was brief, and then it was gone.

Yudai's arms fell to his sides as he sighed, a satisfied sound. His hair stuck up at sharp angles, but there was more color in his cheeks than Tatsu had seen in a while.

"Are you all right?" Yudai asked.

"Yes." Somehow, it wasn't a lie. The jitteriness in his skin reminded him they'd come to the end of things and won. Against all odds, they'd both managed to emerge on the other side intact; not only were they alive, but Yudai's magic was back under his control and the siphon's threat extinguished.

Perhaps victory should have felt more exciting, but all Tatsu registered was exhaustion.

"I'll get the others," Yudai said and turned toward the door.

"No, I'll do it."

The throne—*Yudai's* throne—was lying on its side halfway across the chamber with one arm splintered off and the reliefs broken in several places.

He found Alesh, Ral, and Jotin just outside the receiving chamber in the narrow entryway, huddled behind a small section of stone wall that jutted out into the room. There was no sign of the soldiers.

"They took off after they were blasted out of the throne room," Alesh said with a shrug. "I think they realized things were going to get ugly."

"Or they recognized the possibility of Yudai reclaiming his throne and did not wish to be on the wrong side," Jotin added.

Ral reached for Tatsu's injured hand. He'd forgotten about the cuts in the fallout of the fight, and looking at the blood again brought the dull ache back to the forefront of his thoughts. Ral's fingers gently curled against his as she looked up at him.

"I'll be fine," Tatsu said. His wince probably gave him away.

"Yudai?" Jotin asked.

"He's not hurt. At least, not badly. Nota's dead."

"I'm sorry." Alesh sounded sincere and thankfully didn't say anything more. Ral let go of Tatsu's hand, and the three of them followed him back into the large chamber.

Yudai hadn't moved from his position standing over Nota's body. His hands were clenched tightly at his sides, face set with weariness. Yudai appeared to have aged ten years in the ten minutes he'd been battling.

They formed a small semicircle around Yudai and the husk of Nota's remains, and for a long time, no one spoke.

"So what now?" Alesh asked. "You've won your throne."

"He's won it, but he hasn't actually reclaimed it yet," Jotin said. "The power does not come from the crown itself—"

"—but from those who agree to follow the one wearing it," Yudai finished. "I'm aware. We'll need to gather the court."

"At least what's left of it," Tatsu said.

Alesh pulled her chin up. "And the poor who were given the rich estates?"

"I'll do what I can," was all Yudai said on the topic.

Alesh's resulting frown betrayed her disagreement, but if she was going to say something, she didn't get another chance. The heavy double doors behind them swung open with so much force they shook in their hinges, and a broad Runonian man strode in, iron-spiked boots clanging loudly against the tiles. He stopped before them, first with suspicious eyes and then with a visible unclenching of his shoulders.

"It's true," he said. "You returned to kill her."

"Iharu," Yudai said in greeting. He shifted, widening his stance, and though his hands slid out of view behind his back, the flexing muscles in his forearms let Tatsu know his fingers were still rounded into fists. "That was fast."

"The guards came straight to my chambers to alert me," Iharu replied.

"You were working for Nota?" Yudai asked.

"We thought you were dead." Iharu's eyes flashed as his lips thinned. "It's good to see we were wrong."

An elegant way to sidestep the question. Tatsu might not have had any knowledge of the Runonian court, but he did know the state he'd found Yudai in many months ago, tied to a chair and kept catatonic. That Yudai's torture had happened beneath the court's very noses was offensive.

"You thought he was dead when he originally fell out of your gaze years ago?" Tatsu asked, softly and carefully, as if treading on unsteady spring ice. "Or when we rescued him from Nota's use?"

Iharu's nostrils flared, and Tatsu imagined the man wanted to reply to point out Tatsu's use of the word *rescued* instead of *stole*. Iharu said nothing, however, and eventually turned his gaze back to Yudai.

"The others who worked beneath your father will want to know you're back. Nota's coup splintered the court. It will take time to gather them all again."

"Get started," Yudai ordered. "I've lost enough time as it is."

Iharu bowed at the waist and left the room without another glance.

Alesh swayed awkwardly between her feet while Ral stared down at the remains of Nota's body. Jotin adjusted his leather belt. Yudai, at least, seemed willing to break the silence.

"Will you stay?" he asked them as a group.

"No," Jotin replied without hesitation. "We have seen your journey through, and my own will begin once I return to Moswar. The High Council is keen for my service to start."

Yudai turned to Alesh. "And you?"

"What can we do here?" she asked, more quietly than Jotin, as if she was afraid a raised voice would carry too far in the expansive room. "This is the end."

"Then before you go," Yudai said. "You had an informant when you first came to Yuse. Someone loyal to the Chaydese queen."

"Yes."

Yudai ran a hand through the strands of hair falling into his eyes. "Go and fetch him, if you will. I think we'll find an *awful* lot to talk about."

Chapter Twenty-Two

THE AIR IN the room was now still and strangely quiet. Alesh and Ral had left to find Akao, and Jotin had excused himself to somewhere Tatsu didn't know. Now, Yudai sat on the floor littered with the finely ground dust of the stained glass windows, his head in his hands. Behind him lay Nota's body. A part of Tatsu wanted to move it, though he couldn't identify why. In the end, he didn't reach toward it, and he couldn't explain the hesitation either.

"You won," Tatsu said.

"Then why does it feel so hollow?" Yudai murmured. His fingers shakily pulled down across his skin, leaving red lines behind blossoming bright and then fading to a dull pink before disappearing completely.

Tatsu sat down next to Yudai on the tiles. "I should have asked earlier—how are you?"

"I'm alive."

"There's a lot more to it than that. Don't push me away now."

"I'm sorry," Yudai said on an exhale, and the apology sounded sincere, a far cry from where the two of them had started. "I'm just...overwhelmed. For a long time, I never thought I'd get the crown, and certainly never like this."

Tatsu couldn't think of anything to say. They sat in silence until his knees began to ache in protest, and he shifted to try to alleviate the pressure.

"You should rest before the court gets here," he said.

"There's no time," Yudai said, "not now."

Tatsu knew by the sharp tone in his voice there was no talking him out of staying for the court's return.

"You asked the others if they would stay," Tatsu said instead, without looking at Yudai's face. "But you didn't ask me."

"I didn't," Yudai agreed.

"Why?"

Yudai's eyelids fluttered closed. He took a deep, steadying breath and let it out in a low hiss through rounded lips. "Because I won't be able to function if the answer is no, and it seemed easier not to hear it."

"Did you think I would say no?"

"I don't know. I want you to stay more than I want the throne, but I'm not used to getting much of what I want anymore."

"I suppose not," Tatsu said.

Yudai sucked in a heaving lungful of air. "Tatsu—"

Tatsu leaned over and kissed him, unsure if he was shaken by what Yudai was going to say or by what he *wasn't* going to say. It didn't seem to matter. They were both alive and relatively unscathed, and Yudai's lips parted beneath Tatsu's in a contented little gasp. They didn't have much time before the members of the court would begin to filter back in, but he couldn't stop himself from deepening the kiss, just a bit—a taste that lingered on his mouth even after he pulled away.

Yudai's eyes remained closed long after they'd broken apart.

"There's a lot of work to be done still," Tatsu reminded him. "There's a lot you probably don't know from your time spent under Nota's control."

"And a court split in its allegiance to me and the woman who murdered my father?" Yudai said.

“That’s not including the issue of the drained areas on either side of Runon’s borders, nor the power clash from Nota elevating the poor citizens.”

“Stop,” Yudai moaned piteously, though it seemed only half serious. The beginnings of a smile tugged at the corners of his mouth.

“This is your birthright.”

Yudai shook his head. “That doesn’t mean I’ll be any good at it.”

Tatsu pressed his hands against the sides of Yudai’s face, sliding a thumb across the smooth skin there. “You’ll be fine, even if it takes some time to get a handle on everything.”

“How do you know that?”

“I know you. I believe in you.”

Yudai’s eyes shone in the sunlight streaming in through the empty windowpanes. “I think you’re the only person who’s ever believed in me like that.”

Tatsu leaned forward to press their foreheads together, and Yudai glided his fingers across Tatsu’s until they laced together.

“Are you ready?” Tatsu asked.

“No,” Yudai said and laughed, the sound wobbly, “but I suppose I don’t have a choice, do I?”

THE NOBLES ARRIVED first, looking anxious and worried as they clustered near the raised floor tiles leading to the broken splinters of the wooden throne. Yudai made no move to hide Nota’s body, and as the court took notice, whispering with wide eyes among themselves, Tatsu understood why. As a show of power, the sign of Yudai's right to rule lay strewn across the floor with the broken glass in a well-chosen intimidation technique.

When the first of the mages arrived, something squeezed Tatsu's lungs. He'd not thought of the other mages, the ones who hadn't been part of the coup, and after everything with Leil, it felt like a betrayal. The mages in Runon didn't wear the thick, dark robes or the gold bracelets those in Chayd did. Instead, they were clothed in layered beige tucked into loose-fitting pants like the rest of the court, and the only difference was a thin circlet of silver curving across their foreheads. The first one, a young woman—shaking so badly her iron-studded boots screeched against the tiles—went beyond the waist-bending bow of the nobles and sank all the way to her knees in front of Yudai. With her palms flat against the floor, her sobs echoed in the room.

"Your Majesty," she said in Common, and the tone of the honorific lifted as she switched to babbling in quick, sharp Runonian. She continued for a good minute before Yudai stopped her by stepping off the dais and bending over to place a hand on her shoulder. Whatever he said, it was done in low tones that made the woman cry out once, in surprise more than anything else, and then nod again and again until Yudai stood back up. She followed clumsily and moved to the far end of the dais while wiping at her face with the back of her hands.

Yudai's shoulders straightened when he faced the rest of the assembled court.

"There are to be no consequences or punishments for the mages who were not involved in Nota's assassination of the king." His voice rang out in Common, which surprised Tatsu. It was unclear whether it was the language or the message that brought the agitation among the nobles clustered at the middle of the chamber, but a cry of disagreement rose up in a cacophony of angry words. Tatsu stumbled back, wishing he could escape, while Yudai held his ground, chin held high and looking every bit the king Tatsu had known he could be.

The mage standing behind Yudai looked furtively at Tatsu and then just as quickly away.

As the court went into full chaos, Iharu strode in and pushed his way to the front of the crowd, carrying with him the air of a man used to getting his way. He shouted something at Yudai in Runonian, and Yudai bristled.

"In Common, Iharu," he ordered. "You can translate later for those who need it."

Iharu's eyes narrowed. "Your Majesty, if I may—"

"You were my father's advisor, so speak."

"Runon has been through much in the past year. With so much change comes instability, and should we appear weak to our neighbors, they will seize the opportunity to strike back."

"Strike back?" Yudai repeated as one eyebrow shot up and disappeared beneath his hairline. "An interesting choice of words. You believe those who share our borders will attack us. And would the reasoning behind this imagined retaliation have anything to do with how I was *used as a weapon against my will*?"

By the end, he was nearly shouting, though Iharu remained where he was, holding his ground. Yudai took a menacing step forward, and Tatsu could imagine what was going to follow—a respected advisor dead on the ground and Yudai's rule the most short-lived in Runonian history. He lunged for Yudai without really thinking and caught his arm mid-reach, fingers outstretched in Iharu's direction.

"Yudai," he hissed.

Yudai's eyes flashed dangerously at Tatsu before the emotion fell away. Yudai pulled his arm away as his face relaxed, and he took two steps back.

"This won't help," Tatsu said softly. "You know they aren't the ones to blame."

Yudai stewed on that for several long breaths. When he finally replied, he sounded tired again. "Yeah, I know. You're right."

Iharu was still poised with his hands fisted at his sides, and Tatsu didn't like the look aimed at him.

"What is your suggestion, Iharu?" Yudai asked, though he still didn't look as though he were keen to hear it.

"We need to keep the systems in place. They have existed for centuries and given us standing and power."

"You're referring to the mages," Yudai said, "and the unfortunate poor within the city."

Iharu sighed. "I am referring to everything, including the use of our native tongue at court."

The gathering of nobles had doubled in size, and the stragglers who'd entered last wore the same anxious expression as the ones already present. Three other mages had quietly joined the first group near the back wall, looking confused and out of place. Though Yudai didn't spare them another glance, Tatsu let his gaze linger on them. He wondered how they felt, knowing what one of their own had done—were they afraid of retribution from the crown and court? Or were they mourning the loss in status again, wishing Nota had survived the encounter?

"I will take your counsel into consideration," Yudai said. "For now, let this be a general announcement—I am not my father, and I will not rule in the manner that he did."

"Beginning with...?" Iharu asked.

"Don't assume you still retain your position in the crown's cabinet simply because my father appointed you."

That was the wrong thing to say, and anger painted dark lines across Iharu's face. The nobles standing behind him resumed their hushed conversations, eyes darting from side to side, and all of it was wrong. Court politics existed in a realm outside Tatsu's expertise, but the atmosphere shifted the ground beneath them down, even if Yudai seemed oblivious. He was going to lose the court, and with it, he stood to lose his crown.

"And him?" Iharu asked, jerking his head in Tatsu's direction.

"What *about* him?"

"I suspect we'd all hoped that you'd grown out of this *phase*," Iharu said. "But to allow an outsider to stand next to you as an equal—"

"How *dare* you—" Yudai began, a guttural growl, before he too was interrupted.

"He's Nota's son!"

Every head in the room whipped back to stare at the mage who'd shouted—the first one who'd prostrated herself on the floor in front of Yudai's feet, and then she flailed, hands flying to cover her mouth. Apparently, even she was shocked by the outburst, but her surprise was no match for that of the court and cabinet.

The mage began to shake violently, even as her fingers slid down from her lips.

"How do you know that?" Yudai's voice was very low.

"I-I am sorry," she stammered, the accented Common tripping up her tongue. "But, he...he must be the one. He broke the barrier, and her blood—"

"Is this true?" Iharu demanded of Yudai. "He is Nota's son?"

"The son she *abandoned*, you mean?" Yudai said. "He never knew her, he's not—"

"A blood connection is still a connection!" Iharu exclaimed, and the chamber erupted in arguments.

It felt an awful lot like being in the middle of a vicious, spurned flock of birds. Runonian flew through the room, wings and claws as the nobles turned to one another with shouts of alarm and anger. Tatsu wished to crouch on the floor with his arms held protectively over his head. At the heart of the argument was his blood, his damned blood shared with the woman lying drained on the tiles, the blood he couldn't free from his body.

Tatsu's ears popped, and the chamber abruptly fell silent as Yudai's magic hissed, pulling the glass shards up from the ground and holding them aloft. The court collectively shifted back as Yudai stood sparking, his chest heaving.

"There will be order here," he seethed.

"Yudai," Tatsu murmured, but it was lost. The court, held motionless through fear and mistrust as they stared at the manifestation of Yudai's abilities, seemed unable to react. Even when Yudai dropped the glass back down, the tension refused to dissipate. It clung to Tatsu's arms like an unwanted second skin.

The doors to the receiving chamber opened with two loud bangs, and four soldiers marched inside with a dirty figure shuffling in the middle of their formation. Yudai's eyebrows arched high until Alesh darted in behind the clanking boots of the guards and ran past the nobles to the steps of the dais.

"We found Akao," she said, "but he didn't want to cooperate. It took the guard's intervention to bring him in."

Tatsu recognized Akao then, even with his chin lowered and his hair falling in front of his eyes, no longer sporting the black eye and split lip from Zakio. The soldiers thrust him front and center, forcing him to skid to a halt very near Yudai's feet.

"I see," Yudai said as he clasped his hands behind him. "Well, Akao, my friends here tell me some... interesting stories about you and your allegiance. I'd like to give you the chance to speak for yourself."

"I'm not afraid of you," Akao said bravely, but it was clearly a lie by the shaking in his shackled wrists.

"That wasn't much of an answer." Yudai took a step down, and Akao flinched, pulling back toward the soldiers, somehow the safer of his two options. He glanced up to meet Tatsu's gaze and something hardened in his eyes.

Yudai leaned in, his position on the steps making up for what he lacked in height. "I've got it on good authority that you report to the Queen of Chayd."

Akao said nothing.

"Did you allow Chaydese citizens to take refuge in your home in Runon and smuggle them into the castle for the purpose of stealing..." Yudai licked his lips and huffed a mirthless laugh. "...the siphon?"

"You already know," Akao said. "There's no need for my answer. Why bring me here? Why not just have me killed?"

From the mumbling between the nobles, Tatsu thought the court agreed.

"I'm going to let you go," Yudai said, and this surprised Akao enough for him to jerk his head back, eyes widening. Yudai smiled, the expression dangerous. "You're going to deliver a message to your queen."

"What's the message?" Akao's gaze flickered to Tatsu again.

"Tell her I'm going to call upon her for favors," Yudai said, enunciating with enormous care. "And she will very much want to agree to them. After all, she *owes* me. And she knows why."

Akao drew in a deep breath before replying, "And what of me after I deliver this message?"

"Don't come back."

Yudai straightened once more, and the two soldiers in front brought their armored hands down hard on Akao's shoulders.

"Take him to the border," Yudai said. "See that he makes it across."

"Use the trade roads," Tatsu added, trying to keep his voice quiet enough so only Yudai would hear. "He won't make it through the Weeping Forest."

Curiosity sparkled in Yudai's eyes for a second, and then he nodded sharply. "Stick to the roads. We wouldn't want him getting conveniently lost on his way home."

As the guards pushed Akao out of the chamber, Iharu moved back to the front of the crowd.

"What about the court?" he asked.

"You're dismissed," Yudai said with a casual wave of his hand. "I'll call you back once I've decided what to do about the advisory council."

It took longer than Tatsu had expected for all the nobles and mages to leave, and the young mage who had spoken about him to the court gave him a sympathetic look as she passed. Eventually, Tatsu and Yudai were alone in the room with both Alesh and Ral.

Yudai sank back to the floor, his confidence visibly draining as he wearily rubbed at his eyes. "That didn't exactly go as planned."

It helped somewhat to know the outbursts hadn't been premeditated. However, it didn't seem like the best time to bring up the subject of Tatsu's presence or the court's reaction. Yudai mirrored a skittish youngling bear, and Tatsu didn't wish to reawaken his ire. He turned to Alesh instead.

"And you?"

Alesh held up her shackled arm in response. "We can't go anywhere yet."

From his position on the stones, Yudai glanced up. His eyebrows furrowed. "Ah. I'd forgotten. I suppose I'm meant to judge you now."

"I committed a crime," Alesh said, maddeningly neutral, and her face gave away nothing.

"Yes. You did." Yudai sighed. "And it doesn't matter at all that you were right about Leil. She was a servant to the Chaydese crown and acting under royal orders. At the very least, we should have brought her with us for a proper sentencing."

"And now we can't," Alesh supplied. The corners of her mouth pinched.

Yudai dragged his tongue slowly across his bottom lip. "And now we can't."

"So? What will it be, Your Majesty?"

"You murdered the Chaydese Queen's mage in cold blood." Yudai's eyes shone with what Tatsu read as sympathy, but his voice remained clear and strong. "You can't return to Chayd, not for good. I'll have to report Leil's death to the queen eventually, or else someone else will, and after that, nothing will protect you there."

Alesh crossed her arms over her chest, staring at her boots. "I don't have anywhere else to go."

"I think perhaps it's time you found a new line of work," Yudai said. "Something...more productive to society."

"No offense, but I don't really think we want to stay here."

Yudai huffed out a tiny laugh. "That wasn't what I had in mind. I'll give you a night to think about it. There has to be something better you could do with your talents, isn't there?"

Alesh didn't respond, but something flickered across her expression. Beside her, Ral appeared hopeful, sliding from side to side as she picked her feet up one at a time. Finding a way out of the criminal element had always been what Tatsu wanted for Alesh, and even though the decision had ultimately been placed in the hands of someone else, he was glad for the turn of events.

"Come back here tomorrow morning, and I'll properly sentence you," Yudai said. "And let me go to the treasury and get something for you before you leave."

"That's not necessary—"

"I insist." One corner of Yudai's mouth twisted up. "I remember who helped me."

Alesh's resulting smile was genuine. "All right, then. Get some rest tonight. It's been a long day—shouldn't you already be settling in?"

"Yes," Yudai said, but it lacked strength.

"Yudai fine," Ral said as she reached forward to take both of Yudai's hands. He gave her fingers a squeeze in return, and something shimmered between them Tatsu would never be able to fully understand. Then Yudai gave a small, shaky laugh that sounded so little like him.

"I'll never know how to thank you, Ral," he said. "Promise me you'll take care of yourself."

"Look forward," Ral told him. When he pulled his hands out of her grip, she gently pushed a bit of unruly hair out of his eyes. "Always forward."

Yudai nodded, his mouth a thin line. "I will. Thank you for everything."

He turned to Alesh.

"There are guest rooms here, and some quarters that used to belong to council members. I'll instruct the guards to escort you to a room that's empty. I'm afraid I don't have the faintest clue which ones have been occupied."

"We'll come by tomorrow morning," Alesh agreed. Then she paused before glancing at Tatsu. "Take care of each other."

"Think of something you could do," Yudai told her, his voice serious. "Something better."

"I will," she promised.

Alesh and Ral moved together toward the double doors.

"And if you see Jotin," she added, craning her head over her shoulder, "send him by tonight, will you?"

"Are you giving the king orders?" Yudai asked with a genuine laugh.

"Thank you, Your Majesty," Alesh called as they walked through the doors and disappeared.

YUDAI DIDN'T SAY much as they left the receiving chamber other than to give instructions for the castle guards to clean up Nota's body and the debris from the fight. He and Tatsu made their way up one of the side turrets. Tatsu trailed behind—it was a little different from when he'd previously snuck through the stone-lined corridors. But he was still an outsider, infiltrating the stronghold behind enemy lines. The feeling of displacement weighed heavy in him, even as Yudai took the hallway's twists and turns with practiced speed.

At the top of three flights of narrow, curving stairs, the pathway widened into a short hallway. As there were no torches mounted on the walls, the lantern Yudai held provided the only light. The circle of orange wobbled, casting dancing shadows, as he moved forward jerkily, seemingly guided more by memory than sight.

He reached out to touch one of the worn wooden doors.

"Is everything all right?" Tatsu asked.

"These used to be my chambers." Yudai's voice sounded very far away. "I grew up in these rooms."

He grabbed at the nearest door handle and pulled hard. After a few tugs, the resistance gave way, and Yudai stumbled backward. The portal flew open with a puff of long undisturbed dust that clouded the air, reflecting the lantern's glow back at them. Inside, the stale air smelled slightly of mildew. The rooms hadn't been opened for months, if not years, and Tatsu wasn't sure what that said about Yudai's father and his feelings toward his only son.

Whatever emotions he was wrestling with, Yudai didn't let them stop him from entering the room and moving to the middle, making a wide arc as he took in each corner in turn.

"Everything is still here," he said, his voice low. "Everything is exactly as it used to be."

"Perhaps they always assumed you'd come back."

Yudai's face pinched. "I was never gone. Nota always kept me in the castle so she could be near both me *and* my father."

"Maybe they thought the siphon was temporary," Tatsu said.

"My father never thought that. My father was ready to use my life to extend his own."

Feeling helpless, Tatsu took in the room as well. The ring of lantern light was small but enough to see most of what remained, dust-covered and forgotten: a low bed propped up on curved iron legs, a low table one would need to kneel to use, and a large bookcase crammed with more books and parchment than it seemed a single person would ever need. Leaning closer, Tatsu noticed black ink stains on the tabletop. They darkened when he ran a finger over the dust atop the marks to clear it.

"You were his only son," Tatsu said, standing back up. "You were his heir. Why would he risk the line to his throne?"

"If he were to live for another hundred years, he likely thought he had plenty of time to make new heirs." Yudai's grimace was ugly and angry.

"You meant something to him."

"No," Yudai said and set the lantern down next to a cracked porcelain bowl on a small end table. "I was a *gift*, given to him by the gods to expand his power and control. At least that's how he must have seen me by the end. It wasn't always like that—not until Nota shared the idea of the siphon with my father. Before that, I was just..."

He shifted his face away, gazing at the opposite wall, so Tatsu prompted, "Just what?"

"A disappointment," Yudai said. "Arrogant and spoiled and uninterested in what I needed to learn to be king."

"You were a child."

"I was a *prince*," Yudai corrected. "And princes are not allowed to be mere children."

Tatsu closed his eyes. "Don't do this to yourself, not now. You're in charge. You don't have to stay in your old chambers if they remind you of your worst memories."

When Tatsu pried his eyes open once more, Yudai had crossed the room and was standing in front of him. Even in the dim light, Tatsu could see the mischief dancing in his eyes.

"Oh, I don't intend to stay with all the bad memories," Yudai said. His hands went to Tatsu's biceps, pushing and steering him backward until Tatsu's calves hit the side of the mattress. Tatsu tumbled backward onto the blankets, and Yudai wasted no time in following him, with his knees sliding to either side of Tatsu's hips. Their combined weight on the mattress conjured up a cloud of dust.

Tatsu sneezed, his eyes stinging. By the time his vision cleared enough to see again, Yudai was laughing.

"Sorry," Tatsu said.

"I suppose it's nice knowing for sure no one used my bed for illicit affairs while I was gone."

Tatsu smiled so wide it ached. "'Illicit affairs'? Is that what you had in mind?"

"It's only fitting I make some better memories here, isn't it?"

"Whatever you say, Tatsu murmured. "You're the king."

His thoughts grew fuzzy as Yudai's mouth found the curve of his jaw and worked its way diagonally across his throat. "I have to do what you say."

"When have you *ever* done what I said?" Yudai asked, laughing. The sound was muffled by Tatsu's skin, and the feel of Yudai's lips sent delicious shivers down his back. Tatsu arched up into Yudai's touch, his heartbeat thudding loud and fast in his temples.

"Then I suppose this will be the first time," Tatsu said.

Yudai's breath against his earlobe was hot. "And likely the last."

"Your Majesty."

Yudai muffled whatever would have come next by sweeping in to kiss him.

Chapter Twenty-Three

THE NEXT MORNING, Alesh stood before Yudai in the receiving chamber.

"Have you thought of a way to be a productive member of society?" Yudai asked her.

Alesh's eyes slid to Jotin, who stood at the far side of the dais with his hawk perched on the strap across his shoulder. "Joesar."

Yudai's eyebrows rose. "An interesting choice, considering that's where you committed the crime."

"It's fitting, then, isn't it?" Alesh thrust her chin up, the perfect embodiment of false bravado. "I'll go to Joesar and start an apprenticeship. I can't stay in Chayd, and we'd never fit in here in Runon."

Yudai turned to Jotin. "I assume you had a hand in this."

"She can study under my sister's alchemist master," Jotin said. "Alchemy is a fine trade, and Nalen will lose her apprentice with my sister graduating to the Cabaj-walkers."

"You're asking me to release a murderer into your lands," Yudai pointed out.

One corner of Jotin's mouth quirked up. "Everyone makes mistakes. Her skills will serve her well among the traders."

"Very well." Yudai raised his right hand in the air, and the room swelled. "I hereby judge you, Alesh, guilty of killing the Chaydese mage Leil and sentence you to penance in a Joesarian apprenticeship. May you find a way to help others instead of hurting them."

The iron shackle fell from Alesh's wrist with a clang and an echoing clatter against the floor. Alesh rubbed at the newly exposed skin of her arm.

"You have about a week before I send the message of Leil's death to Chayd," Yudai told her. "I suggest you return to Chayd and gather whatever you wish to keep. After that..."

"I get it." Alesh smiled, though the action seemed forced. "I'm not welcome there anymore."

Yudai's grin, however, appeared genuine. "Take your silver, then. You've earned it."

After Alesh and Ral left, only Jotin remained.

"You too?" Yudai asked. "Returning home?"

"It's time." Jotin smiled. "It has certainly been an adventure traveling with you. I hope the throne is everything you want it to be."

Yudai grimaced, but otherwise, he didn't reply. Instead, he pulled out a small bag made of smooth leather and held it out in front of him until Jotin reached for it.

"A token of my gratitude."

Jotin smiled again and slipped the pouch in between the layers of his shirts without checking the contents. "It was not necessary, but I appreciate the thought."

"You've been a great help," Yudai said.

Jotin gave him a shallow bow. "I am looking forward to working with you during my time on the High Council. May the future of our two kingdoms be a movement toward peace and understanding."

"Take care of yourself," Yudai said.

"Don't let any scorpions get hold of you," Tatsu added with a wry smile.

It felt empty after Jotin left without a backward glance. They'd returned to the way they'd started so many months ago with just the two of them, but after everything, it rang hollow. Even after leaving the others in the Myvar Ruins and setting off on their own, Tatsu had grown used to the companionship. If the expression on Yudai's face was anything to go by, Tatsu wasn't alone in the unsettled discontentment.

"Well," Tatsu said, trying to shake the feeling, "what happens now?"

"Now the real work begins," Yudai told him, one eye twitching before he stood and left the space through the narrow side door.

THEY REMAINED IN Yudai's childhood rooms, and once the castle servants got wind of it, they cleaned and readied the tower with earnest. No one seemed willing to ask Yudai to move instead into the old king's suite, so every night, the twisting staircase up to the top floor was lit with dancing torches, two palace guards standing watch at the narrow opening where the corridor met the top of the stairwell.

True to his word, Yudai called Iharu and the former members of his father's council into a meeting only to dismiss half of them, which sparked a flurry of angry meetings that never failed to devolve into Runonian shouting matches. Tatsu understood Yudai's reluctance to retain counsel who had either advocated for his involuntary use or passively allowed it, but the atmosphere in the smaller side rooms used for the council gatherings was nearing an unbearable level. Seated around the well-worn tables, none of the remaining advisors were pleased with Tatsu's constant inclusion, and they had no problem making their feelings obvious.

Yudai's control over the court unraveled further with each heated argument. Tatsu wasn't sure which part infuriated the nobles most—that Yudai was pushing for better treatment of the mages or that Yudai, a man half their age they must all have remembered from his bratty days, was holding the crown at all. And from Yudai's frantic kisses at night, fingers clawing at Tatsu's clothes like a man possessed, the tension was wearing him equally raw.

After only a week, Tatsu began finding reasons to be absent from the meetings. He didn't understand Runonian, or ruling politics in general, and his presence only fanned the flames. He spent some time in the stables with the royal mounts, hardy draft horses adept at dealing with the sharp elevation climbs surrounding Runon's capital. The other hours, he got himself lost in the castle's hallways and corners until he knew the layout by heart. After Yudai's return, activity in the palace picked up again with a high number of comings and goings, but most of the time, the air hung stifling and wrong. Tatsu longed for the green canopy of his woods; the stone ceilings of the castle were a crushing prison in comparison.

Yudai tracked him down loitering near the kitchens after a particularly long day of meetings that, judging by Yudai's face, hadn't gone well at all.

"I have something for you." Yudai slid his hand into the leather pouch at his waist. "I'm sorry it took me so long to get it—the nobles weren't happy with the decision and took some convincing."

He held out a small silver key which lay glinting against his palm. Tatsu took it gingerly, unable to calm his racing heart.

"You don't want me staying with you any longer?" he asked, which seemed unlikely, as such a wish would please the advisors rather than enrage them further.

"What? No!" Yudai balked. "It's the key to Nota's chambers. No one is sure what to do with everything there, but I wanted you to be the first to go through her things."

A wave of startled gratitude swept warm through Tatsu.

"Thank you." He cradled the key nearer to his chest, fingers tightly clutching the metal. "I—I appreciate it."

Yudai went quiet.

"What will you do with all her things after I go through them?" Tatsu asked.

"Burn them," Yudai replied, voice sharp. His eyes flashed. "I want nothing of hers in this castle anymore."

He fell silent and then huffed a low laugh. "Except you, of course."

The attempted joke fell flat.

"Where are her rooms?" he asked.

"Off the main hallway in the back annex. I figured you'd want to go immediately?"

"If it's such a big issue with the nobles, I should get it over with as soon as I can."

Yudai's expression softened into gentle fondness. "Take all the time you need. I'll see you tonight once you've finished."

After he left, Tatsu unfolded his fingers from around the key, which had left a dark imprint of the outline in his flesh. Part of him wished he could put off the task, and the other craved its completion. Seeing his mother's effects seemed the final step in letting go of all the imagined things she could have been and ultimately wasn't.

The room was right where Yudai said it would be, the second door in the small hallway, and the key slid into the lock with a click of finality.

It was much smaller than Yudai's chambers, with only a single square room jutting off from the narrow entryway that was barely large enough for Tatsu's shoulders to fit through. He pushed inside and found tables piled with books, journals, scribbled notes on ripped pieces of parchment, and bookshelves overcrammed with glass bottles. Whatever he thought he'd sense, it didn't exist—no signs or signals lay within to betray this had been his mother's room, and nothing jumped out at him as a sign of her personality.

Momentarily overwhelmed, Tatsu sat down hard on the low straw mattress, the iron frame squeaking in protest beneath his weight.

Close to the bed on a small circular table littered with droplets of long-dried candle wax was a small leather journal, thinner than the volumes stacked on the wider tables. Tatsu reached for it without thinking and opened it to pages of Runonian characters, the swoops and strokes meaningless to him. From the look of it, the book seemed to be Nota's journal, but without knowledge of the language, its secrets wouldn't do him any good. The only clue he had were the thin numbers at the top of each page: date stamps.

If she'd kept a journal regularly—and flipping through the pages showed several months of consistent musings—then the habit was probably a practiced one. It was possible she'd been in the routine for years—

Possibly as far back as Tatsu's birth.

He tore through the books on the tables, but even after what felt like hours, he failed to find a single one written in the same journal style. Nota's book collection was made up of old spell books and precisely lettered texts, and none of them were in the same hand as her own notes. Even going through all the loose parchment revealed nothing. Finally, Tatsu sat on the slightly grimy floor tiles and looped his arms around his knees, trying to fight his bitter disappointment.

Nota must have been paranoid that any notes about her past would come back to haunt her and gotten rid of the evidence in case the worst happened.

Tatsu wasn't sure how long he spent on the floor, but his knees were aching by the time he finally pushed onto his feet. It was only then he noticed how the underside of the nearest table was thick and low, far too deep to be a single slab of wood atop the legs. He pressed his fingers to the bottom to check it was the same all the way across and then rapped his knuckles against it, which echoed. The box beneath the tabletop was hollow.

With reckless abandon, he grabbed all the books piled on top and threw them to the floor until he was staring down at worn boards. There didn't seem to be any seams or creases to mark a hideaway, but when he pulled at both sides, the tabletop came away with surprising ease.

There, nestled in between the boards, was a cache of hand-bound journals.

As he combed through them, there seemed to be no order to their sequence, and Tatsu had to go through seven of them before he found the year he was looking for. He sat back on his heels as he thumbed the pages, stopping mere days before what his father had always said was his birthday. In the journal, the date came and went. But a week later, there was an abrupt skip—four days went unrecorded—and then the daily note-taking picked up again.

Tatsu took a deep breath. The skip had to be a result of his birth and Nota's physical state following it, but he couldn't read the characters to be sure. Still, the discovery felt meaningful, and he closed the journal while running his fingers slowly over to the smooth cover. Somewhere in those pages was a hint that, at one point, his mother might have loved him.

He restacked the books on the table but didn't bother to put everything back in place. If his instincts about the court were right, they would probably tear through the room searching for notes about the king and his murder. They wouldn't care if the books remained in the same haphazard order they'd originally been in. Tatsu slipped the journal into the innermost pocket of his shirt, hoping the top layers disguised the strange bulge of its corners, and then he left Nota's rooms knowing he'd never go back.

After he locked the door once more, he turned, and started, almost dropping the silver key when he saw the mage standing only a few paces away. It was the same young woman, Mairi, Tatsu had later learned, from the receiving chamber a week earlier, and she looked as nervous as she had in front of Yudai and the court. The silver circlet on her forehead shimmered in the torchlight.

"I'm sorry," she said when Tatsu pressed his hand against his chest, heart racing. "I didn't...mean to scare you."

The clipped ends to her words and the flat tone of the long vowels betrayed her lack of practice in Common. Tatsu had grown so used to Yudai's nearly flawless accent he'd forgotten many in Runon weren't educated as highly. That Mairi would seek him out despite the language stumbling felt ominous.

"Is everything all right?" Tatsu asked.

"No, um—the n-nobles. They are t-talking about a c-cousin."

"A cousin?" Tatsu's mind flew wildly with the implications. Did he have more family in Runon he didn't know about? Could Nota have had more children?

"For the throne," she continued. She wrung her hands together.

Tatsu's stomach dropped. "For the crown. To replace Yudai, you mean."

"Yes."

"And they have the power to do this?"

Mairi's silence was confirmation. Yudai had barely held the title for a week, and already the court wanted to overthrow him. The earlier they did it, the less consequences there would be for the unsteady kingdom. Yudai had been held captive for years, perhaps assumed out of reach forever. He was an unknown entity to the nobles scrambling to keep their influence. Of course, a known cousin would be both easier to control and less likely to buck the status quo.

"They say he is too weak," she said.

"And you're telling me because...?"

"You are."

"I don't understand. I'm what? I'm..." Recognition dawned. He swallowed painfully. "I'm his weakness."

He buried his head in his palms, but even the offered darkness didn't help the twisting inside.

"I'm the reason they want him gone," Tatsu said, mostly to himself despite the woman standing in front of him. "I'm the blood kin of the woman who killed the king and threatened to strip the court's power, and I'm an outsider. I'm everything they fear, and I have Yudai's favor."

Again, Mairi didn't answer. Tatsu raised his head again to look at her and tried to ignore the sympathy visible on her features.

"Why warn me?" he asked.

"The king cares about mages." Her eyes darted across the floor. "The court doesn't."

Yudai's decision to fight for better treatment of the mages was fueled mostly out of a sense of responsibility to Tatsu and Alesh rather than his own feelings on the matter, and Tatsu knew Yudai well enough to recognize it. If Yudai needed to crumble on something, then the mage issue would be one of the first things to go. The young mage had come to find him because she was desperate not to lose the only advocate she had.

"Thank you," he said, though his tongue was thick, thudding against the back of his teeth as he tried to get the words out. "Thank you for coming to tell me."

Mairi gave him one last look before darting around the nearest corner and scurrying down the hallway, leaving him alone in front of his mother's rooms. Tatsu turned to stare at the closed door behind him. He pressed two fingers against the journal held snugly within his shirt, but it wasn't until he'd made it back to Yudai's chambers in the turret that he knew what he had to do.

Yudai was seated on the floor in front of the low table going through stacks of parchment Tatsu couldn't hope to read. He looked up when the door opened, the light from the fire hearth illuminating his smile in faint orange and reflecting back in the silver of his eyes.

"I wasn't sure how long you'd be," he said and shuffled a few of the papers away. "Did you find what you were looking for?"

The truth was, Tatsu hadn't known what he was looking for, and he'd gotten far more than he wanted. He thought about taking the journal out to show Yudai but decided not to. Somehow, sharing his mother's words with the man she'd abused felt wrong. He turned to shrug his shirt off and kept the leather out of sight, slipping it beneath the layers as he folded them and laid them on the iron-footed dressing table.

"You're quiet tonight," Yudai said. A second later, his warmth pressed against Tatsu's back and his arms slipped to Tatsu's waist. "Was it hard to see all of her past?"

"No." It wasn't a lie. "It made me think about things."

"Don't think too hard on it. You aren't your mother, and you aren't bound to carry her sins."

Yudai kissed the back of Tatsu's neck gently, like a feather skipping along his skin. "Come to bed. Things are always worse at night."

But lying in the darkness and staring up at the black of the ceiling shadows, Tatsu's mind sagged heavy with guilt. Yudai was going to lose if the nobles overthrew him, magic or no. He had the power but not the desire to beat the court into accepting his rule; he'd lose his crown because of the softness remaining in his heart. Nota had taken the throne through force and fury, and the nobles were not going to forget it anytime soon. Yudai had been gone from court for too long to be a symbol the advisors could control. The last thing they wanted was another loose cannon making decisions.

Their fear was Tatsu, the man the king listened to above all others, the outsider and the traitor's son. Tatsu shivered despite the heat of the hearth and the comforting warmth of the body lying next to him.

His presence in Runon was the noose around Yudai's neck.

THE NEXT MORNING, as the castle servants prepared the iron tub with hot water, Tatsu worked through collecting his things in the room, slowly but methodically, trying not to arouse suspicion. There was so little he owned that it didn't take much time. His bow and quiver were the last of it, both propped against the far wall, and Tatsu stared at the taut string for a long time as he packed his mother's journal and the remnants of his possessions into his shoulder sack.

Pressure was building in his chest and pushing against his sternum.

He'd thought perhaps he'd get more time to ready himself, but Yudai was too shrewd to let Tatsu's actions go unnoticed. As Tatsu tugged the drawstring closed, Yudai rounded the bed to stand in front of him.

"What are you doing?"

"Go and wash first," Tatsu tried, "and after that, we can—"

"What are you talking about?" Yudai's face tightened as his gaze moved between the full pack and Tatsu, who was wearing the cured layers he'd left his father's cottage in. "You're—you're leaving."

"Yudai..."

Yudai's head whipped to the two servants near the tub and the painted partition screen, trying to blend in. "Get out."

They scampered out of the room, and the door slammed shut behind them.

"You shouldn't yell at them like that," Tatsu said.

"You're leaving," Yudai repeated, ignoring everything else. His body tensed, as if preparing for a fight, a cornered fox baring its sharp teeth. "Where are you going?"

Tatsu couldn't answer, even though the word *home* was on the tip of his tongue, a lost and foreign concept he didn't think he'd be able to feel again.

"Are you coming back?" Yudai's voice held a tight edge of fraying patience, his temper barely held in check.

"No," Tatsu whispered.

Yudai recoiled as though slapped. He sucked in a deep breath, ragged even to Tatsu's ears, and pressed a hand against his chest as though he could stop the onslaught of what was coming next.

"You're not coming back," he said to himself as he stared down at the floor tiles. "You're leaving me."

"I'm not leaving *you*. I'm leaving *this*."

Yudai's chin jerked up. "It amounts to the same thing, doesn't it? This *is* me—this is who I am and who I was born to be."

"And you need to be able to be this person. Me being here is ruining your chances of controlling the court."

"You can't leave." Yudai's face crumpled. "Tatsu, without you, this all means nothing. Without you, this is all meaningless."

He stumbled forward with fingers outstretched and caught hold of Tatsu's shirt.

"Please don't," he pleaded. "I need you, Tatsu, *please*."

Tatsu curled his fingers around Yudai's, which were balled so tightly in the linen they pressed hard creases into the fabric. His heart pounded out a drum rhythm too loud to hear anything else over, and as the pressure in his stomach expanded, his body struggled painfully to accommodate the swell.

"You promised," Yudai said. "You promised you wouldn't give me this if I couldn't keep it."

Tatsu had, and that was why it physically ached to open his mouth and say, "I can't stay here with you."

Yudai stared at him for a long moment, eyes wide, and then abruptly shoved Tatsu away with so much strength Tatsu tumbled backward into the wall. Yudai's expression hardened as his lips curled away from his teeth.

"Then go," he demanded. "Go and leave me! Go run away to your woods the same way your father did."

"Yudai," Tatsu said, but Yudai was beyond reach.

"Get out! Get out and don't ever come back!"

Blindly, Tatsu reached for his pack and slung it over one shoulder. As he made his way to the door and his bow and quiver, scarcely able to breathe, every footstep seemed to echo loudly enough to bring the whole tower down.

"You're a coward," Yudai said behind him, and the venom in the words curled Tatsu's toes. "You're a coward just like he was, and I never want to see you again."

Oh, he'd wanted this to go differently. In Tatsu's mind, he'd left with the good memories stretched out between them, a bit of extra strength for both to turn to when the nights grew cold. But he'd been a fool to think Yudai would accept anything less than his all, and he should've known better. He wrapped his fingers around his bow, though the familiar grip felt suddenly foreign.

The tension in his chest threatened to overwhelm him entirely.

He pushed at the door, pausing halfway out the opening to turn back and take one last look at Yudai. His face was contorted in fury, but still, he was one of the most effortlessly beautiful people Tatsu had ever seen. Yudai's ghost would haunt every one of Tatsu's thoughts, both waking and in dreams.

"I love you," Tatsu said, unplanned and horribly timed.

If there had been any vulnerability in Yudai, that was all he needed to overcome it. His voice was the unflinching demand of a king. "Get out. Don't you ever come back here."

Tatsu did as commanded.

He made it to the first floor of the castle with its white walls and burst through the double doors leading to the courtyard before everything caught up with him. Stumbling, he threw a hand out to catch himself on the wall and misjudged the distance. His knees hit the dirt with a pang that reverberated up through his hips, but the throb couldn't compare to what was happening inside. He was being ripped apart, piece by piece, torn and flayed until nothing remained.

A moment later, his stomach seized, and he vomited into the weeds, choking on the hot sting of tears and the bite of acid. His vision went red and wavered dangerously, and it was only through controlling his breathing and casting all his focus on his lungs that he kept his body from pitching forward entirely. Each lungful was a knife in his gut, and he was the one holding the weapon—he'd done this to himself.

He'd just succeeded in breaking his own heart.

An awful keening noise broke free of his throat and he slapped a hand over his mouth. He was only lucky it was early enough in the day for the courtyard to be deserted; an audience for the lowest moment of his life would have been too much to bear. Tatsu stayed there without knowing how much time had passed until the jelly feeling of his legs was under control enough to walk with. Then he pushed himself up to his feet and pressed his palm to his forehead. There was no hope of fully steadying himself, not with the unabating ache in his chest.

As he fumbled his way out of the courtyard and into the streets of Yuse, he knew he had to look a fright but couldn't find it in himself to care. By the time the sun was high in the sky, he'd left the narrow streets and close-set buildings behind him, moving through the scattered farms trailing away from the city. Walking along the road was easier than moving near the mountains, and he made better time than they had sneaking in through the woods and shadow.

Each thud of his boots, an echo of the desperate pain within, left everything he loved further behind.

Chapter Twenty-Four

USING THE ROADS, it took a week to get back to the comfort of his woods, even when giving the Weeping Forest a wide berth. As he stood beneath the canopy, the sweet smell of wet soil surrounded him, a cocoon of memories stirred free by the chirping of birds and the rustling of branches. Tatsu had to stop an hour into the trees to try to compose himself, but the effort produced little success. The hollowness inside might as well have been a physical wound for how much it hurt, a renewed throb with each step toward his cottage.

He'd thought he'd feel better once the cabin came into view, but his stomach sank lower. He stood outside the weathered wooden walls and stared at the remnants of his previous life. Isolated for so long, the jarring onslaught of emotions surged into being with so much force it'd knocked the wind out of him. He ached for when his biggest problem had been the softened longing for his father. Standing outside the house, Tatsu couldn't set his thoughts in order; the clarity he'd hoped to rediscover was nowhere to be found.

He pushed the front door open, pleased to see that an almost full season of rain had washed his front stoop clean.

The cottage remained exactly as he'd left it, with the addition of cobwebs draped across the corners and ceiling. Tatsu spent some hours clearing them out and putting his things back in place, though the table he'd destroyed before leaving was a lost cause. Then he sat on the straw mattress, head in his hands, questioning why he ever thought returning to his old life would feel the same—returning was impossible, prompting a sour backwash of all the things he'd run away from.

He slept for a long time.

During the night and the next morning, he woke intermittently, overcome with fear the queen's guards were on his doorstep. When they didn't arrive, the anxiety refused to fade away, and instead, solidified into a constant nervousness. If the guards weren't going to show the next day, it would be the one after that, and so on. Tatsu would be a fool to think the Queen of Chayd would allow a traitor to return to her lands without facing punishment. He kept his mother's journal on hand always, just in case they arrived to haul him back to Aughwor.

In the meantime, he waited restlessly.

He hunted for what food he could find in the winter chill. The cooler temperature was nothing compared to the bite of snow on the mountains but still a shock after spending so long in the desert sun. The straggling game in the woods ensured he never went hungry, and he found several berry caches to supplement on the days when protein ran low. Fear of the guards' arrival kept him from ever going too far away from the cottage in case they found him in the woods and overtook him there.

Often, he would stand under the trees and stare up at the leaf cover thinking of Yudai. On those days, the ache in his breast grew too strong to ignore, and he hid beneath the blankets in his bed trying to force the thoughts away.

Day by day, the soldiers failed to arrive, and the rest of Tatsu's warring emotions became stronger than his fear.

It was two weeks before he was brave enough to return to Dradela.

IT FELT BOTH familiar and oddly foreign to weave through the traders' brightly colored caravans set up at the edge of town. Memories of a life he'd long since left behind. Tatsu made it to two guards posted at the sandstone archway into town, his breath catching, but other than a sideways glance, neither soldier moved to stop him. Trying to push his misgivings away, Tatsu walked quickly along the well-trodden paths through the city until he came to the storefront he wanted. The building had the same whitewashed brick as all the others, and aside from the faded red awning providing shade for the entrance, nothing about it stood out from any other. Tatsu paused outside the door, drawing long, slow breaths to calm himself. He'd have to move forward, discomfort or no, so he pushed through the swinging doors that didn't completely fit the arch of the entrance.

He stood alone in the shop for a moment before anyone walked out from the stocking alcove in the back. The man, broad-shouldered and bearded, his coarse hair peppered with gray, looked up with practiced disinterest and then did a doubletake.

"Well," he said and leaned against the wall. A slight smile tugged at his mouth. "I have to say, it took you a lot longer than I figured to finally show up here."

"Hello, Drel," Tatsu said.

Drel set the wooden box he'd been holding onto the countertop. He seemed in good health, at least as far as Tatsu could tell, but then again, Tatsu hadn't visited the shop since Hesch died all those years ago. Losing the last friendly soul who'd known his father had been too much to handle; Tatsu chose to expand the distance between the Chaydese in Dradela and himself. "It's been a long time, Tatsu."

"I wasn't sure if I would make it here," Tatsu said. "The guards—"

"Are under orders to keep their hands off you."

When surprise locked Tatsu's muscles in place, the hint of a smile on Drel's face expanded into a full grin.

"Didn't know that, huh? You've made a very powerful friend who seems keen to watch out for you. This order came straight from the queen."

Yudai and the favors he'd threatened. Knowing Yudai had used some of his demands to protect the man who'd deserted him left a bitter taste. But Tatsu hadn't come to find out why the guards hadn't yet arrived on his doorstep. He shook his head, frowning. "How do you know this?"

"I pay attention," Drel said with a shrug, "and I have my sources. But you didn't come to hear about that, and you've got some explaining to do. Why didn't you come sooner? I've been waiting for you for years."

"Hesch—"

"My father would have been furious that you took his death as an excuse to hide yourself away from everyone."

Tatsu winced, feeling like a young child being scolded. "For a long time, I thought you'd be angry. It was Alesh who brought that fate on Hesch."

"I've never blamed Alesh," Drel said. "She came a few months after the accident to apologize, crying her eyes out. We've kept in touch since then."

"She never told me."

"For a while there, she made it seem like you wanted nothing to do with her."

Tatsu sighed and rubbed his hands over his face. His control of the situation had spun wildly away; the visit wasn't supposed to dredge up most of the things he was ashamed of.

"You didn't come here to talk about Alesh," Drel said.

"No. I came here to ask about my father."

Drel sat in one of the low-backed chairs and gestured for Tatsu to do the same. "What do you want to know?"

"Did you know my mother?"

"No," Drel replied. "But my father spoke of her sometimes—the lovely Runonian mage who had stolen your father's heart."

Lovely and terrible, though Tatsu wondered when the last trait had truly come to life.

"He loved her," Tatsu said.

"I think they both did, in different ways."

"And how did the queen know about me?"

Drel sat back, looking strangely satisfied, as though he'd been prepared for years to answer this line of questioning. "When your mother sent you here from Runon, she put you in a basket and gave you to one of the last trade carts allowed in the kingdom readying to return home."

"How did she know I'd be delivered to my father?"

"I don't believe she did. The trade cart arrived at the palace with a baby of half Chaydese descent, and the trader took you straight to the old king. I think you stayed in the palace with one of the cooks who had recently given birth until they figured out what to do with you."

Tatsu squeezed his eyes shut as he opened and closed his hands on his lap. "And then?"

"My father got wind of the situation and put the pieces together. He went to the king to appeal for your release."

"Hesch." Tatsu breathed out a nostalgic sigh for the man who'd always been kind to him. "I was released to my father's care?"

"By the time that happened, there were quite a few people who'd heard of the whole thing. It'd caused quite a stir in court, as you can imagine. And all the attention—"

"My father would have hated it," Tatsu said. "That's why he kept me away in the woods."

Drel frowned and leaned in closer. "He was *grieving*, Tatsu. I don't know all the specifics of his relationship with your mother, because he always kept that to himself. But I imagine he felt like he'd lost everything before you arrived. Runon had begun to shut its borders, and he had little hope of getting back in, and no hope of a mage of the crown ever getting out."

When Tatsu didn't answer, Drel cocked his head a bit to the side, the salt and peppered hair of his beard dragging across his lapel. "Do you have any experience with a heartbreak like that?"

The question seemed too innocently posed to be coincidental, so Tatsu leveled Drel with a steady stare, hoping his face shut down any further line of questioning on the subject.

"My father never spoke Runonian," Tatsu said.

"No, he never learned."

"Did you?"

The inquiry seemed to catch Drel by surprise. "Some, yes. I needed it when we went into the markets before we were all removed."

"Can you read it?"

"Enough," Drel said.

Tatsu pulled his mother's journal out and held it between both hands, running his thumbs lightly over the cover. "Then I'd like to ask you to help me with something, if you'd be willing."

FOUR DAYS AFTER Tatsu visited Drel, a knock on the door threatened to stop his heart completely as he convinced himself Yudai's favor had run out and the queen had sent her guards for him. But after he opened the door, he was met only with Alesh's disapproving frown.

"Tatsu, what are you doing here?" she asked without preamble. "When Drel told me that you'd stopped by, I thought he was lying. You should be in Runon with Yudai."

"Are my whereabouts a public topic?" Tatsu asked. Ral, a few paces away from the front stoop, caught an early spring butterfly between her hands and caged her fingers around its wings.

"He told me when I went to say good-bye," Alesh scoffed. "People have better things to do than sit and talk about you."

Tatsu let her in by opening the door wider, the action reminiscent to her initial arrival that had sparked the undoing of everything he'd thought he'd known.

"Off to Joesar, then?" he asked.

"Yeah," Alesh replied. "I wasn't wild about the idea at first, but Joesar is a fresh start for both of us."

"And Ral?" Tatsu asked, glancing over his shoulder at her.

Ral smiled and spread her fingers wide, palms up toward the sky. "Learn things."

"Remember the fortune-teller in Moswar?" Alesh asked. "She's like Ral. Maybe she could help teach her."

Then she shook her head. "But this isn't about me. I know what I have to do. Why are *you* here, Tatsu? Why did you leave?"

"It's difficult to explain."

"Bullshit. You're running again."

"I'm doing this to help him!" Tatsu cried. "Leaving was the only thing I could do to make sure he kept his crown. My presence in the capital was only causing problems."

"That's how life works! You fought for him and then you stopped when it really mattered."

Tatsu fell silent, glaring at the floor with growing frustration, and when Alesh spoke again, her voice was gentler. "Tatsu, he needs you."

"He needs to be able to hold his title more than he needs me."

"But Tatsu did," Ral added from the far side of the cottage where she'd sat on one of the still-standing chairs.

"Did what?" Tatsu asked.

"Yudai's title," Alesh said. "You did that—you were the one who gave that to him. You changed his future and you changed Runon's, don't you see? It was all because of the actions you took."

Instead of feeling good, Tatsu's stomach felt heavier. "I'm nobody. I'm the child who was abandoned by my mother because I had no use."

"Maybe you don't have magic, but that doesn't make you useless. Look at what you did. Yudai is a king now."

The resulting quiet crept like a dark shadow over Tatsu's heart.

"Tatsu," Ral began.

"I made my choice, and so did he." Tatsu ran a hand through his hair. "He never wants to see me again."

"You don't honestly believe that, do you?" Alesh asked.

"It doesn't matter," Tatsu said wearily. "That's what it is. And you should go to Joesar."

Alesh's features softened. "Will you be all right on your own?"

"I always have been, haven't I?"

She pursed her lips but didn't push the subject.

"Come and see us sometime," she said.

Tatsu wouldn't have trouble keeping that promise. "I will. And be safe on your way to Moswar."

Ral stood from the chair and gave him a tight hug, squeezing her arms around his waist with gusto. When she pulled away, Alesh surprised him by hugging him as well.

"Go back to him," she said, stepping back.

"Good-bye," was all Tatsu said, and he watched their retreat from the front porch until they disappeared completely in the darkening brush of the woods.

HE STARTED MEETING with Drel on a weekly basis to translate his mother's journal, and after the first few times, his nerves calmed upon entering the city. Whatever strings Yudai had pulled to keep Tatsu out of prison were still there, and though Tatsu knew the queen had to be seething at allowing him to retain his freedom, there was nothing she could do. She'd kidnapped Yudai to use for her own gain as a magical slave, and now he was sitting on Runon's throne. Her actions would have been just cause for retaliation, and she probably feared the angry, vengeful young king enough to honor his demands.

Tatsu wasn't sure why the thought always made him smile, but the situation contained a strong pulse of satisfaction, even if not wholly for himself.

Drel found an old book in Runonian Hesch had used as a study tool with notes and translations in the margins. What parts of the journal he couldn't read they would compare to the symbols in the book, sometimes stumbling across a passage Hesch had annotated.

Slowly, week by week, they made their way through the passages up to and after Tatsu's birth.

Later, when he was alone in his cabin listening to the cool spring rain, Tatsu would read their translations over and over until he knew the words by memory, and even then, he would read again, as if the words could fill in all the holes left in his past.

I could feel the child stirring inside me today—it must be nearly time. It's getting harder and harder to make excuses for my absence from court, but the troubles at the pass with the Joesarian splinter forces keep the king occupied, and my servant Hida weaves tales of crippling head pains. Sometimes, I press a hand to my belly and whisper to the child, hoping that they can hear me through the magic that binds us.

The entries before his birth were easier to read because Nota hadn't known yet about Tatsu's lack of magical abilities. He always turned the pages anyway, despite the ache the words summoned inside.

I performed a test with the baby today, and my worst fears are true—the baby has none of my abilities. I placed him between the candles as we do with all infants of the court and whisked the fire with my magic until it was nipping at his ears. He should have reached out with his own magic in fright, the skill manifesting to protect himself, but he did nothing but cry. He wailed until I had to stop for fear of being caught.

If the king discovers the baby's lack, all my work will be lost. There will be no hope of convincing the king of how wise it would be to marry a mage in order to produce magical children. I have to get rid of the baby, or I will lose everything I've fought for.

But when I steel myself for the horrible task, his tiny hand wraps around my fingers, and I can't bring myself to go through with it.

AS THE SEASON fully blossomed, the forest floor grew a carpet of tiny white flowers and ball-like berry buds, and Tatsu expanded his hunting circle. The renewed life of the land lacked the promise it used to hold, but still, something about the air felt right as he slunk silently between tree trunks while tracking a hare. At least the pain when he thought of Yudai had subsided enough to allow him to go through his day without being hobbled. It was a victory that, for a while there, he hadn't thought he'd get.

Still, he took time before returning to the high cliffside overlooking the Turend Mountains and the spikes of coniferous trees between them. When he finally reached the overlook, he wasn't sure what to expect. The last time he'd stared over the sloping hills, the trees and brush had been gnarled and withered, drained dry of life and left to fester.

Standing on the edge of the drop, Tatsu surveyed the still-brown and drooping land. Then he knelt by the sickly line dividing the drained foliage from the healthy parts, a stark contrast beneath his boots. The grass across the line was dead, but nestled beneath the remains was something green.

Tatsu dug at the earth and grass until he'd cleared a small patch of the withered stalks. There, poking through the soil, were tiny green buds of new, healthy growth.

He sat back on his heels, gazing out at the rest of the destruction. Out there beneath the dead plants lingered the signs the land would eventually return to the way it had been, even without any of the stolen energy being returned. The sides of the mountains would eventually revert to their living state and invite back in the animals that had fled. Over time, the trees would splinter and fall, and in the decaying trunks, new sprouts would emerge to tower proud and tall.

Tatsu ran his fingers lightly over the green buds protruding from the dirt, took a deep, steadying breath, and smiled.

Epilogue

IN THE WOODS, the insects of midsummer were in full chorus, their calls a heavy sort of sound he often thought he could reach out and touch. They helped to mask his footsteps as he slipped between trees to check his snares, though the silence following his path also tended to give his location away. Luckily, he'd already caught what he needed with his traps, and resetting the wires wasn't a task that necessitated stealth. His pack was weighted with a ground squirrel and a pheasant unlucky enough to have landed while Tatsu crouched with his bow ready, along with a handful of bright summer berries and some edible green roots.

Once he finished resetting his lines, he hefted the pack over his shoulder and started back to his cabin. The last of the evening sunlight filtered through the tree canopy and painted the ground with its yellow-orange hue, and the air was just reaching the point of being sticky. The summer promised to be a hot one, with several months remaining before the temperature would start to drop. As difficult as it was, the uncomfortable stuffiness helped keep his hunting lucrative well into fall, and the assurance was worth dealing with the humidity.

Overhead, several white songbirds circled one of the larger tree trunks. Tatsu watched their erratic loops around the branches until they chose one they liked and disappeared within the green of it. He didn't bother trying to disguise his footsteps on the way back, which quickened the return, but as he neared his cottage, the chirping of the insects abruptly faded. Tatsu stilled, waiting for the noise to start up again, and when it didn't, he leaned in closer to the grass and weeds growing wild from the soil.

Bits of the brush were bent and flat, evidence of having been trampled by someone wearing boots heavy enough to sink into the soft upper layer of dirt and embed the stalks. Tatsu stayed for a moment in his hunched position, hoping the fuzzy-looking tops of the weeds hid him well enough. He waited, listening for the sound of armor clanking through the woods.

It took a few moments for him to pick it out, so whoever had created it had to be *attempting* to be quiet. It wasn't entirely working, though—the clanking was on his left, perhaps three minutes away if he moved slowly.

Tatsu rose, fingers tightening on the straps of his full pack, and crept diagonally away from the soldier to approach his cottage from the back side.

On his way, he found two others lingering in the trees, and neither of them seemed to notice him. The smooth iron of their chest plates was out of place in the green of the trees and easily spotted when the dappled evening sun reflected off the metal.

When he came across two boot prints in the dirt, undisguised by trampled leaves, small, deeper holes dotted the print—iron clamps welded to the soles.

Tatsu trailed a finger across the bumpy dirt and the marks, huffing out a short, breathy laugh.

When he reached his cabin and pushed the front door open, he wasn't surprised to see a figure seated in the chair nearest to the unlit fire pit.

"Your guards aren't very good at hiding in the trees," Tatsu said, surprised he could make his tone so light. He dropped his pack and the carcasses onto the repaired table without glancing over at the fire pit, afraid doing so would shake all his courage free.

"They haven't had much practice with creeping through the woods. I'll put it on the next training to-do list."

Tatsu turned to face him, clasping his hands behind his back. Yudai was sans crown, and Tatsu wasn't sure if the lack had more to do with traveling in relative secrecy or hoping to appeal to Tatsu as an equal. His clothes had been upgraded to a darker-colored shirt seemingly made out of slick silk, and the white ends of his hair had finally been cut off so the black strands were all that fell across his forehead. He looked healthy; his cheeks glowed with more color than Tatsu could ever remember seeing.

Tatsu had seen Yudai's face every night since he'd left Yuse, but the real thing before him still stole his breath away.

"You look good," Tatsu said.

"So do you."

"What brings you here to my cabin?"

Yudai's tongue darted nervously out to wet his lips, and then he looked away, taking in the stack of smooth skins Tatsu was going to take to the traders in Dradela during his next visit and the pile of still-drying wooden bowls and plates on the far cabinet. He stood up before he met Tatsu's gaze again.

"I know you left because you thought I needed you to in order to keep control of the court," he began, "and I *suppose* you believed you were doing the right thing—"

"I was."

Yudai rolled his eyes, but the action seemed good-natured enough. "But I've come here to report that things have settled down and most of the issues with the nobles have been resolved."

"You fixed everything in only four months?"

"More or less." Yudai shrugged. "Some of them required more persuading than others."

"Tell me that you didn't magically throw any of the nobles into the rafters and leave them there to prove a point."

A genuine grin spread over Yudai's face, though he didn't deny it.

"The point is, your reason for leaving is no longer an issue."

"You told me you never wanted to see me again," Tatsu pointed out, shifting his weight to his left heel and crossing his arms over his chest.

"Yes, I know what I said." Yudai waved his hand in front of him, an action no doubt used often with advisors he wished would stop talking. "And you know me. You know I was angry, and I didn't mean it."

When Tatsu didn't answer, Yudai ran a hand through his hair, eyes flitting from side to side again. Tatsu had never seen him so nervous—not when standing on the hill overlooking Yuse and knowing he had to face Nota, not when waiting for Hysus and his mages to push his head beneath the water of the pool. Seeing Yudai rattled and knowing it was *his* doing made Tatsu want to smile, but he tamped the inclination down. Better to let the other man stumble his way through whatever he was trying to say. After all, he'd come all the way out to the Chaydese woods with a company of heavy-footed guards to say it.

"Look, I...I'm not happy without you there," Yudai said. "I mean, I'm doing what I need to do, and things are under control, but it's not... I'm not happy. You were the only thing that made it all worth it, and I want you to come back."

Again, Tatsu kept quiet, and the silence visibly agitated Yudai all the more.

"I know I'm not the easiest person to be with," he continued, "and I know that I'm...complicated, with my situation and the crown, but you were able to look past all that at one point, and I'm hoping you can do it again."

Tatsu pulled his gaze away, which caused Yudai to cross the distance between them and then pause, lingering just out of reach as though he wasn't sure he should continue.

"If you come back to be with me, I'll give you a title and everything."

The silence stretched between them, tense and heavy, meaningful in a way Tatsu had missed in his long months alone.

"I'm prepared to beg," Yudai said more quietly. "But please don't make me do it. It's not very becoming of a king."

Tatsu looked at him again, at his silver eyes desperate for an affirmative answer and the shiny black of his hair so unfamiliar after so long with the bleached strands. Yudai was a fool to think Tatsu had ever been able to stop thinking about him—his pendulum mood swings and razor-sharp wit and bright smile. Yudai was a fool to believe his ghost hadn't haunted Tatsu's days for all the time they'd been apart.

Tatsu took a step forward, bridging a little of the space between them.

"The day you left, you told me you loved me," Yudai said, almost a whisper.

"I did."

"Do you still?"

Tatsu pulled Yudai in for a searing, needy kiss that Yudai returned with enthusiasm for some time before pulling away, lips pink and swollen.

"That wasn't really an answer," he said. "Do you still love me?"

"Yes," Tatsu told him, curling his hands at the sides of Yudai's face. "Always."

"Good," Yudai exhaled, a rush of air. "Because I seem to be so hopelessly in love with you I'm unable to properly function alone. Say you'll come back to Runon with me."

"I'll go with you."

Yudai's expression smoothed, all the lines and worried tension easing away.

"How angry will the court be with my return?" Tatsu asked.

"*So* angry." Yudai laughed, and it said a lot that his reaction was of glee instead of frustration. He really had gotten the advisors under control and the kinks worked out if he was happy to put up with their condescension. "How much time do you need to pack?"

Little in the cabin meant enough for Tatsu to mind leaving it behind, and all of the important things would fit into his pack. "Not long. How much time do I have?"

"As much as you need," Yudai said. The answer was accompanied by another airy wave of his hand.

"Won't the court be expecting you back?"

"I'm the king. I'd like to see them try and scold me. Besides, this gives me plenty of time to come up with your official title."

Tatsu sighed, dumping out the berries and greens from the pouch and pulling free his mother's journal from the lopsided bookshelf. "Please don't make it anything embarrassing."

"Oh, come on, where's the fun in that?"

Yudai sat back down in the chair and stilled, face growing more serious again. "I missed you."

"Yeah," Tatsu replied, a pleasant warmth bubbling up from his stomach. "I missed you too."

"Well, hurry up so we can get on with this. I have so much to tell you about the last months."

"I'm more anxious to hear about how you stuck advisors up in the ceiling beams."

"That only happened once, and it was entirely provoked," Yudai said, and Tatsu let the lightness in his feet carry him around the cottage to collect his things as the sun slid down the painted sky and disappeared behind the horizon.

Acknowledgements

The original *Life Siphon* duology was a real labor of love, and perhaps even more so as I reached the end of the story. I've never been very good at knowing when to say good-bye, so the third installment happened without much conscious thought, and I'm beyond excited to say this isn't the official end of Tatsu and Yudai's story, but merely the opening of a much larger world!

The biggest thanks for this book goes to Caroline Ziegler, who is still my initial first draft beta reader. Having someone you trust to point out weaknesses is something you can't put a price on, and I'm so grateful that Caroline was excited to be on the second part of this tale with me. Thanks also to Miranda Van Minnen, who sorted through the early chapters and gave her feedback on how to improve the beginning.

And a massive thanks to Rob Rowland, my unofficial publicist slash weird brother-twin, who convinced half my colleagues to read the first book when I was still too self-conscious to even mention that I'd written it. (At least I know now that I shouldn't try to write anything after wine *nomihou*!)

To my family and friends, who don't defriend me on Facebook when all I talk about is books and writing and try to convince them to buy a copy for everyone they know: you are the best for putting up with me all the time!

Thanks for reading what I write, even if you aren't particularly interested in the subject matter.

And my husband, Masaki, the rock that keeps my feet steady on the ground: all the thanks in the world. You're always my number one.

About the Author

Kathryn Sommerlot is a coffee addict and craft beer enthusiast with a detailed zombie apocalypse plan. Originally from the cornfields of the American Midwest, she got her master's degree and moved across the ocean to become a high school teacher in Japan. When she isn't wrangling teenage brains into critical thinking, she spends her time writing, crocheting, and hiking with her husband. She enjoys LGBTQ fiction, but she is particularly interested in genre fiction that just happens to have LGBTQ protagonists.

Email: ksommerl@kent.edu

Website: www.kathrynsommerlot.com

Twitter: @KSommerlot

Other books by this author

Ibuki

The Life Siphon (The Life Siphon, Book One)

Coming Soon from Kathryn Sommerlot

The Loyal Whispers

Excerpt

Choked with debris, the waves lapped at the fire-blackened hull boards left behind, and worse yet, bodies bobbed in the spaces between splintered wood. They quivered up and down with each crest, clothing billowing around motionless limbs, and Ravee had to turn away with one hand pressed to her mouth to keep her meager breakfast down. The air smelled of burning softwood and singed flesh interwoven into an overpowering and inescapable tang that did nothing to help her constantly queasy belly.

"*Gods above,*" Captain Wret hissed under his breath. When Ravee peeked over her shoulder, his knuckles had blanched white, fingers clamped to the deck rail. "What happened here?"

The answer seemed very obvious: the worst. The lingering fear of anyone who took to the seas was a shipwreck, whether by pirate attack or the unforgiving elements, and the evidence of just such a tragedy lay strewn around their vessel in the whitecaps. But no storms had darkened the sky in the past week, only a clear blue horizon with favorable winds, and pirates tended to strip the ships of both treasure and hostages before destroying them. Among the remnants, broken shards of porcelain dishes floated alongside the wood, and anyone searching for profit wouldn't have left something so valuable behind. The knowledge should have helped soothe her nerves, for the *Sheersilk* and her passengers were far less safe with their trade cargo if pirates roamed the Oldal Sea, but the uneasiness was slow to dissipate.

As her stomach stopped roiling at the grisly aftermath, Ravee turned back to peer over the ship's side. If it hadn't been pirates and couldn't have been the weather, few other possibilities made sense. Ships didn't simply spontaneously break apart, and the sea serpents had already entered their dormant months. A horrible pall settled over the remains, as though not even the sun's bright rays could touch the bloody mess.

"Look!" one of the deckhands yelled. "Rad-em colors!"

The outburst prompted a scrambling of boots across slick boards as the sailors searched for something to reach the floating silk with. Eventually, the cloth drifted near enough for a man to fish it out with one of the long deck mops, and while Ravee's heart skipped at the sight of her kingdom's flag, the shock paled in comparison to what came up after it. More silks, strung together on the single rope line, tangled in a mess of clumped, torn fabric. Ravee had never heard of the northern kingdoms sailing under a united banner, not even in the oldest orated history lessons. She whispered a prayer under her breath as the crewman struggled with the cord, grateful her hands weren't visibly shaking.

Captain Wret pushed the sailor aside to grab at the bulk, his hands steadier than the deckhand's had been. He pulled the Rad-em colors free, and then the rest one at a time, peeling the sopping layers apart until four flags lay spread across the deck. Four silk banners, fraying and burned on the right side as though they'd caught fire as the ship went down and only the briny seawater had stopped them from being completely devoured.

Four silk banners representing the kingdoms of the southern coastline.

Ravee's stomach twisted again with a painful throb.

"Rad-em," Wret said, pointing, "Chayd, Runon, and Joesar."

"Impossible," one of the men argued. "They'd never sail together like this. And under united colors?"

All the flags had been displayed on a single vessel, and to have such a bold showing could mean only one thing.

"They were on official business," Ravee whispered, speaking before she could stop herself. Wret's head snapped in her direction, his eyes sharp, but he didn't stop her from continuing, which was something. "In an official capacity."

"Yes," Wret said. "They were traveling as ambassadors. Peaceful ones, likely, given the treaty negotiations."

"Who would attack a ship containing peaceful representatives from all four of the coastal kingdoms?" the sailor nearest to Ravee asked.

Wret's gaze shifted to the broken, charred pieces of the ship still floating out on the sea. "The easiest way to answer that is to figure out where they were going."

Then his expression morphed, cycling through surprise and shock before hardening in resolve. He crossed the space to the side of the rail with long steps and hesitated only for a moment, scanning the water, before shouting, "Get a lifeboat dropped! Someone's alive in there."

In the resulting chaos, Ravee was pushed back, shoulders bumping into her arms with such force her skin would bruise. She couldn't see around the sailors to confirm for herself, and she knew better than to try and fight it. Captain Wret was already displeased enough to have her aboard his ship, accompanying her family's goods, and hadn't bothered to keep his feelings quiet. Making her presence known could result in banishment down in the sectioned sleeping quarters afforded to her.

A lifeboat splashed onto the sea and a few of the sailors started up nervous muttering, but it wasn't until several moved to the rigging that Ravee felt confident enough to slip through the small crowd to the railing again.

The sailors in the lifeboat were pulling a body out of the water, and despite Wret's earlier outcry, the man looked very dead. He didn't so much as twitch as the sailors rowed back toward the ship's side and prepared the dinghy to be lifted back up. When one of the crew hauled the man over the rail and deposited him onto the deck, his head lolled lifelessly to one side. Bits of his shirt had been eaten away as if by flames, and a nasty-looking cut sliced across his forehead, the red of the still-flowing blood mingling with the seawater clinging to his skin. The sailors spent a long moment staring at him in silence.

In the stillness, the air above the ship's deck shimmered as shivers ran down Ravee's spine in a familiar tremble. Bithlad, God of healing, pressed against her from behind, all four of his hands ghosting over her biceps as he whispered, *He's alive. Help him.*

Ravee darted in between the sailors, nostrils burning with the lingering smell of the less fortunate passengers, her feet propelled by the murmured command. She flattened her head to the injured man's chest, shoulders sagging at his muffled breath sounds. He *was* alive, but only barely so.

"How did you know?" she asked Captain Wret, who had advanced to hover uncomfortably over her shoulder.

"He was clinging to one of the bigger pieces of the ship's hull, and his position was too unnatural to have been the result of post-death rigor."

Ravee looked back to the man's body. "I doubt he would've lasted much longer out there in this state."

"He may not be the only one. The lifeboat's already prepared—we should search the area for more survivors," Wret said, and he walked away to bark the orders at his crew.

Ravee stayed where she was, kneeling with one hand on the man's shoulder, wishing she could will him to wake up. His eyes stayed closed, though it was comforting to see his chest rise and fall, even if his breaths were shallow. The lack of movement gave her a better opportunity to check him for injuries. Though bleeding steadily, the cut on his head wasn't deep, but when she peeled back the soaking layer of clothing from his torso, she exposed a fresh wave of crimson. Along his side darted a dark gash, and it seemed his shirt had been the only thing holding what remained of the skin together. Ravee pressed her hand against the wound in shock as she shrieked for help.

Also Available from NineStar Press

Connect with NineStar Press

www.ninestarpress.com

www.facebook.com/ninestarpress

www.facebook.com/groups/NineStarNiche

www.twitter.com/ninestarpress

www.tumblr.com/blog/ninestarpress

www.ingramcontent.com/pod-product-compliance
Lightning Source LLC
Chambersburg PA
CBHW032202180726
48284CB00001B/148
* 9 7 8 1 9 5 1 0 5 7 6 2 6 *